TK

TK

Published by Roger K Sutcliffe 2022

Copyright © Roger K Sutcliffe 2022

All rights reserved. No part of this book may be reproduced in any form without permission.

This is a work of fiction. All characters are fictitious and do not relate to any real people, living or dead.

TK

The Epic Story of a Wild Spirit

Roger K Sutcliffe

Contents

TK Book I

London, May 1812	9
Six Months Earlier. Winter in Spain	15
Hackett	27
The Duel	35
The Thames	45
The Ladies	51
The Severn Village	55
Dorset	61
Waterloo	67
Dorset	79
The Severn Village	83
The Bow	87
Farewells	97
Departure	109
The Lydia	113
Pirates	117
The Storm	127

TK Book II

New York	131
The Jewels	159
Assembly	177
Departure	195
Wild Boar	205
Lucy	211
The Red Cliffs	215

Wolves	225
Parting of the Ways	229
The Dutch Settlement	235
Oregon	243

TK Book III

Fort Vancouver	255
Fort George	261
Gold	285
The Return	295
South Pass	303
Back to New York	307
England	311
America	325
Buffalo	333
The Settlement	343
West	347
The Main Seam	351
The Privateer	359
Going Home	367
Mustangs	375
Another Convoy	387

TK BOOK IV

St Louis	393
Hostages	401
Ambush	415
Guy Davenport	431
Leaving St Louis	441
The River	451
New York	471

TK Book I

London, May 1812

'You are a damned cheat,' she said.

Nell sat on a golden chair at a small table with her back to the window. The evening sun shone onto her light brown-gold hair and onto her mother's sapphires, which matched her eyes. She sat straight, showing her figure to advantage, in her mother's dress.

Her aunt laughed. She had looked over her niece's shoulder, seen an old man hobbling towards them, and called, 'First.' The game was that each called a number and the other must marry a man of that number that passed their table.

They were in a large fashionable house adorned with the latest wallpaper and hangings. Chandeliers hung from the high ceilings and all were lit, even on this summer's evening, at no regard for the expense.

Nell was nineteen and an orphan. Her aunt, Elizabeth, was twenty-five, an orphan and a widow. She was taller, slimmer and darker but very beautiful in her widow's black and her mother's diamonds. She had a beautiful smile. They were great friends and lived together in Dorset in comparative poverty, and they did not care. They had their house and they had their horses. This was their first London reception and they were fascinated but refused to be overawed. They were in town to find husbands, a mission that they were not taking too seriously. Their infectious laughter caused smiles around the room.

Their table was in a small salon off the main hall of the house in St James'. Their laughter echoed as a murmur went around and their escort, Sir Robert, quickly stepped up. He explained that the young man whom they could now see through the glazed doors was in uniform and likely to be called out by the Count. Their hostess was a Duchess and the Count was her companion on these occasions. She was a rich English widow. He was a mid-European bachelor. He was known to induce a duel with any British officers, particularly if they attended one of the Duchess' receptions wearing their uniform. Many promising officers had died at his hands. Word had spread that it was not safe to wear uniform at the receptions.

Sir Robert explained this as Nell gazed at the young officer and fell in love. He had dark red-gold hair cut short, very broad shoulders, and a deep chest, which made him appear shorter than his actual height. His broad face bore deep blue/grey eyes. He had a broad nose, broad chin with and short strong teeth. He was a captain and wore a dark green jacket. He appeared unconcerned.

Suddenly a cold chill spread across the rooms. The Count had arrived. He was very tall and very blond with pale blue eyes. He had a scar above and below his left eye. He wore his civilian clothes like a uniform and his eyes were chilling. He was in his late thirties, very strong and very confident. He strode, in cold fury, straight up to the young officer and his companions.

In nature, when a predator takes one of the herd, most of the herd remain at a safe distance and watch in fascination, as the victim is killed, not necessarily very quickly. They do not run. So it was at the reception. As the Count bore down silence fell. The guests drew back, watching and listening in dreadful fascination. But they did not run.

Sir Robert had slipped away to see the confrontation. As the silence started to lift, with a murmur and then a buzz, Sir Robert returned with the story. There would be a duel. But not as expected. The Count had immediately confronted the young officer and his companions. Wasting no time, he had made derogatory remarks about his unfashionable regiment and the poor state of his jacket. The young officer had smiled and thanked him for his opinions. The Count had replied that anyone but a coward would have called him out. Again, the young officer thanked the Count for his opinions. The Count raged and towered and glared with his ice blue stare. He was met with steady deep blue grey eyes looking contemptuously down the captain's nose. The Count protested that he was being mocked and made the challenge. The young officer had smiled and asked for confirmation that he was being challenged and that he could choose the weapons.

'Yes, damn you!' said the Count. He was known to excel with both pistol and sword.

'Very well,' said the young officer. 'Sabres on horseback. Bring your own sword and your own horse, no armour.'

The Count was silent for a moment and then smiled. He had been an officer of heavy cavalry, used to heavy horses and heavy swords. He saw his advantage and agreed, although, in fact, he had no choice. A glance at the officer's companions confirmed his suspicions. A tall dark curly haired young man was clearly an officer from one of the best regiments in civilian dress and the other, older, weather beaten and battle scarred, was probably a duel master. Well, they would soon realize the mistake that they had made. One of them was going to pay with his life.

Nell told Sir Robert that she would like to meet the young officer. Sir Robert said that this may be thought ghoulish, the young man was expected to be killed early one morning quite soon, but he would try, and he hurried away again. He returned with the young officer, who introduced himself as Captain Tom Kynaston, from a poor manor and a poor regiment, and feared that she would find him poor company.

'No,' she replied. 'I am from a poor farm and my military family have left me poor and we may get along very well discussing the cost of bread.'

He saw the reckless smile and laughed, and her loins yearned in the face of his confident blue-grey eyes, strong teeth and broad-dished chin. She asked why he had chosen a cavalry duel.

'There is more to go wrong,' he replied. "When things go wrong, I take advantage. This is not the world of the Count. He requires control."

She asked if he hunted and he replied that he had been brought up with no choice. His mother had died hunting and his father would be happy to die the same way. His ambition was to hunt six days a week and die poor.

The duel would be held very soon, and he asked

whether he could call upon her afterwards at the house of Sir Robert, if all went well. Her beautiful face looked troubled.

'Don't worry,' he said, and smiled again, and her loins lurched again. That night she prayed for the first time in years.

In the meantime, rumour and opinion raged. Who was the young officer? How had he come to be invited? Had he deliberately provoked the Count? His companions had been officers from one of the best regiments, in civilian dress. He was staying at the barracks. Apart from his conversation with the protégées of Sir Robert, he had made no social effort. Clearly, he was poor. He came from a poor regiment. Why had he been invited to the reception?

Behind the fans and the nosegays, the debate raged. The time of the duel became known. The Count had been seen exercising on horseback, tall and imposing. But nothing was seen or known of the young officer.

He was unknown to polite society, so should polite society have any care of him? Yes, it seemed there was a general suspicion of the Count, great fear for the young officer, and a furious anticipation of the coming duel.

Six Months Earlier. Winter in Spain

It was cold and wet. There was snow on the mountains and rain in the hills. And mud everywhere.

General McLaren had been sent by London to discuss the conduct of the Peninsula War with the local commanders without recourse to pen and paper. He was also visiting the separate armies in the Peninsula to assess the morale and potential weaknesses.

He found the armies in Spain cold and damp but spoiling for a fight. They believed they were close to a French army and were hoping to engage them. One evening the commanding officer, Colonel Fitz-Warwick, interrupted their discussion to receive a report from a young cavalry officer. The young captain was summoned into the presence. He was not very well turned out and he was not invited to sit. Before him sprawled the Council of War, lounging in order of seniority. The least vertical was the general in a blue jacket, next the colonel in red infantry uniform leaning slightly towards the general, finally, the adjutant sitting stiffly in a red cavalry uniform, at his desk. The colonel explained that the captain had valuable information regarding the likely position of the French army. The captain told them that that they had been searching the mountains that bordered the Spanish plain before falling down into Portugal. They had found a French build up. With permission, he intended to go out again the next day to take a closer look. The commanding officer agreed, and the captain was dismissed.

When he had left, the commanding officer explained rather shyly that he had found a use for a cavalry group from one of the unfashionable regiments. They were from the West Midlands along the Rivers Wye and Severn and had particular skills in surveillance that seemed to be founded in the art of poaching. The commanding officer had not enquired too closely but had separated them out and had been impressed with the results. They were now camped at a farmhouse a couple of miles from the main camp. They were scruffy but well fed, and their equipment was immaculate. The time that they saved on spit and polish and drilling they spent riding hard in the surrounding hills hoping for a contact. They also provided a point of contact with the guerilla bands that had formed in the Spanish hills. Today they had made a lucky contact with the French. Tomorrow they would go out again and report in full.

The general had been a brave and successful cavalry officer in India and America. He asked to be attached to the group for the day. The commanding officer did not like the idea. Not least because of the apparent lack of discipline in the group, which he had allowed to develop in the interest of not diminishing their effectiveness. Also, he did not want the group and their methods to become generally well known. He had hoped to make something of it and gain some military praise.

However, he was outranked and wise enough not to

argue. He again warned the general not to be shocked and sent for the young officer to return.

He explained the general's request. The captain shook his head. He looked at the general and shook his head again. He would not be able to keep up. He could be killed. The mission would be compromised. Also, if he was captured, all his secrets would be lost. This was not insubordination but a brutal statement of the facts. A frankness not generally seen in the British army at that time when preferment and promotion were dictated by deference to superiors. The captain had done a calculation and reckoned that they needed him and his patrols and would not jeopardise the arrangement by being too rigid. So far, he had been proved right but he was careful not to overstep the mark. He only did what was necessary to protect the patrols. He was asked to retire. When he was recalled he was told the adjutant of the general would accompany him. The adjutant was young, a good horseman and did not know too many secrets but would report to the general on what he saw. He would accompany the general to report to Sir Arthur Wellesley.

'Very well,' said the young officer, 'but I must have command of the expedition regardless of seniority, and the conditions might be very harsh.'

The adjutant asked what he was called.

'Everybody calls me TK.'

TK insisted that the adjutant should return with him to their camp. The start the next day would be very early and he wanted to ensure that he was properly equipped. He could eat and sleep with the group, which was what the general wanted. The general wanted to know it all and he guessed that the adjutant was in for a shock.

On the short ride through the mud to the farm the adjutant apologised to TK and promised not to be a burden. TK replied that he should not worry. The group would do what it would do. The adjutant could observe, the rest was up to the fall of the cards, and TK would make the calls. TK asked the adjutant what he would like to be called informally and in the heat of battle.

'Otto.'

TK smiled, 'We don't have any other Ottos, so Otto it will be.' And he held out his hand.

The adjutant was not much older than TK. He was taller and slimmer with dark curly hair, a moustache and a deadly smile.

Otto had expected to be led to a tented camp. Instead, he was led to an old farmhouse. The second surprise was to smell a terrific meal cooking. The third surprise was that, apart from the kitchen, horses appeared to be in all the downstairs rooms. In the outbuildings, there were more horses and several tack rooms in beautiful order with men working on the equipment. They smelled and looked perfect. In the kitchen, two men turned spits, boiled pots, filled ovens and attended fires. Tonight, they would be cooks. Tomorrow they would be killers.

Before dinner, TK called the men together.

'This is Otto, he is the senior officer here. You will call him Sir. He will not give orders and he will do what we tell him. But if any man is insubordinate or even just rude I will punish him harshly. Do I need to say more?'

He looked for a challenging eye, but none met his.

'Very well, Otto is with us to observe. We will not ask him to cook, clean or fight. He will not engage. If he is captured, he must be killed just like the rest of us.'

TK drew Otto aside. 'You will see things that may shock you. Things that are not in the manual and not in the rules of chivalry. Please do not intervene and do not judge us until you see the results. Then I will rely on your discretion. In the meantime, your life is in the hands of these men – trust them.'

TK instructed two of the men to take Otto and find him a dark jacket, dark breeches, dull boots and a place to sleep. Tomorrow he would need one of their saddles and one of their horses. Otto knew the significance of fighting out of uniform and realised that he would be a spy, outside the etiquette of warfare and outside the protection of its rules.

Otto was shown a selection of dark jackets and dark breeches with well-waxed but unpolished boots. He found a set that fitted. He was surprised at the quality, officer standard that was out of character with the dull colouring. He was surprised, and then not surprised, to see stitching of cuts in the cloth and staining through the dye. He wondered how this could be the same army that drilled and flogged its men to March and fight in columns and squares in perfect uniform. The colours roughly matched the green coats and black britches of the regiment.

Dinner was pork. The best that Otto had eaten for months. 'Don't ask,' he was told, and he did not.

He was woken in deep darkness and told to dress and join the group. He went down and was given hot soup and bread. A man led up a horse and a blackened sword which he was not expected to use. He became aware of tension among these calm men. A dark red horse without a trace of white stood in fury with ears flat against her head in a separate stall. She was having her head pulled down to the crib so that she could not bite. A man banged her in the ribs and lifted her nearside front foot so that she could not kick. A saddle was dropped on. TK sat on from the edge of the stall. A bridle was slipped on and the bit slipped in. The horse's fury calmed, and the front foot was lowered. The head collar was released, and TK swung out of the stall like a riding instructor showing his paces. The red mare danced. One of the men told Otto quietly that the Red Bitch is a killer until she has a rider. Then, so long as it is a good rider, she was as good as gold. But God help the rider if he fell off. The Captain always takes her out when he is expecting action. You may see something special today.

Each horse had a roll behind the saddle with blankets for men and horses, bare rations, several tight twists of hay and horseshoes. TK told Otto that each horse carried its own spare shoes. When the horse was shod, a couple of spares were made to the exact size. If a horse loses two shoes it might be shot. If it loses three shoes, the blacksmith might be shot.

Six of them rode out with Otto before dawn. They headed for the hills in the grey damp morning. After four hours, Otto began to feel some new muscles. They rode on, staying behind the ridge of the valley. They rode all day through wet bracken, gorse and copses, around rocky outcrops and along swift streams. They ate cold bread, cheese and bacon and drank cold water. That night they slept in their cloaks in the rain. The next day they approached the ridge of another valley that TK thought may contain a French contingent. They stopped and then moved forwards slowly. Otto could hardly breathe.

They heard the French patrol before they saw it. The French patrol came trotting and jingling round a bend on the mountainside below them. Ten French cavalry strung out in single file.

The order came immediately, in a harsh commanding growl.

'Otto, under that tree. Hackett and two go left. Two right with me. Charge!'

And with that TK rode down on the French. The red mare was far ahead and seemed to fly over the steep rough ground. Then, just before they engaged she seemed to do a step in the air and change the line of her attack. The French were put off balance. They had turned to receive an attack from one side and it came from the other. TK's sword flashed in small jabs and slices and Frenchmen fell. Three down. Two broke to the left and were cut down by Hackett and his companions. Hackett sat tall in the saddle and crashed down relentlessly, tirelessly with his sabre. Resistance faded in the face of the onslaught.

TK's pair arrived and crashed into the remainder, knocking them off balance and slashing down with their sabres. One survivor, an officer, broke to the right and spurred away down the hill. TK swivelled the red mare and followed. The officer had a good horse and rode well along the mountain track, but the red mare was faster and nimbler. Even so, there was some doubt as to whether TK would catch him before he reached the crest. Suddenly the path turned sharply round a rocky outcrop. The French horse slowed and stumbled. The Red Bitch danced level and TK stabbed the Frenchman through the heart from behind. He left his sword in the Frenchman's back, steadied him in the saddle and taking the reins turned and walked back with the Frenchman sitting upright, just as he had left.

In a few minutes, the group had killed every Frenchman. The French had been unprepared and died in shock. The group quickly tied the French corpses to their saddles, using the Frenchmen's own stirrups. Then they threaded the reins through the bridle rings. Two of the group had been cut by French swords. They were splashed with brandy, sewn up and put back in the saddle. It was their reluctant task to lead the French horses back to the camp. They knew the routine. Collect the valuables, take the boots, strip the uniforms and drop the bodies off a cliff. The horses would be added to the group's stock for evaluation. The best were retained and the weakest were sent back to the regiment.

TK beckoned Otto down and they followed the Frenchmen's tracks back towards the French army. They were careful not to go over the ridge line at the point where the French patrol had left the valley. They expected to find a large army. First, they smelled them, and then they heard them.

TK kept the horses back behind the ridge, neatly pulled a rider into Her Ladyship's saddle and dropped down. TK, Hackett and Otto crawled to the top of the ridge. The French army was being assembled in a shallow valley below them. Otto started to pull out a telescope, but TK pushed it down, pointing to the sun breaking through the mist. In surveillance, telescopes were two-edged swords. They provided brilliant detail and clarity, but they provided a reflection off the lens that could be picked up by watchers far removed from the target.

Otto and TK estimated the numbers of men, horses and guns. They estimated the food and the hospital activity. They looked at the discipline, the uniforms, the routines. They watched the patrol groups riding in and reporting. As it broke through, the evening sun lit up the French army in fine detail flashing on metal among the blue and white uniforms, white tents and the black of the guns. However, a large area, lower down the valley, was shrouded by trees and there was no way of knowing what they concealed.

Otto said that they had seen enough. Their report would be invaluable. TK disagreed. He wanted to know more. He knew that Otto would refuse to be sent back unless he came with him. He decided to send Hackett with two men to ride hard below the ridge line to the head of the valley and look down over the other side to see what was below. He assumed that it would be a plain with converging army units preparing to enter the valley.

He called Hackett and explained his proposal. Hackett stood as he rode, upright with his head straight and eyes ranging, missing nothing. They gave Hackett extra food and extra blankets and sent him off as the evening sun started to fade. Two men were instructed to remain to look after Hackett's horse and to provide support on his return or to try to kill him if he was captured.

TK hopped up behind Her Ladyship's rider, who slid off and mounted his own horse. TK, Otto and the rider, set off back towards the British camp. They rode until dark and then slept in their cloaks until dawn. Cold and hungry they rode into the farmyard the next morning. Again, Otto was excited at the smell of good cooking. Again, he was surprised as TK and his men did not rest to eat until the horses had been rubbed down, fed and watered and the tack cleaned. However, they did not work alone. The whole team joined in to help.

Over their meal TK and Otto discussed what they had seen. Otto was amazed to hear the detail that he, the observer, had missed. However, strategically he was able to conclude that the French army was assembling for a major battle down on the plains below the valley. However, at this stage the activity on the plain was only conjecture. Again, the food was delicious and now accompanied by local wine. Otto now knew better than to ask how they managed this.

Otto said "You must have enjoyed the fight."

TK replied "I do not enjoy fights. I enjoy lovely ladies, good company, fine food and fast horses. But fighting is my profession. I fight to win. I do everything necessary. I do only what has to be done."

"Where did you learn to ride and fight?"

"Riding from my mother. Fighting from my father, and a few others.

Otto took the opportunity to ask TK about the sword

that he had used. TK showed it to him and explained that his father had brought it back from India. The tip was broken off like the prow of a Greek warship and the blade was only slightly curved. The blade was hollowed and had a heavy reinforcement on the upper edge. When it had been brought back it had no hilt, but his father had liked the look of the blackened steel. The local blacksmith had been an armourer and he put on a standard hilt, balanced it and sharpened the blade and the broken end. TK loved the balance and the edge.

Otto asked about the stabbing sword strokes. TK laughed and said that Otto was pressing a bit too close to home. But he explained that he had been shown by the local butcher where to cut arteries and tendons. When his mother died and his father was away with the regiment he had been adopted and protected by the local community, including the butcher, the blacksmith, the huntsman, the gamekeeper and the river warden. They had taught him a lot, including the huntsman teaching him how to ride hard and the butcher teaching him how to kill. But much more, they taught him how to live off the land on both sides of the law. TK then looked Otto in the eye and told him that his training had equipped him how to deal with gossips. Then he smiled, that charming deadly smile, but Otto had got the point.

The next morning, back in uniform, Otto rode his own big grey horse down to the English camp to make his report. He could hardly contain his amazement at what he had seen. Mostly relating to a cavalry officer who rode a red horse that could only be mounted on three legs and carried a broken sabre that he used like a rapier. The bond between TK and his men, and how TK had attacked eight French cavalry knowing that his men would follow. How they looked after their horses before themselves and the constant teasing and joking among them, but clearly subject to an iron code of mutual preservation. The men clearly worshipped TK and would follow him anywhere. Discipline was absolute. The greatest punishment would be to be sent from the troop. But above all, Otto was amazed at TK's horsemanship and swordsmanship. He had never seen anything like it.

The CO's worst fears were being realised. How could he explain that he was running a bunch of spies under the British flag?

However, the strategic information that had been provided completely outweighed any concerns about his management.

The assembly of a French army must be reported immediately to Wellesley and then in London. This information could change the course of the war on the Peninsula.

But also, the General was beginning to form a plan to deal with a problem in London, relating to losing young officers and the stealing of state secrets that had been tolerated for too long. It was time for him to leave. And Colonel Fitz-Warwick breathed easy at last.

Hackett

The team consisted of Lieutenant Hackett, Sergeant Smith and Corporal Evans. The best of the group.

At the head of the valley, where the French were assembling, was a mountain. The easternmost edge of a range that went from east to west. That range was the start of a series descending south. The range concluded with a series of valleys leading down to a major river valley. The French were in the easternmost valley. Hackett's led his team as far as he could up the parallel valley to the west. Here the heads of the valleys came close together. He told them to set up camp but stay out of sight behind the ridge, and no fires. Also, he told them to be prepared to move behind the next ridge line if they saw any French. He explained that he was going to go up to the tree line and work east to get a view of the route that the French were using to enter the valley. He could not move fast on foot, so it could take several days.

He took cold bacon, cheese and bread and a big water bottle. He left his sword but took a big knife. He climbed slowly but steadily to the head of the French valley. He started to follow the route of a stream, now merely a trickle of meltwater.

After two hours he was still far short of the tree line when the stream turned sharply, and he walked into a level area occupied by two French soldiers sitting down to lunch. The first one to stand was the first one to die.

Hackett hit him in the throat and broke his neck as he fell. The second reached for his musket. Hackett dived across and forced his hand into the lock as the hammer fell. Hackett forced his free hand over the Frenchman's mouth as he extracted the other hand from the lock. He then put the freed hand over the other hand and pulled the Frenchman back until his feet lifted off the ground. Without his feet the Frenchman could not exert much force and Hackett maintained the suffocating hold. The twisting became more frantic and then began to subside as the pounding of the Frenchman's heart grew faster, peaked and then faded. Hackett twisted the Frenchman's head, lowered him and then jerked upwards. There was a snap and Hackett dropped him.

If Hackett' comrades had seen it they would not have been surprised. It was absolutely in character for this black-haired, hawk-nosed, strong chinned, straight-standing whipcord soldier who never took a step back. They didn't really know him, but they bound him in as one of their own. They called him 'Ackit'.

Hackett checked the pockets and satchels of the Frenchmen. He found nothing but bread and cheese which seemed a bit fresher than his own and some sausage. Also, some letters that he could not read. Another lost love.

Hackett searched downhill and to the west and found a steep gully. He dragged each Frenchman to the edge and dropped them down. Then he had to climb up slowly and painfully nursing his bruised hand.

He ate the Frenchmens' lunch and then continued upwards and eastwards. At dark he wrapped in his cloak and finished the last of the Frenchmen's food. At dawn he crawled to the shoulder of the mountain and saw the valley below him and beyond that, to the east, the plain. He saw that the valley was far bigger than they had supposed. Below the point that they had observed, it turned west and opened out into a wide lower valley heavily wooded and capable of hiding a huge army and all its support and equipment. There was a smaller valley to the East opening onto the plain. There he saw bullocks towing heavy guns and heavy horses pulling laden carts between the copses of oaks.

They were heading for the entrance to the valley. They formed long lines snaking across the plain, appearing and disappearing with the undulations of the terrain, with herds of horses, cattle, sheep and a few straggling pigs tended by Spanish horsemen.

Hackett knew that his information was important, and he must not be captured or killed. He decided to go back round the back of the mountain, much longer and slower but he assumed, safe from view. He climbed to the tree line and turned left. He was in cover and able to move more quickly as he headed south and west.

After one hour the spasms struck. He dropped his pants and an explosion erupted. He crouched in shock. He washed from his water bottle and set off again. But he felt far weaker. Then again, another spasm. Again, he washed and went on. But slower and weaker. He had to secure each foothold and handhold before moving to the next. He used branches, rocks, roots and heather stems. Time and again he was overwhelmed. Each time he washed off and resumed. Each time slower and weaker than before. And now, with no water. At last he was crawling, two or three yards per minute. All he knew was that he had to keep going around towards the west.

After another hour he came to a trickle of meltwater. He washed himself and sat in the stream until he was numb. Then he filled his water bottle. He abandoned his breeches which were rubbing him raw and wrapped in his cloak and rested. So, warm against the chill of the spasms he closed his eyes and slept. He woke as the sun began to set. There were no more spasms, but he did not risk eating any of his English food. He just drank water and then set off again, crawling west. But now, his weakness was amplified by his pain, from his bruised hand, his empty stomach and now, his sore bottom. He soon realised that it was impossible to make any meaningful progress in the dark and he would be better to rest. He stopped again, wrapped in his cloak and slept. At dawn, he ate a bit of wet bread and started to crawl to the west. Now, to add to his injuries, his bare legs above the boots were being scratched. Hour after hour he staggered and crawled forward. In the late afternoon he came to the cliff that formed the western flank of the mountain. A scree of loose stone offered a way down. He slid and rolled to the bottom. Now he had cuts and bruises to add to his wounds. The bread might have given a little strength but had resulted in more spasms. Even so, for the sake of his strength he ate more bread and drank more water. He knew that he must keep drinking.

And so, he crawled through the boulders. At the rate of one yard per minute he might get to the ridge by dusk where he could rest safely. Each yard was a nightmare of effort and pain. He left a trail of blood on the stones to mark his path.

Sergeant Smith found him behind the ridge the next morning. He was huddled in his blanket and unconscious. Smith had followed a kite. If Hackett had opened his eyes he would have been blinded. Smith cradled him in his arms, struggled onto his horse and rode slowly to the camp. They were shocked at his condition, but Evans remembered similar conditions in India where they treated the victims with water, black tea and sugar. Smith's grandmother had recommended a little salt as for boiling potatoes. They thought it could do no harm. They found a bit of salt with the food and a bit of sugar with the tea, mixed it with lots of water and dribbled some into Hackett's mouth. His reflexes worked, and he swallowed.

They made a cushion from a folded blanket, wrapped him in a cloak and Smith cradled him on the cushion, across the saddle inside the cloak. And so, they set off across the valley.

They rode carefully through the copses, rarely having to cross open ground. But it was slow and wet. At last, they rode over the western ridge line into comparative safety. They rode down into the valley, laid Hackett to rest and lit a fire. They warmed the mixture for Hackett who swallowed it but did not gain consciousness.

They rode on, stopping occasionally to change horses. Smith was in balance and could continue after each change. As the light faded they planned to build a big fire in a hollow, so that its flames would not show and the smoke would not be seen in the darkness. They slowed to look for a suitable place when they heard a call.

'Ooo-eee.'

They waited five seconds and then drew their swords and called back, 'Eee-ooo.'

They heard horses approaching fast and six of their colleagues rode up. They were the search party, led by Smith's twin brother.

The British regiment was a day away. The new team took over building the camp and the fire. They made a bed for Hackett and prepared hot food for Smith and Evans. They now had plenty of men to stay mounted as guards through the night.

The next morning Hackett opened his eyes and drank the mixture. They did not wait to cook but set off, as before, with the other Smith on cradle duty. Two men rode ahead fast to get things ready at the farmhouse and to ride down to the medical tent to ask for advice and medicine.

When they arrived at the farmhouse they had a bath ready and then a warm bed close to the fire. Water and sleep had been confirmed as the right mix and dry bread was ready for Hackett to try when he woke. The country remedies were not included but the team gave them anyway, because that was the way they lived, and died. The next morning, Hackett woke and wanted to report to TK but could still hardly speak. It could wait until tomorrow.

The next morning TK came down and sat with him to hear his report. Clearly, the French were assembling for a siege. TK rode down and reported to Colonel Fitz-

Warwick. He passed on Hackett' view that the size of the guns and the amount of supplies indicated that the French must be preparing for an attack on a major fortification, accessible either along the bottom of the valley, or, more likely, back out onto the plain and driving north.

In the meantime, the French were hiding in a trap.

TK rode down to the British camp to provide the final piece of the jigsaw. Colonel Fitz-Warwick told him that the general and his entourage had left two days ago. He agreed that TK should ride after them with the new information.

TK rode back to the farm and chose two of his best riders and six of the best horses. The Red Bitch would stay behind this time. They would ride hard all day and into the night to catch up with the general. And so, back into the saddle and back into the rain, they cantered in pursuit with the news that it would be a major battle from the plain.

The Duel

The morning of the duel was beautiful with clear sky and hazy sunshine. It would be hot later. But as TK watched dawn break at the barracks he knew that he would not be bothered by that. The duel would be over before most people sat down for breakfast.

All around the barracks the first sounds of the day gradually built up. It was a special time. The sunlight lifted the spirits. In the stables, the warm peace of horses munching hay. Outside, the rattle of buckets, the ring of horseshoes on flags, quiet voices talking to horses and colleagues and the occasional cheerful laugh. The best of times.

Evans had brought TK coffee and hot water to wash and shave two hours before dawn. His jacket, the same one that he had worn at the reception, was still presentable. He would need only that jacket, black breeches, boots to below the knee and short spurs. He would need no helmet, no belt, and no gloves. Apart from the spurs he could be going for a walk in the park.

He had brought Evans with him from Spain because he worked best with the Red Bitch.

'How is Her Ladyship this morning?' asked TK.

'On her toes, Sir. She seems to be up for it, or something. The sea cruise seems to have done her good. Would you like a bit of breakfast, Sir?'

'A lot please, Evans, and more coffee. I would like to crap before we leave.'

'I can only organise the breakfast, Sir. But that won't be difficult. Everyone in the barracks wants to help. Otherwise, you are on your own'.

Otto and the older second arrived with the coach soon after dawn and the beautiful moment was past. TK took charge of the departure. This involved careful procedures to avoid the Red Bitch injuring anyone, or more importantly, at this moment, herself. Damn, he had no reserve horse. His life rested on her eccentric talents. Only now, when it was too late, did it begin to dawn on him that there would be no second chance. No borrowing a spare horse or sword. He would be on his own.

Evans had heard the talk in the Barracks. The Count would be a formidable opponent. He was tall and strong and rumoured to be a brilliant horseman. Evans knew that TK would need all of Her Ladyship's footwork to avoid trouble and, possibly, gain an advantage. He admired and respected TK and he was going to do everything in his power to help him. He had brushed Her Ladyship's coat until it gleamed, he had cleaned and oiled her hooves and he had soaped the saddle and bridle to prevent any breakages. He had done the first part of the preparations. Next, Evans pulled her head down through a hole in the stall. Then, when he was sure that she could not bite, he lifted her nearside front foot and secured it by a rope around her neck. So far so good. Next, Evans put on the numnah and the saddle, skillfully manoeuvring her away from the side of the stalls where she could trap him. Then the girth had to be tightened, always a worrying moment in case she had found a new trick. Again, so far so good. Finally, he slipped the bridle on over the head collar. There was no bonding between horse and groom and it was not elegant, but it worked. Evans stepped off a stall rail into the saddle and released the foreleg. TK released the rope of the head collar and passed it to Evans. Her Ladyship stepped daintily out of the stall with her head up and her intelligent eyes sparkling. Otto noticed that the dark red of her winter coat had been replaced by the dark pink of summer. She was spectacular. TK would ride in the coach and Evans would follow closely with Her Ladyship.

Otto's companion used the time in the coach to go over the formalities with TK once again. Their main concern was that the Count should not try to use his seniority to gain an advantage by introducing new rules.

The scene in the park was surprising. Dozens of coaches were drawn up behind the narrow road along the edge of the field. The early morning sun shone on the dewy grass. The coaches made quite a spectacle with lacquer and brass gleaming in the sun. Grooms attended to the horses. The occupants strolled and chatted together. The ladies had taken the opportunity to dress up and the gentlemen had added a bit of colour to their outfits. Some bets were being made. Apparently this quarrel was not going to be settled privately.

On the other side of the road, in the field, the Count's coach was drawn up and the Count was exercising on a big chestnut horse that was prancing and pawing the ground, sweating and blowing froth. The Count held the horse in with a heavy bit and double reins.

'Too much oats,' said Evans.

'Good,' said TK. They drew up near the Count's coach and Otto and his companion stepped down to conduct the formalities.

Back in one of the spectator coaches, painted with a coat of arms, a boy looked out with wide eyes at the Count. He marvelled at the tall figure on the big horse: the tall leather cap; the blonde hair falling in ringlets at the side of his head; the piercing blue eyes picking up the blue of his coat; the shining tall cavalry boots and the gleaming spurs. And then there was the sword. He looked in awe at the long broad blade of the heavy cavalry weapon shining in the early sun. His parents smiled at his excitement to see the best duellist in the world and the privilege of seeing him perform. He did not doubt for a moment that the Count would triumph. His mother saw it as an endorsement of her position in society when her friend the Count would prevail. And kill one more British officer, thought her husband.

The protagonists presented themselves. Otto invited TK to object to the hard leather cap of the Count. TK declined but asked to see under the Count's white gauntlets. The Count was wearing heavy leather wrist protectors, again defying the instruction against wearing armour. Again, TK declined to object. And at the sight of TK bare-headed, in his shirt and stock on a smaller horse with a black sword without a tip the Count simply sneered and turned away.

'Damn,' thought TK, 'on top of all that he is left-handed.'

The Count was no fool. He had guessed that the

encounter at the Duchess's reception had not been an accident and he had been manoeuvred into making the challenge. Sabres on horseback were not unknown between cavalry officers but in his case it was exceptional.

He usually engineered to receive a challenge and chose the weapons. Pistols were most reliable, but foils were sometimes advantageous because of his length of stride and reach. Some of these advantages had been taken away. However, he could still rely on a big horse, a big sword, exceptional strength from his tall frame and his long reach. He was also left-handed and skilled in manoeuvring to take advantage of this. He simply had to play to his strengths and not get involved in trials of horsemanship or swordsmanship where, presumably, his opponent felt confident.

TK had two advantages: his horse was fast, nimble and well-trained; and his sword was strong, exceptionally sharp and beautifully balanced. If either failed, he was doomed.

So the Count's strategy was to use his big horse to intimidate the mare and to keep his opponent on his forehand. From there he could use his long heavy sword to crash down from a great height with a weighted stroke that would break wrists, swords and skulls.

It started well for the Count. TK did not attempt to avoid the Count's forehand and the Count was able to use his reach to crash down heavy blows. But TK used his horse to extend the range and used the reinforced back of his sword to divert the strokes without receiving the full force. All the Count's violence was being diverted away. The Count persisted, and TK's arm grew weary. Perhaps he should get out of range for a while to take a rest. But on the next charge the Count changed tactics. He moved closer and swung upwards with huge effort. TK leaned away and parried upwards, but the Count's tactic had worked. The force of the Count's drive and the weight of his sword deflected the razor-sharp edge of TK's sword against his left eyebrow. Instantly, the eye filled with blood and his vision was lost. The Count was reinvigorated at the sight of blood and charged and charged again with mighty swings, driving TK back onto the Count's forehand.

All was action and fury. The Count's big horse foaming, sweating, and throwing up clods on the turns. The Count standing tall and crashing huge blows down. TK working his legs and feet to keep the red mare out of range and twisting his wrists to divert the Count's blows with the back of his sword. After each charge, TK cleared his eye and got most of his vision back. But having to turn his head was adding to the strain.

The Count was using great strength and energy and appeared tireless in his attack. TK was working hard with his legs to position the dancing mare to keep out of range and to parry the strokes. The mare seemed fine but his wrist was losing strength. Then the Count mustered all his strength for a repeat of the upwards swing that had almost succeeded previously. This time he tried to get even closer and to lean further across. But this time TK leaned far out of his saddle and skipped his horse away from the swing and allowed the Count's sword to slide up the back of the black blade and away. TK began to doubt whether he could outlast the Count at this game. He touched the mare's flank for the turn and was relieved to feel her keen response. TK forced his arm up and stiffened his aching wrist ready for the next attack and wiped his eye. He blinked, but yes, the Count's horse had shuddered to a stop, its chest heaving, its neck drenched in sweat and foam and its flanks drenched in sweat and blood. The Count jerked on his reins to pull himself upright, but his sword arm dropped as he strove to regain his balance.

TK saw his chance. The red mare spun around, and TK gently used the sharp side of the sword for the first time to slice the tendons at the top of the Count's hand above the guard of his big sword and below the leather wrist protector. He cut through the white gauntlet leaving a swelling red line. The big sword dropped and hung on its lanyard from the limp bloodied hand. Then TK pressed the mare against the bloodied flank of the Count's horse. The Count looked up at the red gold halo of TK's hair in front of the early morning sun. He did not notice as TK gently prodded the chisel-sharp tip of the dark blade into his lower right abdomen.

And so, the duel ended with the Count slumped in the saddle cradling his ruined hand with his sword dangling on its lanyard and his double reins dangling from the sunken head of his horse. A broken man on a broken horse. TK cut the lanyard and hooked the sword through its guard with his own sword. Then he took one of the reins and led them slowly back to the coaches.

TK's doctor cleaned the drying blood from his eyebrow, declared that it was just a scratch and did something that made it sting quite painfully. The Count's senior second came up and formally announced that the Count had suffered a wound to his left hand and could not continue. Honour was satisfied. The duel was concluded.

TK took Otto aside and told him that the Count had fought his last duel. His hand would never recover. This was symbolic. More important, the Count would be dead in three days. His appendix had been pierced. This would become apparent during the next few hours and the Count would have three days to put his affairs in order. So the rats would start to run.

Her Ladyship had danced the Count's huge horse to a standstill and she was hardly blowing. TK took her for a gallop round the park. Mostly to thank her, but also just for fun. Her put her through her paces and could not believe what he knew, that without a rider she was a killer. Even so, she was a joy to ride. The spectators then saw the skill of horse and rider that had defeated the Count. TK returned to the coach and put on his jacket over his bloodied shirt. He decided to ride the mare behind the coach back to the barracks.

Along the way he passed the decorated coach which had been pulled up to watch the duel and saw a young boy looking out. The boy saw the man who had defeated the Count. He saw the dark, red gold hair, the broad brow, the broad nose, the broad chin and the short strong teeth now smiling from the suntanned face and he wondered how the Count had ever dared to ride out against such a man. He looked down and away. His mother looked down and away and her shoulders sagged to see the man who had caused her such loss. His father appeared disconcerted.

The Thames

Later that day, as the news of the duel travelled like wildfire, a rumour started to circulate that the Count had been mortally wounded. Agents of the Crown were positioned around the front and back of the Count's house. First the doctors came and went. Then members of the administration and the nobility started to slip in and out carrying document cases. Each was followed as he slipped away.

In one case a man who appeared to be a doctor had a coach drawn close to the rear of the house. He emerged with a footman carrying a chest. He was followed to St James' where he got out of the coach and his place was taken by the man who had watched the duel from the decorated coach that morning. He was very well-connected in the highest government and social circles. The agents hesitated, and the opportunity was lost. The coach set off and the agent hurried to report to Otto. He was furious and rode into the barracks to find TK.

He was lucky. He found TK talking to Evans near the stables. Otto pleaded with TK to go with the agent to establish the rendezvous and stop the escape of the spy and his chest. They found a cavalry horse for TK while he collected his sword and they set off in the direction of the coach. Otto had guessed that they would be heading to the river to escape by ship. They headed that way and caught up with the coach as it left the City and headed east. They followed at a distance.

As TK rode along the riverside the traffic gradually thinned as the buildings became poorer. The cobbled streets flowed like open sewers. And the open sewers did not flow at all. A line of dogs trotted past with the heads down in strict order of precedence, led by the biggest and ugliest, off on a mission. Eventually TK was following a single coach through terrible slums. Even the beggars stopped begging. People sat in filth and despair. And the stink was overpowering. TK wondered how these buildings had ever been new, who built them, and how they had fallen into such decay.

Eventually the coach pulled up alongside a riverside inn. The wooden floors and walkways lurched at unrelated angles. The riverside was covered in planks leading to a floating jetty where a four-oared boat waited. The occupant of the carriage had stepped out into the mud and sunk over his buckled shoes as he hurried towards the boat and called for the boatman to carry the chest down from his coach.

TK drew his sword and drove his horse down towards the water's edge. But from nowhere children gathered round him with fast fingers pulling at anything that they could reach. They even unbuckled his spurs. Knowing well that his boots would be next, TK stood in his stirrups and swung at the urchins with the back of his sword. To no avail. They would scrag him if he did not start cutting. And the boat was starting to push off. He would have to drive his horse on to the boat. This was going to be messy.

'Belay!'

The order was bellowed with such force that TK froze with the sword raised. The urchins slipped away. A big, bearded, barrel-chested, figure appeared on the jetty. Behind him a Royal Navy skiff had pulled up with twelve oars standing perpendicular.

'You must be Captain Kynaston, Sir. I am Boson Fairburn, Sir, ready to receive your orders, Sir. The launch is ready, Sir, and under your orders, Sir.'

TK was concerned for the coach, its driver and its horses, also the agent and their horses. He asked whether the boson could provide two guards. In response the boson summoned two teenagers, gave them a coin and set off for the skiff. TK followed. He confirmed that they were after the row boat, its passenger and the chest. The boat was manned by four big river men and the helm was held by a piratical figure who lashed them with his tongue.

The bosun nodded and declared that they must be headed for the Dutchman anchored in mid-channel. The Dutch were supposed to be neutral but hired out to either side.

TK asked whether they could cut off the row boat before it reached the Dutchman. The bosun replied that they could cut them off with five minutes to spare and never come within pistol shot. TK was dumped in the stern of the skiff and the bosun started to bellow orders including that the main object was the chest which must not be lost at any cost.

TK need not have worried. The skiff cut through the tide and caught up with the escaping boat as though it had been standing still. Sure enough, as they approached the chest was thrown overboard. TK wondered whether the bosun could bring the skiff alongside the chest before it sank. But as they approached an order boomed out from the bosun and an oarsman dived in and grabbed the chest. A line was thrown to him and the chest and oarsman were pulled aboard.

The skiff pulled alongside the escaping boat, scattering its oars. TK got ready to draw his sword, but on the skiff, men pulled out short heavy batons and the boat surrendered. It was all over. Almost. The coach passenger dived overboard and under the surface. Again, an oarsman stepped from the skiff onto the boat and dived into the water. He came up with the passenger. He was thrown a line and sailor and passenger were hauled in. Under the gaze of the Dutchman, the rowing boat was put in tow with two naval oarsmen to encourage the crew.

Back at the tavern TK was relieved to see the coach, its horses, driver, guard and the government agent together with his own horse all happily rescued, fed and watered. The bosun explained that the tavern was provisioned from the river and a regular stopping place for the skiff. It was therefore a safe place to eat and drink. TK was relieved to accept the bread, cold ham and weak ale that was being supplied to the crew.

The boat crew and the piratical helmsman, who had been very subdued, were thrown into the river for the fun of it. The helmsman could not swim, at least not with his boots on, and was last seen with his boots floating in the sewage and filth and his tricorn hat floating where his head was last seen.

TK sent the coach, with the cavalry horse tied behind, back to the barracks. He told the driver and the agent to ensure their safe journey back to Chelsea where they would all have questions to answer. TK rode in the skiff back to Chelsea with the spy and his chest. They were in safe hands and would make good speed on the tide. As TK looked back he saw the Dutch ship raising its sails as the sun started to set. So much for identifying the rendezvous.

TK returned to the barracks late, tired and hungry. He had not eaten properly since breakfast. He had resisted the temptation to eat more than a snack at the riverside tavern. He had handed over the spy and his box and waited for the coach to return. There was no sign of Otto. He was very angry. He thought Otto had been inefficient and lazy. He had asked too much. And be damned to rank, he would tell him so tomorrow. So he ate bread ham and cheese and went to bed still hungry and still angry.

The next morning, he got a decent breakfast in the mess. When Otto turned up he got the broadside. Otto apologised and explained that the instructions for TK to be involved in the riverside adventure had come from above. TK should be pleased. He was not. With the duel and the riverside adventure, he had become an unattached, unacknowledged adventurer at the beck and call of Otto's faceless masters. He was supposed to be an army officer. Otto did not know what to say and TK started to contemplate life outside the army.

The Ladies

An invitation arrived from Sir Robert asking him to his house for tea that afternoon. His first instinct was to refuse because he knew nothing of London manners and had only his old uniform to wear. However, the prospect of seeing Nell cheered him up and he accepted. Evans and a team from the barracks shaved him, cleaned up his uniform and arranged a carriage.

Tea was not what he expected. Sir Robert sent his apologies. The ladies tried to tease him about the breach of formalities and the likely damage to their reputations. "You will have to marry us both". They looked beautiful in summer dresses and their laughter tinkled in the sunshine. He started to relax, and the ladies turned the conversation to his red mare whose reputation, as far as they were concerned, was almost as great as his own.

He relaxed and told them a little of the patrols that he rode and how one day the red mare had appeared outside their camp after a battle. She ran off when they approached her and then came back. When they tried to catch her she fought furiously, kicking and biting, bucking and rearing. It was clear that she was a beautiful animal, but they doubted whether it would be worth the time and effort required to tame her.

They had used some tricks to confine her and were amazed when TK got into the saddle to find that she was transformed. Her head came up, her ears pricked forward, and she stepped out beautifully. They had no idea who had trained her so well, why she behaved impeccably when she had a rider and why she tried to kill any pedestrian when she did not have a rider. She had responded brilliantly to his training for cavalry manoeuvres and would respond to leg and saddle pressures without need for the bit or reins. She would step sideways and turn sharply at the slightest command. This made her invaluable in battle. He explained that these were the nimble manoeuvres that had enabled him to keep himself and his horse fresh while the Count had exhausted himself and his horse with thunderous charges.

They discovered a mutual love of hunting and the ladies explained how they used the aunt's Navy pension and Nell's small farm rents to support a lifestyle dedicated to hunting several days per week. They loved to tell stories of their adventures and misadventures during the hunt and the social confusion that they caused. TK was very taken with Nell whose joy and enthusiasm was infectious. And the aunt was wicked. He agreed to introduce them to Her Ladyship the next morning, before his departure to visit his father, up on the River Severn.

That night he dined in the mess. He enjoyed the gossip, the jokes and the tall stories. The regiment were proud men, proud of their status and proud of their wealth. There seemed to be an understanding not to talk about his own regiment and circumstances. But they certainly wanted to know all about TK. Where he had learned to ride and fight with a sword. He told them about his mother, a brilliant horsewoman killed trying to stop a fight between horses during a hunt. And he told them about his father, a colonel in his own regiment, a good rider and a brilliant swordsman who had taught him the skills that he had used in the duel. He also told them about his time in America and the Americans' obsession with sword fighting. He told them of hunting and being hunted by American cavalry patrols. He explained their preoccupation with manoeuvring the cutting edge of the sabre and how, to counter this, he had learned to use the back edge of his own sword. But he did not tell them about his other skills learned in his childhood and now being used, unconventionally, to support the army in Spain.

By the time he went to bed he had drunk more good wine and good brandy than ever before. But, as far as he could recall, he had not given away any secrets.

The next morning the ladies were amazed to see the procedures required to prepare the mare for her outing. Finally, Evans was in the saddle, Her Ladyship's head was up, her ears were pricked, and she stepped out. Evans took her for a canter in the park.

TK chatted with the ladies. Nell turned the conversation towards village life. Did the village people not seem happier without all the rules of status, protocol and respectability that burdened the aristocracy and professional classes? It seemed to her that village boys and girls had more fun, more romance and had fewer concerns than their counterparts. The lives of the clergy and teachers seemed to represent the worst of all worlds – no money, no status and yet the obligation to observe all of the rules. How could anybody marry a clergyman or a teacher? Surely life as a tradesman or a farm worker would be much happier. TK told them of his childhood among the village people who taught him their skills, and a lot more, while the lady of the neighbouring manor taught him English and arithmetic without the need to go back to school.

When Evans returned, the ladies were amused to see how easily TK and Evans swapped places. TK showed them the footwork that made Her Ladyship so special. The stepping out to avoid barging, the stepping in to avoid sabre cuts, changing step to keep her in balance when changing direction, stopping and turning to avoid danger. He showed how the Count had tried to barge and crash down with his heavy sabre.

And he showed how Her Ladyship had stepped away, giving TK space to parry the Count's devastating blows until the Count's horse had stalled and the Count had tired. The ladies were thrilled to see such horsemanship so lightly demonstrated. TK and Evans swapped places and TK explained that Evans would be in charge of Her Ladyship for the journey back to Spain.

And so, they said their goodbyes. Nell stood close to TK and he sensed the exciting perfume. She told him that he had to visit her in Dorset. He gained a very clear impression that it would be very different from the constrained environment of this time in London. TK explained that he must visit his father, the fox-hunting colonel, and then rejoin his regiment. However, he would try to visit her before he left. He would look forward to it. A bond was sealed and there was an exciting expectation between them.

The Severn Village

In a small village not far from the River Severn the villagers were enjoying a typical early summer's evening. It was six o'clock: work on the farms was over for the day; the horses were back in their stables; the workers had eaten their evening meal and now young and old were relaxing around the village green. The children had their own games; the teenagers were circling and teasing and hoping; and the adults were sitting on benches, drinking beer and cider in the late sunshine.

At the edge of the green stood a strange structure with a long low thatched roof, tiled upper walls and earth-covered lower walls, a low door and small dark windows. Moss, grass and flowers grew all over it. This was the village pub. Inside, in a dark back room, a group of men sat around a long table strewn with tankards and jugs of cider and beer. This was their place. The blacksmith was a huge dark man with a beard and a hook for a left hand. Next to him sat his left-hand man, a small wiry fellow with fingers like talons. They worked as a pair, each complementing the other. Hammer and Tongs.

The left-hand man said he had heard that TK was back. The butcher, heavy and florid, said that he had heard that he was on his way but had not seen him. The huntsman, tall, slim and slightly stooped, reckoned that he would know soon enough at the stables. The ferryman assured them that he was not coming by river. They remembered how, in the beginning, TK would turn up at their work to ask what they were doing and could he help, which were his tools and could he come again tomorrow? They remembered how he had turned up one night when they were settling snares: could he help; which was his job and why were they being so quiet?

They remembered how he had been sent away to school in the city to prevent him from becoming completely wild; how he had escaped with just a knife, a ball of string and a few other bits and pieces from the school kitchen; and how he had walked by night and slept by day as he came up the river, living off fish and rabbits, to join them one night while they were working. They had not even heard him coming. His father was fighting abroad, as usual, his mother was in the graveyard and they had agreed with Lady Anne at the Manor that they would keep him out of trouble or, at least, not let him get caught, if she would take him in and try to educate him.

It had worked well. By the time he was sixteen Lady Anne had taught him to read and write, the blacksmith had taught him about swords and guns, the left-hand man had taught him to fight with a knife, the butcher had taught him the anatomical niceties of artery sinew and tendon that would enable him to kill or disable any man or beast with a sword or a knife, and the ferryman had taught him the secrets of the river and how to live off its fish and animals. Finally, the huntsman had taught him to ride purposefully over any country and to jump and breast any hedge or thicket. Above all, on their nights out, they had taught him to survive. He was ready to join the regiment.

His father had resigned his commission and TK had inherited it without having to make payment. His father had brought back some 'souvenirs' from India. These included a strange black sword blade with a broken tip and some knives. The blacksmith as a former armourer had seen the quality of the black steel of the sword blade. He heated it, hammered it and sharpened it so that it cut like a razor. He bonded a standard cavalry hilt and guard to produce a perfectly balanced sword. He then refined it to Tom's exact circumstances for a perfect fit.

TK's father, the Colonel, spent the first year of his retirement drilling Tom endlessly. He taught him every aspect of fighting with sabres on foot and on horseback. He also taught him all the manoeuvres possible on a cavalry horse to defend and attack.

By the time they were all finished Tom Kynaston had been ready to go to war. He demonstrated his skills by dissecting a pig carcass hanging from a tree on horseback. "Arr" they said "'e shunna coom to mooch arm". He was posted to America.

And then there had been Kate. And now, again, there was Kate.

'Now Tom, it's quite big and it's been a long time. Gently, please. There, that's a start. Now, let's wait a moment. Gently, gently, gently. Now, try to find the top. Yes, there you are. Off we go. Good, good, good. Yes, yes, yes. Ooo. Welcome home, Tom.'

They lay in his bed at the Manor. They had picked up where they had left off when he went to the Peninsula.

'Was the last time really with me?'

'Yes, I've been saving myself. Keeping pure. Waiting for you.'

'What about all those camp followers and Spanish whores?'

'They turned me down. So here I am. What about you?'

'Pretty much the same. Not more than twice a night, normally.'

They were the same age and had played together and explored together. And they could make music together, from soft notes to crashing climaxes. When rumours started about how they were spending their time, Mrs Smith had sent for them and explained the facts of life. She had also given them some invaluable advice about how to get the best out of it, and she had given them some lotions and potions to help them on their journey of discovery.

Kate was very beautiful with dark curly hair and pretty, crooked, teeth.

She was quite tall with firm breasts slim strong legs and a firm bottom. So, when she started to scratch and nuzzle, TK rose to the occasion and they started again. This time TK took the lead and conducted the pace with slow introductions and exciting finales. Then Kate moved on top and TK held her firmly as she made her own pace. As she finished he looked up and saw the beautiful smile that he remembered so well. Then they tried some other movements that they began to remember until TK felt that the time had come and led once more through slow and quick tempos to the grand finale.

They lay back and rested in special companionship.

'Can anybody else do that?'

'Only your father.....'

TK made a final tour of the Manor, starting at the back with the kennels with the constant yapping of the hounds, then the stables and the warm quiet munching of the hunters, then the dairy with its smells of milk and cheeses, then the kitchen with the constant smell and bustle of cooking and he smiled at the trestles and benches where the staff that he had just visited sat down for meals and above them the elevated table where the family would eat informally, but separately. He remembered the outrage on all sides when he had hopped down to chat with the huntsmen. Finally, he went through the big door to the front of the house and said goodbye to his father and Lady Anne.

Then he rode south along the east bank of the River Severn, heading for Dorset.

He had been pleased to see his father and Lady Anne so happy, bonded by their hunting and their squirearchical social life founded on it. They had no need or interest in the aristocracy. They did not want to be invited to balls. They just wanted to hunt and hold hunt parties and they were very happy together, most nights.

He thought about Kate. They were old friends and would always help each other as they had done in the past. Their sex life was fantastic. He did not know anything else, but he assumed from male conversation that it was exceptional. So why was it not love? From his side he realised that she did not ride and had no interest in horses, except how much they cost to buy and how much they cost to keep. She did not hunt. She walked. She walked all over the riverbanks and the hills. Often to her friend and mentor, Mrs Smith, who had advised on their sexual experimentation and got them out of trouble very often. She walked for hours, but she did not ride. And, from her point of view, why did she not love him? If he had asked her, she would have told him that he was just trouble. Exciting, but trouble.

He thought about Nell. Bold and beautiful, and she loved horses and hunting. If she was as brave as he expected he could be fulfilled. And so, he rode to Dorset.

Dorset

Going south down the eastern bank of the river, twisting and turning above the red cliffs and willow trees. In the fields country life went on with laughing and singing. Hay being mown, turned, bound and stooked, cows being brought in for milking, pigeons billing and cooing and boys and girls maneuvering. Below him geese and swans floated on the river. On the western side, the meadows were covered in geese. That night, goose was on the menu at the inn, its strong flavour balanced with onions, wild garlic and herbs. A special welcome to early summer.

Down past Bridgnorth to Ironbridge. TK sat above the town with its new iron bridge connecting between the coal in the west and the iron in the east. He had never seen anything like it. The furnaces and the hammers, the engines and the pumps, the smoke and heat and noise. The river was discoloured for a long way downstream.

He wondered why they would go to the trouble of hauling coal, hauling iron, smelting and rolling it all to produce struts for a bridge that could be provided by wood closer and easier. The modern steam engines could cut the wood faster than the iron could be forged. Certainly, iron was essential for bolts and fittings and the new coking furnaces here made iron cheaper and more adaptable. But surely it would be easier and cheaper to build the bridge out of wood and hold it together with bolts of iron. He was only a soldier and had little prospect of meeting anyone who could answer his questions. So he rode on.

He considered riding down to the town and boarding a barge to ride downstream. But he preferred to bypass the town and remain in the open country. So he rode on down the river road.

At Arley he saw a large ferry transporting sheep from one side of the river to the other. A steel cable was strung between big trees and the ferry manoeuvred by steering into the current. He stayed at the local inn. Roast lamb was on the menu for supper and bacon and eggs for breakfast. He rode on down the river.

He came to a point where a stream joined the river. Upstream, a dam of tree trunks had been constructed, much wider than the stream itself. The stream flowed over the dam, back into its channel and down to the river. He asked workmen at the dam what they were doing. They replied that they were collecting gravel. When the stream met the dam it spread out into a pond and slowed and the gravel fell to the bottom. There it could be collected through sieves. It was used to repair the roads. The process was continuous. TK was fascinated.

He rode past Worcester and Gloucester. Below Gloucester with all its river traffic he turned up the escarpment along a twisting road through the woods and glades to a long straight road to Cirencester and on to Chippenham. His progress increased to eighty miles per day across open country and long straight roads. It was highwayman country but they did not try to stop him.

He rode along a stream towards the coast. Some

children shouted at him for disturbing the trout. He stopped, left the horse in the stream and took their net on its pole upstream, taking care that his shadow did not touch the water. He came to deep reeds at the river's edge. He stepped in quickly and swung the pole under the reeds and brought up three good trout.

'Where did you think they would be?' he asked as he handed them over.

And so, he came to the village near the coast. He found the house with two reception rooms, one each side of the front door, and kitchens and dairies at the back. But it was deserted. No horses in the paddocks; no pigs in the yard; no crops in the fields and no sheep on the hills. It appeared to have been abandoned.

He rode to the inn which was thatched and welcoming, just what he would have expected in such a lovely rural village. The innkeeper was in character: big, rosy and jovial. He explained that the ladies from the farm had gone away. There had been a claim from Farmer Jackson, the biggest farmer in the area, relating to the sale of horses, hay and oats. The claim had been upheld by the judge, who was a close friend of Farmer Jackson. The ladies could not pay and the farm had been forfeited. It was a local scandal. It was rumored that the farmer and the judge had offered to settle the whole thing through marriage arrangements, but the ladies had left.

'Where have they gone?' asked TK.

'India.'

****

Dorset

Dear Tom,

Your friend Otto insists that you would wish me to address you thus.

I hope this finds you safe and well, back on the Peninsula. Well, there is so much to tell. In order of events, it transpired as follows.

Liz and I left to stay with our patron, Sir Robert, in London. We did not dare to challenge the barefaced fraud by Farmer Jackson and Judge Hendricks to steal our farm. We announced that we were off to India to avoid signing over the farm. After a few weeks we were visited by Otto, who had received your letter and offered to help to restore the farm. We travelled with him back to Dorset and stayed at the hotel in the town. There we heard stories of a cavalryman who had ridden up to Mr Jackson's farmhouse, walked in and taken the farmer and his housekeeper into the dining room. There he drew a sword and proceeded to shave the left side of the farmer from top to bottom – quite literally, they say! Then he rode up to Judge Hendricks' chambers, took him and his clerk into the courtroom, locked the doors and shaved the judge in the same way. The housekeeper and the clerk say that the sword strokes were so quick and so accurate that the farmer and the judge were left naked and half-shaved within moments. They both remember that the removal of the eyebrows and the moustaches with the flat tip of the sword was exquisite. In each case he is reported to have whispered into the shaven left ears of his hosts, who remained seated and silent long after he had left. And then, just after the bald wretches were beginning to emerge, much diminished, dear Otto arrived in full uniform to arrange cancelation of the sale of the farm, withdrawal of the claims, calculation of compensation, the relocation of the farmer and the resignation of the judge. They were very meek. And now they have gone.

I must say that Otto pressed our case for compensation very firmly and we were paid out for losses that we hardly knew that we had suffered. So, we are rather better off than we were before, buying horses, hay and grain for the new season. Otto told us that you had written to him post haste and called in a few favours. So, we owe you many, many thanks.

Otto seems very taken with Elizabeth but she will let him trot along for the time being.

In the meantime, there has been great excitement in London. It transpires that the Count was a thoroughly bad lot. He had a group of spies in London, including some in the Army and some in the Government. Following his death they have been arresting them for treason. Apparently, each has been implicating the others in the hope of leniency. But no public hangings yet.

We were all thrilled to hear of Wellesley's latest victory. Apparently, he caught the French on the hop and they are retreating to France. Were you involved? Did you survive? No doubt Otto will keep us up to date when he visits.

Your friend (I hope),

Nell

Waterloo

TK formed up with his company, looking drab among the glitter and plumes of the other cavalry regiments. Looking small next to the big men with big swords on big grey horses of the Scots Greys. It was a cold damp morning in May that preceded the battle of Waterloo near Brussels. A battle for which the British army had been recalled, to fight the French, yet again. A battle between big armies formally lined up against each other. A battle for which TK felt ill suited.

'Ah, Major Kynaston. Welcome to the world of real soldiering, cannon fire and column volleys, fixed bayonets and the whites of their eyes. No cantering in the countryside for you today.'

TK studied the handsome face of his commanding officer for a sign of humour, and found none. Asking him if he had enjoyed the gallop at the Dutchess of Richmond's ball a couple of nights ago might not be appreciated.

'Thank you, Colonel.'

'Very well, first off you can charge some guns. The French are assembling a battery of horse artillery on that ridge over there. Take your men and spike the guns and kill the artillerymen. All of them.'

TK knew that good gunners were invaluable and irreplaceable. 'Very well, Colonel.'

'And Major, be very quick. They have lancers in

support, so you will be on your own. See it as a chance to enhance your reputation."

TK called Captain Hackett and Lieutenant Swan and ordered them to assemble the packhorses and tools and to organise a troop of fifty men. Then he studied the terrain and made his plan. When they were ready he told them what they were going to do. Those who knew him well grinned in anticipation.

They rode fast, round behind the left flank of the guns. Hackett led the killing party and made short work of the crews of the eight guns as they made their preparations. The Smith twins and their helpers disabled the first six guns by hammering metal pegs into the touchholes of the flintlock firing mechanisms and breaking a couple of adjacent spokes on one wheel. The guns lurched and pointed impotently into the air. Evans' team stayed mounted and held the horses of the men on the ground. Evans slipped onto the back of the Red Bitch and TK dismounted. Lieutenant Swan's team manhandled the two end guns to point down the narrow track that had been used by the horse artillery. They found powder cartridges, cannisters filled with musket balls and bags loaded with grapeshot and priming powder for the locks, all laid out by the French artillerymen. The Smiths sawed through a couple of spokes which would break when the guns fired. TK supervised the loading of the guns with both grapeshot and cannister and set the aim for lancers at twenty yards.

TK worked frantically, and he and Swan were running back the firing lanyards when they heard the thunder of the French lancers. Hackett and his team rode in front of the guns to conceal them until the French were one hundred yards away – and unstoppable. Then Hackett rode behind the guns. Evans held the horses for TK and Swan. At twenty yards TK and Swan pulled the lanyards and without waiting to see the result leapt for their horses. The reports were still echoing as they got into full stride

And so they ran for the shelter of an infantry regiment guarding the Allied flank.

TK glanced back and saw the chaos of the dead and wounded men and horses and the broken guns. He saw that the uninjured horsemen were coming through to give chase, but the twenty yards had turned to two hundred and the French were in shock so they should make it to safety – so long as no-one fell off. One did fall off when his horse went down but a colleague scooped him up.

These horses were at the back of the retreat because they were slow and tiring. The double load of two riders was going to be too much. One lancer officer, wearing a decorated green uniform and a crested brass helmet had been reluctant to give up the chase. He saw his opportunity, lifted his lance and spurred forward. TK swung the Red Bitch back to defend the attack.

TK had the principle of doing what had to be done, and no more. However, this situation provided an opportunity to test sword against lance. He thrilled at the challenge. He cantered forward and then stopped. A lancer has the great advantage that the long lance can cover an arc of almost one hundred and eighty degrees. A small adjustment by the lancer can cover almost any movement by the target. By stopping, TK had reduced the speed of convergence. Also, he had narrowed the target. Now he sat with his sword upright at chest height out in front. He had to judge the moment when the tip of the lance would be level with the sword. Then, he leaned away and swung the back edge of the sword towards the lance. The back of the sword met the lance about a foot behind the point and diverted it a few inches. TK had learned a few inches. That was enough. The point of the lance went past. But the back edge of the sword slid along the shaft, cracked on the knuckles of the lancer and, as the sword lifted, TK turned the blade and sliced at the throat of the lancer.

TK swung the Red Bitch and as the French horse hesitantly continued its charge towards the British troop, TK seized the bridle and booted the rider from the saddle. The lancer clattered to the ground in a spray of blood. TK led the French horse up to the broken horse and threw the reins to the cavalrymen. He was just thinking that it had gone quite well for the cavalry, when an English shout warned him of the approach of a second lancer. He was closing fast. TK could only turn away and hope that the lancer would follow. Then perhaps Her Ladyship's speed and agility could help him to attack from behind. But the lancer rode past and the stranded Englishmen would surely be killed.

The shot came as a surprise. It had been fired by an English cavalryman standing without a horse with his feet apart holding a big French saddle pistol in both hands. He had stayed calm and waited until he could be sure of his shot. The big ball hit the lancer in the chest, continued through and caused some affront by singeing Her Ladyship's shoulder as it expired. The lancer's pace carried him on and the cavalry man had to dive out of the way. TK emptied the French horse and led it back. So, the two French horses replaced the broken English horse and carried the riders to safety. The winded horse slowly tried to follow.

TK did not usually dwell on his victories, but this had gone very well. He was proud of his men.

And so they made it intact to the shelter of the infantry regiment who were drawn up below a low ridge. The ranks separated to let them through. TK reported to the commanding officer in charge of the infantry regiment and was pleased to meet Colonel Fitz-Warwick again. And now they sat looking down through the mist onto the main French columns getting into position, while the French cavalry regiments attacked the British positions. The French cavalry could not break the squares or the British fortifications. And so, inevitably, they saw Napoleon's main weapon, the infantry columns forming up and wheeling to march towards the British positions.

Sure enough, they saw a French column wheeling to attack the flank where they were standing.

"Well, Major Kynaston, you missed Salamanca. Otherwise engaged, we hear. But Hackett led your troop and skirmished very well. And now you are back. I thought that you had been sent on a suicide mission at the guns, but you pulled it off and gave a display of sabre against lance to cheer us all up. But I fear that you are going to die with us this time." said the Colonel. 'No, we have come to fight with you,' said TK. 'When this column makes its attack, we will deal with their skirmishers and, when the time comes, we will attack the front ranks of the column while it is marching. We will make ourselves useful. Every time you fire two volleys we will attack while you reload. If all goes well, they will lose momentum. We will slow the front ranks and you will kill the front ranks. The more they lose, the slower will be their advance and the more you can kill. We can beat them.

'If you agree, you will simply have to hold your fire while we cross the line. I will take my chance on crossing before you are ready to fire. I will lose men and horses, but we will kill the French. The slower they advance, the more you will kill.'

'I wish I could share your confidence, Major. But I like the idea and we have nothing to lose unless we come under cannon fire. So here are the mathematics: we have one thousand men and the French column will be fifteen hundred men, or more; we start our volleys at two hundred and fifty yards; on plain ground the column can advance at one hundred yards per minute; uphill and through high vegetation, say fifty yards per minute; so five minutes to reach us; we can fire two volleys per minute at least, ten volleys; ten thousand balls but we are only hitting the front ranks, say ten ranks at best, half down is two hundred and fifty men; if you can slow them to two hundred and fifty yards per minute, twenty volleys and five hundred down, plus whatever you can kill, we are on equal terms when they reach us; and I would back my men against the French with bayonets. I will take your offer. Good luck'.

The British would probably be outnumbered but they were well-placed, away from the French artillery. The French column, at the point of attack, would, in fact, be a solid block of up to twenty five men wide and over fifty men deep. However, prior to engaging the British, they would advance in a wider column to engage the British line. Now, ahead of the column, groups of skirmishers started forward to make targeted attacks to weaken the British line. Some of these groups contained light cavalry to attack any breach in the British line.

So, as the French column started to move forward, a group of French cavalry shot out of the advance, riding up the hill to attack the infantry on the ridge. As they made their attack, TK rode out from behind the infantry and the French skirmishers were driven off.

The French responded by sending a larger group of foot soldiers with cavalry in support. Again, TK hit them before they could begin their attack. Again, there were few survivors. This was easy work for the veterans of the Peninsula patrols.

Finally, the French sent cavalry units to attack the British flanks. The British infantry formed up into squares that are safe against cavalry and fired two volleys. TK's teams then cleared off any French survivors.

So, the time had come for the attack by the main column following the eagles, driven on by the drums and shouts of "vive l'Empereur". TK split his group into two units to attack the front of the French column from alternate sides. TK led one team and Hackett led the other. The French would not stop to fire or reload but their bayonets presented a serious problem. The front row presented a formidable line of ready bayonets. An impenetrable wall of steel.

TK planned to attack by using his sabres to attack the hands and arms that held the French bayonets. If he attacked after the British volleys, the French line would be confused and the wounded French would obstruct the advance. On each pass the front of the cavalry line could hit hands and arms. The following horsemen could then get closer and hit heads and faces. The end of the cavalry line were free to attack the remnants of the front row of the French chopping below the bear-skins. And the French advance would be slowed.

Surprisingly quickly, the French column came within musket range of the British ranks. Everything now depended on timing. TK's teams must not attack until after the second volley and the infantry should not fire their next volleys until the cavalry had got clear.

Theoretically, each infantryman could fire three shots per minute. With three ranks they could fire a volley every twenty seconds. In practice this was not sustainable and the thinner ranks were less devastating. So, with two ranks firing every thirty seconds the infantry was well within its capabilities. The big question would be whether the cavalry could complete their runs across the French column in thirty seconds while the infantry were re-loading. And the French column was getting wider.

After each volley the French column regrouped and marched on, as ever, driven on relentlessly by the drums. They marched over fallen colleagues towards the British line. As the cavalry made their pass they barged into chaos and left more chaos. And the column marched on over ground and crops churned up by the cavalry passes and over fallen colleagues, fallen cavalrymen and dead and wounded horses. Men and horses thrashed about in pain. And still the column advanced. But they slowed. And the infantry fired more volleys and the cavalry made more passes. And the chaos and the carnage increased. Gun smoke and the smell of blood hung in the air.

At the front, the solid block of blue and white was fragmenting into individual soldiers to be targeted by the muskets and slashed by the cavalry.

TK was content. So far so good. The French column was slowing and therefore taking more casualties. The plan appeared to be working. However, he was losing men, so it would lose its effectiveness with each pass.

Then, damn, he let his concentration slip for a moment. He had seen a big French infantryman with a big black moustache and a big grin. TK thought that he should wipe the grin off his face rather than just cut his hands. He leaned out swung hard and missed as the Frenchman leaned back. Then he felt the jolt as the bayonet struck. The Red Bitch fell. He stepped out of the stirrups and tried to parry and cut against the French bayonets. He fell and rolled and rolled and rolled again, then got to his feet ready to run from the French advance when a big light bay blocked his path and a big left arm hooked down.

He hooked in his left arm and was swept up onto the back of the bay. Saved by half of the Smith twins. He continued to slash at the French as they leapt away. As they cleared the French column, musket fire from the British infantry whistled behind him. As they readied to form up TK pointed to a big grey mare with long ears and feet like soup plates. Smith rode alongside and TK slipped into the saddle. He adjusted the stirrups and was ready after the next volley. He did not know that Smith's brother had been riding the grey. It would be the last charge. The British were fixing bayonets and the cavalry would have to get out of the way.

Then a cheer went up as a Prussian unit entered the battle. The French stopped, turned and ran. TK took his men forward to consolidate the retreat and the remainder of his men took terrible revenge on the retreating French.

TK called over Lieutenant Swan. 'Take your chance at glory. The Eagle of that column is in retreat. Take three men and bring it back to the infantry regiment commander with our compliments. But be careful, they are defeated but they will still fight for it, and they have been chosen to defend it.' Swan grinned with pride and spun away.

Suddenly there was a roar of victory from the main battlefield as the Prussians made the final push. It was over, and the Allies had won.

The survivors of the troop filtered back having harried the retreating French down to the bottom of the valley where the allied armies were organizing the French surrender.

An infantry officer and two men approached, leading Lieutenant Swan slumped on his horse. With the colonel's compliments and their thanks for the Eagle they were sorry that the lieutenant had died as he had handed it over. Apparently he had stretched out for the eagle and got picked. If he had waited, it would have fallen into his hands. They offered food and medical assistance.

TK was wracked with guilt at what he had done. However, he remembered to send thanks to the Colonel and accepted his offers.

TK rode down into the field of dead and dying men and horses. He was shocked to find that already the British camp followers were cutting throats and stealing coins – French and English. Some carried sacks but many simply tied up their skirts to make a pouch. He was surprised how young some of them were, skipping from one body to the next. Speed counted in this trade. He wondered whether any of them ever found their own 'husbands'.

He found Her Ladyship lying among the dead. She was still alive. He drew his sword to ease her end and put out his left hand to steady her head and give it a final stroke.

He rode back with the saddle and bridle and passed two of his men leading Lieutenant Swan slumped on his horse.

TK hung his head at his stupidity. He had given the Lieutenant a chance at glory and had cost him his life. For nothing. And now he had to write to his mother expressing regret at the loss without explaining the honor that could have been won. Without pretending that, in any way, it could have been worth it.

Captain Hackett rode up with the butcher's bill. Eight

dead, now make it nine, and twelve wounded, some seriously. One of the Smiths had died. Also, Evans and others from the Spanish campaign. Brilliant patrol riders caught in a stand-up fight between cavalry and infantry. Not the way they would want to go. But at least half of them had survived and none had suffered the hopelessness of being killed by cannon fire.

TK split the survivors into two. Half to get the wounded over to the infantry hospital and half to tend the horses. Hackett noticed Her Ladyship's saddle and bridle and a wound on TK's arm. He raised an eyebrow. TK shook his head. Yes, she was dead.

'And yes, she bit me.'

Dorset

The farmhouse was smaller than his manor house in Shropshire, but it had all the features of respectability in the form of reception rooms and all the warmth and comfort of the big kitchen with sculleries and outhouses at the back. The workers came to the back of the kitchen and joined the maids for their meals. The workmen and maids were accommodated at the back of the house and over the outhouses. Heavy doors separated the back of the house from the front.

Tom loved the smell of home. Fresh baked bread, coffee and the special dairy background aroma of butter and crumbly white cheese.

Overall, the house had a genuine warmth. It was fuelled by the fires in the kitchen and the reception rooms and by the happy atmosphere between the occupants at all levels. Tom soon put this down to the loyalty shown by Jack Harper, the foreman. He loved his ladies and worked hard to protect them.

Nell showed him round and the tour stopped at her bedroom.

'So, Major Kynaston, that's what it's all about.'

'No, Nell, that's just the beginning of what it's all about.'

It had taken many months after the defeat of the French before TK had been released on leave. Now, at last they were together, and that's how they lay. TK had known that Nell would be brave enough to come to his bed. Nell had known that it was inevitable and had looked forward to it from the moment that she had met him.

TK looked down at Nell's beautiful face plastered with a wave of light brown-blonde hair. Yes, she had been as brave and exciting as he had expected. Now, he began to orchestrate the harmony that they were destined for. And so, he put his hand under her and began the movements from slow introductions to crashing crescendos and then as she floated down he started to build up slowly to the next. And Nell relaxed and allowed herself to be carried along. And there was more to come when he gently helped her on top and helped her to make her own music holding her firmly to maintain the rhythm until he joined in and they enjoyed a perfect climax.

'Not a bad start,' he thought and looked forward to the future.

'How can I live without this now?', she thought, and looked forward to the future.

'So, Nell, at last we are together. Wellesley contrived to send me to every corner of France to confirm that the peace was secure, while he set up court in Paris and conducted his romances. Very selfish. Well, I like it here with you too much to return, so my soldiering days are over.'

"Well that was fun and I'm glad you will be staying for more. How could you be so loving when I know that you could be so ruthless in battle?"

"Soldiering was a profession. I did what had to be

done as well as possible. Away from that life, I take pleasure in fun, kindness and generosity. But I can always do what has to be done."

"Did you start young with the country girls?"

"Yes, luckily a wise old woman of the world, a medicine woman, saw what we were getting up to and taught us to stay out of trouble. Were you locked up in a nunnery?"

"Not quite. When my parents went away, I was brought to the farm and the farmers family looked after me and a tutor came in to teach us. I watched through the window as the country children enjoyed themselves. Elisabeth had been sent to a smart school. She had one untidy night of marriage, then separation and widowhood. So she moved in and we watched through the window together. Later the farmer moved to the cottage. He and his wife still ran the farm and kept a close eye on us. We gained a reputation for being supercilious. But clever old you broke in. I wonder if Elisabeth will change. Perhaps she gets too much fun from her mockery. Did the military life get you into trouble?"

"I was fortunate. In the early days, I was invited to my first mess night that would lead to drinking, gambling and women. But one of my father's friends took me aside and pointed as the officers first got drunk, then started to play cards when they could not think straight, then started falling out and, at last went after the appalling women. It was quite a lesson. I chose to go with him to America to ride patrols and keep away from military entertainment. It always ends the same."

"Good. We are going to get along very nicely. Now, where were we?"

The Severn Village

As evening faded at the village the usual team assembled with beer and cider. Translated from their broad country accents, the conversation went something like this.

'Tom's back.'

'He'll find some changes.'

'His father is dead, the bank has taken over the farms and the manor is to let. What an inheritance.'

'His father died hunting, riding like a mad man, they say, but who would have guessed at the debts he had run up? Mostly, buying horses from sellers that did not own them and then trying to get his money back with bets on slow horses. Lady Anne had no idea. Lord Darling is keeping the stables and the kennels going for the hunt but the rest is chaotic. Kate is trying to sort out his debts, but I am sorry to say that some neighbors have been dishonest. I hope that she will show them up.'

'Tom will not know of her success while he has been away. Nor her engagement. Wait until he sees her in her bonnet and driving her trap and hears that she will be marrying the solicitor in town. That's a lot for our young friend to come home to.'

'Very well, in the meantime, let's settle the meat rationing. It's not going to be so easy when the manor changes hands. And if the keeper changes it will be very much harder.'

And so they went into their huddle, and nobody interrupted their whispers.

A few days later, their usual evening discussions were interrupted when a broad figure loomed over the table. They shuffled up to make room for Tom and asked for his latest news.

'Well it's good to see you all, still together. The warfare became very hard and I lost a lot of good men and friends at Waterloo. But I have found a beautiful lady and I hope to marry her. So, on balance, I am ahead in the great game. My father left a bit of a mess, but it can be managed. The farm rents will go to the bank to pay the interest on the debts so the tenants can stay in place. The manor house must be rented out to pay off the capital in instalments. Luckily, young Sir Robert Darling intends to take it, to bring home his new wife. He wants to be Master of the Hunt and to keep the kennels and stables. I wanted him to pay a lump sum for a five-year lease but he wants to pay an annual rent. Let's hope he does not break his neck. But, seriously, I think he is a good man and deserves our support. I think that he is keeping on our friend the gamekeeper.

'Now look, I need to find some money. So, I am off to America to look for gold in the North West. I led patrols in the East. I know what is involved and all the risks. But I love the country and the people. I have survived so far by looking out for the risks and taking care – just as you taught me.'

'There are three things that I will need from here – a knife, a bow and a box. I hope that you will be able to help. I will be able to pay because I am going to resign my commission. It is not worth much, but I should get enough to pay for your work and make it to America.

'For the knife, I would like a six-inch blade, two inches wide, edged on both sides, not too sharp a point with a good hilt and a good handle. Also, I would like it to balance perfectly on the hilt. In Spain, I saw that you can throw a knife from the hilt like an arrow – no turning, but not very far. Among my father's weapons from India there is a curved knife with a good handle, wood or bone. It looks like good steel. Maybe you could reshape it and rebalance it or use bits of it. I will bring it up to the forge tomorrow to see what you think.

'Next, I hope to get a bow. Just like the ones we use on our nights out, but I would not ask for one of yours. I would like to meet your bow maker. I have an idea to start with a short strong bow and to cut it in half, then bond it together with a metal grip so that the halves can be reunited without loss of strength. I think that it could be done with one folded piece of metal. I will show you at the forge tomorrow. Also, I would like your ideas on how to get some arrowheads in the roman style. I will explain tomorrow.

'Finally, still at the forge, I would like a tin chest to hold my beautiful sword, the two halves of the bow, arrows, arrowheads and possibly a rifle and ammunition.

So, there is a lot of work for the forge. In the meantime, the next round is on me. In fact, all the rounds are on me. I am so happy to be home.'

And they saw his broad, strong-nosed, strong-chinned face light up with a happy smile and the short teeth set in a big grin. Who could doubt him?

And so TK had taken the Arab knife to the forge for adjustment and was delighted to watch them at work heating, hammering, folding and hammering over and over again until it started to take the form that he had asked for. Finally, the Left Hand had sharpened the edges and put forty five degree angles on the point. Then came the shaping and the balancing of the hilt. And finally, the butt. When it was finished the Left Hand balanced it at the hilt on the point of a nail and they all laughed at the perfection they had achieved.

Next came the scabbard. They laid the knife on a sheet of tin and edged round the blade with space for the rivets plus a three-inch tab to make the clip.

The Left Hand cut out the metal halves. He then took them to the cobbler and came back with thin strong leather matching the metal halves. He explained the cobbler had taken the leather from an old riding boot so it was perfectly tanned. Now the Left and Right Hands worked with perfect understanding to bond the two halves with rivets, trying the fit of the knife as they worked. Finally, they folded the clip and TK stuck the knife with its scabbard in his boot. It was a perfect fit. Then, as an alternative, he clipped it inside his belt and it held firm. He was delighted. He would feel a lot safer with this at his disposal.

Then TK made a drawing of the tube and fittings that would form the handle of his bow and an arrowhead shaped like a pyramid with angled sides and a hollow in the base for the shaft to fit.

The Bow

The next day TK rode up to Mrs Smith's cottage. It was on a cliff above a bend in the river. The cottage was low and set back into the hillside with a thatched roof.

There were lots of animals. Chickens, ducks, pigs, sheep and goats. And behind the house, the herb garden.

TK slipped out of the saddle, loosed the girth and sat down at a table looking down on the river. Eventually, Mrs. Smith emerged. She was tall, elegant and had great dignity.

'Tom, my dear, I wondered whether I would ever see you alive again. Stories of dueling and patrolling and the bloodbath at Waterloo were very worrying. But here you are.'

'So, Mrs. Smith, it has all been very interesting. Far from home and hunting and friendships and the way we live. Now, I am just a soldier. My father has left horse-trading debts from selling fine Irish horses that he bought from sellers that did not own them. The farms are already mortgaged and now the manor house must be let for a few years. So, I am off to America to look for gold.'

'Well Tom, I'm sure you have a plan. It is probably wild, but I am sure that you think that you can do it. Will you stay for supper and a bed for the night?'

'That's what I had hoped. You know my story. I would dearly love to hear yours. But, before I forget, I will be away for a couple of days and would like to pick up a big bottle of your "end of the month" medicine on my way back.'

'I look forward to hearing that you have found love. I would wager it's a lady who likes her hunting and understands our country ways. Let's hear where you have been and where you are going.'

The next morning, he rode down through the Welsh hills to a workshop, next to a wood with yew and hazel trees. It was well-equipped. A figure emerged, and Tom explained that he was from the English side of the river. He and his fellows had been using bows from here for many years. And he would now like something different.

'Well, Tom Kynaston, get off your horse before you speak to me. I deal on equal terms. My bows are the best and that is the start point for any discussion.'

Tom stepped down to meet the bow maker. He was Tom's height but wider with a big belly and heavy legs. His hair was long, dark and curly and he had a beard to match.

'I am Robert. I can draw any bow and hit any target. I make bows for lesser men.'

'I am Tom. I can kill with many weapons. But I will listen to you on the subject of bows.'

They shook hands and Tom felt his strong rough hand enveloped by a bigger stronger rougher hand. He found himself thinking of knives and swords. He was always going to lose in a bare-handed contest.

'Robert, I need your help. We have lots of your bows but I would like something special. I am going to America. I will need to be able to kill deer and possibly natives and bears. I will need a short bow with heavy arrows. Also I need it to be in two pieces and joined with the grip. Maybe you can't do it. Maybe you won't do it. But I would like to work with you to try.'

Robert stood still. He looked grim. He sat down in a big wooden armchair at his bench. He sat still for several minutes in a deep calm. TK had never seen such quietude. But so much in character for such a strong independent man.

Finally, Robert said, 'Very well, I will help you make your bow. First, we will make the bow in one piece. If it performs I must be paid. After that it will be your risk. If it performs when it has been cut and joined, you must pay me half again.'

Tom agreed.

Tom showed Robert the grip and explained how the two halves would fit together. He hoped that the tension of the bow would keep it firm in the grip. The shaping of the bow within the grip would be crucial. Again, Robert went into deep thought. Finally he said, 'You have an idea. No more. I will talk to you tomorrow. Go down the road to the farm on the right and tell them I sent you for the night.'

As the light faded Tom rode up to the farm with its muddy yard, through chickens and ducks and pigs and a lone cow. He was greeted in Welsh. He asked in English for stabling for his horse, supper and a bed. In silence they showed him a stable and filled a net with hay. They showed him a pallet with a straw mattress in a back room. They pointed to a seat at the kitchen table and produced cold ham, bread, butter and cheese. He sat down. They brought him clear cold water and he drank it and asked for more. He knew that they understood his English and did not know why they refused to respond in English. As he ate, a conversation lilted in Welsh but they made no effort to include him. In fact, the opposite, he was made to feel like an intruder. But an intruder tolerated for his money. No more.

The next morning, they gave him bacon and eggs. He paid and left. He had felt duty-bound to thank them, but they did not reply.

At the workshop, Robert was a new man. He had thought it through. He had decided that the grip needed to be in two halves, front and back, and gripped together with rings. The design would hold them secure. Robert took Tom to the blacksmith and explained the requirements. Next Robert took him to the arrow maker and explained the need for heavy arrows with good flights to balance the heavy triangular heads.

Finally, Robert explained that the bow would be cut in half at an early stage to allow for the shaping that would be required to fit the grip.

Over lunch of bread, butter, cheese and sausage Robert relaxed. He understood the project and was rising to the challenge. He told how he came from a long line of bow-making archers who had made bows and fought in the wars for hundreds of years. Now the armies no longer asked for bows and he lived quietly with his workshop and his tools making hunting bows for clients who would come to him from great distances. He found it a good way to relax as he grew old. Yes, he knew that he was growing old. He could still pull the bows, but he could not run after the arrows.

Tom told him about the defeat of the British Army in America, the pride of the American gentlemen, their respect for swordsmanship and his evolution as a patrol rider. He explained that this led to the formation of his group in the Peninsula war and the gathering of intelligence. Now he needed to go back to America in the far West in the hope of regaining his property and maybe making his fortune. He thought that he would need the bow to stay alive.

Robert explained that bows were made from yew wood branches. The thickness had to be just right so that the heartwood on the inside of the bow would provide strength and power and the outer wood would allow the length of the draw and the consequent length and accuracy of the shot. The heartwood bent a little and provided great power. The outer wood bent more and gave long unleashed energy to the shot.

Robert produced a bow and asked Tom to draw the string back to his chin. Easy. Next a shorter, thicker bow. Possible, but too hard on a regular basis. Next, a slightly slimmer bow. Perfect.

'Good,' said Robert, 'that pull will deliver a heavy arrow fifty yards or more with good accuracy. It will fire further but the accuracy will be less because you will have to adjust.'

Robert told Tom that he was not going to cut a bow in half. He was going to make two identical half bows from two identical branches. This was going to be special.

Tom would have to trust him on the cost. He used a spoke shave and a two-handed blade with a vice to produce the identical twin half bows. He regularly gripped them together in the vice to ensure that they pulled equally. At last he was finished, leaving only the grip ends for final fitting.

As Robert oiled the wood and started to measure the strings, the blacksmith arrived with the grip and a few extra arrowheads. Robert trimmed the bow ends and pushed them into the grip and they fitted together perfectly to complete the bow. Even so, Robert shaved a little and the blacksmith banged a little to complete the perfection. And it was done. With perfect timing the first of the arrows arrived and fitted snugly into the heads. Robert asked how TK had arrived at the idea of fitting the arrows into the heads instead of fitting the heads into the arrows. TK explained that the shape of the heads came from the Romans and the fitting came with the new casting techniques at the foundries. A one armed blacksmith had put them together.

Finally, Robert measured off lengths of his heaviest bowstrings, knotted the loops and bound off the loose ends with fine twine. He made five and said that if Tom needed any more, he would have run out of natives and wildlife to shoot.

As they finished Robert looked uncharacteristically shy and said, 'Tom, you don't make any great claims and you don't have any great demands. But I think that you have a story to tell. I would like to know where you have been and where you are going. I have a simple cottage, simple food and simple accommodation. But if you would like to stay with us tonight, we would be honored.'

Tom had developed a strong bond with this self-contained craftsman and humbly said that he also would be honored.

Robert's 'cottage' was a big square construction with a large kitchen, open hearth and good oak furniture. They ate from a stewpot with hare, rabbit and lamb and with potatoes baked in the fire. Delicious. Robert's wife was younger, dark, and heavy-breasted with soft downy arms and Tom guessed, with legs to match. And sure enough, there was a young curly haired Robert ready to carry on the tradition.

Robert explained that tomorrow, first thing, Tom would fire the bow at targets at different distances. The bow could not be changed but the aim could be adjusted to accommodate it. But first they would visit the arrow makers.

Robert took them to a long low barn where ladies wearing shawls and smoking pipes worked quietly to make the arrows. Splicing and turning the shafts, rolling them, steaming them, and pressing them. Cutting the lengths, polishing the wood, gluing and trimming the goose feather flights, drilling and sawing the knocks, and, finally, trimming a slight point at the other end to fit into the arrow heads. Tom was surprised to hear a quiet broken voice break into a low song and then the others joined in to produce a beautiful harmony. Tom was deeply moved.

And so, to the butts.

They picked up a few of the completed arrows and rode over to Robert's target area. Robert chose thick straw targets to absorb the heavy arrows at a short distance. He checked Tom's stance and noted that he wore a glove over the pulling fingers. He suggested that Tom should use his back more to draw the bow as he lifted the arrow from the vertical between the knees to the horizontal at chin level. He suggested that Tom should pull with one finger above the arrow and two below. He recommended that the arrow should always be on the same position on the grip and that the distance should be altered by aiming above the target. He gave Tom a short strong three-fingered glove to keep with the bow.

At fifty yards, under Robert's guidance, Tom regularly hit the chest-sized middle of the target. At one hundred yards major adjustments were required but, by aiming higher, Tom finally started to hit the target.

At last, he put the bow and ten arrows in his saddlebags, placed an order for one hundred more arrows with payment in advance and arranged for them to be collected. Then he gave the grey mare a handful of oats and headed back to the river, and home. He cantered easily along the greenways and returned to Mrs Smith. She gave him a large bottle with severe instructions as to dosage. He thanked her and, as he was leaving asked, if she did not mind, what had become of Mr. Smith. 'He died in my arms, dear...'

He stayed at the inn, ate well and slept deeply. They fed and cleaned him in the morning and at last he rode down to the manor. He arranged for his personal stuff, and also his father's, to be kept in storage at the manor.

Two days later the handover was conducted at the

Manor. The house staff, from the manager, the maids, the home farm staff and the dairy maids were assembled in front of the house. Young Lord Robert arrived in his coach with Lady Charlotte to meet the staff. Lord Robert assured them that he looked forward to employing them all. Lady Charlotte said that in addition she would be bringing her personal maids. Tom and the gamekeeper exchanged a quick glance.

They were joined by Lady Anne and Lord Robert. Tom went to the dining room where the papers were laid out for signature. Tom signed as landlord, Young Lord Robert signed as tenant and Lady Anne signed as trustee. Kate and her fiancé signed as witnesses. And it was all done. Young Lord Robert would have the hunt and the manor for ten years and he was very pleased. Tom's debts would be cleared but he was running out of money. His back pay was spent. His half pay would not provide much of a lifestyle. Also, his accumulated leave was running out. It was time to go to America. But first he must visit his regiment and finalize his retirement.

Farewells

'So, Colonel Kynaston, you have arrived at last to tell us that you are leaving. The regiment is very proud of you and will be sorry to lose you. Your secondment on patrolling duties has brought us considerable prestige. The dinner this evening is to show our thanks and the guest suite has been prepared.

'We owe you a few pounds and the sale of your commission has brought in more than expected. Also, we have asked for contributions from the regiment and the result has been remarkable. Even so, it will not fund much of a retirement.'

The food was average, the wine was below average and the speeches were worse. The collection certainly would not fund his retirement but with the other bits and bobs it might get him to America. He had heard of a new style of hunting rifle being produced by specialists in St James'. That was out of the question from his regiment, but he might be able to pick up an ex-army rifle somewhere.

Afterwards he mingled with his fellow officers and tried to answer all their questions. Hackett was the only officer to have survived through the patrolling and the battle at Waterloo. TK finally found him, inevitably standing apart, straight as a ramrod and grim. They could not politely talk for very long, but it was clear that Hackett was not looking forward to a military career in peacetime on half pay. He asked to join TK on the trip to America, but TK explained that he had to do it alone. And, knowing him, Hackett understood.

The next day TK returned to the village and stayed with Lady Anne. They went hunting under the new master, young Lord Robert. They had a few good days. The grey mare was exactly as TK expected. She went everywhere, jumped everything, went through hedges that she couldn't jump and cantered strongly all day. He could not have asked for more. Lord Robert asked to buy her, but TK refused. He escorted Lady Anne to dinner at his old home and was pleased to see the traditions of the hunt being continued. It was all a bit more formal than previously, but he was sure that the new master would be knocked into shape.

At last, he set off for Dorset and London. The river was rising, and he boarded a barge at Shrewsbury and floated downstream to Ironbridge. There he stopped off and plunged into the noise and smoke to find a workshop that could cast one hundred and fifty of his arrowheads. Then, back down the river as far as Gloucester where he disembarked to ride up the escarpment through highwayman country towards Dorset. He was not stopped.

He picked up with Nell where they had left off. Terrific loving, great hunting and a lot of fun. Their friends were the new squirearchy. They refused invitations to Balls at halls and sent invitations to parties at home. Christmas was a whirl of hunting and parties. The best of times.

Again, Tom offered to marry Nell. Again, she told him that she would look at him again when he returned from

America. Tom handed over Mrs Smith's bottle with her instructions and told her to keep out of trouble.

Tom went to London and met up with Otto. Tom assumed that Otto had used his contacts to smooth TK's promotion to Colonel. Otto corrected him. TK had supporters in high places. Otto was just the messenger. But, he hoped, a good friend.

Otto reminded TK that he had found and followed the French on the Peninsula, had fought the duel with the Count, supervised the capture of the chief spy and his documents and had capped it all with a brave but costly defence at Waterloo. The infantry regiment at Waterloo, encouraged by Colonel Fitz-Warwick, had invited him to dinner and wanted him to select a gift. Also, Otto had been instructed to find a suitable gesture of gratitude from his masters.

TK explained that his inheritance had been destroyed by his father, he had sold his commission in order to make ends meet. He had had a terrific season in Dorset and was now off to America to restore his fortune. Otto laughed out loud. It was all so outrageous and so typical of this wild cavalryman. Otto asked whether the infantry regiment and his masters could help to supply the expedition. TK explained that the North West passage had been discovered but was not well travelled. He expected to remain hidden most of the time. But if he was attacked or became hungry a rifle would be a huge advantage. He reminded Otto about the firm in St James' producing hunting rifles with new percussion caps that were quick and easy to use, waterproof and very accurate. But, probably too expensive. If necessary, he would try to get his hands on a flintlock army rifle. Otto said that that was just what he needed to know.

Otto poured wine and asked about Elizabeth. TK answered with brutal honesty. Elizabeth had been enchanted by Otto but the lifestyle that she was now enjoying was far removed from Otto's lifestyle, with the balls, the clubs, the drinking and gambling. She was not convinced that Otto would fit into her lifestyle or that she would fit into his lifestyle. And she was not looking for a fling.

TK was offered civilian lodgings at the infantry barracks and Otto promised to get in touch. Sure enough, after TK had ridden the grey in the park the next day a message arrived from Otto giving the name of the gunmakers in St James' and telling him to choose a rifle, and if it suited him, also a pistol. TK walked over to the gunsmiths and asked to see the new rifles. The staff were clearly not impressed by the young man in his worn green jacket with dark patches where insignia had been removed. They suspected the worst. However, he clearly knew what he was looking for and they showed him the rifles. TK lit upon a short one third inch calibre rifle with double octagonal barrels and a single trigger. He asked them to demonstrate it for him. At last they became enthusiastic and showed him how the trigger would only release a hammer that had been cocked, how the hammer would hit the percussion cap fitted over a nipple with a hole that directed the flash down to the powder charge in the barrel. They showed him the caps and how they fitted over the nipple to keep the powder dry. The rifle could fire the traditional powder and ball, but they enthused about their bespoke cartridges containing a fine powder, black powder and a ball, all to be rammed down with a single push. To activate the cartridge a gimlet was poked down the hole in the nipple to puncture the cartridge exposing the fine powder at the end. The cap would then be pushed on and the rifle was ready to fire at any time.

TK was captivated and, finally, asked the price. They told him the price of the rifle and he went pale. Then they told him the price of one hundred bespoke cartridges and his heart sank. TK put on a brave face and said that he would think about it and wondered whether they made a pistol along the same lines. They showed it to him. The mechanism was identical. The short octagonal barrels were just the same and the grip was beautifully balanced. He promised to return but wondered whether he would ever do so.

He met Otto for dinner and told him about the beautiful rifle and pistol.

He could not afford the guns until he had found the gold and he might not live to bring back the gold without the guns. If he had not seen them he might have died without regret. Otto smiled and explained that the artillery regiment was one of the oldest and richest in a land of old rich regiments and TK's friends in high places had unlimited resources. TK began to hope.

Otto asked again whether TK might be able to help with Elizabeth. TK repeated that their lifestyles were incompatible. TK, Nell and Elizabeth came from similar lifestyles. Otto lived in a world apart. Even Nell was refusing his own offers of marriage. Those girls were going to deal on their own terms.

Civilian life was not suiting TK at all. He was riding the grey mare in the parks and heaths and getting to know London, but for what purpose. He was eating in the mess as a guest and enjoying the male environment and humour. But he would not join in the card games or going on to the clubs and the London men's entertainments. In short, he really did not fit in with the Guards officers.

Fortunately, Otto arrived after a couple of days with good news. The infantry regiment had leapt at the chance to give the rifle. And TK's friends in high places did not hesitate to offer the pistol. Also, the ammunition would come from an unexpected source.

The presentation dinner would be held at the infantry barracks in five days' time. In the meantime, Tom should go to the gunsmiths to order the guns and ammunition for delivery to the barracks. Otto gave him a letter of introduction. Otto would be at the presentation.

The next day TK went to the gunsmiths to order the guns. He handed over the letter and his reception, originally cautious, became enthusiastic.

First, they took the fittings for the rifle. They offered an adjustable sight for the longer shots, but TK chose to have a simple sight and adjust the aim by pointing higher. The fore sight would be a brass bead and the rear sight would be a simple broad V. The bead would fill the V when the aim was complete. Less to go wrong. TK chose the smallest possible hammer system. If the hammer was released before it locked it would return gently. However, after it was locked it would return sharply to activate the percussion cap. They explained that the amount of powder in the cartridge and the weight of the ball dictated the impact. They recommended a charge that would provide great accuracy with the chosen one-third inch ball up to one hundred and fifty yards. TK did not expect to shoot more than one hundred yards, so he would be in credit. The gimlet for piercing the cartridge would screw point first into the end of the ramrod. The gunsmiths were very proud of their brass fittings but TK asked them to darken the brass so they would not reflect the rays of the sun.

TK asked for exactly the same specification in relation to the pistol.

They discussed whether the cartridges for the pistol could be the same as those for the rifle. TK really wanted them to use the same ammunition. The gunsmiths confirmed that this was possible, but he would lose a bit of distance with the rifle and a bit of accuracy with the pistol, but this would be compensated by the hitting power.

They went to a disused open tunnel with one hundred yards' range. The target was a three foot square canvas with a three inch diameter black spot at the centre. They started at fifty yards. They demonstrated the locking with the hammers down. A cartridge was inserted. It was rammed down with a polished cane rod. The gimlet was unscrewed from the butt of the ramrod. The hammers were partially pulled back and the gimlet was pushed down the nipple to pierce the cartridge, exposing the fine powder. A copper percussion cap was fitted over the nipple. The hammer was then returned to rest on the cap.

TK was invited to rest on a stand and take aim. They

advised a slightly wider stance, pulling the stock tight to the shoulder, closing the left eye and then the slightest touch when the bead was in the middle of the V. TK pulled the hammer to the locking position, took aim and fired. Three inches high and three inches to the right. They advised him to keep the stock tight against the shoulder, but to breathe out and relax before touching the trigger.

He tried again. This time he touched the right edge of the black spot. Good enough. At fifty yards TK and the rifle were aiming dead straight.

They moved to a target with a six inch spot at one hundred yards. They advised TK to aim two inches above the spot. He pulled the stock firmly into his shoulder, got the bead in the middle of the V, breathed out and touched the trigger. He hit the spot. They explained that at one hundred and fifty yards the aim should be six inches above the spot. They explained that with a heavier charge he could aim lower and hit harder. However, the pistol would then become unmanageable. TK was happy with the trade-off to kill humans and deer at one hundred yards. He had heard that there were huge deer in the north of America but he did not expect to be shooting them.

They tried the pistol at twenty five yards with the same charge. They told him to stand square on with his right arm rigid. The left hand should cover the right hand and hold it rigid. The shot hit four inches high and four inches to the right. He had forgotten to breathe out and relax. The second attempt nicked the spot.

At up to fifty yards the aim would be the same but less

accurate. After that he would be lucky to hit the three foot square. One shot proved the point. He understood its limitations. Afterwards he was shocked to hear that the cost of the cartridges and caps would be almost half the price of the guns. Apparently the caps were a new invention, there was only one supplier and they were handmade. He remembered Otto's confidence and placed the order.

In theory, as a retired officer, TK could wear the uniform on formal occasions. However, TK had had to remove the insignia in order to use the jacket as a civilian. Otto turned up like a guardian angel. He brought a jacket of about the right size and some notes for TK to use in his words of thanks.

On the night, Otto collected him and led him through the introductions and the formalities. The dinner was exceptional. TK followed Otto through the soup, fish and main courses knife for knife, fork for fork and spoon for spoon.

At last the infantry general, as host, said a few words to introduce the guest of honour. Then, to TK's surprise, Otto stood up and vividly told the story of how they had met in the peninsular, how his commanding officer had guessed that TK might be able to deal with a problem that was undermining the whole government war effort, the Count. He explained the plan to trap the Count into a duel in which he would be fatally injured with long enough life expectancy to summon his accomplices and to give his instructions to destroy the evidence of the spy network. It had been a long shot, based on TK's ability to win a duel on horseback against the Count. TK had taken up both challenges, from the Count and from High Places. He had symbolically disabled the Count's dueling hand and crucially pierced his appendix. The Count was left with three days to live. As expected, the Count had summoned his spies and, as planned, the government's agents had rounded them up.

Then Brigadier Fitz-Warwick told the story of how TK's patrols had followed and reported on the movements of the French in the peninsular. And finally, turned up to help at the Battle of Waterloo. The spiking of the guns, the blasting of the lancer charge and the retreat to defend against the French column were becoming legend. The interplay between the attacks on the front of the column and the infantry volleys were being written into the manuals. And, to top it all, his young lieutenant had brought back an Eagle for the regiment. And there it was in pride of place at the end of the hall.

The Brigadier stood again to thank TK and to say that certain gifts had been arranged. First from the regiment, a new percussion rifle. Second from HM Government, a matching pistol and finally from the Prince Regent, who had been persuaded that TK had helped him win the battle of Waterloo, ammunition.

TK had been grateful for the kind words from Otto and Brigadier Fitz-Warwick but had sat in dread at the prospect of having to speak in front of these Guards officers who might sneer at his poor regiment, his poor uniform and country manners. He looked down at a sea of red and gold. 'Very well, they thought that he had been brave doing what came naturally. Now he really had to be brave doing what came absolutely unnaturally. But, brave he would be.'

He drew on Otto's notes. First, he thanked the regiment for saving him and his men at the Battle of Waterloo. Then he confirmed that he had been pleased to help in a small way. If he had sheltered behind the infantry, he would never have been let back into the cavalry.

He was pleased that the charges across the front ranks of the column had slowed them down. However, the victory was that of the infantry regiment and its brilliant discipline in the face of the French Column. Finally, he was sorry that the Eagle had come at the price of the life of a talented young officer. He blamed himself for not providing him with more support. It had seemed like a great adventure and it turned into a tragedy. But the battle for the Eagle had been won by the regiment and they could be immensely proud of their achievement.

So, what next? He had developed a great admiration for the unspoiled vastness of North America and had heard that a North West passage had been discovered. He hoped to follow that route and, possibly, to pick up a bit of Gold if he found any lying around. He thanked them for the guns. If they heard that the natives were firing percussion cap guns they would know that his adventure had not gone too well.

From a side door a cloaked figure with a high-bridged nose looked down on the proceedings, smiled and said to his companion, 'Well, McLaren we used him hard. He served us well. At last he is getting some reward. Let's wish him luck. I think he will need it.'

"I would not bet against him."

The speech was well received. TK sat down and relaxed as the port started to go round. Otto drifted up beside him and warned him to take only a sip each time the port went around. It would be a pity to spoil the evening.

At the end of the evening they said their goodbyes. From TK nurse-maiding Otto on the field of battle in the beginning, they had finished with Otto nurse-maiding TK through the top level of military life.

Otto, once more, asked TK to remember him to Elizabeth. TK said that he hoped that Otto would help to keep them safe, but not necessarily out of mischief.

And so, TK returned to Dorset and the hunting and the parties and the love-making. His final encounter with Nell left them locked together in joy.

'So Mr Kynaston, I hope that you will come back for more.'

'I will. But will you be waiting?'

'That's just one more chance that you have to take with this crazy adventure. The hope might make you careful, but I doubt it.'

"Nell, I understand that you don't want to be a widow, inheriting my debts and out of the game. But I am going to try to stay alive. I am going to try to make some money and I am going to try to come back to you with a bit more to offer."

"I would be happy with more of the same. But the man that I have come to know and love would not be happy for long. Just remember this moment and so will I. Now, where were we?"

Departure

TK followed the river road on horseback along muddy lanes. He stopped at Ironbridge to collect his arrowheads. Then on up to the village. He stayed with Lady Anne and was pleased to hear that the season was going well and there were no tragedies in the village.

He went to the forge to collect the final item for his voyage. The tin box had been made as he asked with waterproof seals and sections to hold the sword, the parts of the bow, twenty arrows and now there would be space for the rifle and the pistol and the ammunition. The knife could go on top when he was not carrying it. The sections had holes with cords to secure the various items. He would need smaller tin cases for the arrowheads, the cartridges and the percussion caps. The cartridges were in waterproof packs of five and he wanted to carry five packs in the box. The cobbler who had made the sheath for the knife with its sewn-in metal clip would produce a sheath for the pistol. Tom left the pistol with him and when he returned he was delighted to see how the barrels would fit along the top edge without a seam and the seam along the lower edge would hold the trigger guard tight. The sheath would go inside his belt and the clip would hold it in place. It was designed to sit on the left side under a coat. On top of the trunk, he wanted a quilt to compress the contents and, perhaps, provide warmth when required. An oilskin cover for the box completed the preparations.

While the work was going on he had ridden out with Lady Anne and had a last night out with the poachers. He sold the grey mare to Lord Darling, paid his debts, said his thanks and made his farewells. At last he rode north on a couple of workhorses for Liverpool.

He rode due north staying at roadside inns and farmhouses, some better than others, and arrived at Chester. Even in winter it was a beautiful city, proud of its Roman origins. He stayed at the post house, a small indulgence. He walked in the centre and was amazed to find shops on two storeys with wooden walkways at the upper level.

And so on up to the Mersey. The riverside ferry towns were chaotic. The ferry services dictated by wind and tide. However, after two nights in an unpleasant ferry inn, he boarded for Liverpool.

Outside Liverpool he visited three livery stables. He went back to the first and smiled to think that the second and third were even worse. However, they were making the best of a bad job and were honest and helpful. He sold the workhorses and organised a ride to the waterfront. He asked where to go to take passage to America. The stable keeper recognised another horseman and tried to help. There were passenger ships that sailed rarely and at great expense. Some merchant ships had cabins for passengers which were safe and cheap. Some smaller cargo boats took hands to work their passage, some good, some not so good. He had no recommendation. Their berths could be found in descending order along the quays. When they reached the slums and taverns they were to be avoided.

Even with some advice about how to look for a passage, TK was overwhelmed by the size and chaos of the docks. There were so many ships moored and anchored that there appeared to be a solid wall of hulls, masts and rigging. He had to concentrate to distinguish the individual ships. And the dockside was not what he had expected either. A mass of manpower thronged together. But, again, as he looked more closely, they appeared to have a common purpose. They did not crash into each other but worked alongside each other as if with a common purpose, pushing carts, pulling carts, loading and unloading carts and just carrying loads on their backs. And in amongst it all were the horses, hundreds of them, pulling carts, pulling ships and being led from one job to another. There were dogs everywhere fighting over scraps. And through it all cattle sheep, pigs, hens and geese were being loaded onto ships. And the workmen waded through the filth. In the harbour dung and rubbish floated in and out on the tides. The stench was awful.

TK started at an inn close to the top end of the scale mentioned at the livery stable. He joined some masters and captains to ask their thoughts on what would be the best for him. He did not think it strange that he should join them as equals and they did not think it strange that this self-assured young man should quietly start to ask their opinions. He assumed that they would want to help. He respected them and he assumed that they would respect him. A passenger ship would be too fancy and expensive. A cabin on a cargo ship would be slow and boring on a long journey. So, for something new and different it looked like signing on to work his passage. They looked at his hands which worked well in the country but advised him to get two or three pairs of gloves. Finally, the best piece of advice of all, they told him that Captain John Phipps was moored down the quay. He was a good sailor, a fair man and a patient master. His ship was the Lydia. She was a fast little ship carrying high value cargoes between Liverpool and New York. This time she was carrying silks and spices.

TK paid for a round of drinks and left them to walk down the quay, past three masters, past the two masters and so to the one masters, the sloops. These were big boats but simply rigged for easy long voyages. He found the Lydia and walked aboard. Captain John Phipps was surprisingly tall and almost thin but for his broad shoulders. His hair and beard were turning grey and that gave him an air of confidence and authority. He was the commander of his ship. TK explained that he was a country boy, a horse soldier and that was he was excited at the possibility of working his passage. He hoped to learn some new skills on his voyage to America rather than just sit in a cabin.

Captain John Phipps shook his head. He would have a crew of only five. If one of them could not cope there was not enough scope to share the load. TK understood and nodded. Captain John kindly advised him to try one of the bigger ships where they could share the load and the risk. TK understood the logic and accepted the decision. He would go back to the captains tomorrow to ask for a recommendation for a larger ship.

The Lydia

The next morning, he joined the captains and masters ready to ask for their alternative recommendation when they told him that Captain Phipps was asking for him. They laughed and wished him luck.

Captain John told him bluntly that he had seen all the other applicants and could not find anyone better. He knew that TK had been an officer but from now on he would have to work as a deckhand. It would be hard work. TK should bring his own boots and gloves. They would sail the next morning.

The next morning TK came aboard with the tin trunk, and boxes containing arrows, arrowheads, cartridges and a few clothes including his new boots and gloves.

He met the mate, Andy, a bit younger and a bit heavier than the captain but otherwise from the same mold. Very steady. The other members of the crew were Toby, short, very broad, heavily muscled, a big grin and a master of the rigging, and finally, Pat Devlin, a young Irishman with dark red hair, big and strong with an obvious instant competitive dislike for TK.

Hmm, early days.

They would leave on the afternoon tide. TK appeared in sea boots and gloves. Pat Devlin hooted with laughter, but Captain John said it would do no harm to get the hang of them.

Captain John had decided to keep it simple and would

sail out to the north. He supervised the laying out of the sails and explained the procedure for raising and using the booms and sails, each in turn. The jib appeared fairly straightforward but it was very big and heavy. The gaff must have its sails attached and must be raised quickly when the time came. Captain John showed them the ropes to be pulled and reminded everyone of the steps involved and each person's tasks. Heavy canvass, heavy booms, heavy ropes, heavy work, only made possible through use of block and tackle. Human strength alone would not be enough.

They would need to work as a team. And that's exactly what they did. Calm voices directed TK what to do. And so, they sailed neatly out of Liverpool Harbour, North West and into the open Atlantic. No ships, no shores, easy sailing.

Captain John announced the watches. He and Andy would alternate, and Toby, Pat and Tom would alternate but with overlaps. The responsibilities would be shared between one senior and one junior with a reserve at all times.

During a meal break, at one of the overlaps, Pat could not resist a tease.

'So, soldier boy, how do you like life at sea?'

'Very well, thank you.'

'Did you ever kill anyone on land?'

'Very many. We were at war.'

'How did you kill them?'

'With swords and guns and knives and with my bare hands.'

Pat nodded and fell silent. The point had been made

without reducing the crew numbers. TK smiled as he remembered how Hackett had taught him to use his hands and remembered, grimly, a couple of times it had come in useful. He was no longer a soldier, but he hoped that he could survive as well in civilian life.

Captain John and Tom would take the first watch. Captain John explained that the sailing involved many hours on the same course with the same setting of the sails. Tom would be asked to steer the ship by following the same compass setting, but they would not be going in a straight line. They would constantly be drifting down wind and drifting with the tides. Captain John would explain this during the voyage. Every few hours the course would be reset, and the sails would be adjusted. The watches really would involve watching. Watching for sails and floating debris by day and for lights by night.

But they could talk and Captain John would be interested to hear about Tom's career as a soldier and Tom would be interested to hear about Captain John's career as a sailor.

Captain John and Andy set the course and took the wheel for the changes. Pat and TK pulled ropes. Even with the extensive use of blocks and tackles, which could be heavy, it was hard work. Toby was a revelation. TK had never seen such athleticism. In theory it would not be necessary to climb into the rigging. In practice, Toby found every excuse to run on deck and climb in the rigging. He was the sail master.

So they sailed out into the Atlantic, away from Ireland, the South of England and Portugal, rechecking the course and resetting the sails. Gradually, as they left South Portugal behind, the heavy rains and winds became less and the days became sunnier. And the sailing became easier.

Then, 'Sail Ho!'

Pirates

Captain John extended his telescope and shook his head grimly. They were level with the north coast of Africa and this was pirate territory. The ship that they had seen was a caravel rigged for piracy with two masts, lateen sails an extended bow spit and a big Genoa foresail. Captain John explained that they could not escape and that it was only a matter of time before the pirate ship caught up with them. The pirates would be after their ship, their cargo and the crew to be sold as slaves. TK asked how many pirates would be on board and was told at least ten and more likely fifteen. He asked how long it would take them to catch up and was told that if they sailed away from the pirate it could take a few hours. TK asked about the pirate weapons and was told that they would be equipped for hand-to-hand fighting in the hope of taking them alive for ransom or slavery. Captain John told them that the pirate ship was comparatively small but the crew would be big and ruthless. They had few options. They could sail better into the wind but eventually the pirates would catch them.

TK asked whether they had any defenses and Captain John confirmed that a few years ago he had been persuaded to buy a two-pounder cannon to fit on the stern of the ship with round shot, grapeshot and canister for this very situation, but it would do them no good once they were boarded. TK asked whether they could delay the boarding when the pirate ship was within range. Captain John told him that he could make a few turns but once the pirates had grappling hooks and lines on them they would not be able to escape.

TK asked about the weak points of the pirate ship and was told that the steering mechanism and the rudder were most vulnerable. If the two-pounder could hit the rudder fittings it might detach, then it could not sail.

'Very well,' said TK. 'It's the steering mechanism and the rudder and, presumably the men who do the steering. If you can keep away from them at ten or fifteen yards for a few minutes I may be able to do some damage with the cannon at very close range and I can shoot the crew with my guns and bow. First, cannon fire, then the rifle and the bow, then the pistol, then the sword, then the knife, and finally, my bare hands. I like the odds. If you, Andy and Toby sail the ship, and Pat loads the guns I will do the rest. As you say, we have plenty of time to practice. Let's have a look at that cannon.'

His confidence inspired them, and they worked briskly to get out the little cannon and set it up on its swivel with its stoppers. The flintlock looked fine. The first priority would be to hit the rudder mountings of the pirate if possible. For this, they set out round shot. Then, for the later battle they laid out grapeshot and canister. Everything looked very small but TK knew that at close range it could be very effective.

TK checked the powder cartridges and the fine powder for the flintlock. They were dry and ready. He cut the end of a powder cartridge and rammed it down the barrel. Then he rammed in a ball and wadding. He broke a cartridge of fine powder into the lock, set the gun on horizontal and pulled the lanyard. He counted from the flash to the bang and from the bang to the splash. He had all the information he needed. He replaced the balls on the rack. Captain John told him he would only get two shots at the rudder and a few more with the grape and canister. His spirits started to match his brave demeanor. However, he knew that he must be careful. If he was killed the others would also be lost.

He took Pat Devlin into the cabin where they would keep the powder cartridges and priming cartridges. They would have to be taken up one at a time to avoid any damp or spray. Then he opened the tin case. He took out the weapons one by one. Pat Devlin was amazed. TK told him that these would save his life or liberty provided he did exactly as he was told. Nothing more. Nothing less. Just exactly as he was told. Pat had never known such a commanding presence. He started to pay very special attention in order not to displease TK in any way.

First, TK wedged the sword, in its scabbard, upright close to the steps. He explained that Pat should not attempt to draw the sword out of its scabbard but should pass the sword and scabbard up together if asked. By way of explanation TK drew the sword, swished off one of Pat's dark red curls and had the sword back in its scabbard before Pat looked down to see what had happened. Pat shuddered at the realization of what he was dealing with. TK explained that this would be the last line of defense and Pat must not let him down.

Next TK took out the rifle and the pistol. He showed

Pat the ammunition pouches and the percussion caps, the ramrods and the spikes. He drilled Pat with the procedure: clean, cartridge, gimlet, and cap. He drilled into Pat the need to look after the ramrods and the gimlets and the necessity of not fully cocking the hammers before fitting the caps. He made Pat repeat the procedure several times before it was clear that Pat had understood the importance of each step.

Finally, TK took out the bow, locked the two halves into the grip, fastened it and strung it. They fitted arrow heads to all twenty of the arrows. They made a shelf in a dry corner at the top of the steps where Pat could put the loaded guns and TK could return them after they had been fired. The bow and arrows stood nearby. TK stuck the knife into his boot and he was ready.

TK joined Captain John at the wheel. The pirate ship still seemed far off. He had plenty of time to load the two-pounder and to talk through with Captain John the maneuver that would enable the sloop to pass under the stern of the pirate ship. The conditions were in their favor with a light breeze and a gentle swell. The five of them would be able to handle the changes of direction on Captain John's orders, but they would need to be quick and sure. One mistake could be fatal.

Time seemed to stand still. Then, eventually, the time came and everything happened very fast. The pirate aimed to come along the side of the sloop but Captain John tacked sharply, the sails changed with a bang, Andy, Toby and Pat worked furiously to re-set them, TK ran to the gun and they passed behind the pirate ship as Captain John had promised. At close range TK aimed at the top fitting of the rudder and fired on the rise.

Splinters flew but he could not tell whether he had hit the target. He fired the rifle twice at the men at the helm of the pirate ship and saw one fall. He handed the rifle to Devlin and started to reload the two-pounder as the pirate ship started a sharp sweeping turn when, suddenly, it pointed into the wind and stopped with its sails flapping.

'The rudder has gone,' said Captain John. 'It could not take the strain. They will have to gather at the stern by the steering lines. Try the grapeshot.'

TK put down the ball and picked up a bag of grapeshot the size of walnuts and rammed it home.

Captain John brought the sloop under the stern of the pirate ship and sure enough a group of pirates was working frantically behind the rudder. Again, TK fired on the rise and saw the group disintegrate in a cloud of blood and splinters.

'I think we will be safe now,' said Captain John.

'No,' said TK, 'it is our duty to finish the job, no loose ends.'

Captain John reluctantly agreed to stand off and let TK use the rifle, but he hated to court further danger in case their luck ran out. He feared the worst when a tall black figure, completely bald with a big gold earring, swung a grappling hook that locked onto the stern of the sloop. But he dived for cover and pulled a boy down with him when he saw the rifle barrels swinging towards him. Andy cut the grappling rope. Other pirates were not so quick as they lined the rail of the caravel to swing the grappling hooks and one by one TK started to shoot at them while Andy and Toby ran up and down the side of the sloop cutting the ropes or throwing off the hooks. While Pat reloaded, TK slipped on the glove and fired the bow straight at the targets and was pleased to see some hits. But it was the rifle that was really doing the job. He could lean it on the rail and get good accuracy. It was not a fair fight. The pirates still wanted the crew of the sloop alive, but TK wanted the pirates dead.

At last, the surviving pirates realised that TK posed the greatest danger and started to shoot at him with guns and bows. TK had to move fast from cover to cover, steadying each time and firing the guns. He could not risk standing to fire the bow. Suddenly, there was a cry from the bow. Andy and Toby were cutting at a grappling line that had hooked on. The line was reinforced and they could not cut it. Four pirates were pulling on the line and the ships were beginning to move closer.

TK ran forward and risked a shot with the bow. He rushed it and missed. One of the pirates raised a musket and TK found himself looking down the muzzle of an English gun. He dived and was hit by a shower of splinters. The bow fell apart in his hands. TK found the rifle and shot low at the man with the musket as the sloop began to rise. He hit somewhere around the chest but the pirate did not fall. He fired the second barrel and hit a pirate high on the shoulder and, still, he did not fall. He put the rifle down and drew the pistol. He stepped forward in the confusion and stood on the grappling line. The tension went from the hook and Andy took the chance to release it and throw it overboard. TK fired the pistol at the pirates from close range and hit one in the throat. Lucky.

The pirates had not given up. Indeed, they became more desperate, shooting to kill with bows, spears and guns. Andy and Toby took cover and TK ran down the steps back to the cabin for re-loading. Time was critical.

Already the pirates had pulled the grappling hook onto the caravel and were ready to try again. Pat took the rifle and followed the loading procedure. TK started the procedure on the pistol but Pat took it off him surprisingly quickly.

TK took the rifle forward and from behind the cabin roof, took careful aim and hit with both barrels. He was starting to return for the pistol when Toby took the rifle and passed the pistol. They were in business. TK could remain in cover behind the cabin and steady the guns to improve the aim. His hits to the chest became more frequent, even with the pistol. The pirates gave up on the grappling hook and took cover. Now it was just a matter of time to find his targets with the rifle and, at last, all was quiet.

When there were no more targets he asked Captain John to put the sloop alongside the caravel. Captain John refused. He said that the job was done and they should not tempt the fates by hanging around. TK insisted. No loose ends. TK took the sword and stepped alongside the pirate ship as Captain John, reluctantly, brought the sloop alongside. He moved carefully and shot one survivor as he stepped out of hiding. Amazingly, the rest were dead or dying and TK helped them on their way. The grapeshot at the stern had done more damage than he imagined. Captain John started to relax as the danger to TK receded. Again, Captain John wanted to call it a day without tempting fate any further but TK wanted to board the caravel. No loose ends. Captain John relented on condition that he would move away again when TK had boarded.

TK carefully made his way to the cabin which was more like a mini stateroom with wide steps. Through the chaos he saw ladies' dresses thrown around a large chest and, behind it, an armchair with a lady tied hand and foot with silk ribbons. The lady fluttered her eyes and asked in Spanish whether he was to be her rescuer. She explained that she was a hostage. The pirates intended to take her back to Barbary and claim a ransom.

TK asked what had become of her ship and she explained with sad fluttering of her eyes that the pirates had stolen the ship, they would sell the cargo of spices and would sell the crew as slaves. She was very sad. TK extended his sympathy, cut her free and offered to show her to the sloop. Again, the smile and the fluttering of the eyes. Perhaps she could have a few minutes to compose herself 'as we ladies like to do' before she might be allowed to join the English ship. TK, still shocked, apologized and agreed to withdraw, with great gallantry.

On the sloop TK explained what he had found and, as he spoke, doubts arose and warning bells began to sound. 'Damn, the ribbons were too loose, the dresses were on the floor, the chest was closed, the black man with the shaven head has not been found, she had no shoes and her feet were brown. Damn me, if she isn't a pirate and I'm her fool.'

TK grabbed his sword and leapt across to the pirate ship. He ran down the steps and just had time to see the lady and the Moor standing in front of the open trunk when he skidded on one of the silk dresses. He fell against the trunk as the Moor raised a scimitar high above his head like an executioner.

'Bad mistake,' thought TK and lunged forward thrusting up with his sword under the ribs up through the heart and lungs to the neck. The scimitar hit the edge of the trunk where TK had fallen. TK used the sword as a lever to pull himself round with the Moor between him and the lady just as the Moor's nose exploded in a red haze and the bang echoed round the cabin. The turn had blocked the lady's knife. Then another bang and the lady sat down with a red stain spreading across her chest.

TK blinked blood out of his eyes. 'Well, Pat, your second shot was better than the first.'

'Ah the first was from four feet but the second was from two feet, so it was. Did I do well? Did I save your life?'

'I don't know about saving my life. I thought that I was doing quite well before you filled my face with bits of nose. But you certainly saved us all a lot of trouble with the lady, I don't know if I could have killed her. You tied up all the loose ends, and that is priceless. Now let's find their treasure chest and we will have had a good day.'

TK automatically went to the stove and started to pull it over when Pat Devlin remarked that it was bound to be in the chest, and there it was. It was a tin box, but it was locked. TK withdrew a black silk ribbon from round the

Lady's neck. And there was the key. The box was half full of gold and silver rings, coins, bits of gold and silver and a surprising amount of jewelry. TK leaned down with his knife and threw in the big earring from the Moor.

So, as the sun started to set, they sat together again on the sloop. The pirate ship was the last loose end. She was valuable, but it would be hard work and risky to get her to a friendly port in order to sell her. Captain John decided it. No loose ends. He and Andy took heavy iron staves onto the pirate ship. They threw oil lamps into the cabin and very quickly jumped back onto the Lydia. As they cast her off, and once again, started to sail south, they looked back and saw her starting to go down with flames leaping up her sails and rigging.

'How will we share the treasure?' asked Pat, rather aware that he had found it.

'Equal.' said TK, and that was that.

'I don't know the rules for bringing in pirate treasure.' said Captain John. 'If they confiscate it, we may never see it again. Let's weigh it now.'

So they emptied it into a flour bag and weighed the contents and the box. Captain John entered the weights in his log.

Finally, TK retrieved the pieces of the bow. They were all there, undamaged, except that the bow string had been broken. He took a spare from the chest. No loose ends.

The Storm

And so they formed into a happy crew. They sailed into sunnier weather and turned west, sailing gently but surely across the Atlantic. They became becalmed, but Captain John, unperturbed, told them to be patient and, sure enough, eventually the sails flapped and the wind returned to push them on.

Andy saw the storm first. He raised the alarm and suddenly the calm turned to frantic activity. They did not have a moment to lose before it would be upon them. First the foresail had to be lowered and stowed securely. Then the storm sail had to be raised. Finally, the main sail and gaff came thundering down, to be lashed down securely. Captain John and Andy double checked that nothing could come loose in wind or waves. Then Captain John turned down wind. Finally, as the first rain hit, they attached heavy woven rope fenders to the ends of two hawsers, very long heavy ropes used to tow the ship into berth, and paid them out over the stern, in the hope that they would provide some drag and keep the ship in line with the wind.

After that it just got worse and worse with no end in sight. They paired up to be lashed to the wheel for short spells. They wore oilskins which did not keep them dry but saved them from the worst chill of the wind that could drain their strength. Hour after hour they were driven before the storm. Sometimes the little ship dived into the waves. Sometimes the waves crashed over them. Always the decks were awash with sea water. As the bow came up through a wave they saw that one of the ropes used to tie the big foresail down on deck had come loose. It would be fatal if it started to unfurl and fill with wind and waves. Toby grabbed a rope, tied himself in a bowline, attached a clip and shot towards the bow. He worked to secure the headsail as waves crashed over him. At last he stood back as the bow dived into a huge wave. His feet kicked in the air. When the water subsided, he had disappeared. The safety line whipped about in the wind. Empty.

TK began to wonder whether they could take any more. It had to relent. But it did not. But they did not give up. They just hung on grimly for two days. Their movements became slower and slower. Their strength ebbed away. They hung on to each other, to provide support and mutual strength, driving themselves to keep going. And then, as quickly as it had arrived, the storm passed. The sun broke through and they sat in puddles as it started to revive them. Each admitted that he had only kept going because he did not want to be the first to stop.

Slowly, over several days they began to put the ship back into full sailing order and to re-set their course. Then, as the wind freshened and the current strengthened, they turned north. At last, more gulls appeared and bits of wood and rubbish floated on the surface. And so, on a brisk spring day, they came to New York.

TK Book II

New York

They did not have to wait long for a berth in New York Harbour. A small ship left and they dropped into its place while other larger ships had to wait.

And so they moored up and put the gangway in place by evening. Captain John announced that the ship would pay for dinner at his favorite inn. So they got cleaned up with shaving and beard trimming and shaking out shore clothes.

Tomorrow would be a busy day with the documentation of Toby's death, the declaration of the pirates' chest and the unsealing and handover of the cargo.

Captain John explained that after months at sea most captains and their guests would want fresh meat cooked the American way on open fires. The beef was the best. So that's what they chose. TK drew on his experiences in Spain and France to find an accompanying wine that was drinkable. It had travelled a long way. And they relaxed for the first time since they had left Liverpool. They toasted Toby with thanks and agreed to give his mother an extra share. Then they moved on to recall their adventures on this voyage and other voyages and TK answered a lot of questions about his life as a cavalry officer in Spain. He did not dwell on the horrors of Waterloo. Captain John and Andy told of their life in command of a Royal Navy frigate at the battle of

Trafalgar and did not dwell too long on the slaughterhouse conditions on the gun decks. The evening was drawing to a close when Pat declared that he needed Irish whiskey, so he did. And he knew just the place for it, so he did. Captain John and Andy shook their heads knowingly. The others did not drink whiskey. So, Pat left with a promise not to mention the pirate chest.

The next morning Pat had not returned when the others were eating eggs for breakfast. Lots of eggs bought with fresh bread and butter on the harbour side. They were disturbed by boots on deck and a harbour constable marched on board to place them and the ship under arrest. They would be required to go quietly. A warrant was nailed to the mast. Without discussion the constables removed the pirate chest, TK's tin chest and the ship's log book. The charges were theft, piracy and murder.

Captain John scribbled a note to his agent, Adam Hillstrider, asking for help. As the constable continued to search the ship TK took the note on deck in order to hand it over to a likely courier. Among the morning chaos TK had hoped to find one of the harbour lads to carry the message. But right in front of him was a handsome gentleman smiling at the warrant fluttering on the mast. Yes, he knew Adam Hillstrider and yes, he would deliver the note. And yes, they would meet again Mr Kynaston. A tip of the hat and he was gone. Clearly, Pat had been talking.

So the pirate chest, TK's chest and the log book were confiscated and they were led under the gaze of the harbour folk to the Harbour Master's office. There they were led into a bare room where Pat sat pale and shame-faced in a corner. The door was locked. Tk was enraged. He prowled like a caged animal and would not be calmed. He had not lived through all his patrols and campaigns just to risk hanging at the hands of the opportunist Harbour Master of New York. He was going to escape and take his chance. Up and down, up and down, hour after hour. His mood was worsening and his determination increasing. He would not listen to the suggestion that the charges could be withdrawn and they could be released. Just the possibility of being hanged was enough to convince him that action was required. To wait and see was not an option. The first chance of escape would be his best chance of escape. He prowled and waited.

At last the door opened and TK moved forward. The harbour constables carried truncheons and an assistant carried food and blankets. No chance this time.

The next morning the four were put in chains under heavy guard and led to the hall of the Harbour Master's office. And there he was, sitting in a high chair. He was huge. Tall, broad, heavy-stomached, red-faced with a purple nose and big whiskers. This was Horace Locke, the Harbour Master.

A clerk read out their names then the Harbour Master boomed out, 'You are charged with theft, piracy and murder. How would you plead?'

Captain John spoke for all of them, 'Not guilty in each case.'

'Very well, we will proceed, and I will see you hang

before nightfall,' snarled Horace Locke.

TK looked carefully around the room and its doors and windows. He concentrated on the guard who had the key to the chains. He thought that the constables would be off guard while he was chained.

Charles Craddock, a lawyer, introduced himself and stated that he would present the case against the crew. He was also big and fat and red-faced, but not quite as big and fat and red-faced as Horace Locke. The charges were theft, piracy and murder. The penalty would be confiscation of the ship, its cargo, its contents and the hanging of the crew. He would start with the taking of a civilian ship carrying wealthy European passengers on the high seas.

He was preparing to introduce his first witness when the door opened and a young man called loudly, 'You may not proceed. This court is not properly constituted.' He was the gentleman who had taken the note.

The young man introduced himself as lawyer, Ben Horseman, who had been appointed by Adam Hillstrider to defend the accused. Then he announced that Judge MacMillan had ordered that the case must be transferred to his State Court.

Horace Locke stood huge and announced that he was damned if he would give way. Ben Horseman signaled to the door and State Court officers and soldiers came into the room. Ben Horseman read out Judge MacMillan's letter directing that the hearing would be transferred to his Court the next morning. Horace Locke cursed them loudly and withdrew. Ben Horseman gave orders for the chains to be removed and introduced

Adam Hillstrider who was was tall and slim with curly brown hair. He and Captain John greeted each other as old friends. Ben Horseman explained that following Pat Devlin's stories at the Irish bar, Horace Locke had moved fast to make the arrests and he had gone down to take a look, as any good lawyer would. And he grinned. He hoped that the crew would confirm his appointment. They did.

Ben Horseman explained that he had found Adam Hillstrider in a coffee shop frequented by lawyers and agents. It was clear that Horace Locke was up to no good and was exceeding his authority. They pulled in Alan Alexander who was an expert on the new Constitution and the powers of the civic authorities. He had been standing quietly with the court officers and soldiers and now stepped forward to be introduced. He was very small, good-looking, fair-haired with bright blue eyes. He carried himself with the dignity that small men often reserve for themselves, and he was respected by working lawyers and judges alike. Ben Horseman explained that Alan Alexander would try to show the limits of the Harbour Master's powers. It was Alan Alexander who had drawn up the application to the judge to have the case transferred.

TK smiled for the first time and said that if the lawyers could win the case they might, just, save the life of Horace Locke. They all knew that he was not really joking. Alan Alexander turned a little paler.

The lawyers gave their word to the senior court constable that they would attend court with their clients the next morning. But the constable asked for a note of confirmation and it was handed over. At that, the lawyers withdrew to prepare their case and Adam Hillstrider and the crew went to an inn recommended by the agent. TK told Pat Devlin that if he went out of TK's sight, he would be sorry not to have been hanged. Captain John told him that even if he recovered, he would never go to sea again.

The inn was crowded with agents, merchants and ships' captains. They came up to express their support and to pass on the rumors that they had heard. In short, Horace Locke was in debt. He had heard of the pirate chest following Pat's night out and had resolved to seize it and hang the crew before anyone could object.

The State Court House was a fine two storey building. The offices and cells were located on the ground floor. The upper floor consisted of a large court room with a public gallery at the front and the judge's offices behind.

The next morning the courtroom was already crowded with spectators and the air was thick with tobacco smoke. The morning sun shone through the windows giving blocks of smoky brightness in the gloom. Judge MacMillan was grey. He had bushy grey hair, bushy grey eyebrows and bushy grey whiskers. Judge MacMillan called the court to order and called in the jury. He asked whether any members of the jury had any connection with the case and there was no response so he could proceed. He directed Horace Locke to explain his case. Was he not, as Harbour Master, prosecuting the case against the accused? Horace Locke agreed.

'Then, Mr Locke, you cannot sit in judgement. Nemo judex in causa sua potest. No man can be a judge in his own case. Do you wish to proceed with the prosecution?'

Horace Locke fumed and demanded the right to prosecute the accused for theft, piracy and murder, and to confiscate their stolen property.

Judge Macmillan said, 'Very well, the case will be heard in this court before me as judge. Not you. Do you agree?'

Horace Locke grumbled and agreed and asked to appoint a lawyer to present the case. He would give evidence in his role as Harbour Master and he expected proper regard to be given to his position.

'No, Mr Locke. In this court you will be treated the same as any other witness. We will consider the weight of your evidence.'

Charles Craddock stood and stated that he had agreed to present the case for the prosecution. Ben Horseman whispered to his team that Craddock was pompous but straight. And then he stood and introduced himself as the lawyer for the defence. With the agreement of the Court he would be assisted by Alan Alexander.

'No, Mr Horseman, I am not having lawyers popping up and down all over my court. There will be only one lawyer for the defence. You will just have to do your best, Mr Horseman. Now, Mr Craddock, let's hear what this is all about.'

Charles Craddock introduced his case and explained that it had come to the notice of the Harbour Authority that the Lydia had engaged in a fight at sea with another ship; that the crew had taken a chest of valuables off the other ship and in the process had killed the passengers and crew. Thus, the charges were piracy, theft and murder. He would, as requested, call Mr Horace Locke as his first witness.

Charles Craddock asked Horace Locke to explain his position of Harbour Master and his powers and duties that had led to the present case. Horace Locke explained that his appointment charged him to prosecute offences under the law within New York harbour. Piracy was against the law. Theft was against the law and murder was against the law. Invited by Charles Craddock, Horace Locke stated that he had been made aware of claims that a member of the crew of the Lydia had been telling stories in an Irish bar about his exploits in a battle on the high seas. He had dispatched his constables and their report had led him to believe that crimes had been committed. He had therefore ordered the arrests of the crew and the ship and confiscated the chest as proceeds of crime.

Ben Horseman had been in deep whispered conversation with Alan Alexander. He had been told that he did not need to engage in argument with Horace Locke. He merely needed to obtain answers that could be rebutted by evidence for the defence. Accordingly, he asked Horace Locke to produce the document of his appointment. He then asked about the powers of confiscation. Presumably, confiscation was not for the personal benefit of the Harbour Master. Horace Locke puffed up in indignation and bellowed that any confiscated property would be held on behalf of the Harbour Authority.

Surely the Harbour Authority would be holding the

property on behalf of the City Council, asked Ben Horseman.

'We'll have to see about that,' said Horace Locke.

Ben Horseman asked, "Did you see any act of piracy?"

"No but there is overwhelming evidence that the Lydia had attacked an innocent civilian ship"

"Did you see any act of murder?"

"No but there is clear evidence that the Accused murdered the crew and passengers of a European ship for their own gain."

"Did you see any property being stolen?"

"No but the Accused have no honest claim to the valuables that were clearly taken from the innocent passengers of a European ship."

Ben Horseman glanced at Alan Alexander, received a nod and sat down. Charles Craddock's next witness was a harbour employee who had been at the Irish pub and heard the defendant, Patrick Devlin, telling how the Lydia, a British ship, had attacked another a ship, killed the crew and taken a box of treasure. Thomas Kynaston had led the attack. That would do nicely for Charles Craddock and he sat down.

Ben Horseman asked whether Devlin had described the ship or its crew and was told that he had not. His purpose was to describe great acts of seamanship and fighting. Under the rules of hearsay the witness could not give evidence as to the truth of what Devlin had said, only that he had said it. Ben Horseman asked the witness whether Devlin had said what became of the other ship and was told that it had been sunk.

'So, you have no other information about what Pat Devlin said in the Irish bar?'

'No sir, I have no further evidence.'

'No doubt there will be other witnesses who may have different or better recollections,' said Ben Horseman. Up to that point Horace Locke had been looking pleased at the performance of his employee. However, now he became agitated and summoned one of his men and whispered urgently in his ear. The man left, and Horace Locke scowled at the court.

The next witness was a ship's chandler and constable who had arrested the Lydia. He had been sent by the Harbour Master to arrest the ship and its crew and to collect evidence. He had found a tin chest containing valuables and a tin trunk containing weapons that could be used in an attack on a ship. Also, the Lydia was equipped with a cannon for which there could be no innocent explanation. They were submitted in evidence. He had inspected the Lydia for signs of a fight and found none. The only visible damage were signs of past repairs which were consistent with a ship of the Lydia's age. She was in good condition. Charles Craddock asked if there were any signs of storm damage to the ship and was told that there were none. The ship was in good condition.

Charles Craddock asked about the men of the Lydia crew. He was told that they were all British. One had been an officer in the British army and two had served in the Royal Navy.

Ben Horseman asked whether the repairs that the witness had referred to had been carried out at the same time or at different times. The witness replied that it would be usual to repair any damage between voyages.

Finally, Charles Craddock called a jeweler, who confirmed that all of the items in the tin chest were of European origin. The coins were mainly English but included some French and Spanish. All were gold or silver. Also, there were watches, chains, rings, bracelets and brooches. All could have come from passengers on a European ship.

Ben Horseman asked whether the valuables had anything in common and was told that they could have come from a wide range of passengers. Ben Horseman asked about the large gold ring. Surely this could only have come from the ear of a large pirate, but was told that it also could have come from the wrist of a slim lady. Ben Horseman sat down.

Charles Craddock had no more witnesses and Ben Horseman asked for a recess for lunch. The judge cheered up and agreed that the court would reconvene in three hours.

Ben Horseman called them together and stated his priorities. First, Adam Hillstrider should find as many as possible of the drinkers at the Irish bar when Pat told his story. Second, they needed to find the carpenter who must have done the repairs to the Lydia. Third, they needed the log book of the Lydia to be produced, but so far the Harbour Master had not admitted that it had been confiscated. Clearly the Harbour Master was making a fraudulent case. They must leave no stone unturned to expose his dishonesty, thereby casting doubt on all of the evidence. He must be challenged and exposed at every point. There was a lot of work to be done.

Charles Craddock had done a good job. He had made a prima facie case, based on the available evidence, that it was entirely probable that the Lydia had attacked a private ship. He had also established that some of the crew had been in the British armed forces which would indicate fighting capabilities that would not endear them to the American jurors who may be inclined to presume them guilty. Now they urgently needed evidence to contradict those assumptions and prejudices. And at this moment they had none.

The three-hour break flew past and, far too soon, the Court reconvened.

Out of character, Ben Horseman introduced his case at length. He explained the charges against his clients and the evidence that would be required to prove their guilt. He then explained the evidence that would be required to prove their innocence. He had to cast reasonable doubt on the conclusions drawn by the Prosecution. All the time he was watching the courthouse door.

At last he had to proceed. He called Alan Alexander to give evidence. Charles Craddock leapt to his feet and protested that a lawyer could not be a witness. Ben Horseman pointed out that Alan Alexander had been excluded as a litigator but could give evidence as an expert witness regarding the Constitution. Judge MacMillan scowled at the challenge to his authority. Then his scowl cleared as he saw the reasoning that Alan Alexander had clearly provided to get himself heard as a witness. Finally, he smiled at the ingenuity of these young lawyers. Before he could laugh out loud he grumbled his agreement.

Alan Alexander explained that the appointment of the Harbour Master constituted a delegation of authority from the City Council. Accordingly, the Harbour Master had a duty to prevent piracy, smuggling and theft. In support of these duties the Harbour Master had powers of arrest and confiscation. But questions of guilt and ownership of the confiscated items were a matter for the court. This court. Accordingly, the question of the guilt of the crew of the Lydia and the ownership of the ship and its valuables must be decided by this court.

Charles Craddock half-heartedly pointed to the appointment of the Harbour Master and the words of his authority to do 'all things necessary'. Alan Alexander replied that the City Council had no power of confiscation without a court order and accordingly could not delegate such right to the Harbour Master. The City Council had no right to hang anyone and so that right could not be delegated to the Harbour Master. Charles Craddock recognised that he was not going to win an argument with Alan Alexander about the Constitution and delegation of powers so he raised no further questions.

Again, Ben Horseman glanced at the door and reluctantly called Captain John Phipps. He asked about his career as a sea captain. He asked about his relations with the merchants of New York and his agent, Adam Hillstrider. He asked about the formation of his crew and how he had chosen Toby and the men now facing charges of piracy and worse. And all the time he watched the door.

He asked about the sighting of the pirate ship and how

he had recognised the pirate rig. He asked about the preparations for the battle, the understanding that they would be sold as slaves and how Colonel Kynaston had taken charge. Yes, the defendant had been a colonel in King George's army and fought at Waterloo. Captain John explained that he and his first mate had been in command of a British frigate carrying communications at Trafalgar. He explained how TK had set up the little cannon and how he had sailed under the stern of the caravel, and how they had shot at the rudder fittings. The judge did not appear to be impatient, but Ben Horseman watched the door.

Captain John told how they thought that the shot had missed but the rudder of the caravel had failed under the pressure of the turn required to keep the pirates in a dominant position against the Lydia. He explained how he had taken the Lydia under the stern of the caravel and how TK had fired grapeshot at the group trying to repair the rudder. He explained how he had stood off from the caravel and how TK had shot the pirates as they tried to attach their grappling hooks and how Toby and Andy had fought to cut the ropes. He explained that the crew of the Lydia had an advantage because the pirates did not want to kill his crew because they wanted to sell them as slaves and they did not want to damage the Lydia too much because they wanted to sell the ship and its cargo. At last the pirates had identified TK as the source of danger and had tried to kill him and the Lydia had suffered a few chips and scratches in the process but no major damage. Ben Horseman had just asked him how the pirate leaders had been killed when, at last, the courthouse door opened and Adam Hillstrider arrived with two companions.

Ben Horseman continued the examination of Captain John Phipps, who explained that Colonel Kynaston had discovered a lady hostage, then told how he suspected that she might be a pirate and had gone aboard the pirate ship to investigate. He did not see the subsequent encounter, but he received a chest of valuables from the pirate ship. He and his first mate, had sunk the pirate ship and they had sailed for New York.

Ben Horseman had just asked whether the incidents had been written up in the ships log and Captain John confirmed that every detail from the first sighting of the caravel had been written up. Ben Horseman asked whether details of the pirates gold and jewels had been recorded and Captain John confirmed that the gross weight of the chest and its valuables had been recorded in the ships log. Ben Horseman sat down. At least he had established an alternative account of the events at sea. But that would not be enough.

Charles Craddock asked Captain John Phipps why he had not tried to run from the pirate ship and Captain John explained that they had run as fast as they could. He had not expected to escape but they had used the time gained to prepare their defences. But eventually the caravel, with its lateen sails, had caught them within a few hours of the sighting.

Charles Craddock had asked about the two-pound cannon. Why on earth would a trading vessel be carrying a cannon? Captain John explained that with the end of the Napoleonic Wars the Royal Navy had far fewer ships at sea and the Barbary pirates had resumed their attacks on merchant shipping. Redundant Royal Navy armaments had been sold in the harbours to raise funds for the Royal Navy and to help the merchant ships with their defences. He had been persuaded that the two-pounder with grapeshot and canister might give him a chance against pirate attack. He had never had to use it.

'Very convenient,' commented Charles Craddock, 'that you happened to be a British naval office and you happened to have the cannon and you happened to have an ex-soldier with a trunk of weapons aboard.' Charles Craddock looked triumphantly at the jury and was pleased to see at least one look of fury from a juror with a wooden leg that he had identified as a probable veteran from the war of independence against the British who had cost him his leg.

Charles Craddock asked why there were no marks of battle on the Lydia and Captain John replied that there were marks from the grappling irons, a few chips and holes from the musket shots and a couple of arrow hits. As far as he knew they had not been repaired. Charles Craddock pointed out that they had already heard evidence to the contrary.

Finally, Charles Craddock asked why they had taken only the chest. Surely there had been other items of value on the other ship. Perhaps they could not take them because they would be incriminating evidence, he remarked. Captain John replied that a pirate caravel was a fighting ship and was stripped down for battle. It carried no items of value or comfort.

Charles Craddock submitted that the whole of the

defence case relied on the existence of a ghost caravel that passed without trace. If you discounted the ghost ship the defence collapsed and the crew were guilty.

Charles Craddock had made his points and sat down well pleased with his work.

Ben Horseman asked for a few moments to confer with his team. Adam Hillstrider did most of the talking. Ben Horseman turned away with a smile and called Captain Alexander Finch.

"Captain Finch, how are you generally known?"

"Captain Hawk Eye."

"Please tell the Court how you got that name."

"I was the Harbour Master before Horace Locke. I built a house overlooking the harbour with a big veranda. I set up a powerful telescope to look over the harbour at all times. So I always knew what was going on in the harbour."

"And do you still keep an eye on the harbour?"

"Yes, I watch over it every day."

"And have you noticed any unusual goings on lately."

"Yes, harbour constables have taken regular customers from the Irish pub to a hulk on the deserted, seaward, side of the harbour. Food and drink have been delivered. The constables appear to be holding the Irishmen prisoner. They patrol the hulk and the Irishmen do not appear on deck."

"Has anyone else been taken to the hulk?"

"Yes, a carpenter, Ned Wheelmaker, has been taken to the hulk and I have not seen him on deck."

Ben Horseman had no further questions.

Charles Craddock asked whether the harbour had been

well managed by Horace Locke and Captain Hawk Eye confirmed that until the imprisonments in the hulk, the harbour had been well managed. He had no further questions.

Ben Horseman then called Edward Longstaff to give evidence.

"What is your profession Mr Longstaff?"

"I am a broker in stocks and shares. I buy and sell for commission on the New York Stock Exchange. My clients are companies or individuals who wish to buy or sell certain securities. We are regulated by the Buttonwood Agreement, signed in 1792 by the original members of the NY Stock Exchange. We are personally liable to settle the trades that we make.

"Did you make trades for Mr Horace Locke?"

"Yes, I did. He bought a certain stock but its value went down. He doubled up and it went down again."

Charles Craddock protested that this must be confidential information and not admissible in evidence.

"Not in this court when men's lives are at stake." said the Judge. "Please continue Mr Horseman."

"Has Mr Locke settled his account following these trades?"

"No, settlement is overdue. He told me that the amount due is more than he is worth and asked for time. But now he says that he will have the amount to settle in a few days."

"Is this likely?"

"We have discussed his finances and there is no likely source of finance. He has gambled on the Exchange at my expense and lost."

There is a general rule that in advocacy you do not ask a question unless you already know the answer.

Charles Craddock had no further questions.

Ben Horseman then asked for an order of the court to send officers and soldiers to the hulk and to bring any occupants to the court the next morning. He leaned down to whisper to Alan Alexander then straightened and said, 'Sub Poena Habeas Corpus, judge.'

The judge smiled. "Well done Mr Horseman". Charles Craddock did not argue. Horace Locke fumed and the judge granted the order.

"Also, Your Honour, may we please have an order for Mr Horace Locke to deliver to the court the ships log and any evidence in his possession relating to the items taken from the Lydia. Sub Poena Duces Tecum your Honour. And perhaps the Court might order officers to accompany the Harbour Master to assist in the discovery." The judge rolled his eyes and granted the order.

"These orders are not new, you know. And don't be flippant before me, Mr Horseman."

The next morning the courtroom was crowded with scruffy but sober Irish drinkers and a ship's carpenter and, also, two harbour constables. The search of the Harbour Master's office had produced the log book and a bag of coins.

Ben Horseman tried to identify the most respectable of the Irish drinkers. It was a hard choice but eventually he called on one of them. The Irishman repeated Pat's full story of the pirate attack, the defence and Pat's brilliant shooting. In particular, how he had saved TK's life by shooting the pirate leader dead centre. There was no mention that she was a lady, shot at point blank range. The Irishman confirmed that he had been arrested by the harbour constables for drunkenness and held in the hulk. Ben Horseman submitted that the Irishman's evidence coincided with the evidence of Captain Phipps. Also, the ships log book confirmed that account of events.

Finally, the carpenter confirmed that he had been commissioned by the Harbour Authority to carry out repairs to the Lydia. These had consisted of damage to the sides that could have been caused by boarding hooks, bullet holes and splinters and a few arrow heads.

Ben Horseman turned to the judge and stated that this concluded the case for the defence of the crew of the Lydia. The ships log would confirm the evidence given by Captain John Phipps. The log book and the other results of the search of the Harbour Master's office would be relevant to the next phase of the proceedings. He submitted that the charges of a pirate attack on a European ship, murder and theft had not been proved.

The Judge then summed up the case for the jury. Either they believed the evidence of the crew of the Lydia, including the fight with the pirate ship and the capture of the chest, or they believed the proposition of the Harbour Master that the pirates did not exist and the Accused had attacked a European ship and murdered the passengers and crew, but bear in mind that there is no direct evidence to support that proposition.

The Judge then asked the jury to decide by a show of hands. All decided "not guilty" except the war veteran who voted "guilty".

The Judge summoned a court officer and whispered in his ear. The officer went over to the one – legged juror and talked quietly to him but the juror shook his head. Ben Horseman leaned over to his team and explained that the Judge liked jury decisions to be unanimous – especially in murder cases. The officer was explaining to the juror that the only reason for him to be excused was if he became incapacitated. The officer would then offer to show the juror the stairs – a common cause of incapacity. That usually did the trick.

The Judge asked the jurors to vote again. This time they were unanimous.

Horace Locke exploded in a torrent of oaths and headed for the door. Ben Horseman called to TK to stop him and asked the judge to order him to be detained. The case was far from over. The judge called Horace Locke back just as TK was preparing one glorious act of revenge. They both stopped and the judge rather wistfully told Horace Locke to take his seat.

Ben Horseman asked to address the judge on the residual matters arising from the case relating to his clients. First, the pirate box had not been tested against the ship's log which had been taken from the Lydia. Second, the ownership of the box and the right of the Lydia crew to bring it ashore had not been decided. Finally, as part of its campaign against pirates the US government had been giving rewards for pirate ships captured or sunk and pirates captured or killed.

The judge sighed and agreed that orders would have to be made. Ben Horseman suggested that this would be a good point to break for lunch.

Judge MacMillan cheered up and agreed and the court recessed for lunch. The judge loved having these young lawyers in his court practicing their skills but they were very tiring and a break for lunch would be very welcome.

Over lunch Adam Hillstrider recounted how, when he had left the Court he had headed for the coffee shops where the merchants met to trade and gossip. Something was clearly going on in the harbour and the constables were everywhere, grim and alert. The merchants told him that Captain Hawk Eye might know what was up. There was no love for Horace Locke who was greedy and a bully. It was rumoured that he had been speculating and was in debt. A chat with the brokers might throw some light on his behaviour. And so he had met Captain Hawk Eye up at the top of the harbour and Edward Longstaff down in a coffee shop by the Exchange. It had been hard walking and now he needed a long drink. There was no shortage of offers.

And so after lunch they turned to the ship's log and the bag of coins. Captain John pointed out the entry with the weight of the box. Ben Horseman asked for the box to be weighed. It was less that the log book entry. Then he asked for the bag from the harbour master's safe to be added to the scales it almost made up the difference. But not quite. Ben Horseman asked to see the contents of Horace Locke's pockets. Charles Craddock objected but the judge agreed.

Out came a watch, bits of bread and cheese, all sorts of smoking stuff, a magnifying glass, notebooks and pencils, some U.S. coinage but no European coins. Ben

Horseman's heart sank. If the log book and the weight of coins had tallied the case would have been perfect. He felt a tug on his sleeve and leaned down as Alan Alexander whispered in his ear. A lifeline.

'And the little horizontal top pockets, please. Perhaps a court officer can assist.'

Horace Locke bellowed in rage and indignation but the Judge said that his record now did not warrant any sympathy. He could submit here and now or downstairs in the cells. Horace Locke relented. An officer stepped forward and poked a finger in the top left pocket. Nothing. Ben Horseman shrank a little. Then the top right pocket and out came an English guinea. The little quarter ounce coin was added to the coins on the scales and the scales balanced. And there was the proof of theft.

Ben Horseman turned to the ownership of the box and said that it was a trophy of the battle with the pirates and should be retained by the Lydia crew. The judge asked whether there was any basis of claim on behalf of the city or the state. Nobody was aware of any basis of claim. The Judge asked whether there was any prospect of finding the original owners and was told that his writ would not run on the Barbary coast.

Ben Horseman then pointed out that correspondingly the crew could claim a reward for destroying the pirate ship and killing the crew. The judge took the bait, shook his head and agreed to make an order vesting the pirate chest in the crew of the Lydia on the basis that he would not have to listen to any more legal arguments that day, particularly in relation to rewards for countering piracy.

Horace Locke would remain in custody until charges

were filed. The judge closed the case and withdrew.

As the Lydia crew and its defence team relaxed, expressing relief and joy, Charles Craddock strolled over to congratulate the lawyers. He said that it was a pity that the, now, famous Colonel Kynaston had not given evidence and had wondered why not. Ben Horseman explained that under cross-examination Charles Craddock may have stumbled on TK's record as a British soldier fighting in the War of Independence. Charles Craddock's bellow of laughter provided a fitting end to hostilities.

They celebrated at the Plymouth Inn near the Harbour, an old rambling wooden building that survived from day to day one spark from total destruction. It was a meeting place for professionals and traders and had been a source of much information for Adam Hillstrider in his search for evidence.

The mood was one of relief rather than joy, an understanding of how different things would have been without the care and effort of the team. They told their stories. The New Yorkers were fascinated by TK's career. He played down the glories of war and stressed the random nature of success and failure, the fine line between heroism and death, the wholesale carnage of cannon fire and the give and take of infantry battles from lines to squares to bayonets. In turn TK made clear his admiration for the way that the lawyers had taken control and set the agenda, and how Adam Hillstrider had solved the problems that the lawyers had identified, far beyond the usual duties of a shipping agent.

The New Yorkers were shocked at John and Andy's

accounts of battles at sea. In particular, Nelson's tactic of gaining wind advantage and then engaging at close quarters, relying on the British ability to fire faster and for longer than the enemy. Captain John emphasised the huge size of the ships of the line and the number and weight of guns that they carried. He emphasised the random nature of life and death in the cannon fire and the murderous splinters wreaking havoc among the hundreds of sailors required to man the ships.

The agents and lawyers emphasised the amount of legal input to get the merchant ships to sea, the harbour rules, the mercantile contracts, the insurance contracts, the rules of salvage and of course fraud, theft, murder and piracy. In New York all this know-how was condensed in a few small offices and coffee shops. Men of finance, banking and stockbroking traded in neighbouring offices and coffee shops in a professional community mirroring the City of London. It was another world.

TK and the Lydia team gained a privileged insight into that other world. The point of contact between those worlds was the agent, and Ben Hillstrider was an agent. Ben had brought together all these worlds to save their necks.

Through adversity they had formed an unacknowledged deep bond of friendship.

The next day Captain John, Andy and Adam Hillstrider went to arrange the unloading of the Lydia to count the cargo and identify any necessary insurance claims. The Lydia was a sound vessel and her holds were tight. However, among the silks and spices there was bound to be some damage after the great storm and claims would need to be prepared.

TK and Ben Horseman lodged the treasure chest at the bank. Ben then left TK with a member of the bank and went back to work. TK and his new companion separated the gold and silver coins and passed them for valuation. Next, they separated the rest of the gold and silver such as chains, rings and fobs which had value only for melting. This left the jewels in their settings which were left in the box.

TK was directed to a reputable gold trader. The trader enjoyed explaining the tests which he would need to make. Once upon a time, a Greek mathematician called Archimedes was summoned by his cruel king. The king was having a gold crown made. However, he feared that the goldsmith might cheat him by including a lesser metal such as silver into the gold to reduce the cost and pocket the gain. On pain of death the king told Archimedes to prove this one way or the other. Archimedes thought long and hard but could not see a test until, one day, he was sitting in the public baths. He watched the overspill from the bath. He realised that your volume determined how much water you displaced, regardless of your weight. By measuring an object's displacement of water you could determine its volume. The weight of one material would differ from the same volume of a different material. The weight of the volume of the crown in gold would be greater than its volume in an alloy of gold and silver. 'Eureka!' he shouted, and ran home. He had saved his own life but, it transpired, he had cost the life of the goldsmith.

So, they put TK's gold in a measuring jar half-filled with water and calculated the volume from the raising of the level. They then weighed the gold. The volume-to-weight ratio was 92% as that for gold, so TK would be paid 92% of the gold value of the weight of his items. Even after commission it was a lot of money, paid in gold coins which TK took back to the bank.

That left the jewels. He met up with the team that evening at the Plymouth Inn, not by arrangement but through a mutual accord that had grown between them. TK loved the quiet professional companionship that was evident at the different tables in the different rooms of the inn. So different from the bravado of the military gatherings that he had known.

TK joined the team table. He reported the values of the coins and gold which raised their spirits. Captain John and Adam Hillstrider announced that only one tenth of the silk and very little of the spices had been damaged, and this raised their spirits further. So now they only had to sell the jewels.

Adam Hillstrider had arrived late and rather bashful but gave no explanation. He was tall, curly, and amiable with a magnetism that invited confidence. He slipped away to another smoke-filled room and joined another table. He chatted at some length and finally came back with the overview. There was a lane where the jewelers were located. Most of them were small traders and worked closely together. However, at the top end of the lane, adjacent to the larger shops were a couple of larger traders who dealt at the top end of the market. Even so, it was necessary to understand that there was a limit to how much stock any trader could carry. With the small traders working together and the larger traders limited by how much stock they could carry it was doubtful if they would be able to sell all of the pirate jewels.

It was agreed that the seafarers would conclude their business, the agents would settle the deals, the lawyers would provide the documentation and TK would take a few specimens in his pocket to visit the jewellers' lane. After that, the evening slipped into the usual comfortable scene of grilled meat, punch and tobacco.

The Jewels

So, the next morning, well-slept, well-breakfasted and well-directed, TK set off for the jewelers' lane.

The establishments at the lower end of the lane were, as he had been told to expect, small, gloomy, one-room outfits where at one he would be given a value and, as he entered the next he would be overtaken by an urchin and would be given the same value. On the third occasion he understood the rules of the game. Even so, the standard prices that he had been given each time seemed substantial to TK. He missed out the rest of the lane and walked up to the top. There he found two large shops with grills over the windows and entrance halls with grills above the counters. He looked into both and, for no particular reason, chose one and walked in. He was met by a spectacular trader. The man was tall, angular, red-haired, big-eared, big-nosed and he had a big, big-toothed smile. This was David Daniels.

'Good morning, Mr Kynaston, so you have walked up the lane and been given some valuations and each matched the others, children have run from one shop to the next and you suspect that they are colluding. Well, they are. Not to cheat you, they are protecting each other against mistake. The prices you have been given are fair. I might beat them slightly but not by much. I would guess that you have not shown many items, but you have used up the buying power in the lane. You see, if you are buying and selling potatoes, you turn over your stock every day, you make a little profit each time and business is steady. At the end of the year the little daily profits add up to a decent profit and that keeps you in business. If you are selling jewellery, you may buy one day and not sell for a year. So, you need to buy cheap and sell dear to make your profit. But all the shops in the lane and these two stores up here have limited money to invest in stock to hold for a year. So, Mr Kynaston, the little shops in the lane and my store, and the one across the road will only be able to buy a few of your items at about half of what they would eventually sell for. So that's the way of the world. I can organize the traders in the lane and the store across the road to buy your pocketful of jewels at about half the resale value. You will have the money, free and clear, and we will have the stock and the problems. Even then, we may not be able to take them all.'

TK laughed out loud. What a brilliant, honest summary of his position. He could not have asked for more.

'Well, Mr Daniels, here are the items that I have been showing in the lane.' TK pulled a few items from his pocket.

'And these are the rest.' TK began to pull a bag from his pocket.

'Oh dear, oh dear. In the front office here, the items are owned by the customer and it is his loss if they are stolen. In the back office we show the items that we have bought. There the loss is ours. Let me lock the door to reduce your risk.'

TK laughed and thanked him. David Daniels looked

through the bag of jewels that TK had produced and shook his head in wonder.

'These are more than the whole lane and our two stores together could buy. You would need to sell over a period of months or years. We can't do it.'

TK wanted to talk more to this extraordinary man but there was nothing more to say. He knew where he stood. He had a problem. Now it was in his nature to find a solution. He gave his thanks and left.

The solution came that evening at the Plymouth Inn. The team had reassembled without arrangement. Pat had slipped away in search of whiskey, Captain John and Andy had drifted off to join the seafarers, so TK sat with the lawyers and the agents enjoying their conversations. He passed on the brilliant analysis from David Daniels. It was Alan Alexander who solved the problem.

'Let's break it down. It's too big for the jewellers but in small items for private buyers it would be manageable. Let's hold an auction.'

'Brilliant!' they agreed. The sellers would get their money immediately and the price would be more than they would receive from the shops. The buyers would pay less than the price in the shops and the auctioneers could have a commission. There would only be winners.

TK arranged to move to the Plymouth Inn and hired a cab to drop off his sea chest and, then, to take him on to the river. He needed to cross over to meet Tony Parsons who was assembling a convoy of wagons to travel west to the Rocky Mountains, where he would hand over to another guide, to cross over into Oregon and on to the west coast. The cab dropped him at the ferry, and he crossed over to the west side. Here the emphasis changed from commerce to agriculture. The warehouses were filled with produce, the traffic was mainly carts and wagons and the clothes reflected the change. TK noticed lots of leather trousers and boots. Black had changed to brown. He felt rather out of place with his coat, britches and boots. Even so, he had little difficulty in finding a light cart to drive him to the point where Tony Parsons was assembling his convoy. It was further than TK had expected. He had to travel through the warehouses and stores, through farmland and then out to the woods and grassland. TK realized that he was going to need a horse.

At the assembly point Tony Parsons was clearly in charge and was clearly going to stay in charge. He was very tall, very thin and wiry. He had very fair hair that was sun bleached almost white and fell forward. It made a dramatic contrast with his deeply bronzed weather beaten face. TK was much broader – a much more substantial presence. But Tony Parsons took no notice of presence. He was confident in himself. Also, he was clearly not impressed by TK's appearance.

TK introduced himself and asked about the convoy. TP, as Tony Parsons introduced himself, had clearly not heard about the pirate battle and the trial and was unsure whether TK was a serious candidate for the expedition. But, as he asked the usual questions, he began to take note of the unusual replies. A few more questions and he realized that TK had a lot of relevant experience. He had ridden along the eastern mountains. He was quietly confident. He knew where he wanted to go, and he expected to deal with any problems that he encountered.

TP recognized his experience and started to relax.

Even so, TP thought that TK was going to get himself killed in the north-west.

They talked about the sort of vehicle that TK would need as he travelled west and north. They agreed that a light trailer with mules would be most suitable. When the trailer could go no further, equipment for the crossing of the mountains could be transferred to backpacks for the mules. TP explained that a northern pass existed and had been quite well used by fur hunters and, more recently, missionaries. These travelers had reached the Rockies via the Missouri River. Travelling overland would be a bit different but a light trailer and then mules should be able to make it. His main problem would be with the natives. They were becoming unwelcoming because of the plundering by the fur hunters and the intrusion of the missionaries. He would be vulnerable on his own. The upper Missouri was a war zone.

TK asked where he could buy a decent saddle horse. TP hesitated but remembered that he was dealing with a different type of customer and directed TK to a large livery yard where many horses were bought and sold. They agreed to meet again. It would take several weeks to assemble the convoy. TK would need to be well prepared, and TP would help him put together what he needed.

At the livery yard TK explained that, for now, he needed something steady and capable

For travel and battle. The owner clearly knew his business but trotted up a couple of horses that were steady but not capable. Then he got the message and led TK to a group of ex-army horses. At once TK saw what he wanted – a big dark bay gelding that moved in a certain way. They saddled him up and TK swung on for the first time in several months. It was perfect. TK sat easily and the horse moved easily at his instructions. It was as if they were dancing together.

The owner explained that the horse had been a star in the cavalry but had been retired because he could not canter all day, day after day, but in short bursts of up to an hour or two, he was unbeatable. TK bought him. He would be H1. TK asked for a recommendation for a livery yard on the island where he could be kept for TK's stay there. The owner had finally understood what he was dealing with and made the recommendation.

TK rode H1 onto the ferry where he stood steady during the crossing. TK followed the directions to a livery yard and explained that he wanted H1 to be kept overnight, delivered each morning, to the Plymouth Inn, with a fresh hay net and to be collected each evening, for return to the yard. The owner understood what was required and called over a teenage boy who would be the personal manager of H1. He would ride him to the Plymouth Inn, leading his own horse and would then ride it back to the yard. In the evening he would reverse the process. TK liked the look of him, and the boy seemed to recognize a good customer. They rode together to the Plymouth Inn and TK handed over H1 for delivery the next morning.

The team met again that evening and TK told them what he had been doing. They rehearsed the proposal which had to be made to David Daniels and TK stayed for his first night at the Plymouth Inn.

The next morning H1 was standing at the rail outside the inn munching hay but saddled up and ready to go. TK hopped on and rode up to David Daniels, and could not help but smile as the big grin welcomed him into the store. He explained Andrew Alexander's proposal for an auction and the grin widened. Yes, he would manage the valuations and the reserve prices. He would also instruct the auctioneer. His rate of commission seemed very reasonable to TK. They agreed to meet that evening at the Plymouth Inn. David Daniels was a family man but looked forward to meeting the team. He would bring the owner of the other store who would work with him and share his commission.

Miles Kasparin was the exact opposite of his neighbour. Instead of tall, angular and red, he was short, round and dark. But he shared the big honest smile that set them apart. They were a bit older, but they bonded with the team at once. There was a mutual recognition of professional competence. And a mutual excitement at a new adventure.

The start point was that the jewelers would draw up a list of items with estimated sale value and reserve prices. Ben Horseman would draft a handbill confirming that the items were awarded by the court and were being sold under the authority of the court. To add spice, the bills would be headed 'Pirate Treasure'. Underneath, the inventory from the jewellers would be listed.

Adam Hillstrider would arrange distribution through his contacts as far away as Boston to the north and

Baltimore to the south. He also knew a property auctioneer with a sort of honest humour that could set the tone at the auction. He would put him in touch with David Daniels. Alan Alexander was given the task of finding a venue big enough, and exclusive enough, and secure enough to encourage real buyers to believe that they were being privileged to be invited, and to exclude those who had no interest in bidding. Alan Alexander was also asked to find a suitable place to exhibit the items by day and to secure them by night. Eventually, he identified a shiny new bank that could meet the requirements. Unfortunately, they were rather pleased with themselves and made outrageous demands. However, Alan called in TK to discuss the deposit of the money from the sale of the gold and the potential money from the sale of the jewels. They exchanged the short term for the long term and a deal was done.

'It's a funny thing about banks,' said Alan Alexander, 'They always have a price, but you always have to help them find it.'

Alan Alexander put his analytical brain to work to find a venue. As the options narrowed, he laughed out loud. Of course, it had to be the Court House.

The auction was set for four weeks ahead. This would allow Captain John and the Lydia crew to find, buy and load the return cargo. It also allowed time for the story of the auction to mount. New York had never seen anything like it. And New York was ready to give its best response.

Alan Alexander and David Daniels co-ordinated the project. Each evening the team, now including the jewellers, met to refine the details.

The excitement around the auction built up so that it was the main subject of conversation between the ladies and gentlemen who would be the potential bidders. The lawyers filtered out expressions of interest and issued invitations to the most likely bidders. The jewellers stood beside the display at the bank and answered questions. And the tension mounted.

On the day, the lawyers' team vetted the visitors and allowed in the likely buyers and excluded the mere spectators. TK was called to exclude a team of thieves who clearly were not trying to get in but wanted to know about the security arrangements.

The bidding started well with items generally achieving their estimates or better. All was going well until an emerald ring was announced. Bidding picked up quickly to the estimated value, when TK and Ben noticed that Adam Hillstrider was bidding. But he was being outbid by a tall, elegant southerner in a tall black hat with a silver-topped cane. He was standing beside a small, beautiful blonde lady with curled hair in a matching green outfit of dress, hat and shoes. She seemed determined to win the bid, stamping her little green feet and instructing her companion to bid again after each of Adam Hillstrider's bids. Eventually Adam Hillstrider dropped out of the bidding. Then TK told Ben Horseman to bid and keep on bidding to win. But the bidding went on, out of control. TK edged over to Adam Hillstrider and told him to withdraw the item. The auctioneer made the announcement and the result was amazing. The lady in green demanded the ring and called to her husband to challenge, and call out, anyone who opposed them. Her husband stood tall and elegant. He looked carefully at those involved in the fiasco and calmly and clearly assured her that this was not the end of the matter. They then left.

When all the bidding closed, the day had gone well, and the team were pleased with the result. A few items had not reached the reserve, but the bidders would be approached for a private sale. Adam Hillstrider rather bashfully explained that following the trial he had been visiting Captain Hawkeye and his daughter. They had much to talk about regarding the harbor and its traders. More particularly, Adam had developed a devotion to Miss Finch and had hoped to buy the ring in order to propose to her. Without hesitation TK declared that he could buy the ring for the estimate price, and he would deal with the co-owners. They wished Adam Hillstrider luck with his proposal. However, in the following hours, stories began to come in that Mr Paul Delamaine, who had failed in his bid for the emerald ring, was determined to seek satisfaction from the organisers of the auction. He was focusing on Adam Hillstrider and Ben Horseman. He was calling for a duel.

Paul Delamaine was a very rich tobacco farmer from Virginia. His wife was the daughter of a plantation owner from the southern states. Her father, Boss Clay, owned thousands of acres and hundreds of slaves. She took pleasure from getting her way, right or wrong. Paul Delamaine was renowned for his skill with a pistol, and a feared duelist, with many kills to his record. Many of the duels had been instigated by his wife. They had come on their own ship with a cargo of tobacco from Baltimore. It had sold well, and they were on a spectacular spending spree which, she had thought, would come to a spectacular climax at the auction.

'There will be no duels,' said TK, 'even if I have to kill Paul Delamaine like a mad dog in the street.'

TK arranged for Adam Hillstrider and Ben Horseman to move into the Plymouth Inn and to stay there until Paul Delamaine had left the city, or had been buried in its cemetery. He would deal with the problem. No question, and no help, please. Just stay inside the inn and out of the way of Mr Delamaine.

Late the next afternoon the reception at the Grand Hotel was overwhelmed, as Mr and Mrs Delamaine and their entourage returned from her usual shopping expedition, with boxes of all shapes, sizes, colours and patterns. All tied up with ribbons and bows. Mrs Delamaine ordered the hotel staff and her slaves to deliver the items to her suite.

The hotel manager coughed politely and whispered to Mr Delamaine that there was a visitor to see him, over there, sitting by the window with a newspaper. Paul Delamaine recognised TK from the auction, nodded and approached. He stood tall and aloof, tapped his cane, and gave his name. TK stood up and replied with 'Thomas Kynaston'. He suggested that they sit but Paul Delamaine declined, thus demonstrating his superior height and status. He demanded to know what business TK had with him. TK felt a bit shabby in this elegant presence but, as ever, he was not going to give way on this, or any other, point.

'Mr Delamaine, I have wronged you in the auction of the emerald ring. All the decisions in that matter were mine and mine alone. I fully and wholeheartedly apologise for any offence given to yourself or your wife. If I can announce any apology to your satisfaction I will willingly do so. I was in the wrong.'

Paul Delamaine sneered at this perceived sign of weakness. He knew that his position and his wife's humiliation would only be satisfied by a calling out and a killing.

'No, Mr Kynaston, I demand satisfaction.'

Before he could elaborate, he was met with a response, the like of which he had never previously encountered. A chilling, killing, controlled rage.

'Mr Delamaine, I and my companions are staying at the Plymouth Inn. If any of your friends or representatives call on us, I will take a horsewhip to them in the street. The ebb tide is tomorrow afternoon. If you and your wife and your entourage are not out of this hotel at noon, I will take a horsewhip to you in the street, outside the hotel. There will be no duel. If you want to fight, you will have to fight me in the street among the horse shit and the dog shit, with the cats and the rats and the vermin, and I will kill you in the street like a dog. Do not talk to me of honour. You know nothing of it. Good day, sir.'

Paul Delamaine recoiled, recovered and said, 'Even so, I demand satisfaction.'

TK replied, 'Then you must seek it in the street and there will be no honour in it.

That night, sure enough, two southern gentlemen

called formally at the Plymouth Inn and asked for Mr Thomas Kynaston. In response, TK came to the reception carrying his sword in its scabbard and, without any preliminaries, set about the heads of the gentlemen and drove them out of the hotel, off the boardwalk and into the street.

In the street stood three big men, two with horse whips and the leader with a pick-axe handle. Again, no preliminaries. TK shook off the scabbard and herded the two gentlemen with the back edge of his sword towards the men. The nearest man, Ed Smart, was a stockman. He was skilled with a whip and was ready with his whip, but not ready for the onslaught that followed. TK drove the gentlemen towards Ed Smart. He hesitated. It was enough for TK to step forward from behind the gentlemen and slash the lash from the whip before Ed Smart could swing it. He got a crack on the ear from the back of the sword on the return swing.

John Roth was the foreman with the pickaxe handle. He raised it to strike as TK booted Ed Smart into him, broke his wrist with the back of the sword and broke his nose with the hilt.

Broderick Dodds, the slave master, was of mixed race – the product of a white owner and an African slave. He had no friends and had become cruel. He was an expert with the whip. He danced to maintain his distance and angle. As TK booted Ed Smart forward, he stepped aside and cracked the whip. TK saw it coming but was not quick enough. He dived but the lash hit his shoulder and the back of his head. As he came up bleeding, Dodds struck again and hit TK across the back as he dived forward again. This time Dodds could not step back quickly enough and, on the rise, TK hit him between the legs with the back of the sword. Dodds doubled up involuntarily and took a blow to the kidneys. Now it was his turn to roll in the dust. TK stepped on the lash and Dodds dropped his whip and hobbled after the two gentlemen, Ed Smart and John Roth, down the street away from a fury that they had never known. And now TK had a whip, and he cracked it to send them on their way.

TK limped back to the inn where they cleaned up his wounds and made some crude repairs to his coat.

At noon the next day a carriage and two carts were lined up outside the Grand Hotel for the departure of Mr and Mrs Delamaine and their entourage. Ed Smart was driving one of the carts with a bandage round his head, John Roth was sitting beside him with his right arm in a sling and his left hand holding his stave. The cart was loaded with chests. Broderick Dodds was in the second cart with a new whip supervising the loading of the shopping boxes by the slaves. It was not a joyful scene, but a tall, muscular, handsome slave moved easily about his work regardless of the tension and the humility of his position. He just grinned and joked with his companions. TK rode up on H1 and sat twenty yards away watching the scene. He held the whip in his left hand with the reins. He was equipped for a fight with his pistol and knife in his belt and his sword and rifle behind the saddle for all to see.

Paul Delamaine emerged from the hotel escorting his wife and carrying a mahogany case. He handed her into the coach. Then he leaned into the coach with the case but did not enter. This is it. TK put H1 into a leaping surge towards the carriage knocking everyone aside. He rode up onto the boardwalk in front of the hotel and stopped next to the coach just as Paul Delamaine stepped back from the coach with a fine, rifled dueling pistol in each hand. He looked up to see the muzzles of two rifled barrels with a brass bead on top and two deep blue/grey eyes looking straight into his eyes.

'If you raise a pistol I will shoot you between the eyes like a dog in the street, as I promised.'

Paul Delamaine's shoulders dropped. He looked up to John Roth in fear that he might precipitate the fulfilment of the threat and shook his head. He stepped into the carriage and gave the order to set off.

For no good reason, Broderick Dodds flicked his whip at the tall handsome slave, who was putting the last of the boxes on the wagon. As it moved forward the slave slipped behind the wagon and then into an alley beside the hotel, as the wagon passed.

TK rode a hundred yards behind the convoy down to the harbour. As the loading began he rode into the deep shadows of a warehouse and smelled the rich tobacco of Paul Delamaine's imported cargo. He replaced the pistol and drew the rifle.

When the loading was completed and the ship was preparing to leave, Paul Delamaine appeared at the stern rail with his pistols. He searched in vain for TK who watched him from the darkness of the warehouse with his rifle pointing at his chest. In exasperation Paul Delamaine saw an old bucket fifty yards away, fired at it and heard the clang of a hit. Then again with the second pistol and again the clang of a hit. At last, in fury, he turned and went below. The ship slipped from the anchorage under its jib sail and raised more sail as it headed out of the harbour.

TK rode down to the harbour's edge and saw the bucket. Two half-inch holes only two inches apart right in the middle. TK smiled as he realised that he would have been lucky to hit the ship at that range.

As he watched Paul Delamaine's ship leave the harbour, he saw a fast-looking low sloop with a high mast and long bowsprit raise anchor. With a puff its sails filled out as it followed out of the harbour.

TK rode H1 to the empty berth and drew out his pistol. He aimed carefully and firmly with the brass bead at the centre of the bucket and fired. H1 flinched and then stood steady. TK fired again with the second barrel. This time H1 did not flinch but stood steady. TK rode up to the bucket and saw that he had missed with both barrels. He realised that if H1 had not been so quick and brave in barging up to Paul Delamaine's coach, before he could raise his pistols, he might be dead. But there again…. And he gave H1 a pat.

That night, at the Plymouth Inn there was no celebration. The team were in shock at the explosion of violence that TK had unleashed. They were in awe, horror and deep respect. TK explained that he simply did what needed to be done. No more, no less. He would live or die by that standard, regardless of honour or reputation.

At last they were beginning to accept that they could

go back to normal, when Adam Hillstrider joined them. He put his hand on the table and dropped the emerald ring and said, "Miss Finch said No".

Apparently Miss Hawkeye wanted to stay with her father in the eyrie so long as he needed her and would not promise beyond that. They were so sorry. TK immediately said that at his own cost he would buy the ring at its estimated price which Adam had paid.

Changing the subject, Adam reported that Captain Hawkeye had identified a suspected privateer following Paul Delamaine from the harbour that afternoon. He did not like the cut of her jib. It was likely that the spending of Paul Delamaine and his wife had been passed on and the privateer was intent on capturing them near the Chesapeake, robbing them and holding them to ransom in one of the remote creeks that fed the estuary.

TK told Ben Horseman that when it was all over he should send an intermediary to offer the ring at the reserve price to Paul Delamaine. They would sort out the details later.

Two days later TK rode down to the harbour to say goodbye, good luck and thank you to his old shipmates before they caught the tide for their return to England. They were loaded up and sealed down with a cargo of tobacco, cotton and sugar. They were carrying back papers for redemption in Liverpool so that Pat would be able to start buying a cottage for his mother, Captain John and Andy would be able to pay off their debts on the Lydia, and they were all richer for their experiences.

Finally, Captain John asked TK to go forward to meet the new crewman. TK went forward and peered into the gloom to see two big eyes and a big grin.

'Well bless my soul, a stowaway. Give him my boots and stuff.'

That night, at the Plymouth Inn, Judge McMillan called TK over. 'We have word that you have become a target for glory seekers. It's time for you to move on. I don't want to see you in my court again.'

'Thank you, Judge.'

A year later, when the ransoms had been paid and the owners, the ship and its cargo of shopping had been released, Paul Delamaine received a parcel and took it to his wife as she drank coffee from a porcelain cup poured from a silver pot at a table covered with the finest lace. She sat on the terrace of an impressive mansion. In the paddocks in front of the house beautiful horses grazed and in the distance slaves bent over rows in the fields.

'Finally, my dear, you have your emerald ring.'

'You still do not understand, Mr Delamaine, that the ring was never important. It was the loss of dignity and respect. When you failed to win the bidding and when you failed to call out those New Yorkers that damaged us so much. And to be run out of New York, with all our entourage, by one man was unforgivable. Daddy is still furious. And then to surrender to a no-good privateer, without a fight, really was the last straw. Daddy had to pay the ransom and he holds you in contempt. It is a matter of shame. You are not restored to my affection.'

That was the moment when Mr Paul Delamaine began to plan his wife's fatal accident.

Assembly

And so, the next morning TK arranged to leave the most respectable of his outfits at the inn, paid his bill, loaded up H1 with two panniers containing all else that he possessed, lots of spare arrows and bullets and the tin box, and rode out to take the ferry to the mainland.

H1 did not take kindly to being a beast of burden but walked on. On the way, TK called at the livery and paid his bill. He added something extra for the lad who had delivered H1 to the hotel and taken him home to the livery without fail every day. One slip on the day of Paul Delamaine's departure would have been fatal.

On the crossing, as always, H1 stood steady with TK standing at his head among the chaos of the voyage. H1 was beginning to trust TK and TK was already trusting H1.

On the mainland, up-river from the harbour, order was lost and a form of consensual chaos emerged. The living accommodation went from harbour slums to semi-respectability along the same roads, all interspersed with every type of business and industrial premises. And yet the various activities seemed to co-exist without much disharmony. Perhaps because there was no shortage of land the activities sprawled away from the river. The only concentrations occurred along the riverside where frontage was valued and contested. Away from the river and beyond the businesses arable fields and pasture sprawled away with rickety fences, rickety barns and solid home-made houses. Among the chaos there were some small stalls selling individual produce and larger markets selling combined offerings. There were stalls with cheese, butter, eggs, meat, flour and vegetables. And all would come together at the food markets on the designated days of the week.

Far out from this untidiness, on the plain, beyond the fences, Tony Parsons, was assembling his convoy of wagons to go west.

So, beyond the chaos and further chaos, prospective travelers were forming separate camps with wagons and animals. In some cases there were great flat-bedded carts to be pulled by teams of huge oxen and each followed by groups of livestock. They were small mobile farms.

TK was directed to Tony Parsons. He could not mistake him. He was as TK remembered. He was the centre of his own area of chaos. He was a striking figure. He was just as TK remembered. He had dark, weather-beaten skin, bright blue eyes and a shock of fair hair that kept falling forward and being swept back. But now he was in perpetual motion, striding from one situation to another, arms waving, fingers pointing and, above all, a strong clear voice giving orders. And then there were the teeth. When he was happy he grinned widely. When he was angry he snarled. He was in charge and was going to stay in charge.

TK rode up and stepped down. Tony Parsons shouted a final order and stepped forward to greet his visitor. TK re-introduced himself as 'TK' and Tony Parsons re-introduced himself as 'TP'. There was a moment when it could all go wrong. After a pause they both shrugged and shook hands. TK confirmed that he was hoping to follow the North West passage. TP explained that he could take him some of the way and point him in the right direction, but for the rest he had reservations about the north-east Rockies. They sat down, drank coffee and gave a little background, then a little more, and a mutual respect began to develop. It was not friendship, but it was getting close.

TP had been on many expeditions across the Great Plains and up the Missouri. He knew the directions to take and how to survive. TK explained that he had ridden patrols along the eastern mountains and in Spain. He thought that he ought to be able to survive if he knew where he was going. TP grinned and nodded towards H1 grazing quietly nearby and asked where TK would sleep. TK said that he would find a spot with a little wood and a little water and would be very comfortable. They agreed to meet the next morning to equip TK for the journey.

TK rode out towards some parkland and eventually found what he was looking for. It was a small meadow sheltered by a low outcrop of grassy rock with a few trees sheltered from the wind and easier to defend than the open plain. There was a small stream nearby.

First, as always, he tended his horse. Then he arranged the site for defense. Finally, he ate some cold food and wrapped for the night.

At dawn TK made a good breakfast of ham, eggs and bread with coffee. Then he rode over to TP's camp. TP offered breakfast. TK declined but accepted coffee.

So they sat together in a period of calm before TP would start his usual hectic day. TK explained that he still wanted to travel to the north-west and into Canada. TP told him that the original expedition that had reached the Pacific over fifteen years ago had travelled mostly by river. That had been their mission. TK said that he had hoped to travel mostly by land up the east side of the Rockies, then across into the plains. Rivers could be a problem on either side.

TP advised that he could get a long way in the convoy with a light trailer and mules as they travelled west. When they reached the Rockies TK would have to turn north. Theoretically he could travel a long way north on the east side of the Rockies but there were just thousands of miles of lakes and rivers leading further and further into Canada. TK said that he would like to travel by land up the east side and then cross over and go west to the Columbia River and the sea. Then he would go north into Canada. TP said the original expedition had roughly followed that route using the rivers but later visitors had alienated the natives by stealing furs. By river or by land the north west of the Rockies was a dangerous place. TK said that he was hoping to find what he was looking for further north and west. TP said that as far as he was aware Canada was no more developed to the west of the Rockies than the east so he could take his pick. Perhaps they had better talk again on the journey west. TK did not mention that he would be looking for gold.

TP offered to take TK into the chaos of the river frontage to find the right places to buy the equipment that he would need for the voyage. TP asked about money and TK said he was carrying a couple of gold coins. The first visit was to a money changer who broke up the gold coins into smaller gold coins, silver coins and coppers. One gold coin would have been plenty.

TP declared that they should start with a trailer. For TK this should be light but strong and could be drawn by mules. This would provide speed and flexibility. Mules had the advantage that they were cheaper, had more endurance and were more adaptable. Usually it would only take one or two mules to pull the trailer at most with two in reserve so four would be enough. When the time came to cross the Rockies the mules could continue with backpacks and the trailer would have to be left behind.

TP took them to a wagon yard and pointed to a light wagon which would be suitable. However it would need a lot of reinforcement around the wheels and chassis before it would do. The wagoner knew TP well and rolled his eyes when the adjustments were spelled out. However, for a price, he would do what was required and do it well. TK felt that this was a well-rehearsed negotiation but was happy to agree the deal.

Next TP took him to the mule yard. Here he saw the stallion donkeys and the serving pens where the mares were brought for breeding. The resulting mules were a mixed lot. But, by good luck or by good judgment, a few of the mules appeared to be young, strong and energetic. Between TP and TK four were selected and again the deal was done. TK asked to take the most well-behaved immediately.

So, on to the harness maker who understood the

requirements for the trailer fittings and did not need much reminding of the fittings for the backpacks. He would visit the mule breeder to get the measurements for TK's animals. TK asked for a backpack for his chosen mule immediately and a suitable pack was produced. H1 sighed and gave a little buck when the panniers were lifted off.

TK felt that with the guidance of TP he had got good quality from these traders at a good price. However, TP had not finished. Indeed, he had hardly started. Clothes would be next. TK's coat, boots and britches would not do. This was not Europe and something different would be required to cross the prairie.

The raw hide store came as a shock. First, the smell when they entered was overpowering but not completely unpleasant. The choice of weight ranged from soft doe skin to heavy buffalo hide. Also, the patterns varied widely. TP took charge. TK would need several pairs of buckskin trousers with full legs down to the ankle and reinforcement inside the legs. Next he would need light jackets. TK insisted on a double-breasted front with the possibility to button across at the chest, just like his military jacket. Finally, two long coats and again TK insisted on ties at the bottom to secure the ankles, also again the double-breasted style with a button to secure across the chest at the top and, looking around, TK demanded no fringes. A few measurements were taken and he was promised that they would be ready in a couple of days. So much for fine tailoring. In the same store TP suggested a couple of pairs of low boots for the trousers to tuck in and TK no longer had the will to argue.

And it was the same at the clothes store. Shirts, underclothes, socks were piled up. But TK asserted himself briefly to buy strong straw hats that would shade the sun and allow the wind to blow through. Even so, TP added a couple of fur caps.

As the shadows lengthened TP called in at the grain store and ordered flour, oats and barley. TK added an extra sack each of oats and barley. TP said that they would buy cured bacon before they set off.

TK had been amazed at the speed and energy at which TP had led him through his shopping and spent his money. TP said that he had to go back to camp to organise more details of the convoy but they could meet again next day.

That night TK rode back to his camping place on the plain. He fed H1 and the mule and cooked a good supper with bacon, eggs and potatoes.

The next morning TK rode into the convoy assembly area. TP was flying around, as usual, giving instructions mostly with calm but occasionally with a little menace. It all had to be done his way. And now.

TP stopped for coffee with TK and, out of some respect, they were not interrupted by other travelers. A moment of calm.

TK explained that he would need another horse. H1 was brilliant in short bursts but TK needed a horse that could run all day. TP directed him to a horse trader further out onto the plain. He did not ask TK for his reasons. He had come to expect that this man knew what he wanted and should be helped. However, he told TK to come back in the afternoon to go shopping.

The horse farm sat beyond the pasture and crops with good fences and good barns. Some decent horses grazed in the paddocks. TK rode up to the main barn which had a boardwalk in front of the tack room and stores. There he met the owner. Short, bow-legged with heavy shoulders, bald and weather-beaten. TK recognised an old soldier immediately. And the old soldier recognised H1 as an old military charger before he even bothered to look at TK and recognised a cavalryman at once.

TK smiled in recognition of a fellow horse soldier and the old horse soldier looked carefully and then slowly smiled back. They introduced themselves. They were both called Tom so they had to deal on equal terms. The handshake sealed it.

TK explained that he needed a horse that could run all day. No manners, no manoeuvres. Just run. Old Tom grinned to reveal teeth that were rather haphazard but made up a complete set. Yes, he had just the thing and wondered when a buyer would arrive. She was terrific if you could manage her. She was not bad but she had personality.

He led TK to the rail and they looked her over. She was a dark bay like H1 with a small silver star on her forehead and a sliver of white on her offside rear foot. Otherwise there were no white patches and no pink on her face. She had dark intelligent eyes and ears that made her look beautiful when forward but evil when laid back, and they changed momentarily with her moods.

TK liked what he saw and asked to ride her. TK was reminded of the Red Bitch when the hands moved her to the fence before putting on the saddle and the bridle. All accompanied by flat back ears and glaring eyes

TK walked to her head and stroked and talked to her. He stroked longer and more firmly until she stopped trembling. Then he stepped into the saddle and took the reins. He applied his legs and her ears pricked forward. He nudged her and she stepped out. Just beautiful. He moved her into a trot and then the canter. All smooth and easy. He rode her out onto the plain and loved her easy stride. He would need to build up to a long ride but everything looked fine. He rode back to Old Tom. He checked her teeth, she was seven years old, perfect.

TK sat on the verandah with Old Tom. So, she had been brought to the yard by two Irish boys who had bought her from a racing yard. She had stamina but no speed. She lost her races but was always going well at the end. The owner sold her to the boys at brood mare price. They mortgaged their souls to raise the money.

Then came the trick. A brilliantly successful stallion was being kept at a yard a few miles away. They waited for her to come into season and, at dead of night, rode her over. They did not have to break in. The stallion broke out. Actually, he just hopped over the fence and worked his magic.

Being Irish, the boys avoided the hooves and teeth. No introduction, no foreplay, no post-coital gentleness. It was over in moments.

The boys sent the stallion back over the fence and rode the mare into the night.

When they were sure that she was in foal they rode her for three days to bring her to this yard. They had no money but all her papers were in order. So the deal was that they would leave her, in foal, to be delivered and kept for eighteen months. Then the boys could collect the foal and leave the mare to cover the cost. If they did not return, Old Tom would keep the mare and the foal. Old Tom had scrawled out some bits of paper and the boys had made their marks.

Sure enough, they turned up on time to collect the foal, a fine colt. So the boys rode off with a potential dark horse to win races at long odds and then be hired out for stud fees and eventually sold as a successful stallion at a price that they could only dream of. And the boys would be rich. That was the dream that was driving the boys. It would make them rich.

So Old Tom had a fine mare with stamina and proof of ownership. TK just laughed and laughed. He remembered his father's failed dealings and now this fell into his lap. It was agreed that TK would work her in over the next few days and, if it went well, Old Tom had done a terrific deal and TK had found H2 who could run all day.

TK arrived back at the assembly area in late afternoon to found TP still moving and shaking and waving. But he stopped to drink coffee with TK and hear his news. TP said it was a good moment to go to the tool store.

In a world of chaos the tool store was remarkable for its chaos. Certainly, items were grouped together with others of the same kind. But otherwise TK could not see any form of order. The barns were ramshackle, the tools were piled up ramshackle and the rules of trade were ramshackle.

The owner was John Smith. That was the first name that occurred to him when he started the business with a cart load of stolen tools all those years ago, and he had stuck with it. He may once have been tall and young, but now he was old and bent and grey with a long beard and long hair. But he had bright blue eyes. He did not talk much but he communicated by shaking his head and spitting. Short sharp spits and long slow dribbly spits, with all sorts of spits in between, as the occasion required. But he did speak to give his prices. There was no discussion and no negotiation. TK started with the pickaxes. Some were old and some were new. They were distinguished only by their prices. Next the hammers with the same apparently haphazard range of age and price. And there seemed to be no relation between the spits and the prices either. TK said that he would come back later.

On the way back to his camp TK smelled grilling meat and followed his nose to another haphazard arrangement that turned out to be a tavern with a pig grilling on a spit and tables with benches and chairs randomly set around, men talking quietly and girls and women moving between them taking and delivering orders. With joy he saw beer and cider on the tables. He tied up H1 with the other horses and went to see how he could get served. The customers were wearing a variety of clothes, but none wore breeches and boots and he wondered whether he would be turned away. Then he saw a wave. Old Tom from the stables had recognised him. He was invited to join a group of horse workers. What luck. They would be talking the same language.

Among others, he was introduced to a farrier called John Lewis. He did not look like a farrier. He had curly fair hair, blue eyes and a big smile. However, closer inspection showed that the smile was a bit blackened and overall, he was a bit darkened with soot that had not been completely washed off at the end of the day's work. He was square-built, almost as broad as he was tall. A happy bear. You could not fail to like him.

TK asked Tom quietly whether he could trust this man to shoe his horses for the great journey across the prairie plus three sets of spares. Tom whispered, 'Yes, no problem. He is the best.'

TK stepped aside with John Lewis and asked him whether he would be able to do the shoeing. TK also asked whether he would be able to go with TK to the tool store to pick out the decent items through John Smith's barrage of prices and spittle. The big grin gave way to a huge laugh. No problem, he would make the time and he would bring his file but he would charge by the hour, so TK had better be ready to start and make up his mind during the performance. They agreed to meet first thing the next morning at the store.

TK ate pork with fresh bread, dripping, gravy and beer. It turned into a pleasant evening with everyone having extra beers and ciders.

Finally they broke up and Tom explained to TK that John Lewis would not be going home. He had married a spoiled child who admired his property but could not come to terms with his physicality. She had gone back to her adoring parents. So John would be staying, as usual, at the tavern.

TK took pork, bread and dripping for breakfast at his camp and as he looked back he saw John Lewis going into the tavern with a fine, strong girl and TK smiled.

At dawn TK led the horses to the farriers and set off with his wagon to the tool store. John Lewis was waiting.

John Smith spat and led them round. TK had his list: medium pickaxe and small pickaxe; medium sledgehammer and lump hammer; medium shovel and small shovel; medium saw and small saw; blocks and tackles with heavy ropes and light ropes; bundles of knives and, on a whim, he included an old cavalry sword that would fit nicely behind his cavalry saddles. John Lewis worked his file, checked the quality and made his choices, very often the oldest and rustiest. They added a few buckets, pots, pans and grills, a bag of nails and they were finished. TK started to add up the cost, but John Smith stated a figure and there would be no discussion. TK paid up and bit back his surprise at how cheap it all was. One last spit and they were gone. As they left, John Lewis said that he had been told that John Smith chose the name when he first set up his store with a barrow load of stolen items. He had become legitimate but had retained the name. The bundle of tools would serve him well.

TK left John Lewis to work on the horses and got a ride to the camp. At the camp the trailer and mules had been delivered. TP rode up and advised TK to join the convoy camp for protection, so TK made a little base round the trailer. Later he took the trailer and mules to pick up the horses and the spare shoes. John Lewis checked the mules and found a hairline split in one of the hooves. It would never make the journey. The mule would need complete rest for several weeks. TK took it back to the mule station. They did not argue with JL's assessment and handed over a fine tall mule in exchange. Finally, he went upriver to the native traders and bought a big bag of knives, beads, chains and brooches. TK was inclined to go back to the tavern to see what they were roasting that evening, but TP advised him to stay to meet the other travelers.

That evening was a revelation. TK had been an officer but a working soldier all his life. Dinners in the officers' mess had been rare. The visits to the Guards had been an exception. Mainly he had stayed in camps or taverns, some grim, others worse. It had all been part of the life that he chose to lead. Now he was invited into a camp formed by three huge ox carts pulled together. Large blonde men made him welcome. Beautiful tall blonde ladies served his meal. He was immediately included in the group. They spoke English and put him at ease. They were Dutch and were going west and he was welcome to join them. TP joined in to make some introductions. All the men were called Jan, but not just Jan, always Jan-something. Often the names were reduced to mere initials and then converted to a monosyllable. The women kept apart but joined in when the singing started. Good food, nice people and a warm welcome.

Finally, it all came together quite quickly. The trailer and the mules had been delivered. He had picked up his clothes in bundles, John Lewis had delivered the tools, sharpened and repaired with surprisingly few new shafts, and he had delivered the horses on new shoes with sacks of spares. The food arrived in small sacks of flour, potatoes, onions, bacon, ham and coffee, lots of coffee. Also, there were bags of charcoal which TK would not have thought of. JP had specified quantities of oats and barley for the animals and TK had doubled them. TK had asked for all of the items to be delivered in small sacks so that they could be transferred onto the mules if and when necessary.

Over the next days, two smart wagons with New Yorkers arrived and were joined by two poorer wagons with Scottish farmers from the east. TP said that the convoy was now complete. TK noticed that all of the wagons had restorations and reinforcements for the journey. They were all in good order. Clearly TP would settle for nothing less.

On the final evening TP encouraged people to walk among the wagons to make their introductions and bring their food. The children were far ahead of their parents in breaking the ice but quite soon the Dutch pulled everyone together for a shared meal. Every wagon contributed. That night TK made camp on the trailer under an awning and slept well.

At last, the next morning, they were ready to go. TP stood on a wagon and gave them the rules. They were very simple. They were a team whether they liked it or not. If anyone got into difficulties the whole team would join together to resolve the problem. The convoy would not progress until the problem was resolved. If meals became communal, and he hoped that they would, each wagon must contribute its share. If any wagon was not contributing it would be very clear. No wagon would want to be excluded from the team. They would each contribute food, effort and assistance according to their capabilities. Nobody would ask for more, or settle for less.

The New Yorkers were heading for California. They would go to the foothills of the Rockies at South Pass with this convoy and would then join a new convoy to go west.

The farmers were heading for South Pass. They would leave there and look for land to farm either close to the Pass or at the British settlements far to the north on the Columbia River.

The Dutch wagons would turn north at the foothills of the Rockies and would look for farmland to set up a community.

TK would go north to meet the Missouri river and follow it up to the North Pass and then down towards the Columbia River and the Pacific.

TP would look for business going back east or to the south. His customers would most likely be sad and difficult failures struggling to get back to what they knew.

The route would be clear and pretty safe as they went south of the Great Lakes and north of St Louis. After that they would cross the Missouri and follow the Platte River avoiding the wetlands west of the Great Lakes and the natives who were unfriendly because of the competition with fur hunters.

The convoy would travel at different speeds. But overall the progress would be the same. The oxen would leave first, before breakfast. They would go at two miles per hour or better for ten hours. The oxen would graze as they walked. Breakfast would be delivered by the horse wagons and they would arrive in time for supper. The horse wagons would leave after breakfast and go faster but stop earlier so that the horses could rest and graze. The mules would be fastest. They would leave last with the cooking equipment and arrive first to set up camp. TP and TK would ride on horseback to find the trail, mark it with fire smoke and hunt for game.

Finally, TP would hang murderers and flog thieves.

Departure

Now, TP had set out the rules for an orderly progress. However, he did not go into the detail of how the rest of the convoy would be managed. There were children, the ponies and the animals. The children outnumbered the adults and the animals outnumbered the children. There were ponies, dogs, cows and calves, pigs and piglets, goats and kids, geese, chickens and more besides, including songbirds in cages. The wagons followed the pattern, but the children and animals had to be herded along: behind, alongside and in front. Seen from afar it would appear like a rabble. However, the adults managed the children and the children herded the animals.

As arranged, the bullock carts set off first with breakfast cooking on their decks.

The horse wagons remained to complete their breakfasts. The Dutch did very well with the smell of bread and bacon in the air. The Eastern farmers were about the same. The New Yorkers struggled to get organised and used up a lot of eggs and loaves. TP and TK gravitated together to eat bread, bacon and coffee at TK's camp.

After breakfast TP rode ahead to mark which trails they should follow leading from New York, going west.

TK tidied up, loaded the trailer and hooked up the mules to follow. He drove two mules in the shafts and led the other two mules and the horses behind. He was wearing new boots, new buckskin trousers and a rough new shirt with a new straw hat. He took his time to get comfortable with it all.

As they travelled west, the trails started to merge until the one selected by TP clearly marked the way forward. Farmland gave way to woodland, then woodland gave way to scrubland and finally the scrubland gave way to prairie. Eventually the selected trail became less clear and the convoy became a broad group heading west across the prairie.

Around midday TK passed the oxcarts swaying lazily on their way with the oxen grazing, adults and children strolling along herding the animals and ponies cantering up and down scaring off the strays and rounding them up again.

In late afternoon TP arranged for a couple of boys to drive TK's trailer and TK mounted H1 and rode with TP towards the front of the convoy. TP explained that the next few days would be crucial as leaders emerged, the men shared the heavy duties and the women teamed up to do the cooking, child-minding and almost everything else. All TP needed to do now was watch as it emerged and break up the occasional fight.

As if on cue, as they started to make camp for the evening, the dogs started to assert themselves and strive for dominance. It did not take long for the scraps to be resolved and for a line to be formed with the biggest dog at the front and the others following roughly in order of size.

"Damn," said TP, "if this pack forms up we are in trouble. Have you got a whip?"

By chance the whip from New York was still behind TK's saddle. He pulled it out and flicked the dogs until they broke ranks. Except the leader, a big mastiff that snarled and threatened to fight back. TK flicked him a couple more times but he stood his ground. TK hit him harder. He moved back but held firm. Then TK hit him very hard and he whimpered and backed off.

The dog gang had been broken up but the owner of the lead dog, one of the Scottish farmers, came forward snarling and growling. TK could not use the whip, of course, so he stepped down off H1 and stood in front of the farmer. He stood close, slightly to the farmer's right and spoke quietly.

"You are a farmer. I am a soldier. You grow. I kill. If your dog attacks me, I will kill it. If you attack me, I will kill you."

TK did not wait for a reply. He turned his back on the stunned farmer, remounted H1 and rode back to TP who had positioned himself at the centre of the group.

TP said, "If any dog attacks any child or any animal, I will shoot it. Control your dogs or see them die."

There was a stunned silence as the message sank in.

"Now, please, walk about, offer food and offer friendship. You have a long way to go. With mutual support it can be an easy and happy voyage. It's up to you."

And he left them to it.

TK mentioned to TP that he still had some cold pork and stale bread if he would like to share it. TP replied that he was really tempted but would hold out for a better offer. He suggested that they sit tight, and TK would be amazed.

Sure enough, the Dutch got a big fire going and invited the others to bring their food. Each brought more than their share. The women formed into a team. The men fetched and carried. TK assembled what he would otherwise have cooked and joined in.

And the first great game of hide and seek got underway. Lucy, one of the New York children, emerged as the games leader and set the rules. Little ones had to go with big ones. No going outside the camp. When you are found, you join in the hunt. The last found was the first to search next time. It was a joy to watch. The food was cooked and served and then the music started. At first a fiddle, then another, then a banjo, then some percussion, then the children started to dance. Then a few of their mothers joined in to keep them going. TP smiled and relaxed. A team had formed, as usual.

The Dutch contingent comprised several families and several generations. They had prospered in the east and were now moving to prosper further in the west. Their oxcarts were massive platforms with all the daily activities of their communities aboard. Behind the carts came the wagons pulled by good farm horses, carrying stores and supporting the community. Behind the wagons came the trailers pulled by mules, carrying items between the oxcarts and the wagons. Behind them came the ponies helping and hindering and enjoying the adventure. The Dutch were self-sufficient and had every confidence that they would settle in the west and build a prosperous community, with established leaders and a social order.

The Scottish farmers had been less successful. They

had struggled to buy enough land to develop their farms. They were confident that if they could get enough land they would prosper. They were fiercely independent and just wanted to be given a chance.

The New Yorkers were different. They were town folk. They had no experience of the life that they were commencing. They were embarking on their new life for their health. They had run a newspaper in New York and had offended a particular political grouping. Michael Farnish, who was tall and elegant, had fought a duel. He had thought it part of the New York political fashion. He had not even bothered to fire. His opponent was still furious on the day, and his bullet had passed between Michael's chest and arm, nicking both. Michael Farnish could not risk another adventure like this for the sake of his health. He had been shocked. He realised that he had been lucky to escape with his life and now he needed to find a less dynamic environment to ply his trade. Politicians were killing each other in New York and a journalist could easily be added to the list of victims.

His wife, Ella, had been instrumental in his situation. She was tall and had dark brown hair with a hint of red piled high and topped with a hat fixed with a large pin. She was not reserved. She planted her feet and delivered her views on anything and everything in a carrying voice delivered with great humour. Her views, spoken and written, had mocked her husband's dueling opponent beyond endurance. She had been shocked by the duel but had not been shocked into silence. So they had to leave.

Their partners in the second wagon could not have been more different. Arthur and Meredith were short, plump and bespectacled. They set the type and rolled the presses. They were not in danger but they were part of the publishing team. So they were leaving to help achieve a quieter life on the west coast and they were taking the equipment with them.

And so the team formed. The Dutch were the leaders, with great experience and self-assurance. Their carts, wagons and trailers were a mobile self-contained community. The Scottish farmers stood by and took their chance to help with manpower, skills and equipment. The New Yorkers fetched and carried and did as they were told. And they joined in with a good spirit. But their main role developed into running the lessons on the decks of the oxcarts. Ella ran the reading and spelling lessons on one cart and Meredith ran the arithmetic on another cart. And they made it fun. The children loved to be together and hardly knew that they were learning.

At first men and women took turns to drive the light trailers for TP and TK. However, they soon had to hand over to the teenage boys and girls. This left TP free to find the trail and TK free to hunt.

A pattern developed with the oxcarts setting off at dawn and rolling steadily with stoves burning and breakfast served on the move. The horse wagons made the main breakfast and carried extra for the oxcarts when they set off. Finally, the light trailers cleared the camp and followed with the equipment.

TP and TK went their separate ways. At the end of the day TP would light a fire with smoke to guide the convoy. The trailers would arrive first with the grills and ovens; then the wagons would arrive to get started with the cooking. Finally, the oxcarts would roll in and the game of hide and seek would begin. Ella's daughter, Lucy, aged ten, was in charge. She set the territory and made the rules.

Almost every day TK brought back meat. He rode until he found a stream and then followed it until he found supper. He took off heads and guts and carried the carcass on his horse. Sometimes, for bigger loads, he had to ride back for the trailer and the enthusiastic helpers. He was keeping them all fed. After supper came the music. The fiddles played, flutes joined in and improvised percussion and clapping followed. Happy days.

As the docklands had given way to farmland, woodland and brushland, the prairie had opened up. Waist-high grassland shimmered to the horizon mingled with wildflowers. Lots of yellow but also blues and pinks came and passed in patches. Butterflies and colourful birds added to the picture. Birds sang and, in the background, insects hummed. And the convoy moved on relentlessly.

The weather was becoming hot but there was a constant breeze that blew through the straw hats. So, the hats provided shade and allowed the breeze to cool their heads. Also, the hats did not blow off.

Diary entries began to appear on the back of Ella's wagon in the evening. One evening TP had returned to the camp early because he could not find a point to cross a wide river with steep banks in time. TP and TK rode out to find a suitable crossing point for the next day. They found the area that TP had been looking for. The river was very wide, but shallow with shoals and islands. Even so, it flowed fast through the obstacles. It would be interesting.

The next day TP drove his trailer to the chosen crossing point with shallow banks. TK crossed to an island on H1 trailing a light rope. TP unloaded ropes and blocks and tackles and connected a heavier rope with block and tackle. TK rode forward until the new rope with its block and tackle reached a selected tree. TK looped the heavy rope round the tree and attached the hook. He threaded the rope through the block, then attached the light rope to the heavy rope and rode back across the river with the light rope. After that it was all a matter of gearing. The heavy rope was pulled over and more blocks were added to the loop. Then a few horses were towed over. TP put the Dutch farmers to work clearing the routes across the islands and laying the cleared trunks to make paths through the difficult parts. At last they started to send over a wagon. Then the exercise was repeated, to reach another island. And so it went on until they reached the far shore. At every stage the horses and oxen had to work on dry land or shallow water. TK had never seen anything like it, not even onboard ship. TP was organising the towing from both sides of the river and the loads got bigger and bigger. At last the oxen were pulled over and finally came their carts. The last cart carried the last of the equipment and the crossing was completed. There had been a lot of splashing and shouting but TP had managed it perfectly. It had taken three days.

"Mr. Parsons failed to find a crossing over a rather insignificant stream. For some reason this resulted in a very boring exercise involving lots of ropes and other equipment to pull every item over one at a time in order to reassemble the convoy on the other side. Three days of progress was lost and the members of the convoy were inconvenienced.

It is to be hoped that this will not occur again and that in future Mr. Parsons will select an easier crossing point or an easier river."

"That's how she nearly got her husband killed," said TK.

TP laughed, "That was nothing. That was the upper Mississippi. Wait until she sees the Missouri."

After many days of rolling progress, with the oxcarts leading then being overtaken by the horse wagons and at last the mule trailers heading towards the plumes of smoke that would mark the camp for the night, the pattern was broken. They were not greeted by TK with a deer, antelope or gazelle butchered and ready for cooking. He had ridden up and down the rivers and streams along the route but had seen no signs of game. This was not a problem. The convoy had plenty in reserve and there was no weight of expectation or dependence on him.

However, the next day a bulletin appeared on the back of Ella's wagon:

"Yesterday Mr. Kynaston returned to camp empty-handed. After some consideration it was decided

that he should not be sent back until he could return with something to offer. However, this is not the service that we have come to expect. Perhaps Mr. Kynaston should start a little earlier or, if necessary, return a little later."

Wild Boar

A few days later, after normal service had been resumed, famine turned to feast. TK had been riding ahead going along the streams and trails where game had usually been plentiful. As he dropped down towards a big river there were lots of signs. However, one area near a thick thorn copse caught his particular attention. All around the ground was broken. He looked closely and sure enough there were prints from the trotters of wild boar. He remembered the copses in the east and in Spain. There could be good meat but great danger. He smiled at the challenge.

He rode to a low hill fifty yards from the copse. If he stayed mounted he would have a good view around the copse. It was hot in the early summer sun and H2 fidgeted but stayed calm. At last, sure enough, several young pigs came out to play. He had a good view and the range was fine. However, H2 was getting better at the sound of gunshot but with this prize he was taking no chances. He led her behind the hill and tied her to a low bush. He then crawled back to the top of the hill, chose the first shot and a possible second. Then he set the bead on a spot behind the shoulder of his first target, breathed out, touched the trigger, heard the crash and saw the pig rock, but he did not wait but swung onto the second pig before it could react and shot it somewhere in front.

The first pig had been killed but the second lay

twitching as the other pigs ran for the copse. If the second pig recovered enough to dash to the copse it would be lost. This was a dangerous time. Wild boar were unpredictable and horses hated pigs. It was quicker to ride than to reload so he jumped onto H2, pulled out the U.S. sabre and rode fast towards the dying pig ready to swing at the neck. At the last moment H2 flinched and TK's mighty swing missed the neck and hit the skull with terrible force. The sabre stuck in the skull and it was wrenched from TK's grip. He turned H2 back to the slope and reviewed the situation. The first pig was dead, and the second pig lay twitching with a U.S. sabre stuck in its skull. He was getting ready to reload the rifle when the second pig shuddered and lay still.

TK now had the problem of how to recover the pigs from the vicinity of the copse. The parents would have had time to recover and could attack at any time. H2 could not be asked to go back. He could not go on foot because of the threat from the parents. Wild boar had a deadly reputation for charging out of cover and breaking bones and ripping arteries. The dead pigs were twenty yards from the copse so, if the parents attacked he could be hit and killed in seconds. He would have no time to shoot and little time to jump. In any case he would need the trailer to carry the pigs away. He had no choice but to leave the scene and ride back towards the convoy.

He rode through the long grass hoping to cut the trail of the convoy.

He was fortunate to arrive just as the mule trailer was passing the horse wagons. Recently his mule trailer was often being driven by a Dutch girl, past her teens and proud to be taking responsibility. She had a straw hat and a simple blue dress. She had bare brown feet resting on the front of the trailer. Her blonde hair was loosely pulled back. And she had freckles. She had been expecting school to finish and a group of hero worshippers to join her. TP was getting ready to ride forward to choose the camping place for the night.

TK explained that they needed to move quickly. They would need pots and pans and heavy spoons. TP suggested light ropes and eye posts and threw them on board. He offered to ride along to help. They recruited a couple of the Jans from the horse wagon. They could reach the copse in about an hour and pick up the pigs before nightfall. Then TP could choose a camping place and send up his signal where they would convene.

TK exchanged H2 for H1, just to be on the safe side.

When they reached the copse TK directed the trailer to stop between the pigs and the copse. He unhitched the mules and led them away with H2 under cover of the trailer. He rode back and stepped onto the trailer. TP organised the banging of the pots and throwing of the eye posts and dragging them back through the bushes. Sure enough, three young pigs charged out and ran to the stream. Then the sow came lumbering out going faster than seemed possible. TP asked for more banging and more throwing. There was always a boar. And just as they began to doubt, he came out like a bullet heading for the trailer. He hit a wheel with a shuddering bang, stumbled, saw H1 and continued his charge. TK spun away, but a tusk hit H1 on the hind leg and the boar headed for the river. TK dismounted and examined the leg. It was hopeless. Sinews and tendons torn to the bone. TK led H1 away and shot him twice between the beautiful eyes. Theoretically, horse meat could be added to the pioneering menu, but nobody would mention that.

TP and TK examined the wheel. One spoke was broken so it could have been worse. TP extracted the broken spoke and put it on the trailer. They then loaded the pigs. TK brought up the mules and they set off. TP went ahead to find a campsite. TK asked him to choose a place with a tree.

TK went to the trailer and sat on the driving seat with the Dutch girl. The saddle would have been more comfortable and he would have preferred to be alone, but it seemed rude not to share the journey. Her name was Elisabeth, but this had been shortened to Beth. She was tall and slim with an unusual face: longish nose, longish chin and longish teeth. And, of course, the freckles. The overall effect was really quite attractive. She spoke good English and had done a full course of schooling in the eastern settlement.

She had been invited to qualify for the church but was not inspired. She had been invited to teach in the school but would be bored. She had been excited when the elders had decided that their community needed to move on to find more land. The Dutch community felt trapped if they did not have limitless land to expand their farms. They expected to find land and they expected to find a market for their produce. That was their belief. They were going to look in an unsettled area and so she would not be bored. Her big-toothed grin was a statement of self-belief. Clearly, she was past her teens and was probably driving the Dutch boys crazy.

She had read some English books and Ella was lending her more. She was fascinated to know about the English life depicted in the books: the castles; the mansions; the balls and the parties; the aristocracy and monarchy. TK explained that you were unlikely to meet them in the street or in their homes. They were so arrogant that they mixed only with each other. But rich businessmen and new landowners were beginning to create a more even society. Conversely the French had been so infuriated by it that they had cut off the heads of the aristocracy and destroyed their chateaux. Napoleon had restored order but then tried to conquer the whole of Europe and be their emperor. The British had stopped all that. However, they had needed the help of Prussia, Austria and the Dutch to beat the French. The French had had a revolution and a despot and still were left with their aristocracy. TK explained about the Catholic Church and its influence on daily life and the peasant communities that it dominated. The cardinals were part of the aristocracy and the priests were the enforcers in the communities. The revolution and the wars had not changed any of that.

So they rode away as the birds circled over H1. At last they saw the smoke signal from TP and drove towards the camp.

TP had found a place with a tree and he and TK hoisted up the hogs. TK gutted and skinned them surprisingly quickly. TP got a big fire going and they were ready when the wagons arrived with the cooking team, shortly followed by the pony club. Lessons were over and the games could begin. As usual, Lucy was in charge.

The games eventually stopped for the roast pork followed by the music and the singing and the dancing.

"Yesterday, Messrs Parsons and Kynaston surpassed themselves by bringing home the bacon... and the legs and shoulders and ribs, in fact the whole hog. And at no small risk to themselves.

Your correspondent believes that she speaks for the whole convoy in expressing their thanks."

The next morning the start was delayed while the committee agreed how the trailer spoke should be repaired. Surprisingly, in the end, it was the Scottish farmers who dug out some rusty screw things to provide the tension for the repaired spoke.

And, so the convoy moved on. Day after day over the endless prairie. Tall grass, wildflowers, insects, heat haze and weary animals trudging on with weary travellers taking it in turn to walk and ride, fanning themselves as they went.

TK kept apart. He needed to be sociable when necessary. However, he was feeling the loss of H1 badly. He was asking himself what he could have done differently. It was tormenting him. He should not have ridden Her Ladyship at Waterloo and he should not have ridden H1 so close to the boar copse. Those horses had saved his life. He would take some time to get over the loss.

Lucy

Then, one evening, TK came into camp with the mules and trailer carrying a young buffalo, which should have been a cause of celebration. But all was silent. No games, no bustle. Ella was sitting and being comforted by the women. The children were wandering around looking under things and the men were busy having ideas.

TP came up to say that Lucy was missing. The children had been playing hide and seek and she could not be found. No animals and no strangers had been sighted. The dogs were under control.

TK walked away to think quietly. At last he asked TP to summon the children. They stood with heads hanging as though they were going to be punished by this fierce man. But TK was gentle. He asked questions and they replied. What were the rules? Did you all count together out loud? Were you allowed to hide anywhere that you could not hear the counting? Were there any places that you were not allowed to hide? Were there any places that you were afraid to hide – like in deep dark places, or dangerous places?

They replied that they never went out of hearing range of the counting. They were not allowed to hide in the private parts of the wagons.

They were afraid to hide deep in the sacks because they were stuffy. They did not like to go high onto the canvasses covering the machines. There were spaces under the flaps but it was difficult to squeeze inside.

"Very well," said TK," Let's ask the wagon owners to search the private areas. Let's shift the sacks and let's remove the canvasses from the machines."

Men, women and children took up the challenge to look again where they thought that they had looked before. At last a call came from one of the children searching under the machinery. "We have found her, and she is dead".

TP took charge to clear the area. Apparently, she had fallen from the top of the machines and had hit her head on a ploughshare at the bottom. She was lying unconscious on the deck of the cart. The ladies took over and found a faint fluttering of a pulse. She was laid in a dim corner of a wagon. She was dribbled water and her head was cooled. Nothing more, night and day for two days.

At last, with a bump on her head the size of a chicken's egg and black shadows under her eyes, she woke up. The care continued and, at last, she was said to be safe. She stayed in her dim corner, but the convoy moved on.

It took many days before the games resumed and even more before the music slowly resumed before quickening to its former gusto.

> *"Your correspondent is pleased to report that Lucy has recovered. Her record for staying hidden is unlikely to be beaten on this journey. Her family convey their personal thanks to all those involved in her discovery and restoration."*

The sun was getting hotter and the pace was getting slower. Only the oxen trudged on without rest. In fact, after several days they became more alert and quickened their pace. They had to be separated and led quietly. They had smelled the Missouri.

TP led the convoy to a point where the Platte River joined the Missouri. It was their first contact with any settlers. And it was not very pleasant. There was a fort a few miles from the river, inhabited by hot, tired, inebriated soldiers and natives.

The river crossing was managed by teams of boat owners, all in competition. The only way across was by boat. Light boats could be rowed. Heavier boats were secured by lines across the current. But the biggest boats used sail to get across and horsepower to reposition on the other side. TP had seen it all before. This was going to take several days and he wanted to keep the convoy close and protected from the river men. He set up camp far away from the river and drew up an order of crossing. He chose TK to cross first to set up a base on the other side and to find food.

So the mules with the trailer and H2 were the first to cross on a barge with lines across to each side and a huge rudder steering across. It went very well. TK stood with the mules and led them on and off. He was really getting to like those mules. He trotted them up the slope and began to look for a reassembling point.

Soon a horse wagon came across the same way. Then the horses. Then they stopped while an oxcart was sailed across and towed up to the landing point. And so it went on. The ferrymen were rough and tough. But they got paid for success. Over three days they only lost only one horse and did a deal to replace it.

The reception camp grew larger and TK rode out along the Platte River to look for food. Fresh meat was back on the menu.

At last they were back in convoy going west. The games were resumed, and the music started again. And so they continued their slow progress west.

The Red Cliffs

One morning TK pointed to a grey line on the horizon. It was the Continental Divide or, the Rocky Mountains, as they were better known. TP said that from now on the natives were unreliable. In recent years the visitors had become less respectful. In particular, fur hunters had started to steal furs and meat. The native tribes were grumbling and preparing to attack the invaders.

One morning, as the mountains grew closer, TK rode up a slope far ahead of the convoy and saw figures on the slope ahead. He dropped back and went on foot to the top of the slope. He saw about 25 native warriors with spears and bows on horses. They appeared to be young and athletic, probably looking for adventure. Boys misbehaving.

TK rode back towards the convoy, keeping away from the top of the slopes. Along a dry river bed he saw low sandstone cliffs with flat land in front. He rode hard for the convoy and was relieved to meet TP in advance, choosing the route as usual. TK explained the situation and suggested they should head for the shelter of the ravine. It would do no harm if it was a false alarm. On the other hand, it could provide a defence in case of an attack. TP agreed. Better to be safe than sorry.

TP would be able to follow TK's tracks back to the cliffs and they could redirect the convoy as fast as possible. They got the children onto the horses and wagons and pushed the mules and horses hard towards the cliffs. The Dutch double-teamed the oxen and whipped them into a trot. It could not last long, but it would not need to. TK went ahead to organise the arrival and TP rode with the Dutch steering the oxen.

As they arrived TK formed a loose arc. When the last cart arrived, he summoned them all forward slowly, gradually. They touched and then bound in a tight arc. They unhooked the mules, horses and oxen and led them into the cleft. They drove in the ponies and animals and at last the children to hide among them. They were close together but there was no kicking or biting and all were surprisingly calm.

TK told them to load everything to the front of the carts, trailers and wagons to make a barrier. Perhaps it was unnecessary, but their defences were secure. All was calm and they organised the smaller details. It was like a little village. But it was a village with very strong defences. TK organised all the men who could fire a gun to load up and stand at the barricade. Behind them, he organised everyone who could load a gun. Then he told them to practice their firing and loading procedures without live ammunition. That was the best he could do.

The warriors at last arrived on the hill above the cleft and sat on their horses watching the activity. They were faced by a solid arc of wheels, wagons, bags and baggage. TK watched them and expected them to ride on. Clearly, they began to argue. Here was a chance to show courage and gain guns and knives and women and the metal with all the other bits and pieces carried by the intruders. But there may be a danger that they did not know and would not know unless they tried. And so, they decided to attack to see what dangers they faced and to test their courage against the intruders.

In the cleft there was concern among the travelers and a fear among the animals. TK went inside and found a circle around a rattlesnake. Some men were getting ready to attack with poles and shotguns were being prepared. He went to the tin box and drew the dark sword. He stepped forward and went towards the snake with the sword extending circling. The snake was reared up with fangs showing and dripping with venom. It was distracted by the tip as it prepared to strike. In a second the tip was in range, the snake reared, the sword flicked and the snake's head fell to the ground.

There was likely to be a nest and a second snake. TP gave them warning. TK stepped on the rock by the dead snake. Sure enough, a second, bigger snake slid forward, rearing and spitting. Again, the snake was distracted by the circling blade. Again, a flick and the snake's head fell on to the rocks. There was silence. In a moment the danger had passed.

TK dropped the sword in the box and climbed up to look at the warriors. They were now getting ready to attack. He readied the marksmen and the loaders and warned everybody to keep down. The chickens, the children, the dogs, the goats, and the ponies were driven back into the cleft and a barrier of tarpaulin was constructed.

TK took the left side and TP took the right. TK told them not to shoot until the warriors stopped. They could ride past all day and shoot their arrows and do no harm. But if they stopped in front of the barricade they might break through. Then they must be shot.

If the warriors had understood the odds they would not have attacked. They believed that if they attacked bravely with their bows and spears and a few guns they could capture the convoy. And if it was not going well, they could ride away.

TK sensed a presence beside him and looked down to see Beth lifting the rifle ready to do the loading. Quickly he loaded the rifle showing her the steps with the ramrod, the gimlet, and the caps. He would need to show her again if he started to shoot but it would give him time to use the bow. He fitted it together and strung it and laid it out with some arrows and arrowheads.

TK took the left side and TP took the right. TK told them again not to shoot until the warriors stopped. Then he would give the order to fire. The impact would be lost and shots would be wasted if anyone fired too soon. When he gave the order they should aim their shots and fire carefully. They should reload and fire again and again until the battle was won or lost.

The familiar mix of excitement and determination lifted him. TK counted 12 guns and a few spares against about 30 warriors with bows and guns and deadly spears.

The warriors galloped past but fired few arrows because they had nothing to aim at.

They rode faster and closer and still there was no response from the barricade. At last they grouped together at the centre of the arc of the wagons. The warriors were building up their courage. The travelers were dreading the attack.

At last a tall strong warrior with a single feather at the back of his head raised his spear and the warriors rode forward. Then he gave a huge chilling war cry and led the charge. The travelers were stunned for a moment then TK bellowed "Fire!" The effect was dramatic. The warriors were hit by bullets and died. They were hit by shotgun fire and recoiled. Horses were hit, wounded and turned. The fire was devastating. Then there was a pause.

The warriors tried to re-group as the travelers started to reload. Out of the group one young warrior came again. He came fast on a fine grey horse and rode on, mounting the oxcarts and leaping the barrier. He landed among the defenders. They had all fired and were pre-occupied with re-loading. TK dropped his rifle and punched the grey horse in the nose before it could rebalance from the leap. It reared and jumped away. The rider twisted and raised his spear. TK dived under the horse away from the spear and pulled on the rider's leg. The warrior balanced, twisted and swung the spear round. TK rolled behind the horse and grabbed its tail. He was out of range of the spear as the rider twisted again. TK leaned all his weight onto the tail and swung against the rear legs. He did not pull the horse down, but it staggered. TK was knocked down in the tangle of legs and hooves. The rider stepped away, still holding his spear. TK saw it as a moment of life and death and rolled and rolled behind the horse. It kicked him in the chest and he fell winded but tried to grab the mane. He missed and came face to face with the warrior, with his spear pointing down. Attack. He drew his knife and staggered forward to attack the tendons of the legs. The rider raised his spear then fell to his knees as TP shot him in the back. Meredith the typesetter had nimbly reloaded. TK heaved for breath and staggered back to the barricade. As he managed more breaths and tried to ignore the pain in his ribs he noticed that Beth had reloaded the rifle.

There was a pause following the reloading. The warriors could turn and come again. However, the leader of the warriors led them back to the rise in front of the barricade to re-organise for the next attack. They came to him reluctantly as he raised his spear. If he led, they would follow. As they hesitated TK recovered more breath. But he knew that the pain in his ribs would get worse as his movements slowed. He needed a decisive move. He saw that the warriors were out of range of the rifle but thought that if he could hit the leader now, with his bow, they were beaten. He fitted an arrow to the bow and took a deep breath and winced in pain as he raised it to his chin. He looked along the arrow at the leader, had him dead on and then aimed three feet above, plus a little more. At that distance, in Wales, he had hit one out of three. The warrior was unlucky. The heavy arrow came down and hit him above the chest. The force knocked him from his horse.

The warriors abandoned the attack and started to collect their dead and gather their wounded. TP and TK gave them time. At last it was clear that their spirit was broken and they were ready to accept help following their foolish adventure. They stepped out in front of the barricade and the line of guns. TP spoke to the warriors and they pointed to a handsome man standing with a spear over the fallen leader. TP spread open hands and tried a few words. The travelers could do as they wished. However, the warrior would kill anyone who injured his brother. TP said that there would be no more attacks from the travelers if the warriors put down their weapons and allowed them to help. The brother of the injured warrior said no. He would kill anyone who approached his brother. TP said that they would both die. So be it, came the reply.

TK stepped forward with open hands. TP whispered to TK that this was not necessary. They could just send them on their way. TK said that they were only boys and had suffered enough. Let us show generosity. TK approached the wounded warrior with a warning that if his companion raised his spear TP should kill him.

Nobody moved. TK saw that the arrow stuck out high in the chest at the shoulder. He measured with his hand and guessed that the arrow had not hit anything vital and would be through to about an inch from the back. He asked TP to send for pliers and spirit. He indicated that he would cut out the arrowhead and then draw out the arrow. The pliers and spirit were brought by a Scottish lady. She also brought laudanum. She put the bottle to the patient's lips and tipped some in before anyone could protest.TK pressed on the back and found the lump. He drew his razor-sharp knife and washed his hands and knife in the spirit. Then, without discussion, he wedged his knees against the shoulders and made a double cut. He dug in his fingers and thumbs and found the arrowhead. He was holding it between the finger and thumb of his right hand but he could not seize it with the pliers in his left hand. The Scottish lady moved in close. She looked at the angle of TK's hand and pushed the pliers in at right angles. She felt the nose touch the arrow head, then opened them, pushed again and then closed them over the arrow head. TK withdrew his fingers and took over the grip on the pliers. He told TP to withdraw the arrow as he held the arrow head firm. TP twisted and pulled, and TK held firm. TP struggled but at last the arrow shaft started to come away. It was only an inch and the muscles on the back of the warrior were very strong but as soon as the shaft had left the arrowhead it started to move more easily. TP pulled and twisted and the warrior writhed but at last the shaft came out. TK then withdrew the arrowhead with the pliers. TK washed the wound with the spirit. The warrior had fainted but slowly began to move. TK stood in front of the warrior with the spear, bent in pain as his ribs cooled, and dropped the arrowhead into the warrior's hand. TP handed him the arrow shaft. The warrior looked down and did not raise the spear. The Scottish lady splashed spirit on the wounds, gave water to the patient and prepared to sew the wounds, but his brother stopped her and called for a robe and his horse. He told TP that the bleeding was good, and his family would treat the wounds. As he was leaving, the Scottish lady's husband brought forward the horse that had jumped the barricade, and its dead rider. The warrior with the spear shook his head. Another brother. Their father would be very angry. He had told them not to approach these visitors.

TK recognised the Scottish farmer who had been ready to fight for his dog the evening before their departure. He thanked them for their help. He had noticed that they had worked quietly and capably on the journey and, even shown some musical talent. He complimented them on their capability. The husband smiled at last and said that in a Scottish croft, when something needed to be done, either you did it yourself or it did not get done.

TP moved the convoy from the crevice to allow the animals to graze. He told TK that he was sure that the war party would not return after their failed adventure. TK shook his head at the waste of young lives. However, TP pointed out that without the cliffs and the crevice those warriors would have scored a famous victory. The men of the convoy would be dead, and the women and children would be starting a new life.

TP withdrew the convoy from the red cliffs and formed a wide circle to allow the animals to feed.

The travellers had survived. They did not celebrate. Only one young pig had been hit by an arrow. It would be killed before any infection could poison the meat. Pork was back on the menu. But not tonight.

Wolves

The wolves came in the night. They had smelled the blood from the fight with the warriors. The dogs raised the alarm. The bigger ones went out to do battle.

Tony Parsons ordered the convoy to tighten the circle. It was chaotic. The oxen could not be moved in time. The horses and mules were frightened of the wolves and had to be led. The animals and their guides needed to be protected. At last, the mules and horses moved the wagons and trailers to tighten the gaps. Men and women worked together to do the job. First the children were pushed down and made safe on the carts and wagons. Then the smaller animals were lifted onto the carts. A few were lost. Then TP ordered the fires to be lit. He wanted small fires around the circle of the convoy. They must sacrifice anything that would burn. He wanted many small fires. As the fires were lit, the eyes of the wolves glowed yellow.

It all took time and they were losing small animals as the wolves braved the fires. The wolves were jumping freely onto the carts to seize what they could.

Finally, TP called for the shotguns. The people of the convoys were farmers and could handle shotguns well. They aimed for the yellow eyes. Nothing else or they might hit their own dogs. The men did the shooting and the women did the loading. Their ammunition was a revelation. There were some balls of shot, some scraps of metal saved from past work and even some hard stones. They did not expect to use their guns in this way, and they were exhausted after the morning's fight. Even so, they did their best.

A young Dutch boy tried to save his terrier from a wolf that leapt onto the deck of a cart. The wolf dropped the terrier and chose the bigger prize. It seized the boy's leg and dragged him off the cart. The boy was being dragged away when a mastiff caught it in the firelight. It had to let go in order to get away. A farmer dropped his gun to pick up the boy and the mastiff chased the wolf. When it caught up, the wolf came off second best without the pack around it for support. Then the mastiff saw another target and moved on. The wolf limped into the night.

The banging and yelping continued as the fires started to die down. The women looked for anything else that would burn. Ornaments and even furniture would have to go.

TK sat in pain on the back of his trailer with his rifle on his knee. Grey forms drifted quickly in and out of view. Yellow eyes flickered and were gone. All too fast. The rifle had its limitations. At last, a pair of yellow eyes stopped near a dying fire, no longer scared of the flames. TK gritted his teeth against the pain that he knew would follow, sighted between the yellow spots and fired. One yellow spot went out and the other fell away. TK lowered the rifle and closed his eyes against the pain.

The fires began to smoke and smell and the shots were fewer. At last, all went quiet apart from the whining of injured dogs and the distant howling of the wolves.

Then TP's voice came through all over the camp as he dashed around giving orders and helping families to regroup. TP came past TK's trailer and found him lying back with his rifle beside him.

"Just resting," said TK, "I think this is my best position now that I have stiffened up, so I think that I am going to need a driver."

TP smiled, "I think there will be plenty of volunteers. I will send a blanket tonight and breakfast in the morning. Enjoy the rest."

TK groaned. It would hurt too much to laugh.

The convoy slowly limped into action the next morning. The horses and oxen had received a few nips but nothing serious. Two chickens and a small pig had been taken.

One middle-ranking dog and two terriers had been killed. Others, including the rangy leader, were receiving treatment for war wounds. The Dutch boy who had been pulled off the trailer had a nasty bite in the calf and his dog had also been badly mauled. All that could be done was to keep the wounds clean and hope.

Beth, with two helpers, brought breakfast and TP brought coffee. The girls selected a couple of mules and harnessed them to pull the trailer. They tied H2 to the back of the trailer. The two younger girls wanted to take the other two mules for a walk to graze in the long grass and maybe to hop on for a ride occasionally. But first, the mules would have to suffer lots of patting and brushing. TK had never thought of mules as pets.

When they were ready to leave, Beth took the driver's seat and the reins.

"No trotting," said TK, "and mind the bumps."

The convoy creaked forward and TK enjoyed the early morning sun. One of the elders came past and talked to Beth.

She called back, "My uncle was a farrier. He says it was only a little horse. The less you move, the sooner you will get better. He should know. Don't be brave."

"Yesterday, Mr Kynaston entertained us with an exhibition of snake-charming and horse-wrestling.

In the meantime, he saved the convoy from a terrible fate at the hands of native adventurers. In the process he suffered injury to his ribs. Your correspondent thanks him on behalf of the convoy and wishes him a speedy recovery and best wishes for the remainder of his journey.

Mr Parsons arranged for us to take the winning side in a dog fight. We thank him for the entertainment and assure him that an encore will not be required. Our sincere thanks go to Mr Parsons and all those who joined in with dogs and guns for our salvation"

Parting of the Ways

The mountains were getting closer and rivers and forests could be distinguished. TP announced that in a few days they would reach a point where their paths would divide. Some would go on along the Platte River to the Sweetwater River and the South Pass. Others would turn north towards the rivers and mountains. The eastern farmers and the New Yorkers would continue west. The Dutch farmers and TK would turn north.

Among the travelers it was agreed that there would be a party on the night before they separated. Immediately, the children, guided by Beth started to prepare their performances. The parents chose the songs and began to practice.

TK sat with TP and asked what he would encounter along the foothills of the Rockies in his path north. The Dutch elders also had specific questions about where to find the best farmland. TP was not an expert. He merely repeated stories that he had heard. The American trappers had travelled up the Missouri and the Yellowstone River and alienated the native tribes. They were accused of stealing the furs and would be attacked whenever they were found. Traders who did not steal but exchanged food and goods were better treated. The position became more difficult the further north that you travelled. For the Dutch there may be an area a few miles north between the Rocky Mountains and the Bighorn

Mountains where they could find suitable land and where the natives may welcome an honest trading presence. For TK, the route along the rivers to the north and west would be nothing but trouble. He might fall in with a group of trappers who knew the territory, but he might be killed with them if they were attacked. TP would not bet on the trappers against the natives.

The Dutch said that they would be pleased to be away from other settlers and expected to make peace with the local natives. TK said that he would take it one step at a time.

The women organised the food. They dug into reserves to lay on something special. The men organised the fires and the music. The children organised their games and the dancing. It was a lovely party. The convoy had bonded well. The men talked comfortably. The women watched over the young men and their daughters. Beth had a group of admirers, including some of the little boys and girls.

It was a happy scene with the convoy gathered around the fires, good food, easy company, and a few dancers swirling in the firelight.

That night Beth came to him in the trailer. She took off her dress and slid under the blanket. He recognised her special aroma and felt the smooth skin and supple body. She found him and he was ready. She remained above him and he held her firmly. There was a simultaneous explosion of pent-up passion. Afterwards he held her close until they were calm. Then she kissed him and left.

Next morning the final bulletin appeared.

"As we go our separate ways, your correspondent extends heartfelt thanks to the Dutch families who have shown such generosity, support and kindness as our mobile community has travelled west. Thanks also the Scottish families for their steady support.

We also express our sincere thanks to Mr Tony Parsons for guiding us so surely and to Colonel Thomas Kynaston for feeding us and keeping us safe. In particular, his management of the barricade, snake-charming, horse-wrestling and archery left us without words, almost."

They were almost ready to leave when TK finally found his graphite and wrote his reply:

"Pens and swords both have their points."

Ella was still laughing as they moved off.

So, TK was left with the Dutch families. They discussed TP's advice to go north and look for a river. TK offered to ride with them to help them find their farmland. In the process he would reach the Rockies and get a feel for the way north. He offered to ride out for a couple of days to find the area that TP had mentioned. The Dutch farmers told him what to look for. The opportunity for a good long ride was too good to miss. They gave him plenty of good cold food: bread; bacon; eggs; and cheese, and he set off with his saddlebags, saddle roll and the tin box. He smiled to think that he was riding alone in the wilderness with guns and swords. After the incident with the wild boar he had re-sharpened the cavalry sword and it sat behind his saddle.

He got H2 into a gentle canter which enabled him to sit deep and relax. With a couple of rests, he rode all day.

In the evening he found the river with good grazing. He hobbled H2 and ate some of the cold food. Then he slept under a tree. It was just like Spain, almost ten years ago, and it felt good.

At dawn the sun gently lit the plains, hills and valleys to the east. To the west, the Rocky Mountains towered closer. To the north another range of mountains rose steeply.

He gave H2 a handful of oats and sat with her by the river so that she could drink and he could eat a cold breakfast.

By midday he was still in grassland, but the grass seemed a bit shorter and a bit bushier. This was still not farming country. H2 and TK had a rest and a bite to eat and then they were off again. The next evening was the same as the last and so was the morning.

At midday he was looking for somewhere to rest when H2's gentle canter brought him to a headland. It was covered in trees and the loops of the river on either side appeared to be what the Dutch farmers had described. He rode closer and his opinion was confirmed. After weeks of prairie grass and bush there was rich green grass, tall trees rising up the slopes to the mountains, and clear water in the streams and river.

He took a long break and walked up the hill between the trees following animal paths. At a vantage point, he looked down and the location looked perfect. He looked further afield and could see nothing better. So, he walked down and rode back.

The Dutch farmers had taken the opportunity to rest and water their animals and clean up their mobile farm. They were relieved and excited to hear of his discovery. They asked him time and again to describe the river, the mountains, the trees and the vegetation. How tall, how green, how did it smell? He had not thought about the smell, but yes, it was fresher.

They would set off in order. First the mules would set off with their trailers. Next would come the horse wagons and finally the ox carts. TK saw the pattern. They were loading up the faster vehicles with men and tools. Later would come the women and the supplies. Finally, the oxcarts would follow with the heavy machinery and the mobile farm. TK and his horses would provide communication and support if any of the vehicles sent up a smoke signal.

TK had ridden to the site in two days. The mule trailers would take five. So they were looking at about ten days with the oxcarts.

After two days, one of the Dutch wagons turned away to a wooded knoll and spent some time before rejoining at the rear of the group. TK waited until his routine would take him past the knoll. Then he rode up to take a look. There his worst fears were confirmed. Two small graves with little crosses marked the resting place for the boy and his dog.

TK used the journey time to exercise H2. Always he exercised his wrist with the dark-bladed sword. He needed to maintain the balance. He fired the pistol to train H2 and she improved a lot.

He hunted up and down the river and found some wild boar to change the menu. He was more ruthless and more careful this time.

He spent a lot of time talking to the Dutch grandparents and hearing about their decision to leave Holland. Many other families had emigrated to South Africa and it was reported that they had travelled great distances and found good land. But these families had decided to come to America to join the community around New York. They had prospered but the pioneering spirit had prevailed, and they were driven to find bigger and better opportunities beyond civilization.

The Dutch Settlement

When they reached the site, it was a revelation. Many acres had been cleared. The long grass was being collected in stooks and the brush had been formed into a kraal to keep the animals and the family safe at night. But the biggest shock was the stockade. It was very large, and it was going up fast. Trees had been cut and pulled to the site and narrow, deep foundations had been dug and the posts were being erected and secured. As he stood in amazement one Jan after another would nod and smile and pat him on the back. Clearly they were delighted.

The location for an ice house on the hillside had been marked and deep privies would be built downstream. They had identified a crossing point to expand the farm across the river. As each wagon arrived, more joined in the project. Men followed by women followed by children. Each night the camp got bigger and the meals to welcome the travelers more substantial.

One of the older men spoke quietly to TK to say that they had seen natives on horseback in the hills but there had been no approach and no sign of hostility.

TK's mules had been working hard and could now have a rest. He checked them over, and apart from a few scratches they were fine. He had been watching their progress and had chosen the two fittest. He really liked those mules. The Jans put his stuff back on the trailer but he did not secure it. He would be leaving soon, and he would not take the trailer and would leave two of the mules. He would be leading two with backpacks. Also, H2 would have to stay. A couple of the young Jans had asked to ride her and had done quite well. That had encouraged Beth to turn up in her brother's clothes to take her turn. She was the best of the lot. She had ridden with her friends in the pony team until the girls were forced to become young ladies and ride in traps and carriages. The voyage had been a release. They would keep H2 busy and that would suit her very well.

There was not really very much for TK to do. If he tried to help with the digging and lifting, he seemed to get in the way, and they patted him on the back and moved him aside. He did not need to hunt because they were still eating the wild boar that he had killed earlier. However, he was able to help with the final details of the palisade. He helped to design firing positions at two diagonal corners to allow shooting down the sides. Also, he helped with the counterbalancing of the gates and the barring mechanisms. The stockade was becoming a fort.

Beth visited him one night and he gently took control and it went well. She kissed him and left. There was never any mention of these visits. It seemed to be part of her statement of independence.

One evening three native warriors appeared above the camp. They did not approach but sat on their horses and waited. TK threw the saddle onto H2, fitted the pistol in his belt and the cavalry sword behind the saddle. He rode up to the warriors. They seemed to know him. But he did not know them. So, he sat still and waited.

At last, a heavily muscled warrior spoke in English.

"We know you. We have followed you. You saved my brother's life. Why are you here? You have not been invited."

TK realised that they were from the band that had attacked them at the red stone cliffs. His mind raced. They could kill him, but they did not appear to be hostile.

At last he said, "I am travelling west to the great sea. My friends are building a farm. I wish to travel in peace and my friends wish to live in peace. I will leave no mark with my passing. My friends will make a farm and they would like to be your friends and trade with you. They bring special food and special skills."

There was a long pause while the interpreter spoke with his companions.

At last he said, "Do you or your friends steal furs or animals?"

"No."

"We understand the farm. I have seen a farm and I have seen the food. That may be possible. Hunting will not be permitted. Why do you wish to travel to the great sea?"

"I will be looking for gold, a yellow metal that has value in the land of the visitors. I will not find it in your land but may find it in the land by the great sea. If I find it, I will trade for it."

The warriors talked together quietly but for what seemed a long time. At last they spoke.

"Yes, you can pass through our land. Yes, your friends can make a farm. But if you or your friends take from our land and give nothing in return we will drive you away."

"Thank you."

"Now, these two warriors are my brothers. We have the same father but different mothers. We have many brothers." And he laughed.

Then he continued, "The first brother will be our next chief. You saved his life. The second saw you work in pain to save the first brother. He wishes to thank you and to help you on your journey. He hopes that he will learn from you. My family are angry with me because I help the fur traders by the great sea. They are the British. They do not steal but they have built a big fort to protect their trade. I will ride with you and my second brother to the great sea. Our father will not be pleased but our first brother will stay by his side. How will you travel?"

TK explained that he had a good horse and two good mules with light loads. He intended to follow the mountains to the north. The interpreter shook his head.

"Too far. Too difficult. Too dangerous. There is anger between the fur hunters and the nations of the north. The north way is for boats. Not horses. I can show you the way for horses. Bring your mules but leave your horse."

TK tried to explain that H2 was an exceptional horse and could travel fast over great distances. The interpreter replied that they had seen him riding. Even so, the horse would not be able to cross the mountains. They would bring the horses but TK could bring the mules. They would return.

TK made up the backpacks for the two chosen mules. He would leave the trailer and the other two mules for the Dutch families. He would also leave H2. He started to give lessons to the older Jans who had admired his riding. In return they would look after H2 by riding her regularly while he was away. Beth arrived in her brother's trousers and boots. Sure enough, she was the best pupil. By the time that the warriors returned they were all riding well enough to get good performance from H2 without harming her.

He assumed that his native horse would have a saddle like the ones which the warriors had been riding but he had not studied them in detail. Accordingly, he made up his saddle roll with straps. If necessary, he could put it on the mules. He included his cape and blanket and added the cavalry sword. The tin box with spare ammunition and food packs went into the loads on the mules. He also added oats in case the horses and mules needed extra energy on the long journey.

When the brothers arrived several days later, he checked the saddle on his horse. It was a lighter version of the cavalry saddles that he had been using but with leather fittings instead of metal, but it looked sound.

He asked the interpreter to reassure the Dutch families that they would not be harmed so long as they did not hunt for meat or furs. They should be ready to trade.

The Dutch families turned out to wave him off. A special smile for Beth and they were away.

TK had expected more horses. However, he learnt that they were going to meet their father. TK hesitated, then shrugged and moved on. It was clear that the journey was going to be undertaken on their terms.

They travelled through beautiful foothills with trees

and glades and ferns. As they progressed the trees got bigger and the glades more beautiful, with shafts of sun lighting up beautiful flowers and the birdsong increased.

The native encampment came as a surprise. It was located in a wide valley with hundreds of lodges among the trees. It was so much bigger than he had expected. Also, the lodges themselves were much bigger and were spread more widely than he had anticipated. The brothers rode up to a great lodge. Outside sat a big strong middle-aged warrior without finery except the same single feather as his sons, but he had a strong presence. He sent away the women and children as the brothers dismounted and TK followed. The father held up his hand in peace and TK followed. They sat together on carved logs. Food was offered and they ate together. TK did not taste anything amiss. He drank only water. Abruptly the father offered ten wives for a gun. TK shook his head and declined. Then twenty horses for a gun. Again, TK declined. The interpreter explained that their father wanted to offer a generous trade. He believed that it would be rude to simply make a gift. Also, a refusal would be rude. TK said that he needed his gun and he only had one. Perhaps they could talk about a different trade. The father said that he had seen the arrow and the arrowhead that TK had fired. He wanted to thank TK for saving his son. Could he please see the bow. This was what TK had feared. He had a few trade items that he could exchange for the horses that he would need for the journey but if they asked for his weapons he would have to fight. Very well, one step at a time. He explained to the interpreter that he would show the bow and his other weapons, but he would fight to retain them. There followed some argument among the family, but the sons prevailed.

TK went to the tin trunk. He put the pistol in his belt and took out the bow. He assembled it and strung it. It was as tall as he was. Each warrior tested the tension. The father went to the lodge and returned with the arrow and arrowhead that TK had given to the younger brother after the extraction. He tried the arrow on the bow and spoke to his sons. They were discussing the distance of the shot that hit his eldest son. The father shook his head in admiration and handed back the bow. TK quickly took it apart and put it back in the trunk. Then he remembered the journey and the familiar dark colour and shape of the yew trees that he had seen so far from home. At home they had been planted in churchyards hundreds of years ago to provide bows in time of war. Here they were growing tall, dark and wide among the giant timbers. He walked to the edge of the clearing and looked back down the valley and there he saw occasional yew trees, very old, among the other old trees of the Rocky Mountains. He took a saw from the mule pack and rode down, leading the mule with the tin box. It was easy to saw off a suitable branch. He used the cavalry sword to hack it into shape, preserving the hardwood core as Robert had done. He tried to make the top and bottom halves equal. Then he returned and handed it over.

"This is the wood," he said pointing to his bow in the box. The father smiled widely. He had a trade. His sons would take TK to the great sea and he could instruct his bow maker to work on the model that TK had provided.

He asked TK about the warrior on the grey horse who had ridden over the barricade. His wound was in the back. Had he run away? TK remembered the fight and his lucky escape. No, he had died fighting. He was winning the fight when he was shot. The father smiled. "He was my son."

The sons collected more horses. The father looked thoughtfully at the cavalry sword. Would TK trade anything for the sword? TK was about to refuse when an opportunity occurred to him. He did not really need the sword.

He presented it to the father and said, "Protect the Dutch farmers and their families. Save them from harm."

The father smiled and nodded. The trade was agreed.

TK and the brothers spent the night at the camp without incident. The interpreter worked hard to smooth the exchange of cultures. The next morning, they were given food for their journey and they left early. TK, the interpreter and the young brother rode away. The older brother remained, standing beside his father.

Oregon

The paths were the beds of streams. Occasionally with a flow. Generally dry. The huge trees grew smaller. The glades were fewer and smaller. Always there were ferns. Cliffs and rocky headlands poked through. The valleys became steeper. The ascents became more difficult and the descents were longer and harder. Often they simply had to go round sheer cliffs with waterfalls, dry or flowing. Always ahead were the towering mountains.

The interpreter and the little brother began to tie ropes to the head collars of the horses on the steepest parts. They had a technique of looping the rope around a tree and pulling the horses up. The descents were more difficult because the horses would not go backwards. The trick was to have the rope available when they stumbled. The mules trotted up and down unaided. TK really liked those mules.

At last they came to a clearing between the mountains. Ahead the streams started to flow away downhill. Between the two headlands TK saw a new mountain range. On one side he looked up a sheer cliff. On the other side he looked up another sheer cliff. Between them the water course path started to fall gently away.

They stopped and shared food. The natives had dried meats. TK offered cheese, cold bacon and dried biscuits from the Dutch camp. The biscuits were a success.

Soaked in water and topped with a little dry cheese they were quite filling.

TK asked the names of his companions. The interpreter smiled and pointed to himself with his thumb and gabbled in his dialect.

Then he laughed and said, "I am called Dances in Rain but at Fort Vancouver they call me Dick."

The little brother was called Sings to the Moon. TK realised that if he was Tom, and the interpreter was Dick, then the little brother would be Harry. They laughed. "Tom" would be easier than "Fires Long Arrow". They repeated their names and it was agreed.

Tom asked whether there would be a danger across the mountains. Dick said there was some hostility towards the intruders because of the fur trapping but it was worse towards the north. Even so they should have weapons ready. TK drew his knife and they laughed. Harry pulled out a short spear. It had a heavy shaft and a broad blade over two feet long. Tom realised that if it hit you it would go straight through. Dick had the same.

Tom realised that he should be carrying something more. He went to the tin box and showed them what it held. They nodded approval at the double-barrelled guns. They had already seen the bow in its two halves. But Tom took out the sword in its scabbard. They were not impressed. TK drew the sword and flicked twice at a sapling and the top and middle sections hung in the air. They nodded. Carry that.

Dick and Harry took out their elk horn bows. The horn had been straightened and layered with a lot of binding. He tried the tension and was impressed. Good bows, they said, but slow to string. So it was the spears and the sword. TK put the sword behind his saddle and secured the box on a mule. Dick and Harry put away their bows and they rode on.

The descent was more difficult than the ascent because the horses had to be roped more often. The mules made their own way.

Slowly the trees got larger, the glades wider and the paths less steep. But, as usual, they often had to divert to go around cliffs and waterfalls. At last the going became easier and they were able to ride the horses. Tom began to relax. Too late, he felt the path twist and fall away. His horse fell and he dived to the side still holding the lead rope to stop his fall. He looked down to see his horse broken on the rocks in a broad shallow river fifty feet below. He looked up to see the face of the mule at the end of the lead rope, black and tan with furry ears, looking down with planted feet. He really liked those mules.

Carefully they found a glade above the cliff. TK started to take out his rifle to shoot the stricken horse. No, perhaps there may be angry neighbours who want guns. But they needed the saddle and bridle and TK wanted the saddle roll with the sword. It was his horse and his problem. He fetched a long rope and a pulley from the mule packs. He found a tree close to the cliff and secured the pulley. He made a bowline at one end of the rope and threaded the other end through the block. He put the loop over his head and shoulders with the knot in front of his chest. And they lowered him down. The river was fast and rocky but quite shallow. The horse was badly injured and clearly in great pain. Even so, first he took off the saddle and bridle and rested them on its back. Then he took out the wide-bladed double-edged knife and made the cut. The Snake River ran red through the current below him. And he had not even given the horse a name.

He carried the bridle, saddle and saddle roll with the sword to the gravel bank and tied them to the rope. Then he tugged on the rope and called for it to be pulled up. Slowly but surely the sodden bundle swung upwards. He watched impatiently with his boots full of cold water and his, theoretically, waterproofed buckskin trousers chilling his legs.

At last the rope returned and he re-fixed the bowline and stepped into the loop. The gearing of the block made progress slow and he pushed off from the cliff with his feet when he swung close to it. Just over halfway up the rope stopped. Tom was left hanging against the cliff face. He heard voices that became angrier. One in particular was high-pitched and dominant. Suddenly the rope vibrated, and he fell a few feet but then held firm. Tom looked down and saw a drop of about 25 feet to a rocky shore. He looked up and saw a small tree growing from a crack in the cliff above him to the right. He did not want to be cut loose to fall on the rocks. He straddled sidewise with his feet against the cliff until he was below the tree. Then he pulled himself up on the rope until he reached the tree. He could not hold this for long. He was hanging by his hands from the rope and it hurt. He calculated that he could hold onto the rope for a few moments with his left hand while he let go with his right hand and grabbed the tree trunk. That worked but it could not last. Both hands hurt. He pushed his right arm around the trunk and that was better, but he was blinded by foliage. With hands and feet, he managed to get his right arm well round the trunk then he passed the rope from his left hand to the right. This was more manageable. He drew his knife with his left hand and cleared the foliage from around his face. He replaced the knife and could now hold on with both arms. The rope was slack and giving no support, but intact. Perhaps he was wasting his time but, if necessary, he could lift himself up to sit on the tree.

Then the jabbering reached a scream, then stopped and the rope fell down. Then a body fell past him into the river and washed up against the dead horse. It looked like an old native with lots of beads and feathers. He was not dead, but he was choking and spitting blood. He tried to stand in the river but fell back against the dead horse and then forward into the river and he was washed slowly away, bumping against rocks and leaving a pink trail.

Tom pulled himself up onto the tree trunk and cut away more foliage. The rope was hanging down from his chest. He needed to position himself so that he would be on one side of the trunk and the rope was falling on the other. Then he could grab the rope and lower himself down. He lowered himself to one side of the trunk and pulled the top of the rope to the other side. The main thing was that he should be on one side of the trunk and the nearest part of the rope should be on the other side, and that it looped back over the trunk. That looked about right but a mistake would be fatal. He gingerly took the rope in his right hand and saw a continuous loop from the bowline over the trunk and to his right hand. He checked again and tried a few tugs to be sure. Then he made the move. He let go with his left arm and grabbed with the rope above his right hand. Everything held firm. So far so good. He lowered his right hand to grip the rope and then lowered his left hand to grip the rope. The good thing was that he had lowered himself one foot below the tree. On the other hand, it was now out of reach.

But, slowly, hand over hand, one foot at a time, he made his way down. At last he reached the shore without falling. He looked up to see Dick and Harry peering down and smiling at his efforts. They dropped another rope and Tom tied it to the original. He got the bowline on his chest, gave a wave and he was being pulled up. At last he reached the edge and came face to face with Harry, who lifted him over. He was on his hands and knees, dripping wet, not knowing what to expect and being laughed at by Dick and Harry. They gently helped him to his feet and took off the noose.

Dick explained. Spirit Man came with two warriors as they were pulling up. Not friendly. Dick put a hitch in the rope to jam the block and let go. Spirit Man was very angry and kept talking faster and louder. Then a warrior cut the rope. As the warrior cut the rope, Dick cut his throat. Harry pulled his spear and stabbed the other warrior. The Spirit Man was still shouting when Harry stabbed him in the throat. "Stopped talk," said Harry. "In river," said Harry, and laughed. Tom realised that he had not yet learned enough of the language to have said that much. He had better improve.

Dick and Harry had stripped the warriors and gained only knives and tomahawks. They had lost one good horse and gained one good one, one average one and a nag that they would leave behind. They had gained two good saddles and bridles and some rubbish on the nag which they threw away. Tom noticed bloody scraps hanging from the belts of his companions but did not comment.

So they had reached the Snake River. It ran fast and shallow with steep banks and was difficult to cross almost everywhere. Dick said that they must travel upriver for half a day to make a crossing. Then they would loop away from the Snake River to avoid having to cross it ever again. It was a menace. They would divert onto the plain and loop towards Fort Vancouver without any major obstacles.

The crossing was not easy. The banks were steep, and they needed ropes. The bottom was rocky but not impossible. They progressed slowly and carefully. The mules trotted over without help. They just got better and better. If the cavalry officers in Britain could see him now, riding wiry native horses and bonding with mules, what would they think? Well, actually, they would probably not be too surprised. He was back in his element.

They rode out onto the plains. The grass was a little shorter and the streams, hills and woods more frequent than on the great plains in the east, but it was easy going. Tom fed half a handful of oats to the horses and mules each morning and Dick was happy with the progress, but dried bacon, cheese and biscuits was getting boring. Tom was wondering whether they should make a stop to take the bows along one of the streams for a bit of hunting when the grass became shorter and plats of drying, sloppy dung appeared. Buffalo.

They followed the broad path of the herd. It was obviously very large. The path was half a mile wide.

The plats became softer and the flies denser and the vultures flew lower until, at last, they came upon the rear of the herd. That was all they needed. Sure enough, they came upon the stragglers. They chose a young male, big enough to have some meat but not yet tough. Harry speared it but it was Tom who was the butcher. He got to work with his big knife, gutting the carcass, skinning, separating the heart and liver and at the request of his companions selecting special cuts. He cut a section from the hide and tightly wrapped the prize.

They rode on until they came to a stream with an outcrop and a copse. They collected stone and wood and made a barrier around a hearth and waited until dark. Then they made a concealed fire, skewered their choice of meat and had a feast. After they had eaten they made up the fire and skewered more meat to dry out for the journey.

This was really the first time that they had stopped to relax since they had crossed the Rockies. Dick was the co-ordinator. He had met and worked for the British at the fort and harbour on the Columbia River. Tom smiled as he recognised a Scottish twang as Dick talked of Fort Vancouver and the British organisation of the fur trade.

Dick had been employed on the canoes. He was heavy and strong and could work on equal terms with a team of voyageurs on the Columbia River. They were tough men. French, native and Canadian, all proud of their strength and skill with the big wooden canoes that they had mastered. Their hope was that, with camps and portage points, they could find a route far up into the Rockies.

Tom told them that he had heard that in the mouths of the streams in Canada, along the coast, there were signs of gold. Dick had heard of it, but the British were only interested in furs. Harry had to be told about gold, its value in the cities and the greed that it could inspire. In the world of the intruders, gold could buy many things.

They discussed whether the arrival of the intruders was good or bad. They agreed in relation to furs it was bad. In relation to new spirits, it was bad. In relation to new food, medicines, machinery and knowledge, it was good. They should reach Fort Vancouver the next day. There he would learn the difference between the Americans on one side of the mountains and the British on the other.

TK Book III

Fort Vancouver

So they came to Fort Vancouver. Tom had not known what to expect. It was far bigger and better organised than he had imagined. It was built in the British formula on a grand scale. It was over 250 yards long and half again wide. It consisted of a big wooden palisade of solid trunks, very tall and very strong. It had guardhouses at the corners to cover the sides. So far it looked like a fort from the outside but inside it looked like a small town with farmhouses, stables, barns and sheds. It was surrounded by well-tended farmland with crops and herds of domestic animals and, of course, horses. It had a large harbour filled with boats and in front it had two 18 lb guns for protection. The harbour could receive large seagoing ships to deliver stores and export furs. The ships had to sail round Cape Horn for the East coast and Europe or they had to cross the Pacific Ocean for China.

Inside the fort there was a central two storey building with large reception rooms and smaller offices. Along one wall there was a huge factory for receiving, cleaning and bundling furs. Other smaller support buildings around the sides provided dining area, sleeping accommodation, stores and support services. It was a township.

The office block was very busy and well managed. Tom was told by the man in the reception office at the gate that the senior managers were referred to as "the Gentlemen". They were employed by the Hudson's Bay Company and ruled the fort and its harbour with a strong discipline. The company owned everything.

They were offered a cabin outside the fort and invited to join the communal meals provided for the workforce and visitors. Tom noticed that the Gentlemen convened separately in the central building. He would visit them when he had cleaned up.

They unloaded the horses and mules at the cabin and led them over to the stable area and arranged for them to be taken care of. In the evening they ate in one of the canteens and talked to the other inhabitants. Tom discovered a new world of British, French, American and native men with different experiences and different skills all living in harmony under the order of the Company.

The next morning Tom shaved and used the baths and dug out his European clothes. Then he went to the central offices to introduce himself. He was met by a young Scottish clerk with sandy hair and a formal manner. Tom introduced himself and the clerk had hardly left before the door burst open and an almost identical but bigger and older Gentleman Commissioner appeared. He was ushered into an office, given coffee and almost bled dry with questions. He answered them all. He was given more coffee and plied with more questions. And he answered them again. As the interview progressed, more similar figures arrived to join them and ask more questions. Most of the Company men wore European clothes but it was all a bit haphazard and the clothes were in different states of repair with lots of patches. They invited him to lunch, and he joined them in the big room that he had seen the previous evening. Now the dress code improved slightly with all of the Company men wearing jackets and boots. Of course, the seating was based on seniority with the Factor, the most senior of the Gentlemen, as the Company officials were called, at the head of the table. TK was placed next to him, but the Factor did not dominate the conversation. TK wondered whether they were interested in him or just interested in news of the outside world, whatever the source. At first, he suspected it was the latter but as the meal ended and they moved into a large lounge area the more senior Gentlemen congregated around him and began to ask about his background, his career and, at last, what he was doing there. This sparked further excited conversation about how they had come to establish the fort, how they arranged their business and how they hoped to build it further.

They explained that, until recently, there had been great rivalry in the fur trade, first between two British companies and then between the British and the Americans. The British companies had been forced to amalgamate and the Hudson's Bay Company had prevailed. Their instruction had been to secure a monopoly, and the American competition had been eliminated.

This had been acted out in the context of political rivalry between the French, the British and the Americans. The main aim of the British was to control the Canadian territories. There had been a declaration of war but without any real armies or navies nothing had been achieved and eventually the British were left in control of the Canadian territories and this area, called Oregon.

Before the war the Americans had established a base at Astoria on the coast where the Columbia River joined the Pacific Ocean to support their trade. The British had preferred this base, further inland, to secure their trade by ship with Europe. Now that it had settled down, the American trappers from the Rocky Mountains traded freely with the British and the British had maintained a presence at Astoria to control the entrance to the Columbia River, which they now called Fort George.

Tom explained that he had hoped to travel up to Fort George to take a ship up to the Canadian coast to look for gold. They confirmed that from Fort George he would be able to travel by ship up the coast to Canada, but he might have to wait a long time for the right ship. Also, it could be dangerous. A big ship had been destroyed in the Canadian waters after a conflict with the local natives. However, that had originated in fur trading which was always dangerous. Gold may be a different matter.

Dick and Harry did not like the stuffy cabin that they had been given. They ate grilled salmon at the fort and then rode out to the hills above the fort to make their camp. Tom kept the cabin but joined them quite often. They could sit by open fires and grill their food in peace in the late summer evenings. They stayed at Fort Vancouver for a few days.

Tom was invited to dine with the Gentlemen regularly. It was beginning to dawn on them that Tom had had an impressive military career and an interesting visit to New York, so the questions increased. However, they also went out of their way to explain what he should expect on the next stage of his adventure. On the coast of Canada the mountains were steep and the forests were dense and came down to the sea. Also, the natives were hostile.

From their stories after dinner it was clear that the Gentlemen missed their homeland but were not going to waste the chance to explore all opportunities in this beautiful country and to make their fortunes with the Company here. In particular there was a fascination to find a way home to the Hudson's Bay by travelling up the Columbia River to its source in the north west side of the Canadians Rockies and then to cross over into the Canadian wilderness and to travel by rivers and lakes to the Atlantic. One man had travelled it from East to West, but they wanted an established route using boats. It was a sort of mission. Perhaps just a dream. At present they were confined to the Columbia River. They had a relay of canoes on the navigable stretches of the river and pack horses to move between the navigable stretches and trading posts in between. The canoes were manned by "voyageurs" who were a mixture of French, Canadian, natives and Americans. They prided themselves on their ability to paddle hard in the currents. It was an efficient way of transporting furs down to the fort, but from there the furs had to go by sea. And so did the Gentlemen.

They wished each other luck.

A supply ship from Britain was due any time. Tom might be able to meet it at Fort George to get some idea of what would be involved in the next stage of his journey.

Dick had met up with the voyageurs and declared that he was ready to join one of the canoes. But in the meantime, he was happy to travel two hundred miles downriver on horseback to visit Fort George.

Fort George

It took two days to reach Fort St George on horseback. It was not really much of a fort. It had fairly low, wooden palisades on three sides and was open to the harbour with a low earth and stone wall. Inside there was a fortified building on higher ground and a few smaller cabins. It looked as though it had once been rather more significant.

They were greeted by a stocky grey-bearded American wearing buckskin. He was John Potts. He had been appointed by the Company to manage the fort and to arrange pilotage for ships to cross the bar from the Pacific to the Columbia River. He had a garrison of half a dozen helpers.

At the moment of their arrival he was preoccupied with a slow-motion naval engagement outside the bar. There would be fun and games. He pointed to a neat merchant sloop that was being followed by a larger ketch with guns on its desks like a frigate or, more likely, a big privateer.

"That little sloop is delivering supplies, papers and gold to Fort Vancouver. I was expecting it and would pilot it over the bar. The ketch is after it and I was certainly not expecting it. It looks like a privateer and it is well set up. If the ketch boards the sloop we will lose everything. The tide is too low for either ship to cross the bar, even if it knew the passage. The only hope for the sloop is to go aground and to launch a boat which might make it across the shoals while the waters are quiet. So, if we think very hard or pray very hard, they might get the message. Otherwise, they are lost and the Company property will be lost with them. It's all going to happen very slowly and it might end in a boat race and a fight on the beach."

Tom nodded. Dick had not understood this explanation and Harry waited for a translation that did not come.

Tom said, "I am Tom Kynaston, I have some military experience. Is there anything that we may be able to do to help? Have you got any guns?"

John Potts nodded, "We have a couple of six pounders and a few muskets. It's not much because anything that we lose might be used to attack Fort Vancouver. The garrison will not be much use and I have survived out here by staying out of trouble. If the privateers reach the fort I want to be far away."

Tom laughed, "I was a soldier and I know how to fight. I would appreciate a bit of practice. Let's have a look. My companions are Dick and Harry. They have bows and spears. They might like to earn some guns."

John Potts nodded and led the way to the arms store. The muskets needed a bit of oil but they could be made to work. The bullets fitted and the powder was dry. There was no ammunition for the cannons. Tom went to the harbour to look at them. They were in poor shape and would take hours to make good. He asked John Potts to assemble the garrison. They were good lads and a couple of Americans claimed to be able to shoot well. The others would be the loaders. He told them to bring out all the muskets and ammunition and cleaning materials to get the muskets ready.

There was a gap in the harbour wall and he walked down to the water's edge. It was just over fifty yards to the water. The beach was shingle and the harbour bottom was shingle and shelved to about three feet deep in about ten yards. He found a safe place for the horses behind the wall and gave Dick and Harry a few arrows with heads attached for their bows. He explained about the boat race and the fight.

Sure enough, whether through the power of thought or the power of prayer, the sloop headed for the bar nearest to the south bank of the river. It ground to a halt, the sails were let fly and the ship's boat was lowered. The captain dropped in with satchels and cases and then the crew of about ten joined him. It pushed off and the lug sail was raised. The oars dipped and gained a rhythm.

The ketch could not come any closer. It dropped anchor and lowered a two-masted cutter. There was some delay while a crew scrambled in with their weapons. Clearly, they had not been taken completely by surprise, but it was not completely well ordered. By the time that the cutter pushed off, the sloop's boat was half way to the fort. The cutter raised its sails and the race was on.

John Potts explained that the sloop's boat was half way to safety but the cutter could sail twice as fast. All sorts of factors would come into play – the tide, the wind and the loads. He judged that it would be a close-run thing. Someone was going to be disappointed. If the boat thought that it would be safe when it reached land it would be wrong because the fort had only a small garrison and the cutter had about twenty privateers on board. If the cutter thought that it was in no hurry because the fort was weakly garrisoned and, with their numbers, their job would be easier on land, they might be surprised by some resistance. TK pointed out that he would have some surprises for them. So it was certainly going to be a close-run thing.

It all took place in slow motion. The boat became grounded and the crew had to get out to push it off as the cutter grew closer. Then the cutter had to turn to find deep water and lost the wind. So it went on. The tortoise and the hare. It was beginning to look like a draw. The boat reached the beach first with a slightly easier disembarkation. The captain and two crewmen jumped first with heavy cases and satchels and set off up the gravel beach. It was hard going and they were carrying a lot of weight. The rest of the boat crew started to follow. Then the cutter grounded short of the beach and the privateers jumped into deep water to make their pursuit.

Thus the boat crew, carrying their heavy baggage, were half way to the gap in the embankment when the privateers started their chase over twenty yards behind. They carried cutlasses that looked like cane cutters with handguards. They carried pistols but few shots were fired through the splashing.

"Fire!" TK gave the order at last. The two American marksmen hit their targets well and took up loaded muskets for their next shots. Dick and Harry got one hit with their bows and notched up more arrows. TK aimed the rifle carefully and thought that he had made a hit with the first barrel before taking a snapshot with the second. Privateers kept coming. TK fired both barrels of the pistol and ran to his horse.

"Cease fire!" he shouted and jumped the embankment. Dick and Harry followed. TK thrilled to be using his sabre on horseback once again. This was the first time since Waterloo – well, apart from the pig. He drove the horse forward and slashed and sliced and prodded at the foremost privateers. He was surprised to see them stop and turn so soon. Then he glanced back and saw Dick and Harry at work on horseback with the spears stabbing hard and fast. Then his saddle broke. His instinct told him to roll and roll and he stopped at the legs of a privateer. He hunched and sliced for the inner thigh and felt a gentle blow across his back. He looked up to see Dick smiling down as he withdrew his spear. Harry was riding in the water picking off the stragglers.

The privateers ran for the boat and used the oars for a quick escape. They pulled the stragglers in and rowed away. Harry was a revelation as he followed. It looked as though he was going to board the boat. TK shook his head. You could look forever to find a fighter like that. He had found Hackett and a couple of Smiths and now Harry. He raised his sword and Harry raised his spear in reply.

The butcher's bill at the fort was terrible. Only the captain from the boat would survive. One of his companions with the bags, a big strong man, had been hit with a pistol ball deep inside and would not survive.

Another had taken a cut to the neck and had slowly bled away. The rest of the crew had been picked off with the cutlasses in the battle on the shore and there would be no survivors. The privateers had started with over twenty men but only eight had escaped. And some of them were wounded.

TK, Dick and Harry had cuts to their legs and backs. The wound on TK's back was long but not too deep. The wound to his leg seemed to be more serious. John Potts did a bit of stitching, but Tom, Dick and Harry could not ride. They would have to go up to the fort on the cutter. Harry's horse had a cut on the rump. Not too close to the heart, as they say, and could make the journey back in due course.

TK limped back to the harbour with Dick and Harry and the captain of the sloop. Most of the privateers were dead. Tom, Dick and Harry worked quickly to finish the job.

Suddenly he stopped. "No scalps. No honour."

Dick and Harry grumbled together then nodded. "No honour, no prisoners."

Thankfully, it was quick and clean. He collected the arrows, a few pistols and more cutlasses.

Dick and Harry went to wash down the horses, including the one with the wound. Tom went to meet the sloop captain. He was William Llewelyn. He had sailed from Bristol with stores, papers and gold for the Company. He had saved the papers and gold but he feared that the sloop and the stores were lost. It was his sloop, well actually the bank's. The Company had chartered the ship and the cargo. All in all, his first voyage had not gone well. However, between the bank, the Company and the insurers he had not much to lose. Already he was making plans to take the cutter up to Fort Vancouver. He was a handsome man with dark curly hair and a chipped smile, but he was beaten down with the loss of his ship and crew.

TK said that he would stay with the garrison and the horses until the Company sent up replacements. And so Captain William Llewelyn had left with John Potts and a few of the garrison. TK asked them to drop off the corpses on the ebb tide. They laughed when they realised they would be sending them back to their ship.

It was a fine morning in late summer. Across the estuary the banks of the Columbia River were dark with dense greenery. The river was calm but the bar swirled with currents, tides and side shows.

TK organised the remainder of the garrison to reload the muskets and to keep watch. He did not intend to defend the fort and made plans to evacuate it if necessary. The garrison had plenty of food and some rum so they made themselves comfortable. They slept to the sound of an owl and woke to the sound of the dawn chorus.

TK looked at the wound on Harry's horse and found that John Potts had sewn it up nicely. It was looking healthy.

TK had intended to spend the day cleaning up the six pounders. However, the privateer put on a show. They anchored stern on to the sloop, dropped the sails and ran a heavy line across from their capstan to the sloop. They reversed the process with a line from the capstan of the sloop to the ketch. Then they shifted heavy stores to the downwind side at the stern of the sloop and she began to list. Then they started to pump out the sloop. Finally, they took a rest and watched the bodies go past as they waited for high tide. They worked very hard with good discipline and clearly had a plan.

At high tide they raised the sails on the sloop and pulled them in so that she listed further and TK could see the keel. Then they raised the sail of the ketch as if to sail away. But she did not move. Then, over the water, TK heard singing and stamping as the crew worked the capstans. At last a cloud passed in front of the sun, there was a gust of strong wind and the ketch moved. The stamping got quicker and the sloop also started to move. The sails were changed and the sloop floated upright. A cannon fired from the ketch and the ball fell well short of the fort. And then they sailed away. They had won the sloop and its stores.

TK went back to work on the six pounders and he noticed that his leg wound was looking ugly. Dick told him to put it in the river for a while, so he went for a long swim. Afterwards the wound did not look much better.

Three days later two cutters arrived from Fort Vancouver towing a boat and carrying a new garrison and gold. TK met them with his boot off. The leg was not getting much worse, but it was certainly not getting any better. Apparently salt water and air were not the complete cure. Dick had said that they might have to burn it if did not heal.

John Potts had planned to introduce the senior Gentlemen but instead led TK to the medical chest on the Company cutter and went to work. When he had finished it looked better but felt worse.

"I don't remember inviting you to choose," said John Potts.

The senior Gentleman was very sorry to see that the ships had left. He had hoped to buy the sloop and its cargo for gold.

"We are traders first and last," he said.

The new garrison included some natives like Dick and a couple of French/Canadian/native voyageurs so there was a big reunion.

Captain William, John Potts, Tom and the Gentleman joined together and told their stories.

William had been a junior officer on a ship of the line at the Battle of the Nile. Tom had been a cavalry officer at the Battle of Waterloo. John Potts had been a medical officer on the Tonquin which had established Astoria, and the Gentleman had travelled the full length of the Columbia River and seen the pass across the Continental Divide.

The Company garrison had done well. The two Americans and their four loaders had fired a lot of shots and hit a lot of targets before the ceasefire was called. They were unharmed and would be left at the fort with a couple of more senior Company men to review the defences. Tom, Dick and Harry all had cuts from the cutlasses. Harry had suffered a cut across his backside, Tom had a nasty cut to the calf and another across his back and Dick had a cut on his thigh which was not too deep. The horses had come off worst with cuts to their faces, necks, shoulders and hind quarters, but all could be stitched up.

John Potts had handled the first stage of repairs. Now the Company medic was taking over. He needed to re-stitch Harry's backside and some of the wounds on the horses. In particular, he did not like TK's calf.

They decided to leave the horses to rest and go back to Fort Vancouver on the cutter. It was late summer. The geese and ducks were flying south and clouds were starting to build up on the coastal mountains. John Potts said that soon it would start to rain. First a few showers, then heavier rains until at times it would rain all day on and off until next spring. However, it would stay fine for a few days while they sailed upstream to Fort Vancouver.

They made Harry comfortable on his stomach in the bow of the cutter with Dick in attendance and they enjoyed the sailing experience. Tom, with his leg up, sat between William Llewellyn and John Potts and the senior Gentleman, Angus Browne. The company men crewed both cutters so there was time to talk.

Angus Browne had seen the world. He had started as a deck hand on merchant ships out of Glasgow. He narrowly escaped being pressganged in Glasgow and again in Liverpool. On each occasion the tavern got warning just in time. After that he decided to stay at sea. So he signed on for one-way voyages with different ships to different countries all around the world. At last he had signed on as a mate on a ship carrying furs to Hudson's Bay ready for onward shipment to Britain. From there he had signed on as first mate on a six-month voyage around Cape Horn back to Fort George and Fort Vancouver. Then he got caught up in an artificial war between the British, the Canadians and the Americans.

No country had enough ships or men to fight here in the north-west so there were no battles but the trading became slightly hostile until, far away in Europe, the British drew their customary line on the map and the area came under the joint control of Britain and America. The British forced their rival trading companies to amalgamate to drive the Americans out of business. The Hudson's Bay Company had prevailed. Astoria had become Fort George and the Americans had withdrawn their trapping and trading activities to the east side of the Rocky Mountains. Angus had stayed with the Company and had taken charge of the navigation on the Columbia River. This had led him to explore further and further north as the river took him along the west side of the Rocky Mountains and up into Canada. There he found a pass over an ice field that would lead into the vast wilderness of Canada. So far he had got no further than setting up a trading post just inside the border. He had sailed as far as possible, and then used native canoes carved out of cedar trees and manned by voyageurs who were a mixture of French, Canadian and Native Americans. They took pride in being able to paddle their canoes almost anywhere. They were tough and proud of it. He had established posts along the river and it was now under the Company control for its full length. The next step would be to establish a route across the Canadian wilderness to Hudson's Bay. Men had made the crossing individually but there was no established route with the sort of posts that he had established along the Columbia River. This was his ambition. The Columbia route was used to transport furs downriver.

The Canada route would carry men and messages to Hudson's Bay. He was proud to have become a senior Company Gentleman.

Tom remembered Tony Parson's stories of constant friction between the American trappers and the natives east of the Rockies. And yet, here, in a matter-of-fact way, he was being told of a British project based on trade and co-operation. Now he understood that Dick was a voyageur and that was how he had got his muscles. Dick was comfortable with the British visitors. Also, he had come to an understanding with his father that visitors could come to trade and to buy furs and meat but not to steal them. The British worked well with this arrangement, but the Americans were in conflict. There were two different mind-sets on either side of the Continental Divide.

William Llewellyn was the son of a Welsh merchant. His father had expected him to join the firm but William wanted to join the Royal Navy. So his father spoke to a friend who spoke to a friend who arranged for William to join as a midshipman. He showed a talent for arithmetic and applied this to the skill of navigation. He received commendations that earned him a good reputation and an early promotion.

He was Lieutenant on the Goliath leading the landward column at the Battle of the Nile. Nelson had tracked Napoleon and the French fleet around the Mediterranean and, at last, found them anchored in a defensive formation near Alexandria on the Nile delta. Nelson judged that if the French ships could float at anchor close to the shore the British ships could sail close to the French ships on the landward side. This suited Nelson's tactics perfectly.

His main aim was always to get close and fire broadsides. Nelson had split his fleet and attacked from the seaward side and the landward side. Few French ships escaped. William was beside the wheel of the lead ship on the landward side of the group that took the heaviest fire as they progressed along the line. The last French ship got its guns to bear and scored some hits before the Goliath had completely passed the French line, firing as it went. William was hit across the back by a three-foot splinter and was conveyed back to Greenwich for hospitalization. So, he missed the Battle of Trafalgar. However, he was ready for the Battle of New Orleans and was made commander and placed in charge of the Royal Navy longboats that transferred the British soldiers to attempt the attack on New Orleans. It was intended to keep a last trading foothold on the Mississippi River. The boat part went well but the land battle part failed among the swamps and water courses and William received a glancing blow on the ribs from grapeshot during the evacuation. And so, back to Greenwich for hospitalisation. Peace was declared between the British and the Americans in the same treaty that drew the line between Canada and America on the map in the north-west. The Battle of Waterloo ended the war in Europe and the British soldiers and sailors were looking for work. Britain resumed its aggressive trading methods through the East India Company and the Hudson's Bay Company and recruited the decommissioned personnel.

William was discharged from hospital and from the Royal Navy and went home. His father's business had prospered from the war and he was turning his attention to the trading companies. William could play his part. His father spoke to a friend who spoke to a friend who found him a sloop financed by a loan and insurance from friends of friends and William took a charter with the Hudson's Bay Company to deliver a cargo from Bristol to Fort Vancouver. It was all done in slow motion. The order for supplies was received in London, three months later the cargo would leave Bristol, six months later it would arrive in Fort Vancouver. Normally, it would return and six months later the order for supplies would be received in London.

William had sailed from Bristol with a cargo of supplies for Fort Vancouver including guns, knives and axes for trading with the natives for furs. Also, he carried some gold and some papers and, of course, his charts. He had travelled ten thousand miles and had lost his ship within sight of his destination. But he had rescued the gold, the papers and his precious charts. His shoulders sagged and tears welled in his eyes. He had lost his crew and his friends.

John Potts was a neutral. He tried not to take sides and he tried not to fight. He was born in New York with a rich and indulgent father who gave him a boat and he had grown up sailing boats on the eastern shore. When the British captured New York nothing changed for his father or for John Potts. He sailed on.

There is a sandbar running along the east coast of America from north of New York down to Florida.

Inside the bar is an almost continuous inland waterway. John Potts sailed it according to the seasons. He wintered in the south and spent the summer in the north. He camped and lodged and slept on his boat and he avoided the war.

He made lots of friends among the communities along the water course and got lots of advice about the tides, bars, shoals and currents along the east coast. He had a natural talent and developed a skill for reading the shallow waters. After the war he returned to New York and started to study medicine, but the sea claimed him and he went back to his boat. However, he stayed around New York. His reputation for knowing the waters spread and he was hired by Captain Hawkeye, the harbour master of New York, to pilot ships into the harbour. He helped to save many ships from disaster. And so his skill came to the attention of Mr John Jacob Astor who had a problem. Mr Astor was making his fortune as an international fur trader with his American Fur company. He needed a harbour on the north-west coast of America, in order to ship furs round to the east coast and to China. He proposed that the furs would be transported by the trappers down the Columbia River to his new harbour where they would be cleaned and bailed and readied for shipping. He had identified a suitable location at the mouth of the Columbia River but the river had a notorious bar and Mr Astor made John Potts an offer that was too good to refuse. Mr Astor was equipping a ship called the Tonquin under Captain Jonathan Thorn to build the new harbour and fort. He asked John Potts to join the ship to navigate the bar, select the site for the harbour and pilot merchant ships in and out of the harbour. In return he would receive a large fee, a retainer and a share in the Pacific Fur Company which would be formed for this venture. John Potts had agreed.

Effectively he would be a passenger on the ship. However, Astor would provide copies of all available writings about the north-west. Potts thought he might learn a little about the formal science of navigation from the officers. Actually, early in the voyage, it became clear that Captain Thorn was not going to be much help and was likely to hinder any attempt to enlist the help of his junior officers. However, Potts found a kindred spirit in Robert Holdsworth, the ship's medical officer. Neither was getting on very well with Captain Thorn. Each found the junior officers difficult to approach because they had closed ranks to protect themselves against Captain Thorn. So they were thrown together. It was a mixture of opposites. John Potts was a free spirit with a seafaring talent. Robert was an academic with serious training. However, each had an honesty that bound them. John asked to help with the medical work when accidents occurred. Robert asked about John's experiences on the east coast. But the clincher was the cards. Robert had learned to play during his training. John had never played but was fascinated and learned quickly. It gave them hours of pleasure for over six months as the Tonquin veered across the Atlantic and then up the Pacific for six months.

The arrival at the Columbia River had brought them back to reality quite brutally. John wanted to take a boat to get the feel of the banks and currents. Thorn was impatient. John insisted and was given time but as soon as he said that he thought he had found a route Thorn ordered larger boats to be launched. They drifted off John's line and were capsized in the autumn currents. John organised the rescue and Robert picked up the pieces. Some of the crew could not be saved. They tried again but fear of Captain Thorn drove the boat to cut corners and the result was the same. Death and injury. Finally, John devised a plan, anchoring boats as marker buoys to show the channel. That had worked.

John Potts then spent several days using plumb lines to locate the best harbours. Sometimes they were rejected by the fort builders. Eventually a good harbour was matched with a defensible position and the building of Fort Astoria commenced. After thousands of miles and months at sea they were able to do their jobs. Here Captain Thorn excelled. He organised the transport of the timber for the fort and the construction of a jetty. Within six months it was complete and fully provisioned from the Torquin. But they had no furs. The trappers did not yet know that they should bring their canoes with furs down to the new harbour. Rather than wait, Captain Thorn decided to go up to the Canadian shore to collect some furs before heading north. Robert's contract took him with them. John's contract left him to run the harbour. The Tonquin left, never to be seen again. It had reached Vancouver Island, but Captain Thorn had alienated the natives and, under attack, the crew had blown up the ship. So for Mr Astor and John Potts the venture was not showing a profit and John Potts had lost a dear friend. Eventually word reached the trappers in the Rocky Mountains that Fort Astoria was open for business. The cleaning factory was working, and John Potts was piloting ships in and out and reinforcing the channel. But before his fortune was made the war of 1813 brought chaos. Eventually, the Americans ceded joint control of the Columbia River, Mr Astor's company sold out to the Canadians and the Hudson's Bay Company swept up the lot. John Potts went to work as a pilot for the British. He had not made his fortune.

Working for one side or the other, John Potts had become an expert on the navigation of the Columbia River, the North West shore, and the Vancouver Island channel. There had not been much trading around Vancouver Island but John knew the waters.

Back at Fort Vancouver, late one afternoon, as the rain began to fall, two wagons crawled into the fort. Men, women, and children were walking with the wagons. They were thin, dirty and ragged. Some were ill-shod and others were not shod at all. A horse in the shafts of each cart was being led painfully and slowly forward. A third horse limped behind. The wagons had been emptied along the way. They were the two Scottish families from the east. Tom jumped forward to help but he was too late. The families were taken up by the groups of men and women at the fort to be fed and sheltered. The horses were taken away for food and care. Tom offered to go back down their trail with a trailer but that was already in hand. A gunshot announced that their third horse had been put out of its misery. The families were left to rest overnight. During the next few days, as they recovered, their story emerged. They had travelled uneventfully with Tony Parsons to the south pass. Tony Parsons had handed the New Yorkers to a guide who would take them over the South Pass to California. Tony Parsons had pointed the Scots towards the farming community that was developing to serve the travellers at the pass. Then Tony Parsons had joined a group to travel downriver to St Louis. The Scots had not been welcomed by the other farmers. They did not need any help and they did not need any competition. In fact, they were hostile and did everything possible to disrupt the Scots' attempts to settle, including some acts of sabotage. So they had been forced to pack up and start the one thousand mile trek to Fort Vancouver, where other travellers had told them that the British would welcome more farmers. The final indignity was having to trade for supplies from their tormentors on bad terms.

And now, indeed, they were being welcomed. The future they had dreamed of had become a possibility.

Different worlds opened up. Dick joined the team of Angus Browne as a voyageur for the winter mission up the river to set up posts to bring back furs from the trappers. Harry's wound healed and he went on a boat downstream to Fort George to recover the horses. William Llewellyn and John Potts discussed their position with the Gentlemen of the Company. Both really wanted to leave but neither had made his fortune. Tom's wound had healed at last and he saw an opportunity.

The Gentlemen of the Company had been impressed to hear of Tom's organisation of the defence of Fort George and the repulsion of the privateers. They indicated that they expected to show their thanks. Tom explained that the first step should be to give guns to Dick and Harry. If necessary, he would pay for them. Preferably they should be short military rifles. The Gentlemen said that they would find them and they would be given. Unfortunately, rifles of this type had been in the supplies on the sloop and were now in the hands of the privateers. Insult and injury. But they would honour the deal.

Tom asked about the fate of the cutter. Would William have first claim because he had lost the sloop but had saved the gold and papers? Yes, but the Company militia had played a part in the capture of the cutter and the sloop was chartered by the Company. The Gentlemen gently asked who had possession of the cutter and where it was being harboured and, more tellingly, who else would buy it? TK laughed. They were traders. Very gentlemanly, but traders. TK asked whether a three-way split would be fair. Yes, of course. No question. They were traders but they were fair.

TK smiled and said that he would like his share to be the use of the cutter for six months of summer. William Llewellyn said that he would settle for one third of its value in cash. So, the Company would get the cutter, William Llewellyn would get some cash and Tom would have the use of it for six months in the summer. The Gentlemen nodded, they liked to negotiate a good trade.

Whichever way you looked at it, it was fair. The Company had the cutter at one third of its value. They had to pay one third of the value to William. And they had an interesting trade for the use of the cutter for six months, against one third of its value. They really did like to trade.

Tom had overplayed his hand. He had no use for the cutter unless he had a crew and no use for the crew unless he had investors in his venture. He still had a few small gold coins, but he needed co-investors. John Potts was the key. He could steer the cutter through the treacherous sandbanks and currents of the bar to the Canadian coast and Vancouver Island. William Llewellyn could sail the cutter under the direction of John Potts and could pay to fit it out. Their reward would be gold, if they found it, and Tom proposed equal shares. They both agreed. Neither had prospered from his venture so far. There was a chance to get something out of it at last.

Tom explained that he had been advised to look at any situation where fast streams fell down from high mountains into an estuary or the sea. John Potts had seen the coast and said that he could find those circumstances. The gold was another matter.

There was a long cold wet winter ahead. But they used the time well, in their separate ways.

William fitted out the cutter to Royal Navy standard. As he worked, he realised that the cutter had probably, originally, come from the Royal Navy. And he knew just what was required.

Dick moved out of the cabin to join the voyageurs. He needed to toughen up and the boat crews would get him into shape.

Harry moved out of the cabin to pursue a love interest among the mixed-race families of the voyageurs.

William moved into the cabin with Tom. John was happy to stay in his own cabin and watch events unfold. It could be a long winter, not cold, not hard, just long, and wet.

As it grew warmer and the rain showers diminished, Tom and Harry explored the north coast. They rode up-river opposite Fort George and then turned east along the coast. They could see mountains rising in the west and beneath them, a huge rocky estuary with many inlets.

William had bought, borrowed or stolen everything to fit out the cutter for the voyage. He had brought it up to Royal Navy standards. John Potts had collaborated to provide navigational aids for the shallow waters that they would encounter.

Tom had bled the Company and its Gentlemen dry. He had seen and heard all the reports of expeditions to Vancouver Island and the Canadian shore. He had read everything in the Company library about gold prospecting. And he had borrowed a big, cumbersome, griddle that, he was assured, would separate any gold from rocks and sand and silt. He had also bought lots of cheap guns, knives and axes and a few more beads. The Gentlemen provided every scrap of knowledge and materials that he could need. As the fuller picture of his exploits emerged, they took him into their companionship. He was a pioneer and could help the Company in the next phase of its development. So, they would help him like one of their own. They were traders and saw that if he succeeded now, they would benefit in the future.

So, one early spring morning, John Potts declared that

the time was right to set out across the bar. The rain flow had diminished, and the meltwater had not yet started. They would go up to Fort George and wait for the wind conditions to favour them and then they would be on their way.

At Fort George, TK took the opportunity to review the defences at the Fort. The muskets were all clean and serviceable and the garrison was up to scratch. The six-pounders were clean and in working order. TK took the opportunity to remind the garrison that each man must know his duty. The loads, the rammers, the primers and the firers must know what to do under pressure. In particular, the loaders needed to know when to change from shot to grape to cannister. They would need to practise every day. What else would they be doing?

John Potts eventually said that the conditions were right to cross the bar with least risk. Actually, there was very little risk, they ran through the tide and the current and a gentle wind from astern. They had benefitted from the tide and the current and the wind in harmony, all thanks to John Potts.

John Potts stood short and solid at the bow and signaled the directions. William took the helm and set the course and Tom and Harry set the sails. They all knew that John Potts had worked his magic. He smiled shyly as they gave their thanks.

Beyond the bar they sailed across to the Canadian shore with Vancouver Island to the west. They sailed into a huge estuary with rivers flowing in from all sides. They anchored and rested. They could not see what they were looking for. The mountains were too far away and the rivers were too gentle. There may be gold in these estuaries but not in the concentrations that they were looking for.

They sailed up the west coast of Canada, arriving at possible river mouths entering the channel. They stopped and panned on beaches as they went north. They sailed into estuaries with no beaches. They sailed on north looking for the magic formula where mountains were sending streams cascading to the shore. They panned potential beaches. The gravel deposits were minimal, and they sailed on. They tried every stream and every estuary day after day. Clearly, there were deposits but too small and too far upstream to be worth exploring. Day after day, estuary after estuary, creek after creek, they anchored and panned. The days got longer and the water warmed. And so, the snow melt increased. Always, behind the gravel beaches, the tall, dark green, forests towered impenetrably.

Gold

At last, as the channel between the island and the mainland narrowed, they found a narrow river with rocky shoulders and gravel bars at the mouth. John Potts came alive. They anchored the cutter and paddled the tender to the beach and started panning. Harry shouted first. He had never before seen the speckles that showed in his pan. Was this what they were looking for? Yes, he had found what they were looking for.

They anchored the cutter at the stern and ran a line to a strong birch on the shore. Then they used their gears to pull the cutter onto the beach. They lowered the masts and cleared the decks. At last they unloaded their equipment.

They lit a fire and started to make camp on the shore. They sat all day at the water's edge in the early spring sunshine washing the gravel in the pans and gaining a residue of gold each time. They forgot to eat. They knew that ounces meant dollars and they were producing ounces. At dusk they made a small fire on the beach, dried their clothes and discussed how they would manage the coming days. Clearly, they could sit on the beach and pan the gravel all summer. It would pay the rent but not make their fortunes.

Tom explained that if they could go upstream and create a stilling pond the returns might be greater. John and William understood the theory and they agreed to look for a point to build the dam. They would not go home poor, but they might go home rich.

The next morning, they ate cold food and split into two pairs. Tom and Harry took one side of the river and John and William took the other. The trees at the beach were thin survivors of the winter storms. But very soon, going upriver, they grew bigger and thicker. Pines, firs, birch and cedar all growing closely together. The further up the mountain they progressed, the thicker the trees became, and fewer were the patches of sunlight glinting through.

The swords of the privateers, which they had hoped to trade, proved perfect for hacking a trail along the riverbanks. All day the river ran too fast and too narrow. They went back to the camp and ate cold food and slept without joy. On the second day they were ready to start again when they met the children. They stood by their canoe and watched, ready to escape. Harry went up and sat with them and found common words. He asked Tom for a few beads and they paddled away. Harry explained that they could expect visitors, but they should come in peace.

Later that day, after much hacking, they found a place for the dam. As it descended, the river fell down a high cliff and then widened out through a clearing before narrowing again into a rocky channel. The dam would make a lake but the clearing would be wide enough to form a stilling pond. They would need to camp on the beach but they could build the pond up river and work on the narrow bank.

Tom and Harry took the bows along the river and

Harry killed a deer as it came to the clearing in the evening. There was no point in hiding on the beach, so they lit a big fire and ate well.

The next morning, they took their time and divided the first lot of tools between them to carry up to the clearing. But William looked out over the water and saw canoes approaching. They came fast. They were long and filled with warriors paddling steadily. They had high, fierce prows strikingly painted.

"War canoes," said John Potts.

Tom went to the tin trunk and loaded the pistol and the rifle. He stepped forward with the sword and the rifle.

Harry said, "If fight. Kill chief."

Harry went down to the gravel beach to greet the canoes. Each held over ten warriors. They were well turned out and well-armed, but without guns. Their leader was magnificent. He was tall and strong with decorated buckskin, beads on his chest and a feathered headdress. Tom looked at his long-haired, bearded, dirty and shabby companions and felt that the natives had some advantage. But Harry strode to meet the leader on equal terms. He ignored all of the others. This was to be a meeting between equals. Tom noticed that Harry was carrying his big spear and standing tall. Then he stuck it into the beach and stepped towards the chief with open hands. The chief signalled his warriors to stand back and stepped forward, making the sign of peace.

Harry said, "You are a chief. I am the son of a chief. We do not hide. We come in peace. We come to trade."

"What do you bring?"

"Guns, knives, axes and blankets."

"What do you want?"

"Yellow sand."

"Not furs?"

"No."

"I could kill you and take your guns. Why trade?"

"If you fight, you die first. The gun is ready." And Harry pointed to Tom, standing with the rifle.

"How long will you stay?"

"Until the geese fly south. When we leave, we will give you four guns, ten knives, five axes and six blankets. We will meet you here on the beach, when the geese fly south.

This was the point when it could all go wrong.

"Now give one gun, one knife, one axe and one blanket."

Harry laughed and called for the items. The chief asked again why he should not take them all.

"You try. You die. And you die first. Always, you die first. Send children with fish for beads after five days. Always, after five days. We are at peace, until the geese fly south."

"Very well. Until the geese fly south." And the chief signalled to his warriors to re-embark on the canoes.

William had been devastated by the loss of his ship and his crew. He had worked grimly on the preparation of the cutter and had worked quietly with John Potts on the voyage. He was bigger than average. He had dark curly hair, dark eyes and scars on his face. He could have looked sinister except for his smile. It was crooked and charming. It had been rare.

The construction of the dam caused the change. He

took charge. A difficult construction became easy, and, at last, fun. He designed the construction. He ordered the logs. He supervised the placing of the pillars and the horizontals. He used blocks and tackles. He used levers. The unliftable lifted. The unmovable moved. Ropes swayed over the stream. Hooks on pulleys carried logs. The whole construction became a massive exercise in leverage and gearing swathed in ropes. William was in his element. He was in complete control, absolutely confident and, at last, beginning to smile.

Everyone else sawed and chopped and pushed and pulled with spirit. Quite soon the dam was completed, the lagoon filled, and the stream flowed over and down its course. Then they saw the grin light up and William had joined the team.

They needed to leave the dam for some time for the settling to take effect, so they returned to the beach and the digging and panning.

They found that the deeper gravel produced the most gold. Every ounce counted so they dug deep and worked on with the panning and the ounces filled the churns.

The children arrived with fish. They set the timetable. Every five days good fish for shiny beads. In between they hunted for game with the bows. Alternating game with salmon went very well.

At last the days shortened and the shadows lengthened and it was time to test the stilling pond and the Company's griddle.

With difficulty, they marched the griddle up the narrow track that they had cut between the trees. It twisted and turned to go round huge trunks that they could never fell.

William's system of pullies delivered the buckets into the pond and carried them out. Even so it was cold, wet work and less fun than panning on the beach.

The result was ambiguous. Each bucket produced about three ounces of coarser gold granules. They did not try to pan the buckets. It was either panning on the beach or paddling and griddling at the dam. They divided their efforts. Two panned on the beach and two griddled at the dam. The griddles seemed to be winning but it was less fun than sitting in the sunshine, telling stories on the beach. And it was cold work.

It was a happy time. Day after day they grilled on the beach, either salmon or game. They made jokes, told stories and watched themselves grow rich as the gold mounted. At last the evenings shortened and grew cooler. A few V-formations of geese flew over and they packed up their camp ready to hand over the trade to the natives and sail home.

On the cutter, they cleared up and tied everything down. They left only a small cooking base on the beach. William demanded that the heavy churns must be tightly secured at the centre of the cutter. He supervised the positioning and the securing. Then he checked it all again and demanded improvements.

They bundled up the guns, knives, axes and blankets ready for handover. In the meantime, they continued with the panning and waited for the canoes.

A few days later William called out that the canoes were coming. Tom loaded the rifle and the pistol and picked up his sword. Then, just to be sure, he told John to load Harry's rifle and all the muskets. He told William to stand at the stern of the cutter to be marksman in case of any problem. He went over the different guns and their ammunition with John Potts. He was appointed loader and he may have to load for his life. So, with John as loader and William as marksman at the stern of the cutter, they had guarded against the unpredictable.

John pleaded that the natives must be given every chance to honour the deal peacefully before they were attacked. Tom agreed, but it would be his decision. He and Harry would be facing the warriors. John would be behind the boat. John would do as he was told. He had made his point and he had been heeded. He was satisfied. TK reminded him always to load the rifles first, before the muskets. "Always." As he gave his instructions, TK felt that he sounded like his father, brooking no argument when he had to be obeyed.

"John, you have made your point. Now, do as you are told. Load for your life."

"William, please don't shoot until you hear my call. Then, watch our shoulders. I will be on the left and Harry on the right. Don't let any of the warriors get alongside us or behind us. Harry and I will take care of the front. But if you can get a shot at the chief, kill him."

Harry stood beside him on the beach. The war canoes approached with purpose and landed on the gravel. Their fierce prows sent a message and the warriors, with spears, moved with purpose. The chief stepped off first and then stepped back. A big warrior stepped forward. He was tall, heavily built and had the scars of battle. The warriors from the canoe lined up behind him with the chief among them.

"War canoes, war paint, war champion", said Harry.

TK stepped forward with his hand in the sign of peace. There was silence. The tide rippled on the beach and the birds sang in the trees. But between the warriors and their Visitors, there was silence. The next move would be one of peace or war.

"Guns, knives, axes and blankets," said the champion. There would be no negotiation. "We will take them all."

And he stepped forward with the warriors behind. Too confident. Ready to fight. Ready to kill.

"They fight," said Harry.

"Very fast," said TK, "shock and horror. Hands and faces. Fast."

Harry laughed. They may have heard the warning, but it was lost in the sing as the scabbard fell away from the dark sword. TK stepped forward. The champion was unprepared, but he pushed forward confidently, with his large spear. TK stepped aside and hit the spear hand with the back of his sword. He stepped forward, rose up, spun on his toes and cut the champion's head off. The champion's face was still in shock when it hit the gravel.

"Shock and horror!" he roared, but without much parade ground practice, it came out a bit feeble.

Harry bellowed his nation's war cry and the warriors hesitated. TK slashed at faces and across eyes until he felt his lungs would burst and his arm would drop. Harry stabbed for arteries on the neck, spurting blood. The front rank turned away, slashed and spurting, and the second rank fell back in horror, and ran.

TK's victims sat butchered in the canoes. Harry's victims lay dead on the beach. William's victims lay dead or dying on the beach or in the canoes. The chief lay in a flapping crumpled bundle of feathers, beads and blood.

Harry picked up the champion's head, slashed off his scalp and threw the skull into a canoe. TK worked quickly to finish off the rest of the warriors before Harry could get to them with his knife. But Harry beat him to the Chief. His head joined the champion's in the canoe.

As they sat on the beach watching the canoes depart, TK said to John Potts, "John, if I had been wrong, a few innocent warriors would have died. If you had been wrong, we would all have died. Shock and horror, John, was our only chance."

John shook his head. Happy to be alive.

The Return

They decided to stay for a few days to heal a few small wounds and top up the churns. They did not expect a return attack, but they kept a lookout day and night and kept the guns loaded. At last they were ready to go.

William's anchor rope at the stern was loaded with pulleys and the cutter re-floated effortlessly as they pulled in the anchor rope.

As they left, TK looked back at the waterfalls and the late sun lighted them with silver. Then, above the highest waterfall, against a cliff he saw a small sharp glint of gold.

William and John had no concern about sailing at night and there would be good moonlight. The wind would be on the port bow when they reached the open water and it would be an easy day's sailing until they turned for the Columbia River. So, two days from home, in the sound there was a good wind and they sailed close-hauled but without the need to tack. They relaxed.

At about 2am they hit the log. The impact was shocking. William was at the helm. He stopped the boat and they saw parts of the submerged pine trunk and its roots between the waves. Quite soon, water seeped up between the footboards. William put the cutter about very gently and they set sail to run east before the wind. They lifted the boards and started to bail. The level did not go down, in fact, it seemed to be going up. John took the helm and William found the pump and set it up. Two men pumping was easier than three men bailing. Even so, the level continued to rise. The rise was slower but it was persistent. But, they could sustain this level of pumping for hours. Even so, they were in constant danger because any sudden turn could cause a capsize. The higher the level, the greater the risk. And eventually they would be flooded.

Tom said that he had seen a huge estuary on the north coast when he and Harry had ridden out to explore. John said that he had heard about it. But where was it? William reduced sail so that they would not pass it in the night.

Now they had to choose. With reduced sail and slower speed the boat was wallowing badly. And still the water level was rising and the risk of capsize was increasing. William explained that they could continue and hope that they could find the estuary before they sank. Or they could dump the gold and maximise their chance of survival. Tom asked whether they could buy a little extra time in stages by dropping one churn at a time. William smiled. "I thought you might ask. We would need to dump two churns at a time to retain the balance. We would need to pump hard to keep below the present level. There is great risk, but I know that you will not give up your treasure easily. So, two churns at a time, and watch the water level."

So, they dumped and pumped and wallowed downwind until dawn. William's strategy was right. Only a couple of hours after dawn when they increased sail, the boat became more stable and they saw signs of the estuary. The sea got dirtier with silt. Bits of vegetation and timber appeared, and small currents showed as the river pushed back against the sea.

The bay was far wider than anyone had expected. It was almost the same as being in the sound. William made his turns gently and looked for an inlet with a sheltered beach. Despite the vast area, it took a long time to find what he was looking for. All the time, he was having to control the sail so that the new wind direction would not heel the boat. Progress was slow. The weather held fair, but clouds started to build in the west. One good squall could sink them. He could not be too choosy. But he could not find what he was looking for.

By afternoon, he was becoming desperate when, after twelve hours of pumping and scanning, he spotted a possibility. Even then, he could only creep forward with a tiny sail as they sounded the depths. The depth held good and William sighed with relief as they approached the beach. He dropped the stern anchor far out as they approached, and they ground onto the beach. At last they realised what William had been looking for. The beach was quite short and there were trees behind to pull against. All they had to do was secure the cutter. No, the job had just begun. They had to cut trees to allow the cutter to be rolled up the beach. They had to install blocks and pulleys with ropes to drag it up.

It was getting dark when the rolling started. Even then, they had not finished. William demanded that they keep pulling until high tide. Another three hours. Then, they managed to eat and rest at last. As they rested TK explained that they were roughly two or three days' march north of Fort Vancouver. He guessed that it could take ten days to make the march, assemble a repair crew and, with John's help, sail round to start the repair.

William told them to wait. As the tide went down, they could see the water draining from the cutter. At low tide they would see the extent of the damage and then they could make a decision. Nobody argued.

At low tide they saw that a single strip of the clinker built hull had been dislodged. The gap was extensive. But the damage was slight. William organised the repositioning, the hammering, and the nailing to the bulwark.

Then a lot of tar, boiled on the beach. As the tide came in, he said that the cutter was ready to sail. When they reached the top of the tide nobody was arguing with William when he released the bowlines and hauled on the anchor lines with all its gearing and the cutter slid back into the water. They hauled up the anchor and secured it and they were ready to sail. And so, they sailed back into the sound, against its winds and tides. On every tack, William remembered the weight of the churns and turned gently. At last they reached the Pacific Ocean. It was hard sailing but now they could turn for the Columbia River.

At the bar, John anchored for day after day until the wind and the current and the tide were aligned, and then they sailed over the bar, into the Columbia River and up to Fort Vancouver. John Potts had done his job.

When, at last, they docked at Fort Vancouver and relaxed after their adventure, Tom said, "So, William, when you were preparing the cutter with the nails and pots of tar, did you consider the devastating effect of a bow chaser charged with cannister?"

William smiled gently and said, "Well, boyo, we survived without the bow chaser, but you can never have too much tar." And that special grin was back to stay.

The Gentlemen welcomed Tom, William, and John into the central hall for meals and into the enclaves for gossip.

Throughout the adventure, Harry had bailed and pumped; chopped and pulled in grim silence. He sensed the relief when the cutter floated off the beach. The others knew how hard he had worked and how much they owed him. They shook his hand and patted his broad back. Now, it was time to go and rest among his own kind.

Harry rode down to the voyageurs to look for Dick. But Dick was dead. Running down river, his canoe had capsized in the rapids, his head had hit a rock and when he washed up in the shallows, he had drowned.

Harry went into mourning and could not be consoled by anyone. He sat in the cabin and allowed Tom in with food. Otherwise he sat alone.

Time stood still. Tom would not move until Harry rejoined.

In the meantime, perhaps not surprisingly, the Company could trade in gold. They put the churns through more filters and then, because they were traders, they offered a price. Tom pretended to look around for any alternative offers and agreed. "Certainly". They gave him some gold coins and a piece of paper.

At last, Harry re-emerged.

Tom, William, and John agreed that Harry's share must be held on behalf of his nation. Tom and William expected to travel east. Harry expected to return to his nation. John was in no hurry and wanted to stay in Fort Vancouver for the time being. Tom, Harry and William would travel east together.

The ounces from the pans and the griddles had built up into pounds and the pounds had built up into a substantial amount.

It was not a great fortune. However, Tom would be able to redeem his mortgage, but he would not be able to end the lease. William would be able to pay his debts but could not replace his ship and crew. John Potts could buy his cutter but could not make an offer for a partnership in the Company. Harry did not understand the Trust but believed that one day, it could buy a lot of guns and wives.

Tom explained all this, and they agreed that the adventure had been worthwhile.

Then Tom said, "As we left, I saw where the main gold seam is located. It will be difficult to reach but the rewards will be far greater next time, if we return. Can we agree that no-one will mention the location for two years and that, all being well, we will return?"

John Potts turned a little pale, but they had become a team and they carried him along with their agreement.

Tom said "We will need some help. How do you climb a waterfall? William said, "With difficulty. Actually, you do not climb the waterfall, you climb the cliffs. They do it in North Wales. We will need one or two climbers."

"Now", said Tom, "I want to return to England. The Gentlemen tell me that there is a South Pass beyond the Snake River and I will go that way. I must go soon, before winter sets in on the prairie. Who would like to come?"

Harry said that he would like to go as far as the winter camp. William said that he would like to travel to the east coast.

John hesitated and then said, "No, I'm a sailor." William saw the irony and laughed.

John would make his own arrangements with the Company.

South Pass

They kitted William out with full-length boots, bandages for his knees and double underwear with more bandages and a Spanish saddle with a pommel for balance and extra blankets on the seat. He was a bundle. He could not ride but he could travel.

They set off with extra horses and the mules, all carrying food for the men and animals. The Scots had treated the mules well and they were ready to trot on.

They would need to travel over one thousand miles. At fifty easy miles per day, it would take twenty days. Tom hoped for less. On the first day, they travelled forty miles and William's defences worked well. He was tired and stiff, but he had no sores.

They ate cold meat, eggs, cheese, and bread. They slept on buffalo skins. The next day they travelled fifty miles. William dozed towards the end, but he emerged stiff and tired but still without sores.

The next day they repackaged him, propped him in his saddle, and they travelled sixty miles. William stepped out of the saddle unaided. They were on their way.

And so, they rolled forward. The weight of food for men and animals was lightening and their pace quickened. One horse went lame and had to be set free. The other horses and mules shared the extra weight and the pace steadied. Even so, they were ahead of time when they reached the South Pass.

The South Pass was a high shallow saddle between the towering mountains to north and south. It was grassland and an easy passage, far different from the mountainous routes across the northern Rockies.

Tom saw neat farms with good houses and barns, and well-tended animals. Were these the people who had shunned the Scottish farmers?

At the pass, two men rode out in front of them and called for them to stop. They were well turned-out, one middle-aged and one a little younger. They had guns. They rode forward and offered food, shelter, wine or spirits, and even girls if that took your fancy. Tom rode up to him and thanked him, but said that they wanted to make haste.

"Very well, gentlemen, that will be five dollars each for your passage."

Tom whispered to Harry to take the gun from the young man. Harry said "certainly". Then Tom rode forward and took a drink from his canteen. He rode up close to the man and squirted into the lock of his gun. Then he grabbed the barrel of the gun, twisted through the thumbs and lifted it off him. The boy was wondering how to respond when Harry barged into him and lifted his gun. It discharged into the air as Harry took it away. They rode on.

After a few miles they stopped, and Harry put the guns into his pack.

Tom said to Harry, "You said, 'Certainly.'"

Harry said, "Yes, certainly."

And so, they rode on. They followed the Sweetwater River and then turned north. They were heading for the

Dutch settlement at last.

There was frost on their buffalo blankets and on the grass in the mornings, and the animals needed extra food at night and a few more oats in the morning. But they were almost there.

The settlement was transformed. Fields had been laid out, harvested, and prepared for the next season. Animals grazed on the pastures, stacks had been built in the fields and cattle lowed and steamed in the barns.

All seemed well, but Tom did not know if his trade with Harry's father had contributed. He did not know if the Jans would remember him kindly.

The smiles eased his concern and the welcoming hands helping them from their horses and leading them to the central building was a joyful relief. He stood with Harry, expecting to introduce him, but they remembered him and welcomed him.

Then he introduced William. The blonde girls liked the look of William but when Beth saw him, they did not stand a chance. Tom had never seen such instant attraction. William was lost. She took him to the big table, sat him down, brought him food and started the conversation that would last forever.

Tom went to look after Harry. But Harry was being looked after very nicely. The blonde girls had found him and were thrilled to find that he now spoke English. So, Tom sat down with the Jans and talked about the settlement. They explained that Harry's nation was providing protection and trading produce for meat. Also, an army fort on the River Plate was buying produce and sending patrols. They were settling well.

A Janette visited him in the night and he never knew which one.

The next day Tom helped Harry load the horses with all the guns and Dick's roll.

He said, "Thank you. My regards to your father, and give him these arrows. And could you please send down two good horses for my journey east."

"Certainly."

Tom laughed and Harry laughed. "Certainly."

Later, Beth emerged and led out H2. Tom hopped on and was thrilled at the movement. He rode her along the river towards the mountains through the early frost. It was beautiful. He forced himself to turn back. He understood that he must leave soon to run ahead of the arrival of winter in the east.

Back to New York

He rested, ate too much, enjoyed the visit of the Janets, but really needed to leave.

On time, Harry arrived with three good horses, saddled and ready to go. He chose his clothes for the ride. More wool and less buckskin above the waist. He bagged up feed and twisted up hay for the horses. The mules would stay. All four were reunited. Mules had become a special feature of the settlement.

The settlers gave him food that would stage him through his journey. The last stage was hard biscuits and hard cheese and, as a last resort, if he was walking, dried meat. And they sent him on his way.

He mounted H2 and headed south-east for the army fort on the river. It was all rather formal. He passed on news from the settlement, particularly regarding stores available for sale. He had a good meal and a good bed. There was no news of problems along the river. He bought bread and eggs and went on his way.

After a few days he came to the river crossing at the Great Missouri. Traffic was light and he got an easy crossing. He asked about hospitality.

The fort on the Missouri had not improved and St Louis was just too big and too much trouble. So, he set off alone for over one thousand miles of travel.

It was early winter. The natives had moved to their winter lodgings and there were no travellers going west.

He was glad of the buffalo robe at night. If game presented itself, he picked it off but this wasted time gathering wood for cooking so he usually left it. When he cooked the game, he dried the meat and rode on.

He swam the Mississippi holding the tin box and the spare ammunition high. It was an easy crossing.

He rode on and the food for the horses grew low and he was eating hard cheese and hard biscuits when the dead grassland gave way to shrubs, and then light woodland and, at last, the settlement on the river. The first snows were falling as he arrived.

He rode to Old Tom's livery and was relieved to see that not much had changed.

"Well, I was not sure whether I would ever see you again. Did you reach the Pacific?" "Yes, it's just as big as they say. Can you take care of the horses and let me sleep in the hay?"

"No. The horses will be fine, but you will sleep at my house and we will eat at the inn."

At the inn in winter they still roasted out of doors on the great spit under big metal covers, but the meat was served on long tables in the barn. Given a choice, Tom would have hoped for pork. He would never have dreamed of lamb. Wonderful. But where had it come from?

Old friends and friends of friends joined them, and the exchange of news was exhilarating. In turn they were amazed at his stories of the Gentlemen of the HBC and the west coast. And, yes, he had found gold and the HBC had care of it. John Lewis was delighted that H2 had travelled four thousand miles on his shoes. He would visit Old Tom to inspect and renew. Old Tom agreed the arrangements for the horses, in particular special care for H2. He gave Tom a good breakfast and drove him to the ferry.

At the Plymouth Inn, Tom redeemed his semi-respectable clothes and handed in the debris of his voyage for repair and/or destruction. It was a strange mixture of cotton, wool, whipcord, buckskin, rough leather and fine leather, all the worst for wear.

The team heard that he was back and came to the inn. Not much had changed in New York. Miss Finch was still holding out but weakening. Ben Horseman had not yet found the right mix of face, flare and fortune for a proposal. Alan Alexander had started a long campaign to manoeuvre Judge McMillan's daughter into submission.

Stories had filtered back about Tom's adventures on the voyage west. He filled them in about Fort Vancouver, the Columbia River, and the Hudson's Bay Company. And yes, he had found gold.

Tom arranged to go with Ben Horseman to the bank to register the HBC papers. Adam Hillstrider found him a berth on a big ship bound for Bristol in two days. He just made it. He waved from the rail to his dear friends and set sail for home.

The passengers' berths were comfortable, and they dined with the captain each night. They were a mixture of Americans and British. Tom was surprised to find how formal and conscious of their social status the Americans were. Perhaps the British brought the worst out in them. Not only did everyone want to set out their bona fides and not only was it clear that they were exaggerating, but they clearly encouraged each other in the exaggeration. By the end of the voyage Tom's small farms would have become a great estate and he would have become a lord of the manor, without saying a word. This was their world, but it was not his.

Christmas dinner would be served on board. The captain promised to push the boat out. And it was really very good. Appetizers, beef, plum pudding and delicacies, all served with wine and spirits. Lots of toasts and lots of jokes.

The children became over-excited and Tom organised a game of hide and seek to calm them down. Keeping quiet to avoid discovery did the trick. Tom remembered Lucy, heading west.

The adults shyly put on a few performances. Tom had no instrument, he could not sing, and he could not dance. The relationship between the music and the steps was way beyond him. But he remembered a few riddles and one or two beat the other guests, to his surprise.

It was stuffy below decks. Sleeping was difficult, being interrupted by sounds of passions aroused and passions rejected. At last, he slept.

The wind from the west drove them home fast and easy.

England

The trap pulled up at the farmhouse in Dorset. It was late afternoon, in winter. The cattle sheds were lowing and steaming. The stables were blowing and munching.

Elizabeth met him at the door. She was sorry that Nell had disappeared. Yes, they had got his message. Anyway, come in.

The maid led him to his room with a fire and brought in jugs of hot water to fill the washbasins. Elizabeth was sure that Nell could not be far away.

Tom's joy at arriving sank, and he sat on the bed. He had come a long way and he had written letters and he had expected better. He sat in despair.

Then she stepped out of the wardrobe. His heart leapt and melted. He surrendered and she took him gently to bed. Then he asserted himself and she surrendered. Then, as always, they found their rhythm. Crescendo followed crescendo and climax followed climax.

By breakfast, order was restored. Hounds were meeting locally, and it was their duty to meet. The last time he had jumped had been at Astoria and he was thrilled to be back in the saddle taking fences. They had a good day and he did not fall off over the fences.

Tea was served at the farm. Many had heard of Tom's exploits in Europe, but they could only guess at the American adventures. He was guest of honour.

When they were alone and began to relax, Tom laid out his thoughts. It was not yet a plan. Other people would need to agree. But it could be a way forward.

First, he would like to go to London to buy clothes and some guns and to manage his finances. Then he would like to go to Shropshire to redeem his loan and review the management of his properties. Also, he would like to look up some old friends. Then, depending on how his plans were being received, he may need to go to Wales.

Nell gently pointed out that he had been away for over a year. So, unless she was included in his plans, he should plan for a future alone. So, he asked her to marry him. And she refused. Then he explained that he was attracted to return to America, partly to make his fortune in gold, but also because of all the freedoms that it offered. Would she go with him?

And she said, "Yes."

Very well, would she like to come to London?

"No thank you."

Would she like to come to Shropshire and stay with Lady Anne?

"Yes."

A joint Wales visit, in dead of winter, seemed to be out of the question.

"Very well, the next stage would be to sail for America to collect some gold and gain some freedom. Would you join me?"

And Nell said, "Yes."

Elizabeth said that she would go with Nell. "The farm is fun, but America could be just wild."

In London, Tom found Otto living in the barracks on

half pay, unable to pay his gambling debts, ashamed to visit Elizabeth, and desperate to escape. All very well, but would he be able to dig? Tom did not mention the return to America. But Otto had been a good friend after a bad start and Tom would like to return some favours.

The gun shop in St James confirmed that they would start making three new rifles and more ammunition immediately. It would take a month. Percussion cap guns were becoming fashionable and the American story would be persuasive.

The bank knew the HBC and would honour the Company's papers and provide credit. They would arrange redemption of his mortgage. The amount outstanding was less than he had expected. The bank explained that the rent on his properties had been increased and the repayments had gone up quite a lot in recent months. So, with the mortgage paid off and with the increased rental income and the Company deposit, he was quite well off, but homeless and restless. Perhaps one day, when the lease expired, he could think about home. But with the prospect of taking Nell to America, and no money problems, it did not seem important.

He visited the Guild of Goldsmiths. They directed him to a firm of geologists who explained how gold formed in rock strata. They explained how it could be exposed by fast-flowing streams carrying stones and wearing it away over thousands of years. They explained that once the gold seam had been found, the gold could be easily extracted with pickaxes and chisels. They confirmed that the stilling pond should be building up deposits if you took the time to pan for them. Many men would risk their lives for that sort of return. Tom smiled.

They pointed him towards the British society for organising mountaineering holidays. This was a new adventure following peace in Europe. They were particularly interested in the excitement for climbing in the Alps. Through their members, they had heard of a Swiss climber based in Snowdonia who was not happy. Apparently, he had been a guide with one of the British teams in the Alps and had become romantically involved with one of the servants on the British team. He had returned with her to her home in North Wales, but it had not gone well. One member of the society was based at a manor in Snowdonia where he co-ordinated guided tours and mountain rescues. He may be able to provide more details.

Tom spent time at the British Museum library. It was a dark place. Dark wood holding dark books to be read at dark tables in the semi-darkness of oil lamps. All was supervised by men in dark suits and spectacles. They had information about HSBC's proposed expeditions to travel up the Columbia River to the Continental Divide and to travel from there to Hudson's Bay. This was fascinating but not really relevant to his purpose. In particular, they were interested in the fur trade, and he was not. The British had fought and bargained for control of Canada, and shared control of Oregon but, apart from the business of HBC, they had little to show for it. The only benefit that they could recognise was domination of the fur trade and that was enough.

He returned to Dorset and reset the records for lovemaking but, of course, these were unrecorded. And he spent a day out hunting on a good horse that went lame. So much for hunting in Dorset.

He received a reply from Lady Anne, who said that she would be pleased to receive Tom and his two lady companions. So, they set off in a carriage on the muddy winter roads. It was slow and grim, and the inns were bad.

Lady Anne greeted them with big fires, roast meat, good wine and the promise of good hunting.

Tom went to see Kate and her husband. The practice was doing well, and the family was increasing. They had not been sure that they would see him again. Even so, they had kept his affairs in good order.

Tom explained that he had seen the bank and arranged to pay off the mortgage. It had been less than he had expected.

"Ah yes," said Kate. "We heard that Lord Darling had boasted of getting a bargain. We looked around to see where else he could go and couldn't see anywhere suitable, so we doubled his rent. He blustered a bit, looked around to see where else he could go, thought about it and agreed. We have increased our fees accordingly."

Tom laughed. Who would have guessed?

Lady Anne kept her promise regarding the hunting and Tom was reunited with Smith's grey mare. Lord Darling thought that his management of the hunt was under scrutiny and loaned out two good horses for Nell and Elizabeth. He laid on a superb day out. Then he laid on a joyful supper party with all their old friends and Lady Anne as guest of honour. Lord Darling was not bitter about the rent increase. He even gave Tom Smith's grey mare on extended loan.

Tom went to look up Hackett and Smith. Hackett was called Mark Edward Hackett. He was living on half pay, smouldering in the local society, too poor to be acknowledged as a gentleman, unable to vent his fury in battle, and likely to explode at any time.

Hackett had been the son of a wealthy surgeon. He had helped his father in his profession. This involved moving bodies and body parts for experiments in the practice. More and more the practice involved more and more body parts and more and more actual bodies. Fresher and fresher. His father's practice had moved from surgery to trading in bodies and body parts so that this became his main business. At last, word started to spread, until it was suggested that one body had not been dead before it was passed into the trade. Hackett's father did not wait for charges and fled, as an innocent man, to South Africa. There he would be beyond the social rumour mill and the arm of the law. Hackett's mother had bought him a commission in the army to get him out of the way. In the army he was an officer, but he wanted to be just "Hackett". His career in the army had resembled a game of snakes and ladders. Brilliant organisation, fighting, and leadership qualities brought promotion. But this had been followed by demotion and transfers for stubborn insubordination. He would not take a step back. At last he had been offered to TK and the easy relations backed up by absolute obedience to orders and special fighting methods had bound him into the team.

When Tom found him he was in his cottage reading a book. There were books everywhere. They had been his salvation.

Hackett said, "Yes." Here was a chance to ride with his old leader and to find his fortune.

So, he said, "Yes."

TK asked about Smith. Hackett shook his head. Smith had been hanged. "First he got drunk. Then he got violent. Then he got arrested. Then he fought his way out of prison. Then he was hanged."

TK sent Hackett down to Ironbridge to buy more arrow heads. Then to take some money to Mrs Smith. Finally to come to a small Inn in Shrewsbury. Tom would meet him there to travel on to Liverpool.

Lady Anne was delighted with her visitors. She loved Nell's reckless humour and she gradually warmed to Elizabeth's ironic hauteur. She told them they could stay as long as they wished, and she would arrange for them to go hunting as often as they wished.

Snowdonia was going to be a challenge. Tom had written ahead to a local landowner and good manners required that they should receive him, one way or the other. But his reception in the local villages would be another matter.

The next day he set off for Wales. He visited Robert and put in an order for more arrows. Robert asked him to stay and was amazed at the toned-down stories of the use of the bow on the Atlantic and in America.

Robert's house in winter was a joy. A huge fire in the kitchen set the tone. And there was lamb on the menu.

"How many has the bow killed?" Robert asked. Tom

started to count on his fingers and then pretended to take off his boots. Robert was delighted. He was also fascinated to hear that American natives straightened the horns of rams in boiling water to make bows.

The landowner was Charles Davies. He lived in the style of squires in Shropshire and Cheshire and was delighted to receive company of the same sort in Wales. He wined and dined Tom most hospitably. More importantly, he told him about the people of Snowdonia. They were passionate about their climbing and mountain rescue achievements. They took money from visitors who wanted to climb in summer. But they were a closed group. They looked after each other through the grim cold of winter, remembering misadventures of visitors of the summer. And they had only contempt for the English.

The man Tom had been told about was Jean-Claud. He had been a climber in the Swiss Alps. He had been fascinated by a Welsh servant with a British climbing team staying in some style as they were led up the climbs of the Alps. It was a holiday romance. She was pretty and bold. He was a local hero. He had returned with them, lured by his new love and the promise that he would be received as a hero in Snowdonia.

Certainly, the local climbers welcomed him and learned from him but did not take him into their Welsh-speaking group.

His new wife brought in her mother and spoke only Welsh in the house. After a few months she started to beat him. And it had gone on and got worse. He had tried to escape but had been dragged back by her brothers.

Every night he sat alone in the local inn in the local village. Charles Davies gave Tom the details. He would need to make his approach in the evening. Then it would be a long ride back to the manor.

The village was next to a slate quarry by the coast. On that winter day Tom saw a grey sky descending into a grey sea washing up on a grey shore with grey buildings and grey hills. He wondered how it would look in the summer when the flowers were out, and the butterflies were adding their colour.

He found the inn, which was no more than one of several grey stone cottages. He pushed open the door. And it was grey. Grey with tobacco smoke. He stepped in and a grey dog launched itself at him but fell back and slunk under a table on a growl from out of the smoke. Tom relaxed his hold on his knife and asked for Jean-Claud. He was given a nod and realised that he could have guessed. Jean-Claud sat in a corner, miserable and alone with flat beer among the lilt and laughter of the Welsh language around him. He was short, muscular, and lean, and he had a black eye.

Tom sat down. He offered to speak good English or poor French. JC opted for English. His alpine customers had spoken English and it was a defiance against the Welsh all around him.

Tom explained that he wanted to extract gold from a waterfall on a high cliff in the Canadian mountains. There would be a three thousand mile voyage by ship and a three thousand mile journey by horse and trailer across the American plains. It would take a whole summer to reach the waterfall in the cliffs. He would make more money than he had ever dreamt of.

However, he might be killed by hostile conditions or hostile natives. Most importantly, he would need to make the climb.

Until Tom mentioned the climb, JC had stayed unmoved. Then he smiled and said, "Oui."

Tom offered to take him away there and then. And he said, "Oui."

So, Tom put him on the back of the grey mare, and they rode away. They hired a Welsh cob with a trailer out of hours in the Welsh night at double the usual rate. Business was business. They picked up JC's ropes and equipment that almost filled the trailer and rode away. They were followed by shouts and threats, fully extending the limits of the Welsh language as they rode into the night. They did not stop at the manor and were long gone when the Welsh family turned up. They slept on the trailer among the ropes.

At Chester they rested in a hotel, had dinner and got cleaned up. They bought clothes for JC in the town and set off. They talked of mountains and horse patrols. Perhaps each understood half of the other's story. But each knew that the other had a story to tell.

They came to the village on the Severn the next day. There was room at the inn. Well, more precisely, in the barn. But the food and kindness made it a haven for JC. In particular, he was welcomed in the back room to exchange stories. At the Grange Nell, Elizabeth, and Lady Anne were having a fine time. Invitations were pouring in and they had become known as the best of company among the squirarchy and the hunt community.

Tom joined in whenever he could, but it was the ladies that were in demand.

Tom met up with Kate and her husband. The debts were cleared, and he arranged for the rents to be accumulated. As he had planned his return to the gold seam in Canada, he had seen it as an opportunity to put all financial problems behind him, make his fortune and start a new life. He had never spelled it out, but now, as he put his affairs in order, it fell into place. If he repossessed the manor, he would have the house but no income. If he took the rents, he would not have a home. So, his opportunity lay in Canada. He knew what he had to do. He had a purpose and it thrilled him. He arranged a monthly allowance to be paid to Smith's mother. And he made a Will. Had he had a glimpse of mortality as he set off again for the New World? Or was he just tying up loose ends?

Tom sent word to Otto to collect the rifles and ammunition, to settle the affairs at the Dorset farmhouse, and to come on up to Shrewsbury.

Tom met up with Otto and Hackett at the hotel in Shrewsbury. He arranged to meet them again at the hotel in Chester. Tom was not sure that the Severn community was quite ready to have this tall, arrogant Guards officer among them. However, he was sure that on the journey, Elizabeth would mock him down to earth.

Tom spent some time with Lady Anne. They both knew that they may never meet again. He owed her so much.

The team at the inn was a different matter. They fully expected him to survive and return with more adventures to recount. They made the offer of one last night out in the woods before he left. He wanted to go and it was his duty to go. So, he had to go.

So much had changed since they took him in when he ran away from school. He was now a colonel in His Majesty's Army. He wondered whether a colonel could be hanged for poaching, and laughed. Then he realised that on a bad day in a bad court he probably could. But this was different. They would be on home ground and farm animals would be off the menu.

He took the bow and the team led him to shoot a fallow dear. He was pleased to show them the bow in action. And, also, the knife.

Sure enough the game played out. The game keeper heard them first and moved away. Then they heard him and stalked him. At last he waved and turned for home. His parcel would be delivered in the next couple of days.

The team were so pleased to have had him back. The Right Hand ("the hammer") carried the dear. The Left Hand ("the tongs") insisted on carrying the bow. And they went to their den and talked all night.

They all met up at the hotel in Chester and set off for Liverpool. They stayed at the best hotel in the harbour. This was becoming an expensive expedition.

Tom went to the inn on the harbour to meet the sea captains. Captain John Finch was not there, but stories of his adventures were well-known. The captains were pleased to meet the famous TK. He was directed to a ship bound for New York and got berths for the whole team. They were on their way.

Tom's funds were running low. However, there was a

bit of rent in the bank in England and there would be a bit of pirate money in New York, so they should make it to Fort Vancouver.

America

Nell was seasick and so was JC. There were not really any remedies, just water and advice to look at the horizon. It was winter and their only hope was for calm seas in the topics. Eventually, they started to settle and the dead calm of mid-Atlantic finally got them on their feet. The ship's doctors had insisted they had water available day and night and were never left alone. Seasickness could be a nuisance but with dehydration it could be fatal. The drying of the brain made the crazy seem logical, like getting off the ship to avoid the rolling. But after a few days the sun came out and the sea calmed, and the patients sat on deck and watched the horizon. They began to recover. When Nell asked for sherry they rejoiced.

Tom had asked Hackett to deal with Otto if he tried to take liberties with Elizabeth. One day Otto trapped her below decks and started to support his verbal case with a few contacts. A touch, a stroke, building up to an arm around the shoulders. Hackett gently took him by the balls and gave a squeeze. He could have torn them of with his talons, but a squeeze was enough. Thereafter, Elizabeth was safe from any unwanted attentions. But she still loved Otto's company.

So, the team arriving in New York comprised Tom, Nell, Elisabeth, Hackett, Otto and Jean-Claude.

Tom's reunion with the New York team became a

party. The Plymouth Inn became the hub of the reunion. Adam Hillstrider, Ben Horseman, Allan Alexander and David Daniels came to visit. They met in a private room. Tom knew everyone and started with some introductions. Soon they were introducing themselves. All the New Yorkers wanted to meet Nell and Elisabeth. English ladies in New York were special so they were very busy. Ben Horseman brought all his legal skills into play to establish by clever questioning that Elisabeth was not attached. Otto and Hackett were in demand to tell their stories of TK's adventures in the Peninsular War and at Waterloo. The New Yorkers relived the stories of the pirates and Paul Delamaine. Tony Parsons, John Potts and William Llewelyn could have completed the picture, but for now the adventures in Vancouver Sound remained untold.

New York was confusing. On the one hand Tom was a hero and was rumoured to be rich. On the other hand, local fighting men saw him as a challenge and a way to enhance their reputations.

Tom wanted to escort Nell and Elizabeth to the receptions with Otto. Hackett gave him the answer. He would keep watch. Word spread that a killer was watching, and the interest faded. Hackett did not actually kill anyone.

The bank account was better than Tom had expected, so they booked into the Grand Hotel. The ladies enjoyed the lifestyle, particularly the attention of the young professionals, full of charm and wit and not bothered with the pretensions of status. Ben Horsman found that, at last, he had met his match with Elizabeth. Their conversations were like rapier duels and both came out winners.

Miss Kynch was beginning to come round to Adam Hillstrider's point of view.

Alan Alexander was planning a long-range pursuit of Judge MacMillan's grand-daughter. Nothing less would do.

Otto charged straight into the top order of society but was soon found to be penniless. Hackett and John Claude formed a strange companionship. Hackett came from a good professional family but had no social confidence. After the war he had been saved by his books. He would read anything and everything. He already knew a lot of medicine. Now he was becoming fascinated by the law. JC was interested in geology and geography, particularly America. So they scoured the book shops. Jean-Claude had a crazy reckless use of English that endeared him to everyone he met. Hackett was more measured but he loved the company.

They enjoyed their visit and the ladies really liked the relaxed social life. But Tom and Hackett were busy making preparations on the west bank. Old Tom presented H2 in beautiful condition and set out to find other horses for the journey. The wagon master offered a wreck. Tom took him aside and explained that he did not like to be insulted. He explained that he had lost some trust and offered a chance of redemption. Miraculously, a good trailer became available and the reinforcements that Tony Parsons would have required were ordered.

The mule yard had some good stock and Tom chose four good strong mules that appeared to have the stamina that would be required. On impulse, he also bought a tall stallion donkey. Perhaps he would be remembered in the Rockies, long after his passing, for introducing mules to the native stock. And that was the first time that he had thought of any legacy. Mules.

He bought a few spit-rusted essentials from John Smith. Then John Smith added some extras and presented the bill. It was still a bargain.

When the horses were ready, he arranged for John Lewis to shoe them and make spares. Also, he asked John Lewis to arrange some rooms at the roasting yard for a few days before they set off.

That just left the boots and buckskins. He told the store to be prepared for some surprises and to ensure that there were some ladies available for the fittings. Both the buckskin store and the clothes store were surprised to receive order for so many boys' clothes, but they took the orders, piled up the clothes and handed them over.

All the suppliers had kept their promises and, one cold spring morning, they were ready to go. Six riders, ten horses, four mules, and a trailer. Plus a donkey.

As they assembled on the west bank, four men on horseback rode up. They were dirty, bearded, long-haired and wore buckskin. They carried guns and looked very carefully at the members of the team and their possessions. One asked where they were heading.

"West."

"Well, we are heading west ourselves. Would you like us to guide you?"

Tom looked them over. They did not look as though they were going on a journey west. And, they did not seem to care that it was apparent. Oh dear, just another bunch of chancers.

"No thank you."

"Well, it can be dangerous on the trail and you may need our help."

"No thank you."

"Suit yourself." And they rode away.

The team stayed at the roasting inn and enjoyed the company of the regulars. But, one spring morning they had to leave, and off they went.

On the first day they made thirty miles on the soft ground by nightfall. The ladies would sleep on the wagon and the men would sleep in their cloaks. Hackett asked Tom if he had seen that they were being followed.

"Yes, and I would rather deal with them sooner rather than later."

Hackett smiled, "Very well then, I think it's one for me."

"Very well, no prisoners."

Hackett nodded, rode off without any more discussion and without any discernible weapon.

Tom kept watch all night. Well before dawn Hackett rode in with one good horse, two good saddles, and a good heavy rifle. There were no prisoners.

Hackett explained that the followers had camped in a copse and had not posted guards, so he got close enough to feel the warmth of their fire. He had listened to their conversation and got to know them. They had no redeeming features. Indeed their interest in the ladies and their intentions towards them were past redemption. The leader, with the best horse and the best gun (both stolen) had taken to crime after the War of Independence and had assembled the others along the way. They simply followed his orders, so he was the first to go. Without lookouts the others were easy threats. They paid for their laziness. Nobody would miss them.

The next day they travelled forty miles, and the next day, on the prairie, fifty miles.

JC drove the trailer with the mules and led the spare horses and the donkey. Tom insisted that he spent a few hours riding each day. They gave him a deep saddle with a pommel at the front. He was gradually beginning to get the rhythm.

They were eating easy meals each day and did not spend much time cooking. They rode on day after day camping lightly with small fires and light meals. It was so different from Tom's slow progress last time he had travelled west.

At the Mississippi they had to stop. It was too high to cross. They rode upstream. Day after day they waded into the water and returned when it became too deep. At last the river spread out into sandbars and channels. Tom explained to JC that ropes and pulleys would be needed. JC took charge and swung ropes with pulleys to drag the trailer from one sandbar to the next. Even so, the channel between the sandbars was often deep and JC insisted that they wade from one sandbar to the next. Every time, they had to ensure that the trailer would not start to float and potentially lose its load.

Directed by JC, they zig-zagged their way across. It was a big river, but they were fortunate to have found a point where it flowed wide and lazy.

They drifted south-west towards the Missouri crossing. Day after day the grass grew longer, and the flowers bloomed more beautifully. Butterflies added colour and birds added song.

Buffalo

One day, a line of natives rode across the path. TK checked his weapons, but as they drew close it was clear that the natives were not hostile. They were in poor condition. Tom discovered that his time with Dick and Harry had not been well spent. They had perfected their English, but his understanding of their language was still rather poor. However, after many mistakes and lots of hand signs, including much rubbing of the stomach, he understood that the natives were hungry and that there was a herd of buffalo a few hours' ride away. They were pleading for help to kill two or three buffalo to end their starvation.

Tony Parsons had told him that it was a duty to help people in need on the trail.

Tom said that they should take the heavy rifle and he would bring a London rifle. Otto volunteered to carry the heavy rifle. They followed the natives' pointed direction towards the herd. The rest of the team rode on south-west and the natives drifted away.

The herd was not what Tom had expected. The buffalo grazed in groups of two or more, not far apart from other groups as they spread to the horizon. Tom remembered that on the plain, the horizon was twenty miles. This herd spread for twenty miles in all directions.

He rode quietly at a distance towards the back of the herd. Eventually he saw three young bulls well separated from the rest of the herd. Tom and Otto tied their horses to some bushes, loaded their guns and crept forward. At about fifty yards, Tom pointed towards the buffalo nearest to the rest of the herd and told Otto to wait for the call. The shooting would be difficult because they were to the right of the animals and would be unlikely to hit the heart with the first shot. They would have to hit the lungs and the kill would not be clean. He started to sight his rifle on the second nearest. The explosion was terrific. and Otto's buffalo staggered and fell. Tom kept his aim and fired. The third buffalo had started to move when Tom fired again.

So, the first buffalo had been killed. The second ran twenty yards and stopped with its head down, then sank to its knees and died. The third was going well after one hundred yards when its head fell, it staggered, made a few more yards and dropped.

The shooting and running caused a stir in the nearest group of buffalo and they started to run away. Others started to follow. The effect was like a brown blanket being shaken. The ripples turned to waves and the whole blanket shook and moved. The hooves sounded like thunder, pierced by bawling and bellowing. And the blanket was lost in the dust.

Tom reloaded both barrels and went to look. The first buffalo was dead. The second was dying and Tom shot it in the heart. The third was struggling to stand and Tom shot it in the heart. Even the heart shots did not kill the huge animals immediately. As they had explained in London, the rifle had high velocity and would penetrate deep, but the slightly smaller balls would do less damage as they passed through. Otto's heavy rifle with a bigger ball and lots of powder had killed more quickly. Tom's rifle was taking a little longer. He realised that, really, he had always had humans in mind when he chose the specification for the rifle.

Otto was sheepish. "I hardly touched the trigger. I was just getting ready."

Tom laughed. "The trigger tension must have been bravado. We will adjust it when we get back."

They walked back to the horses. Otto's horse had broken free and run off. It would be a long walk. Tom laughed and set him up under the bushes for a few hours' contemplation of trigger tensions and tethering knots and rode down to the youngest of the buffalo. He sliced along the back and removed the fillet. It was almost three feet long. He wrapped it in his cape and rode back to the team.

Chaos was his first impression as he approached. Trailer wheels in the air. Mule legs in the air. Ladies' dresses blowing in the wind, sacks and bags and bundles everywhere.

Hackett was looking after the ladies, the horses and the surviving mules behind a rocky outcrop. This was the same outcrop that had upended the trailer as they ran away from the stampede.

Tom saw that Nell, Elizabeth, JC and Hackett were all safe. The horses and some mules were safe. But the rest was chaos. One mule had been trapped in the trailer and had been hit by the buffalo stampede. The blundering beasts had knocked them over and trampled them underfoot.

Well, somehow, the team had survived. Hackett had saved them.

The broken wood from the trailer would make a fire and the fillet from the buffalo would provide their meal. He saddled a couple of horses and rode back for Otto.

Jean-Claude sniffed among the wreckage for ingredients. Hackett gathered the wood and by the time that Tom and Otto returned a good meal was ready.

As they ate, the stories unfolded. The first sign was the rumble growing louder and getting clearer. Then the dust cloud appeared. Hackett dragged them to the outcrop. JC was driving the trailer. He whipped up the pace but hit a rock on the bottom of the outcrop and turned the trailer over. He had fallen out of the trailer and just had time to release the horses, mules and the donkey that were being led. But the mule in the shafts could not be released. Hackett had pulled him away as they saw the faces of the first buffalo with eyes blazing. The trailer, with its cargo and the mule were hit by the shoulders of the blundering beasts and trampled by the followers. And this had only been the edge of the stampede. The mule had not been killed but its legs were broken. Hackett killed it.

Tom, Hackett and Otto gave their cloaks for Nell and Elizabeth. They huddled under their capes by the fire. If they had analysed it, the team were lucky to be alive. They left steak to cook slowly over the fire of broken trailer wood and settled for a hard night. Tom and Hackett had known worse.

The next morning, they ate steak and biscuits and started to look at the chaos. Otto did his best, but it was not very good. Tom's best was not much better. Hackett was quite practical, but it was JC who quietly brought order to the chaos.

Nell and Elizabeth concentrated on the load from the trailer. They made separate heaps of clothes, food and fodder.

JC and Hackett looked at the trailer and tried to find where it was broken. Hackett used the surviving mules to drag away their dead companion and he rescued the harness.

The natives arrived leading Otto's horse and offering a choice piece of offal. It was very large and not easy to identify. Tom indicated their thanks for the horse, but they could keep their offering. They were about to leave when JC suggested that they could help to right the trailer. Between them, under his guidance, they managed to lift it onto four wheels, but it was a poor, broken thing. They thanked the natives and wished them good fortune on their way. As an afterthought, Hackett directed them to the dead mule.

JC started with the wheels. Then he addressed the attachment of the axles. Piece by piece he found the chassis of the trailer and they banged it into shape. John Smith had thrown in a few spit-covered tools that Tom had forgotten to order. His hammers and nails helped to bring the trailer into shape. They repaired the shafts and laid out a deck. Now, they could carry some of the salvaged bags and sacks.

So, JC had designed a limping thing with uneven shafts and a sloping deck without sides.

Tom did the analysis. First, they must load the spare horses with everything that they could easily carry.

Anything they could not carry would go onto the wobbly wagon or be left behind.

The bundles went onto the horses, the boxes were repaired and went onto the trailer and the unbroken sacks went on top. All the trampled mess of grain, food and clothes were left behind. And they were still one thousand miles away from the settlement.

The team had worked well together. JC had been a revelation. They attributed his technical skill to the Swiss clockmaking tradition. But he explained that his family made cheese. He had a look at Otto's rifle and adjusted the trigger mechanism.

They were now down to a walking pace, leading horses and mules and riding only when the animals were rested. Everything would depend on the animals. The donkey was going well but unburdened. If only he had a saddle.

"Actually," said Otto, "the pack harness from the dead mule could fit on the donkey with a few adjustments, and he could carry some bundles."

Now everyone was playing his part.

They could have travelled south to St Louis. Otto liked the idea, but Tom did not want to appear at a disadvantage in the town. So, they limped down towards the Missouri crossing. This time they would have no alternative but to appear at a disadvantage. Tom was concerned that the traders would see their weakness and try to cheat them. They would have to make deals but their bargaining position was very weak. However, if push came to shove, they would prevail. They found a camping place among trees on a low hill away from the river. Otto and JC stayed with the ladies, and Tom and Hackett rode the empty cart down to the crossing. Their rough condition helped them to blend in and they were able to negotiate hard but reasonably fairly.

They started with the trailer. There was a wagon yard, but it did not have any trailers. However, it did have a graveyard of broken vehicles. The owner took a close look at the trailer and thought that he could rebuild it from spare bits and parts of the smaller wagons. He quoted a price which was about the same as they would have had to pay for a replacement trailer. The clincher was that he said that he could start immediately and would complete it in a few days. They agreed. They had to show their money, but payment would not be made until delivery.

They looked around to see what food was for sale. There was not much choice but plenty of bacon and beans were on offer. Also, plenty of flour. They would survive. There was also plenty of fodder for the animals including oats, so the animals would also survive. They were told that there was a fort on the River Platte that also had supplies. The situation was improving. They rode the mules back to the camp.

Three days later Tom and Hackett rode the mules down to the yard. The trailer was repaired and ready to go. They paid the agreed price, went shopping for food and fodder and rode back to the camp. They loaded up and were ready to go. The next day, they rode down to the crossing and went over without challenge. Nell and Elizabeth in their hard-worn buckskin went unnoticed. Otto looked back wistfully at the store, where he may have got a game of cards and then looked forward only to see more prairie with a low, grey line in the far west.

Day after day they kept to the north of the River Platte and, eventually, stopped at the fort. It was a simple palisade with cabins along the inner walls and a central long-house. They were almost at the point where they would turn north for the settlement. The fort was orderly, and they got good hospitality, good supplies and good company. Of course, Otto had to mention Waterloo and they were all late to bed. Before they left, Tom had a chat with the commander. Tom was pleased to learn that a trading arrangement had been established with the Dutch settlers.

"Now beyond the North Platte and the Sweetwater rivers you have the South Pass. Is that in your territory?" asked Tom.

The commander nodded.

"Well, some so-called farmers are running a bad business there. In particular, they are charging travellers for passage. Now, we will be passing that way. If we are asked for charge for passage, we will kill them. Would you have a problem with that?"

The commander smiled. "I have heard of this. It is a problem. Strangely, they never ask my troops for charge for passage although they appear to charge any other travellers. So, Mr Kynaston, if you happened to be asked for payment and you happened to kill them you would solve a problem for me. Good luck."

They had reached the fort on bacon and beans. They had eaten well at the fort and, ironically, they would be eating food from the settlement as they headed that way.

They were well fed, well rested, and well cleaned as they rode on. They rode for a few days upriver and then turned north for the settlement.

The Settlement

It had been transformed. Outside the palisade a village of cabins rose up the hill. Below, the palisade had become a fort. The gates were impregnable. A small harbour for canoes and small boats had appeared in front and, most amazingly, field after field filled the valley.

They rode into the palisade not knowing what reception to expect. They had not been invited and they were not expected. But in front of the longhouse they recognised William sitting with Beth and a baby. William raised his hat and Beth raised the baby.

Tom need not have worried. They remembered him kindly and welcomed his friends. Beth took Nell and Elizabeth away to be washed. They left as filthy waifs in buckskin and emerged as ladies in dresses. The bath water had to be changed twice.

The men received about the same treatment, but rougher. The haircuts and shaves were brutal. The bathwater had to be changed four times, but they emerged pink and clean and respectable.

The food was a revelation. The farmers had found and traded herbs and ingredients that transformed the usual meat and vegetables into a delicious feast. And this was normal.

Tom introduced JC to William. He hoped that between them they would be able to climb the cliff where they had found the gold. William was fascinated and remembered his agreement at the fort. He could not resist the offer to join the team. Tom gave him one of the London rifles to seal the bond. A connection between the old and the new.

The ladies hardly needed any introduction. Beth welcomed them confidently and they soon started a relationship based on mutual fascination that would go on for months.

Among the men, Otto talked of a world that the Jans had never known. And did not envy. But Tom had credit among the Dutch settlers who remembered the battle at the red cliffs, the hunting, the finding of their site and the building of their palisade. Otto dropped the bullshit and the newcomers were gently welcomed into a new way of life. Nell and Elizabeth did not mention much about the styles of London and New York. But their stories of life on the farm struck a chord. They quietly started a riding school with H2 and the horses from New York. There was some surprise when they mentioned the donkey and the possibility of mule breeding. The ladies appeared in a new light. But the Dutch were farmers and were fascinated by the prospect of a new way of using their skills. A supply of mules would be useful. Also, if the young men could learn to ride properly, they would be well equipped for their new life.

Unasked, Hackett and Otto rode out each day to make a map of the territory with its mountains and rivers. In the evenings, the Janets started to move in on Otto.

There was a common kindergarten and Nell looked out for signs of red in the hair of the mini Jans and Janets. There were a couple of potential candidates. She thought of confronting Tom. And then she thought, so what? They were in a frontier to a new world. She smiled and wished them luck.

Tom rode up to Harry's family's winter camp in the foothills. Of course, they were expecting him. He had been spotted soon after they left the fort.

He handed over a double-barrelled rifle with ammunition for Harry and a bundle of arrows and a bag of arrowheads for his father.

The father proudly showed Tom the yew bows that his craftsmen had made following his model, and he fired a long shot to demonstrate his success. The ram's horn bows had great power up to fifty yards, but the yew bows with their heavy arrows had a far superior range and effect.

Tom thanked them for protecting the Dutch settlers.

The father replied, "They farm. We hunt. Good trade."

Tom asked Harry if he would return with him to the gold workings. Harry laughed. "We are warriors. We are bound together."

Tom described his travels and mentioned the buffalo hunt.

Harry roared with laughter. "You have much to learn."

With some graphic gestures, Tom described his plan to breed mules, which would require native mares.

"Mules travel well. I will bring ten mares in five days. Five mules for you and five mules for me. Good trade."

Tom rode back to the settlement and asked the elders whether Nell and Elizabeth could stay for six months while he went to look for gold in Canada.

The elders laughed. "They are already welcome. Of course, they can stay."

Nell and Liz were delighted. They were not attracted to the idea of another thousand miles of riding on the plains and a summer in a British fort. So that was alright.

Tom was eager to leave. He wanted to travel to Fort Vancouver, then on to the gold workings in Canada, and home before the end of summer.

They would travel light. JC was riding well now. But, even so, they would bandage him up for a long hard ride. JC's ropes and equipment would be packed on the spare horses. Tom was driving hard. As soon as Harry arrived with the horses, they spent little time on their goodbyes. Nell and Beth were distraught to see their men leave.

West

Below South Pass, Tom explained his conversation at the fort. They would have their guns ready. If the farmers asked for payment for safe passage, Tom would raise his arm and they would each kill the man in front of him. Fast and final. JC would stay back.

Otto drawled, "Why don't we just pay them a few dollars for passage and go on our way?"

William said, "In the Royal Navy we attack first."

Hackett said, "I'd rather fight them alone than make a payment."

Harry said, "Fighting is best."

So, they distributed the guns. Otto took the heavy rife. Hackett took one of the new London rifles. William took his new London rifle. Harry took his new London rifle, but he kept his spear close.

The farmers thought that there would be safety in numbers with seven burly men blocking the way. The leader, with a broken nose, made the demand and Tom raised his hand. It did not go according to plan. Tom shot the lead farmer in the head with his pistol from two feet. Then the horses took off. William missed. Hackett missed. Harry got close and hit twice.

Otto missed. Tom hit a young farmer from three feet. Therefore, three farmers, standing on firm ground could take their shots. One snatched and missed. One hit Otto's horse and one hit Hackett. And then Hackett hit him.

Harry heard the sing as Tom drew his sword. Harry laughed and took his spear. This was their bond. Horsemanship and blades. No farmers survived.

Hackett had been hit across the back as his horse turned. A lot of muscle and a bit of rib. Hackett would survive the bullet wound provided he did not become infected. Harry told him to let it bleed.

Harry collected JC's horse as it trotted for home. Otto had to shoot his horse. They found the farmers' horses and took two good ones and three good saddles. And so, they rode on.

Hackett and JC were given deep Spanish saddles. Both hung on. JC was searching for the rhythm. Hackett was hanging on for life. JC got used to the faster pace and Hackett got used to the pain. Harry insisted that Hackett should bleed until he stopped. Nobody else had a theory, so they rode on and Hackett bled on.

After a few days, JC and Hackett were both sitting up straight. And they rode on.

At Fort Vancouver, John Potts was living well and greeted them generously. The Gentlemen, eager for news, invited them to the main building. Harry shook his head and rode off down to the voyageurs. They had stories to match his own, and one story led to another.

The Gentlemen of the Company were most interested in Otto, who told them the gossip from the regiment, Parliament and London Society. They were fascinated to hear how Wellington was getting on in politics. JC's crackling description of walking and climbing in the Alps caused great amusement. Particularly the antics of the tourists who suddenly became experts.

William persuaded the Company to charter the cutter. He got it fitted out to include all of the usual Royal Navy standard equipment and two three-pounder cannons at bow and stern. He would have been happy with two-pounders, but he had to make do with the threes. This involved more reinforcement and recoil suppression. Most importantly, they had grape and cannister to go with them. Finally, William asked for lumber and the gold sifter. The Gentlemen were pleased to provide all this help, at a price.

John Potts agreed to join the party. Tom had wondered whether he would have decided to settle for what he had got after the last expedition, but John had his eye on a Partnership with the Company and would come along.

Before they had completed their preparations, John Potts insisted on taking them on a voyage down the Columbia River. It was spring but there were still heavy rains and strong winds. The river was flowing full. John Potts moored below Fort George and marched them up to a hill above the fort. From there they could see the bar. The chaotic waving and churning of the waters as the flow from the river met the currents from the ocean was horrific. No boat could survive in those waters, never mind the shoals and bars formed by the dropping of sediment as the waters met.

They went back to the cutter and sailed upstream to Fort Vancouver. John Potts explained that they must not be impatient. When the time and the tides were right, he would sail them through these waters like a baby's bath.

The Main Seam

At last, winter turned to spring and spring turned to early summer. John Potts stated that they could cross the Columbia bar for the Pacific Ocean and the Vancouver channel. He would be able to find the golden beach with his eyes closed. However, he was relying on Colonel Tom to keep them safe if the natives turned up.

With his eyes open, John Potts ran them over the bar, down into the channel and up to the beach. They set up the cannons and lowered the masts.

There would be three areas of operation. They would rotate, but JC and William would always be at the cliff face. Two others would work at the dam and operate the gold-sifting machine. Two others would always man the guns on the cutter and sift for gold on the beach. If any natives arrived, the cutter would fire a shot and the others would come down to pick up the rifles ready for a defence.

The stilling dam was as they had left it. William set up some ropes and they arranged a system to bring buckets to the sifter. It was cold work, and they took it in turns to bring in a bucket and then dry off at the sifter. It worked slowly and surely and started to produce grains of gold.

From the stilling dam Tom pointed up to the cliff. JC's face lit up.

"Bien sûr, very well, first we must find a base below the cliff, as high up as possible, then we will make a camp, and then we will start to climb."

The route to the cliff was not easy. They tried to follow the stream but often had to go around cliffs and up and down dips and climbs. They had to hack vegetation and dig footholds. It was up-hill scrambling all the way. But at last they reached the foot of the cliff. They found a base and cleared the area. Then they had to return to the cutter for the ropes and climbing equipment. JC was in charge from now on and he checked every detail. He chose the ropes and equipment from the cutter and he checked them as they arrived at the base after it had been hauled up bit by bit by the team. And then they had to bring up the timber and more rope. JC was certainly in charge. The crackling English was the same but the humour had gone. He was in charge. From now on he must approve every detail, including checking all the ropes and all the equipment, twice. So, they hauled it all up and then JC checked it all again. They would start the next day.

It was slow and careful work. JC led and William readily became his partner. The others went back to sifting and panning.

JC spent a long time just looking at the cliff. Finally, he put on a harness and started to climb, trailing a light rope. When he was steady, he drove in a peg and threaded the rope. It would follow him up, but he could jam it if he fell.

So, he went up hammering and threading. Gold prospecting stopped as he got higher and higher and the others came to watch. At last, he stood above the waterfall. He drove in pegs to make a base and threw down a rope. William attached a pulley and tied on a new rope. CJ pulled it up and then lowered himself with the pulley. A good day's work.

Eventually they were called on to carry up the planks. It was amazing. JC stood above the waterfall with ropes and pulleys. William stood at the base, ready to send up and receive planks and ropes.

William tied the wood into bundles and then, to the amazement of the others, he climbed up the cliff. Then they saw that JC was orchestrating but William understood the tune. At last, he stood at the top. JC and William built a platform above the stream, level with the gold seam. The stream was low so most of the seam was exposed. From the base camp they sent up hammers and chisels and a basket. At last, the basket came down filled with gold. Pure gold. For Tom it was a great relief that his theory had been correct and that their journey across a whole continent had not been a fool's errand.

Now JC and William set up a rotation. Workers went up and down and baskets went up and down. Tom was amazed at the thick gold seam and how easy it was to break it away into lumps to go down in the baskets. The base camp at the dam became a factory for hammering out the gold, breaking it up and putting it into the churns. At the dam they poured the gold granules from the griddle and shook them into the spaces in the churns. The churns became blocks of solid gold.

It did not take long. Each team on the gold face hammered and chiselled and sent down baskets. Then the team at the dam broke the gold into smaller pieces and added the grains. After only a few days the churns were full, and they were ready to leave. Tom asked William about putting more gold into bags, but William explained that the churns would have to be secured low in the cutter and any more weight would make it unstable. They would have more wealth than they had ever imagined and should settle for that. It was amazing and, if necessary, it would be easy to return. For now, don't be greedy.

By rotation, Otto and Harry went up to collect the equipment and timber. First came the planks from the platform. After two loads, the pulley jammed and Harry, at the bottom, jerked the rope to free it. But he was at the wrong angle. The result was spectacular and terrible. The bundle of timbers was wrenched free from its pegs and they failed. The pressure on the next pegs was too much and they failed, successively down the cliff. The timber fell on Harry, who was struggling to emerge when JC landed on him, broke Harry's leg and broke his own neck.

They used the timber to make a litter for Harry and the equipment. Then they carried Harry and the ropes and the pulleys down to the beach. Down through the pathway using handholds and footholds. Down through the dense vegetation that seemed to have re-grown during their short stay. Harry was tied down tight but the bumps and bangs shook him badly. His handsome face grew tight and pale.

Of all the days for the native warriors to turn up in their war canoes full of armed men, this was a bad choice. The team just could not be bothered to meet them. William loaded the stern cannon with grapeshot and shot the bow off the foremost canoe. They stopped, back paddled and turned away.

Hackett set Harry's leg in a splint. John looked at the churns lined up on the beach and wondered whether they should hide half just in case of, well just in case. He went to look for somewhere suitable to hide some churns. When he came back, he brought the bear with him. As he reached the beach, running hard, the bear caught him and swiped him aside as it saw the others grouped together. William ran to the cutter and started to load. Otto picked up the heavy rifle and started to load. As the bear arrived, Tom grabbed Harry's spear from the litter.

"Don't let go," said Harry.

Tom thrust the long blade below the left nipple on the bear's chest. It went in smoothly. The shaft of the spear was a bit shorter than the reach of the bear. The first swipe hit Tom's left shoulder as he threw up his arm to protect his throat, but he managed to hang on with his right hand and extended his arm so that the next swipe missed. Tom fell back against a rock. He held on to the butt of the spear with his right hand and jammed it against the rock as the bear pressed forward again. The bear's momentum was killing it as the spear went deeper but its swipes were getting closer to Tom. He saw the claws, six inches long flashing closer. He had to let go as the bear twisted. The shaft of the spear was wrenched from his hand and lifted into the air. Tom was defenceless as he saw the bear rise up, almost eight feet tall with murderous claws. Then it fell towards him. It was dead when it hit the beach.

So, out of the seven adventurers who had set off with

such hope, JC was dead, Harry had a broken leg, John Potts had an opened back and Tom had a shoulder slashed to the bone.

This was not a good time for the native warriors to rebuild their courage and come again. Three long canoes filled with warriors were approaching fast. The rhythm of their paddling was accompanied by drumming on the hulls.

Hackett took a London rifle and Tom's pistol and ran to the rock. He helped Tom to sit behind the rock, out of sight from the water. He pulled Harry's stretcher alongside Tom. "Spear" said Harry. Hackett retrieved it. It was damp with blood, the bear and Tom had both contributed. He wiped the shaft and laid it next to Harry. He loaded the pistol and laid it next to Tom. They would not be taken alive. Hackett waited for the canoes to reach the beach.

Otto loaded the heavy rifle and aimed at the warrior standing at the front of the lead canoe. Harry had told them that nobody could stand in front of the leader in the canoe. So, he aimed at the leader and saw him fall back into the canoe.

William had loaded the rear cannon and, fired a ball along the length of the lead canoe. It hit the fierce prow and the splinters added to the injuries.

Otto fired a long shot at the leader in the second canoe. He staggered but did not fall. William reloaded with grape shot and fired into the chaos on the first canoe as it hit the gravel. He reloaded with grape again and fired into the second canoe as it approached the beach. He caught it head on. Almost half of the warriors were hit in some way. Otto reloaded and fired at the leader of the third canoe as it approached. He aimed low but a wave dropped the canoe and the leader's head disappeared. But the canoes were still heading for shore and could disperse as soon as they landed. Otto sensed a presence and turned to see John handing him a London rifle. Now they could do some damage. William was firing grape shot and, even as the third canoe drifted sideways, killed the first three paddlers. Otto hit the first warrior to step onto the beach with the London rifle and waited for the next. It was do or die for the warriors. They could not go home in shame.

The warriors tried to assemble behind their new leaders but the grape shot caused terrible damage and Otto was shooting at new leaders as they stepped forward. They could not continue.

Three warriors ran up the beach to hide behind Hackett's rock. Hackett stood up and shot the leader and then the second. He started to re-load but he would be too slow. The third warrior did not know this and turned to run back to the canoes. He made it just as the last canoe left the beach. He had to wade past the bodies of his companions, who had continued to die under the fire of the cannon and the rifles. Later they would tell of the horror of the banging, the cracking and the snapping that brought such horror. They never knew that if they had spread out and then converged on the cutter, it would have been a different story. They left in shame.

Hackett cleaned up. Most of the injured warriors lay in the canoes. Many dead warriors floated at the beach. One or two wounded warriors crawled on to the gravel.

Hackett took Harry's spear to finish them.

They buried JC on the golden beach. They rested for two days. John was not too badly hurt. Hackett tidied him up and thought the cuts would heal. But Tom had deep wounds. Hackett and John worked together to put muscle and skin approximately back in place. They washed it off with spirit from William's medicine chest. They bound the shoulder lightly to hold their work in place but Harry insisted that it must be allowed to bleed.

At last, they had to leave. William and Otto loaded the boat, laying the churns flat and tying them down tight and then double-tying them. John Potts limped in to check them. If they moved during the sailing the cutter would capsize.

They caught the tide and hauled the cutter off against the rear anchor. John Potts took the helm and they sailed away. They were very rich, but their wealth had come at a terrible price. And they still had to carry it home.

John Potts said that they should reach the Columbia bar before the Autumn currents and tides made it impassable. After everything else, he had not expected the privateer.

The Privateer

It was anchored across the mouth of the river, close to the bar. Its long cannons prevented all passage.

They saw the masts of the privateer over a headland and turned back before they were seen. They anchored out of sight and considered their options. They could not pass in daylight. The bar was still quite calm, but the sandbanks made it a dangerous option in the dark. If they became stranded, the privateer would destroy them at dawn. They finally came to terms that their only hope would be to sail back up the Vancouver Passage to the big estuary on the north coast of the American mainland. Then it was a hundred-mile trek to Fort Vancouver. Then one hundred miles back with medical support. Harry could lose his leg and Tom could die. Even so, this was beginning to look like their only option. They anchored for the night and ate cold food. They were preparing to leave when they saw the American flag. It was flying proudly above the masts of a ship of war. They raised the Union flag and sailed out to meet her.

The American ship was a heavy frigate, fast and well armed. The cutter pulled alongside and William made the introductions in the naval manner. He was reluctantly invited aboard, in spite of his unfortunate appearance.

The American captain was not pleased at the distraction. However, in accordance with maritime custom he agreed to take them on board and lift the cutter. He was even less pleased to find that half of them were injured and would have to be sent to his surgeon.

A platform was lowered and Hackett rode up with Tom. Then it was lowered for Harry. Until now, Harry had remained calm in spite of the strange situation. He had seen ships before, but not up close. He looked up at the heaving black cliff towering above him. He saw sailors in uniform swarming like ants – but with a common purpose. He smelled the special smell of tar, salt hemp and polish. He heard the harsh commands, the whistles and the bell. Also, the rumble of bare feet on bare boards.

Otto saw Harry's concern and knelt beside him on the platform and held him steady as they were swung aboard. Harry resolved that if Otto could do it, then so could he. On board he was lifted onto a stretcher, strapped tight and carried by white clad ants down into the gloom of the lower decks. Lower, closer, darker, the world closed in on him. But Otto stood by.

At last, in a confined cabin space grim faced men in aprons held him down while his leg was unbound, unsplinted, firmly pressed, re-splinted and re-bound. Looking around he saw Hackett, grim faced, looking down at another team. The light of lanterns gleamed on implements. Low, urgent voices instructed the movements and their efforts were accompanied by groans.

Then, at last, he was carried back through the tunnels to the open air. Otto greeted him with a smile. He could keep his leg and would walk strong again. Tom and John were still with the surgeons.

The Captain, Henry Harvey, at last started to relax and joined William. He had been chasing the privateer for a long time. At last, he had it trapped on the bar. The cutter was a distraction but the privateer was trapped and so he could talk without distraction. William gave his story and the captain respected the Battle of the Nile, less so the Battle of New Orleans, but he sympathised with the loss of the sloop to the privateer. They had a common enemy.

The question now was how to extract the privateer from the mouth of the Columbia River. William suggested that they should ask the opinion of John Potts who was the river pilot. Now the captain was interested, and John Potts limped in to join them. The question was, how they extracted the privateer without shooting it to bits or losing it on the bar.

The captain, had begun to respect William's calm appraisal of the situation. He would certainly listen to the advice of John Potts, the pilot.

The three talked for some time, looking at charts, discussing winds and tides and, of course, the peculiarities of the bar.

At last, they devised a plan to pretend to attack from downwind, the south. The privateer would have enough water and wind to believe that it could escape to the north. Then the Americans would turn north and force the privateer to turn south where its superior handling would provide the opportunity for escape. However, the Americans would continue west with favourable winds while the privateer battled south-west against the prevailing winds. Then the trap would be shut. The

Americans would turn into the wind, but always on a more favourable tack than the privateer. Slowly but surely, the privateer would be trapped under a headland.

The surgeons checked the raking on John's back and saw that it was not too deep. It was beginning to heal. They liked Harry's splint and thought that the leg would heal well. They did not like Tom's shoulder. He was becoming feverish and that was a bad sign. They cleaned the wound and stitched it up. They put him to sleep and crossed their fingers.

It was a hard fight and the fever took two days. The team came down to visit him, but he was unconscious. Hackett sat next to him day and night. He dribbled water into Tom's mouth and bathed his head. The surgeons told him that that was all that he could do. So that is what he did. On the third day the surgeon said that either he would die, or the fever would abate. Hackett kept pouring water and bathing his brow. Suddenly he went cold. Hackett wrapped him in blankets and held him close. He started to shiver and then he shook. Hackett held on. At last he went quiet. Hackett called the surgeons. They found a pulse and told Hackett to hold on. When Tom woke, Hackett was fast asleep. Hackett recovered more quickly than Tom, but Tom did recover slowly as Hackett went back to nursing.

And still the maritime game of cat and mouse went on.

Tom was sitting up and eating when the privateer was finally trapped under a headland.

The privateer ran aground on a golden beach under the headland.

The crew took to the boats or swam for the shore and

then ran towards the distant cliffs, carrying their distinctive swords and a few guns. Captain Harvey let them go. They were out of range of the muskets and too scattered for the cannons. Conversely, his crew would be safe from the privateer's guns. He sent his carpenters to look for any damage to the privateer. They reported a bit of leaking, but the impact had been slow into the wind and she was basically sound. It was near to high tide, so Captain Harvey decided to wait for low tide to make a thorough inspection. Then, if the privateer was sound, he would bring his ship in at high tide and pull her off when she was ready to float. He laid the tow ropes. He did not expect to use the capstans, but he got them ready on both ships.

Either the privateer did not have much treasure, or the pirates had managed to carry it off. No matter. The ship was the real prize.

At high tide the privateer began to float off the beach and Captain Harvey's ship towed her clear of the headland. Then the new crew sailed her round to head back to Fort George. She did not appear to be too badly damaged. Her captain had run a tight ship. They had seen him in action recovering the sloop from the Columbia bar. Henry Harvey confirmed that the captain had been a good opponent on the chase up the west coast.

Well, he would need new skills if he was going to survive the winter on the coastal hills.

Captain Harvey decided that he would keep the ships together while he sailed back to Fort George. He wanted to assess the condition of the privateer in a good harbour.

She would need to be absolutely sound for the journey back round Cape Horn. If the privateer was sound when they reached the bar, they would drop off the cutter to sail into the Columbia River. If the privateer was not completely sound, then John Potts and the cutter could lead the privateer over the bar and into the Columbia River and Fort Vancouver for repair. John Potts warned that in the latter case it could be a long visit during winter before she could be brought safely back over the bar. It could take weeks for the conditions of current, tide and wind to allow a winter crossing.

In the few days that it took to reach the Columbia River it was clear that the privateer had suffered more damage than expected to her hull and would need to be careened on a beach or docked in Fort Vancouver.

John and William spelled out the options. Careening would involve sailing to the river mouth on the Vancouver Sound. It would be quicker, and they could leave as soon as the work was completed. However, they would not be able to do the sort of repairs that could be done in the harbour of Fort Vancouver.

On the other hand, docking at Fort Vancouver would mean crossing the bar each way. However, the repairs would be complete.

Captain Harvey opted for full repairs in Fort Vancouver. He could take the opportunity to conduct diplomatic relations between the Americans and the British.

So, the battleship anchored in the shelter at the south of the river mouth and the privateer was crewed up for the crossing of the bar.

John was in charge. Captain Harvey joined the crew of the privateer. John explained that the conditions, in early autumn, were still possible. They must wait for the right moment of tide, current and wind. It would be a matter of hours and they must be ready. He would lead in the cutter. The privateer must follow closely. The set of the sails would be decisive, and they must follow his example. William would join Captain Harvey on the privateer. They would be under reduced sail. If they lost the wind, even for a moment, the privateer could drift aground. John would set the sails of the cutter exactly as the privateer must follow. If the privateer lost the wind, she must drop the bow anchors immediately. They prepared a second bow anchor for safety.

They waited at anchor for several hours. At last, the cutter set sail. Just enough to drive them through the conditions. The privateer followed with matching sails, spilling wind to keep its distance.

The first turn went well. The sails of the privateer matched the cutter. The waters were very strange. Still patches, currents, eddies and waves. The sails had to drive the boats through the conflicting elements.

On the second turn the privateer stood still. The sails flapped and they dropped the anchors. From the cutter, John saw the problem, lowered his sails and dropped anchor. Then John set a small sail to get the cutter sailing slightly against the current. William and Captain Harvey did the same. Both boats sat in the current and waited. John realised that the cutter was carrying a fortune in gold and that raised the stakes.

After an hour he was still waiting. After two hours, he

was still waiting. When the tide changed, anything could happen. But as the tide started to change, the wind changed, and he saw an opportunity. He set the sails on the cutter and the privateer quickly followed suit. They hauled up the anchors and sailed to the next turn. John took it slowly and clearly, and the privateer followed. They were almost over the bar when the privateer ran aground. They had neglected the pumping and paid the price. Both boats dropped anchor and lowered their sails.

They were only an hour short of high tide. They had to wait and they had to pump. Then John set the sails to catch the maximum wind at the height of the tide. He set the sails so that the wind would heel the boats. Sure enough, the privateer heeled and floated free. The cutter tacked and sat in deep water to see if the privateer could follow. The crew were new to the ship, but Henry Harvey had sent his best men and William had a feel for the waters. She shuddered, almost stopped and then, at the last moment, turned to catch the wind and she was free.

In the safety of Fort Vancouver William asked John, "Why did you not pilot the privateer?"

"And where was the gold?" asked John.

Going Home

The Americans were welcomed graciously at Fort Vancouver. Captain Harvey extended all the charm of a visiting warship captain. There was a formal exchange of pleasantries.

As always, the Gentlemen could not wait for news of the world. Captain Harvey was engaged for hours in answering their questions. In the meantime, the shipyard welcomed the new challenge and went about its business.

At last, they discussed the problem of the gold. Indeed, it was a problem. There was just too much of it.

Tom said, "Let's take it one step at a time. First, let's value it. It may take a little longer, but the process will be the same. In the meantime, let's secure it. Surely, there must be space in your strongroom. Next, presumably it must be transported by sea. Caution requires that it must go on the returning ships a bit at a time."

The Gentlemen saw the way forward and devised a plan. Small amounts could be transported within the insurance limits of the ships. The gold was not much more valuable than the furs. Captain Harvey agreed to carry the first, substantial, instalment to New York. The Gentlemen were reassured.

So, the Company issued its bits of paper and took its commission. It was huge and at headquarters the Company would be pleased.

The team discussed the instructions that they should give regarding distribution. They agreed that their shares would be equal. Otto and Hackett insisted on making transfers to cover Tom's investment in the venture. Then they considered their succession. Tom nominated Nell. William nominated Beth. Hackett nominated the team. Harry nominated his Nation. Otto, ever the reckless gambler, nominated Elizabeth in the hope that she would think better of him after he was gone. That was how he lived. But of course, if he lived, he could always change his mind. John could buy his partnership and the HSBC would take care of his affairs.

Tom's shoulder began to heal. The Company surgeons liked the work of the US Navy surgeons. His arm was in a sling, but he was recovering fast. John was given a clean bill of health and Harry started to walk without his spear. But he did not let go.

The privateer was repaired and provisioned so it was time to move on. John piloted it down to Fort George. They waited several days before he declared that they would run the bar at high tide the next day. It went well and they lowered John's boat and his assistant and he made the best of the conditions on the return.

So, at last, as autumn turned the forests to red and gold, Tom and his companions could make a dash for the Dutch settlement and Harry's winter village.

John would stay to pilot the bar with his own boat and buy a partnership in the Company. He was fulfilled.

So, one crisp late autumn morning, Tom, Harry, Hackett and Otto set out with packhorses laden with food, fodder, the tin box and lots of gold coins.

They made good progress, riding hard and eating cold food.

At last they came to the South Pass. Sure enough, riders came out to meet them.

Tom said, "I have lost patience with these people. They imperilled our Scottish friends. And now, for the third time, they seek to rob us. We will not honour them with any stray chance of injuring us in combat. Let us use the advantage of our rifles and shoot them down without honour where they stand."

Harry held the horses. He was good with horses. The others took the rifles and made themselves comfortable. Some were standing, some crouching and some even lying on the ground. Otto took the heavy rifle. Tom, William and Hackett took the double-barrelled rifles.

Tom said, "As we stand. From the left, me, William, Hackett and Otto. Harry will hold the horses. No prisoners."

"Certainly," said Harry.

And there were no prisoners. Otto's shot was perfect. Others needed a second barrel, and a few needed a reload. Hackett had to mount his horse to prevent his target from escaping. But, from a safe distance, they cleared the way.

As always, they collected the horses, saddles and guns. They did not look back as the vultures gathered.

"You said 'certainly'," said Tom.

"Good word," said Harry.

They turned northeast and after a few days they were in sight of the settlement. Harry signalled them to stop and went ahead to where he could see the settlement. He came back.

"There are Missouri warriors around the palisade. It is not an attack, but they are waiting."

Tom went forward with Harry to take a look. It was not an attack. It was not a siege. The warriors were just waiting for an opportunity.

There were too many and they were too scattered for an attack. Harry said that they must wait, and he would ride up to his village for help.

Harry led them up the hill until they had to dismount. Then he led them a little further.

"The warriors from the Great River are far from home. They will not get off their horses. If they lose them, it is a long walk home. The Missouri people live in houses. They burn well. I will bring warriors from my village." And he left.

So near and yet so far. They camped back in the hills and Hackett watched.

Two days later, Hackett led them to a viewing point. Harry had arrived with thirty warriors. They sat on the hill on the other side of the palisade in battle formation.

The Missouri warriors started to withdraw. There would not be a fight.

As they left, William spurred down to the palisade and reached the gate. As he jumped from his horse and banged to be admitted, one of the Missouri warriors, wearing a fur waistcoat, looked back, notched an arrow to his bow, swung up, aimed high, let fly, turned away, bent low and jogged back to join his band of warriors. He did not look back. The arrow flew high and hit

William in the back, nailing him to the gate. When they opened it, he was dead. Still transfixed.

Tom, Otto and Hackett rode down slowly. Tom raised a hand to Harry and his brother. Harry raised his spear and his warriors went back to their winter village.

At the settlement, concern at the siege had turned to relief at the rescue, and then despair at William's death at the gate.

Tom rode in. Before he met Nell, he met Beth with her baby in her arms.

"Death follows you, Tom Kynaston," she said and went away.

Tom found Nell in their cabin, but their joy was flattened by the sadness for Beth and her bitterness. The settlement was in mourning. And Tom had lost a friend.

There was resentment that Tom's adventure had cost the life of Beth's man. But gradually, they understood that Tom had brought William back safely. William had returned as a rich man. He had died because he had loved Beth too much and had rushed to be reunited. At last they understood.

Tom waited quietly for the mood to settle. Tom and Nell made love gently. The unbridled passion of their usual encounters did not seem appropriate. It would explode later.

Otto proudly told Elizabeth that he had returned as a rich man. He could settle down and cut out the clubbing and gambling.

Elizabeth laughed, "Where's the fun in that? I like your rakish manners and your dangerous lifestyle. This is the Otto that I know, enjoy but do not love. I like you to be my charming, dangerous friend. I want you to flirt and I want to tease you. Just as before."

And that's that, thought Otto. And London seemed a long way away.

Hackett sat with Elizabeth. He told her about the expedition, and she told him about the mule-breeding. But their sense of humour did not coincide. He did not know what to make of her mocking, teasing manner. What worked for her was a return of the same, but it did not come. Elizabeth seemed to be perfectly content to smile and tease both men from a distance.

Hackett started to ride up to meet Harry in the winter village to go hunting.

Tom was fascinated by the settlement that the Dutch had built. Not only the toilets, but an icehouse and a smokehouse. They had missed Christmas, but the joints of ham and bacon and other joints from the pigs that they had killed were hanging in the smokehouse over the diffused heat and smoke of the wood fire. The doors were sealed tight to keep the smoke and heat in, and to keep scavengers out. They checked every day and added wood to the low fire. Tom was amazed to see so much meat hanging in the smoke.

The Jan in charge said, "We cure everything but the squeak. Not too slow, or it rots. Not too fast, or it dries. These hams and shoulders and bacons will last for a long time. Certainly, until we are ready to kill another pig. In summer we will have more pigs than we can eat. Then we can trade the cured meat. This is farming, Tom."

The icehouse was a revelation. Tom knew that every village had one and he had helped to collect ice from the

River Severn. But he was amazed at this. It had been built into the hillside. As the freeze set in, the lagoon along the river froze. The Jans left it until it was very thick. Then they went to work.

The icehouse had been built in those late summer days like a mineshaft. It had walls of props supporting a roof of timbers. On the floor, sloping back to the entrance, were wooden rails. And, in between, a drain. At the entrance were two pairs of heavy double doors.

Now, in winter, they worked to collect the ice on sledges pulled up by the mules and pushed along the rails to the end of the mineshaft. Then the ice was unloaded and stacked deep and high to the roof. It was a long tunnel and the ice froze deep. They filled it until it was full. They left a chamber at the entrance to hold food in the summer. One of the Jans explained that if the barley crop went well, they would be drinking cold beer from now on and life at the settlement would be complete.

Tom trudged around in his New York boots which got wet, got dried, and got oiled.

But he had noticed that the Dutch settlers wafted above the snow and slush in wooden shoes. They were wearing clogs with thick wooden soles worn with thick woollen socks. The workshop was making the clogs bespoke for each settler from young to old. The style was the same to ensure that all of them stayed dry. The soles were reinforced with nails providing grip and long wear. They all walked very upright. And they stayed dry.

So, following their arrival at the settlement, Nell and Elizabeth had been welcomed for their different inputs.

Nell had a special way of dealing with the horses and an infectious humour that spread around the settlement. Everything became the subject of fun. Elizabeth had joined in the fun and started the teasing. Then the Dutch had joined in with their dry irony. In this mix the mule breeding and toilet arrangements were a constant source of laughter.

Tom, Hackett and Otto joined in the daily routines. They were not farmers, but they lent a hand with a good humour and that was appreciated.

Mustangs

One winter morning, Harry arrived with the usual trade team carrying game. The Dutch were happy to exchange game for cheese. They did not expect too much. Any game went into a big pot with lots of herbs and vegetables. The cheese could be spared. The protection of the warriors was priceless.

Harry was delighted to meet Nell and Elizabeth. Particularly when Tom introduced him as the great warrior who had lived with him, fought with him and saved his life many times.

Harry had come to invite Tom, Hackett and perhaps, Otto, if he was interested, to a capture of wild horses. They were on the plain, moving north as the snow receded. Harry's family would drive them into a dead-end valley and trap them. Then they would release the ones that they did not want and keep the others. However, the stallion usually had a different point of view.

Tom said, "Yes."

Hackett said, "Yes."

Otto stretched and said, "Maybe next time."

Harry had brought extra horses. H2 would not be going along. Tom and Hackett made up their saddle rolls and they were off. It was now or never. As they rode Harry explained that his nation were great horsemen, horse tamers and horse traders. Their skill brought great wealth and great prestige. They met the team on the plain. A middle-aged, middle-sized, sinewy warrior who appeared to have become joined to his horse was in charge. They rode further on to the plain to find the herd. It was kept together by a roan stallion who kept them moving. He bit and reared and kicked to impose his will. He was a terrific sight. And clearly dangerous.

The horse captain divided the team into two halves to form a "V" formation to persuade the stallion that he wanted to drive his herd towards the open end of the "V". This would lead to the valley.

And so, the stallion drove his herd into the valley. At a narrow point the ground crew had prepared a tree barrier to be pulled across the valley to trap the herd inside. It was a big valley and went far deeper so there would be no panic. Sure enough the stallion drove the herd past the barrier. After the herd had passed the young men pulled the barrier into place. They worked in pairs on horseback. And they worked fast. The stallion started to patrol his territory. In the meantime, the ground crew had built a gateway in the barrier with horizontal poles that they could open and close. Outside the gateway they released some tame mares. The stallion saw them and went to bring them into his herd. He snorted through the gateway towards the mares and the gateway closed behind him. Warriors leapt on the mares and rode them to safety. The stallion did not know which way to turn. He wanted to return to the herd, but his way was barred and he had lost the mares. He was not pleased.

He was even less pleased when he saw that the mares had been ridden away in different directions. He was running in circles. The main herd was in the valley so he turned back. He pawed the ground to sharpen his hooves. The ground crew stayed behind the trunks and poles as the stallion raged against them. They wondered at the blazing eyes, bulging neck, sharp hooves and snarling teeth.

For the young warriors it was a chance to show their bravery as they stood on the other side of the barrier without flinching. But one or two did jump back as the hooves crashed in front of them. This fury was what had made the stallion the leader and kept him as leader.

In the meantime, the horse captain had led a team including Harry, Tom and Hackett, down into the valley to separate some of the old mares. They led them up and pushed them out through the gate. The stallion calmed a little. Then they sent through the young males. Finally came a few unwanted young mares. They kept all the pretty ones and the pregnant ones. In the process, poles fell and young warriors risked life and limb to replace them. They joyed at the opportunity to show their skill and bravery. As young warriors fell, other young warriors leaped forward to replace them. This was their game.

This was orchestrated by the horse captain. Harry knew the job and led the team working hard to separate out the unwanted mustangs. Tom and Hackett started to understand the procedure, rode hard and made themselves useful. In front of Harry, it was a matter of pride.

The horse captain drove the remainder of the herd down the valley towards its end. The stallion collected the released horses and drove them away. So, the horse captain had collected several dozen young and pregnant mares, had got rid of the old and unpromising mares, and the young pretenders. The stallion would start again. That was his destiny.

Tom thought that the entertainment was over for the day. But Harry led them up the valley to the horses that had been retained. There were a lot of them. Over a hundred, at a guess. The young warriors now really started to show their skills. Each horse had to be conditioned so that it could be ridden for the rest of its life. They did it with numbers.

Four boys would surround a horse and bully it into submission. They forced a bit into the mouth and then one was lifted on to the back. The others stayed close and leant their weight until the horse stopped fighting. It was a battle of wills that the boys had to win. And, eventually, they did. But in the process, they fell off, got knocked over and, sometimes were kicked or bitten. They worked in teams and enjoyed every minute. It was part of their coming of age and every minute would be lived and relived, told and retold.

They camped at the barricade. They grilled meat with, courtesy of the settlement, the perfect complement, bread.

Harry interpreted. He was pleased that his friends had not let him down. The horse captain came to give his thanks. Harry was proud of his friends.

Tom asked whether the boys on the ground had survived.

Harry said, "Yes, they kept well away from the

stallion and getting knocked over by the others is part of the fun. They will stay here until all the horses can be ridden. And the leaders will start to be found."

Back at the settlement, as the evenings lengthened, Tom began to walk to a cliff looking west in the evening towards the setting sun. Nell joined him and it became a special time for them.

One evening, they mutually started to discuss where each saw the way forward. They had lived for the present but, together, they began to look to the future.

Nell said that a baby must come along soon, and they would need to decide where it would be born and how it would be brought up. The settlement was fine but, perhaps they should look for something more sophisticated for their child.

Also, Elizabeth had become something like a character from one of the contemporary novels. She had found a bond with Ben Horsman and had given him hope. Now they were two thousand miles apart. Her fate needed to be twisted to get her back to New York. So, gently and gradually, they decided to return to New York.

The settlers traded regularly with the fort on the River Platte. They learned that Tony Parsons would be travelling east and had been invited to make a visit.

This was all very tentative, but a momentum began to develop. They talked to Elizabeth, who replied that she would be going back to New York and they would be welcome to join her if they wished. First a raise of the eyebrow, then a chuckle, then a giggle and finally, the laughter rolled over them. They would be going to New York.

At the cliff looking west down a valley towards the setting sun Tom started to count his blessings. He was not religious, but fate seemed to have treated him kindly. He looked forward to the fast conversation of his friends in New York and started to think that the railways, coming west, might be his next interest.

Nell joined him, and they sat with their backs to the cliff looking down the valley to the west and enjoying a precious hour of the setting sun. They saw the fringes of green creep up the hillside. They saw a dusting of green in the trees strengthening as buds formed and leaves started to open. They heard the small birds starting to sing. Bigger birds were pairing up and starting to preen and call. It seemed like a perfect time to join them.

One evening Tony Parsons rode in. He was riding to St Louis on a hard trail from California. He had left his companions at the fort on the Platte and turned back to make a visit. He was made welcome. He was remembered kindly. Not least, because he had suggested where they might look for the settlement. He was amazed at what they had created.

He met Nell and Elizabeth. He seemed slightly conscious of his buckskin. Little did he know that they had looked just like him when they arrived. He met Hackett and recognised the same inner determination that he had seen in Tom that had served them so well. He met Otto and could not quite work out how this relaxed dandy had survived. Perhaps he had hidden depths. He heard about William and how he had built the palisade only, then, to die at its gate.

He heard about Harry and Dick, the Gentlemen of the

Hudson's Bay Company, and heard about the gold. He warned that along the trail he had heard stories. For desperate men, a few gold coins would be a fortune to kill for. Tony was leading a team of fur hunters who were carrying a fortune in pelts. Tom and Tony talked and realised that they would need a big team going east to deter attack for gold or furs.

Tony mentioned that his convoy through Arizona to California had survived only because of its size. There would be mutual benefit in joining up for the last leg to St Louis

When Tom told Tony about his solo ride to New York Tony laughed, "And you could do it again tomorrow on H2 and cold rations. But if you want to take the ladies, you will need numbers. I have a good team resting at the fort. We are heading for St Louis. If you join up you might be safe, at least that far."

Tom thought about his conversation with Nell and the ultimatum from Elizabeth. However, he kept calm and said, "I think that that could serve us very well. Elizabeth has an interest in New York, and I would like to see St Louis."

One evening Tony drew Tom aside. "This is a joyful scene. The farming and the prospecting have gone well. But I must give you a piece of bad news. Then we will discuss how to pass it on to our Dutch friends. I delivered the New Yorkers to South Pass and handed over to a good guide who would take them through the Rockies and on down to California. They were the last to join the convoy. The Scottish farmers would look for land below the South Pass. I returned down the Platte to the fort. They had a job for me.

When I returned in spring, they told me that a group of so-called "farmers" from below the South Pass had started to demand payment for safe passage. The Scots were too poor and were not allowed to farm. They were driven off. The convoy to California was halted. They were not fighters. After several days a payment was agreed, and they set off. But late. They got caught high in the Rockies by a terrible storm. It was unprecedented. Here is Ella's diary. See the last entry. I am sorry."

And Tony handed over the book and went away, leaving Tom alone. He opened it at the last page.

*We have burned all our fuel. Our guide assures us
that this cannot go on. We have suffered for four
days. We sleep with the horses for warmth.
Tomorrow we must start to burn the wagons. But
no fire can provide warmth against this icy
blizzard. Lucy is brave but fading. We cannot last.*

Tom's broad head sank on his shoulders. His broad shoulders sagged above his broad chest and his broad chest shuddered. He had lost men in
Spain and had lost half of his team at Waterloo. But they were soldiers and here was an innocent bright spirit full of hope and energy taken away. He went up to his cliff. Hackett found him cold and alone. It was news that Tom would have to bear alone. Hackett led him gently back to the settlement.

Tony Parsons organised the departure. He had visited the native village with Hackett to trade for horses. It had gone well. Tony knew his business and the natives trusted him. Hackett introduced Harry. Tony had heard all the stories.

Harry smiled, "I think we met after the fight at the red cliffs. I was going to spear you because you spoke my language so bad. Even now…." And he laughed.

Tony said he was pleased to meet in happier circumstances. The horse trade was good.

Harry said, "Yes, you are riding with fur hunters. They have not hunted on our land and can pass. Do not bring them back onto our land. Go in peace. And thank Tom for your passage."

Tony said, "I am sorry. I did not think that you would know or care."

Harry said, "We know a lot and we care a lot."

The rebuilt trailer and the surviving mules would be going home. Tony waved his arms and ran from one group to another. He was back in his element. The Jans were sorry to see him go.

Tom sat quietly with Beth among Williams possessions. He told her about William's naval career. About his exploits at the gold workings. How they had come to love his reborn happy grin. How sad he was to lose him. The fortune that he had left was no consolation. But she was a special lady. She was young and she had their boy. He was sure that happier times would return. Tom said

"Beth, you are also a very rich lady. William nominated you to receive his share of the gold. It is worth more than ten of those big farms back east. If ever you need gold for yourself or your community, this paper can be exchanged in small instalments at Fort Vancouver or for a full credit at a bank in New York. Harry has a similar paper and even less need for the money. However, circumstances may change. You may need to work together. Harry knows Fort Vancouver and you may need to visit New York and I will be there. I will say the same to Harry. Tony says that we can send letters through the fort on the river. It will be slow but if you or Harry need anything, write to me at the Plymouth Inn in New York. Finally, this rifle is very special. Harry also has one. In due course you may wish to give it to your son. In the meantime, one or two men in your community could learn to use it. Again, talk to Harry. I will send ammunition. So it is goodbye and good luck."

The elders thanked Tom. They were sure that he had left a lot for them to remember him by. And they smiled.

So, they set off, heading for the River Platte. But Tom turned H2 back and galloped to Harry's village. He shook Harry's hand.

Tom told Harry that Beth would know about their money and the letters. There was so much to say. And nothing to say.

Harry said, "Damn, Tom. I have learned your talk damn good and you can't even say goodbye in my talk."

Tom racked his brains for the word, remembered and proudly said it.

"And greetings to you also," said Harry. Tom's broad shoulders sank. Now of all times he was lost for words. Then he saw Harry's smile. Tom's broad brow cleared, his grey/blue eyes twinkled and the short, broad teeth grinned.

Harry drew his knife and cut a fine line across his left palm. Tom recognised the gesture and did the same. They grasped their hands together. "We are brothers" said Harry.

A hug seemed appropriate. It was like grasping a marble pillar in sunshine. "Good luck little bear" said Harry. They laughed and off he went. They would remember their laughter.

As he rode away, Tom realized that he had not been leading Harry into their battles. Harry had been minding him. He turned to wave and saw the great warrior lift his fearsome spear in salute.

Another Convoy

The little fort was overcrowded. Soldiers, fur traders from the mountains and now the English. Tom and Hackett made camp away from the fort. Nell and Elizabeth would sleep in the trailer. Tom and Hackett would sleep under the trailer, taking turns to keep guard. Otto would stay in the fort and play cards.

Sure enough, one of the trappers came to try his luck. Hackett was on guard. No weapons were used but the mountain man would take a long time to recover.

There was no point in delaying. The weather was crisp and fine. They had horses and provisions and fodder, so they set off.

As they left, Tom spoke quietly to the captain.

"Living below the South Pass are some 'so-called' farmers who are guarding the pass and taking payment for passage. They have done harm to two groups that I know, and I have fought them off three times. Perhaps you could take a look and maybe close them down."

The captain replied, "I hear that we would be too late. A band of Missouri warriors paid them a visit. They killed a few old men and took away boys, girls and women. There will be no pursuit."

Tom said, "Thanks. That sounds like justice to me."

Tony led. Then came a few soldiers returning home on leave. Then the English team with a trailer and packhorses. Finally, four fur hunters leading packhorses brought up the rear.

The English were carrying some gold, but the value was far exceeded by the furs. Tony had said there would be safety in numbers. However, the furs piled on the packhorses must be a target and they slowed the convoy down. So, the fur hunters provided manpower but created a problem.

Tom rode with them. They were from the eastern mountains via St Louis. They had been part of a large group travelling and hunting in the mountains along the Missouri and its tributaries. They had been attacked by natives in the north. They had escaped but were separated from the main group. They feared that the group had fared badly. To save themselves, they had headed for a pass close to the source of the Missouri. They had continued hunting on the west side of the Rockies and they had followed the Snake River south. They knew that it led to the South Pass. They had been harassed a couple of times but had survived to the South Pass. They had met up with Tony, who had led them to the fort.

Tom said, "Well, you have been lucky and done well. You are almost home. But we are approaching the Missouri and that is still a battleground. I hear that you fur men have certainly stirred up the natives. We need to take great care. If we have to run, you will lose your fortune. I will talk to Tony Parsons and make some suggestions. Will you do as we say?"

They agreed.

As they prepared to camp for the night there were some surprises. Tony said that TK would be in charge of their defences. Tony told everyone to do as TK orders. "Yes, orders. Now listen."

TK gave the orders. There was no room for discussion. Tony, Otto and Hackett recognised the tone. That tone gave the orders that had saved their lives. If you disobeyed, you would die, one way or the other.

First, they would not be camping near the river that they were following but far inland.

They would cross to the south side. Next, there would be no fires. They would eat cold food. Next, the horses would provide their protection. They would be tied in close to the trailer and the group would be in the middle round the trailer. Tony Parsons would ride ahead to scout the route. They would travel slowly, and the horses would graze as they travelled.

Next, there would be hidden guards around the camp. If there was an attack, everyone would group inside the horse barrier. Next, all the guns must be loaded all the time. Next, they would travel in the same formation with TK at the front and Hackett at the rear. The trailer with the ladies would be in the middle. The soldiers would be in front of the trailer and the frontiersmen would be behind the trailer. Otto would drive the trailer with the ladies. They would practice the defensive formation with the horse barrier in the early stages to ensure that everyone knew what to do if they were attacked on the trail. Finally, if anyone touched one of the ladies TK would kill him.

Tony Parsons remembered the same sort of orders at the red cliffs and told the group, "Do as TK says, and you will live."

Progress was much slower but much safer. It would take longer to reach St Louis but, in case of attack, they would stand a far better chance than if they were straggling along like most convoys.

A few groups of warriors watched them and moved on. Only once, a band of warriors started to approach. TK herded the convoy into its defensive formation. Everyone formed up quickly and the band of warriors was met with a wall of horse rumps with guns pointing between. The warriors rode on. TK wondered whether the warriors or the horses would have been most dangerous if the guns had been fired.

The convoy was fortunate. The big battle groups from the Missouri were located to the north where they were confronting big groups of fur hunters.

And so, they slowly came to St Louis. Then everything changed.

TK BOOK IV

St Louis

Their first impression was bad. Along the river to the west of the town was a random settlement of fur cleaning factories, fur trader's offices, taverns, cabins, shacks and tents.

"I despise this place", said Tony. "Our trapper friends will go to the offices, get paid for their skins, go to the taverns and lose their senses, lose money at cards, go to the whores and lose more money they will continue the round until they lose it all and then go back to the offices to join a canoe to go back north."

So it transpired. The fur trappers became reckless and rushed to sell their skins. The soldiers lost their discipline and went home. Tony slipped away to his usual haunts among the frontiersmen. The ladies changed into smart outfits. Tom, Otto and Hackett changed out of their buckskins and trimmed their beards.

The town itself was comparatively civilized. Tom and the team booked into one of the best hotels. There was some hesitation at the reception desk until Otto started to count out some gold coins.

The ladies called for room service and baths. The men went into town for the baths and the barbers. Then they went to the tailors.

They went to the banks to test the value of the Company's papers. The clerks went to the managers and the managers went to the directors and the message came back that they were welcome, but they could not handle the Company's paper at the moment. This was partly expected, and Otto drawled that they would have to turn out their pockets to complete the journey to New York.

As they walked down the quay, marvelling at the steamboats, a lady rode down on a tall black pony led by a tall black slave in livery. She was very fine in a feathered hat with a riding suit. She carried a silver-topped black cane. The harness was decorated with silver. She was riding side saddle.

As Otto made eye contact and tipped his hat, a youth ran past and snatched the valise from the lady as she approached the bank. He set off down the quay.

Tom quickly lifted the lady from the pony and Hackett swept away the saddle. Tom threw the cane to Hackett, and Hackett jumped on the pony and set off after the youth. He drove the pony hard, skittering and sliding on the cobbles. Even without a saddle he rode with a straight back, as always. At last, as he was just catching up, the boy turned up a gangplank into a steamer. Hackett skidded into the turn and drove the pony up the ramp. He caught the youth just as he was starting to climb the steps to the upper deck.

He stopped with the pony's hooves on the lower steps and the black cane across the shoulders of the youth.

With caning around the ears and nudging by the pony, Hackett drove the youth back, still holding the valise. The return journey was slower. The youth and the pony were heaving for breath. Hackett drove them to join the others.

Hackett hopped off and threw the cane to Tom. They reassembled the saddle and Otto very gallantly helped the lady back into her seat.

Tom handed the cane to the lady. "A quarter turn, I think," he said.

She smiled and nodded her dark curls. Hackett handed up the valise.

"Thank you, gentlemen. I am Madam Biencours. I keep the Harbour Assembly Rooms. Please visit me when you wish."

And she signalled to the slave, and the slave led the pony away.

Hackett quietly pushed the youth away with a clip on the ear.

Otto was lost. A beautiful lady who kept elegant reception rooms, presumably where cards were played, might be his dream come true.

They returned to the hotel but, very quickly, Otto drifted away to look for the Harbour Rooms.

The Harbour Assembly Rooms were in an old French building with tall windows and tall doors. The rooms were all finely furnished with tables and chairs, curtains and chandeliers. They provided reception rooms for the better-placed to meet for tea and coffee, and to play a respectable game of cards. Otto found the tables.

Otto also found Madame Helena. She had heard rumours of Otto's wealth and the combination of that and his assured air and good looks proved irresistible. They were getting on very well.

However, at the tables, four sporting gentlemen were

finding themselves displaced. So, they started to cheat Otto. At first just a little, but then more and more. Otto was used to some give and take on the tables. However, this was proving too much.

One evening Otto had just lost again. He and the other players threw down their cards as the dealer reached for his winnings. Otto slammed down his fists. The room hushed.

"Five kings on the table. The game is void," said Otto, "Come to think of it, there are also two tens of Hearts."

Too quickly, the sporting gentleman said, "You are calling me a cheat and I demand satisfaction."

So it had all exploded. Rivalry in cards, rivalry in love, a challenge, an acceptance and Otto was going to stand in a duel. One of the sporting gentlemen made the arrangements. He specified a glade above the harbour. They provided the pistols and they set the rules.

At the appointed time the sporting gentlemen were already at the venue, dressed in black, like crows. The challenger was vain and handsome. He was of average height, with fair waving hair, good features and a strong chin with a dimple. He strode around the glade, anxious to take centre stage and to make his kill.

The gentlemen had appointed a duel master who fitted the bill. He was very dark, very tall, very thin with big hands and a long scrawny neck. Among the crows he was a vulture. He wore a top hat.

The third gentleman was small and thin and ugly. He really was unpleasant. But he was good with cards. He jumped around and made hostile remarks so that Tom smiled at the thought that they could postpone the duel while they strangled him. He glanced at Hackett and saw the murderous hands tensing.

The fourth sporting gentleman was solid. He was slightly taller than average, slightly fatter than average, very dark with deep brown eyes, straight hair and a clean round face. Darkly handsome, thought Tom.

The duel master asked for introductions. Otto stepped forward and languidly introduced his friends. Tom and Hackett attended as friends of Otto. They had taken him by coach in the British way

The duel master asked who the challenger was. The dapper blonde gentleman stepped forward and said, "I have been wrongly accused, insulted and I demand satisfaction. These are my friends." And he introduced them.

Otto said, "I have been cheated. I agree to fight. These are my friends".

The duel master, out of form, asked whether there was any possibility of apology and reconciliation.

"No." The voices were simultaneous. It was clear that the vain challenger and the languid challenged were determined to see it through.

"Very well. Will the challenged opponent please select his weapon."

Otto looked at the fine pistols and casually picked one up. The challenger picked up the other with a flourish.

"Gentlemen, stand before me, back to back. When I say, 'Proceed', take ten steps to my count and on 'ten', turn and fire."

Otto stood tall and languid with his back to the challenger. The challenger stood stiff with his pistol raised. Tense and ready to step out.

The duel master called "proceed." They took their paces as the duel master counted. "ten."

They turned. Otto lined up on the white shirt of his opponent. But he disappeared. Otto lost his target as the challenger dropped to one knee and fired.

Otto was hit in the chest. Tom was going to protest. Then Hackett put a hand on his shoulder.

"This is not finished."

Otto was badly hit but still alive. Tom knelt beside him and raised him to rest against Hackett's legs.

"Otto, can you see the target?" he asked.

Otto saw the white shirt of the challenger standing with his friends. He nodded. Tom helped him to raise the pistol to rest on his knee.

"Otto, can you take your shot?"

He nodded.

"Otto, set the sights, breathe out gently and touch the trigger."

The crash of the pistol shocked the sporting gentlemen. The challenger fell, hit in the chest. Tom and Hackett remained still. Otto was dying.

"Well that's taught him a lesson" said Otto. "One that he will not forget in this lifetime" said Tom. Otto laughed, coughed, haemorrhaged and died.

The friends gathered over the challenger. At last they turned, outraged. They were met with the two octagonal barrels of Tom's pistol and Hackett' empty hands. Both ready to kill.

The gentlemen blustered. "Our friend is dead. It was not a fair fight. The duel was finished when your man fired. We will seek satisfaction."

Tom replied, "Your man was kneeling when he fired, and our man was sitting when he fired. That is the end of it. There will be no satisfaction. Any nonsense and we will kill you all."

The duel master said, "You have not heard the last of this, Sir." They turned, took the pistols and collected their dead companion.

Tom and Hackett loaded Otto into the coach and drove him down into the town.

Nell and Elizabeth were shocked and deeply saddened to hear the news. Otto had been so calm and confident in everything that he did. It did not seem possible that he had lost the duel. When they heard the circumstances they were outraged. But Otto had killed his man, so the matter was concluded. Tom and Hackett did not mention the threats of the sporting gentlemen. It was a sad night at the hotel.

They arranged a burial, and were interested to see who would turn up. Sure enough, by the wall of the cemetery, three black-clad figures stood apart. "They are too stupid to relent," said Hackett. "They will encourage each other and believe that by cheating, they will get revenge. It cannot be helped." Tom said "If they give me an excuse, I will kill them. In fact, I am not sure that I am inclined to wait for an excuse." Hackett said "Revenge is a meal best eaten cold."

Madam Helena attended on her black pony, wearing black and led by her black servant. She did not dismount and did not speak to anybody.

So, back to the hotel. There would be a period of mourning. Eventually, Tom and Hackett went about their business. In particular, buying better clothes, ready for New York. All the time they watched to see if they were being followed and regularly caught glimpses of the sporting gentlemen. They had been through a lot with Otto and had grown to love his rakish ways. As Otto had predicted they had to empty his pockets for money to complete the journey.

Nell and Elizabeth were deeply saddened at the death of their friend. They wore black scarves that did little to show the depths of their loss. But they would not be beaten down. They remembered, in particular, how he had helped them when Tom was in France. But eventually they got back into the spirit of the town. Dress shops, shoe shops, and hat shops were all plundered for what would suit them best. Nell laughed as she rejected anything ridiculous, and Elizabeth scorned anything pretentious. They enjoyed it so much that they started looking for anything ridiculous or pretentious to maintain their game. Even so, they bought a lot of suitable outfits. Finally, Tom had to show them a small heap of gold coins. At this rate they would arrive in New York as paupers.

Even so, they hired a gig. It had two very large wheels and it was pulled by a well-turned-out dark gelding who trotted beautifully. They became the talk of the town, and invitations started to arrive. Tom was very wary of the fur traders who dominated the town. They were the source of the hunting expeditions that were causing such bad feeling among the natives living to the east of the Rocky Mountains.

Hostages

Then one morning, as the ladies trotted out in their bonnets and parasols to ride out of town, they disappeared. They did not return for lunch. Also, there were no signs of the sporting gentlemen. Tom and Hackett rode out and could find no signs. Tom went to Tony Parsons talking among the buckskin-clad frontiersmen. They turned immediately to a native hunter. He was flattered to be asked and set off immediately to look for a trail. He examined the roads leading out of town. Even among the tracks of all the carts and carriages, he found the tracks of the gig and its high-stepping gelding. He saw the footprints and hoofprints where the gig had stopped and then followed the trail away from town as the road was reduced to a track as the houses and farms became more sporadic, and finally gave way to prairie. The track continued for about five miles to a large, abandoned barn. The tracker did not approach very closely, but returned with the news that the gig was in the barn and that there were many men around the barn. Far more than the three whose prints he had found where the gig had stopped. The barn stood dilapidated among groves of trees between the St Louis hills. He had cut back in the direction of the river camp and found tracks leading towards the barn.

Apparently, a few miles downstream from St Louis,

on the river, was a small forest with a camp. Here, the dropouts from the town and the river traffic congregated and lived in huts and tents and sheds among the trees. It was a large camp with many men, women and children. They had horses and canoes. They survived by stealing. They stole from houses, shops, workshops, fur factories and boats. In particular, they stole from the steamboats and their cargos in the harbour. They lived beyond the law and were too dangerous to approach. If the militia attacked by land, they left by river. If the militia attacked by river, they left by land. Whenever they lost horses or boats, they stole replacements. And they always returned.

So, the sporting gentlemen appeared to have hired some help. An approach by night could lead to chaos.

Tony Parsons came to the hotel to say that the sporting gentlemen had been buying fodder and food in town. They were expecting to stay for some time. So, there was no hurry. Unless the ladies were being harmed. Then the letter arrived.

"We have your women. Bring your gold to the barn five miles due south from town."

They were joined by Tony Parsons and they talked into the night. What if this, what if that?

At last, they concluded that it would be an ambush. The gentlemen had no idea how much gold they might have, and they did not specify a sum, so it was not a ransom. Whichever way they came, openly or secretly, with or without the gold, they would be killed, and the ladies would suffer and would also be killed. They had no way of knowing whether the ladies were already suffering but they had to hope that they were being held as live bait. From these conclusions, Tom and Hackett knew what they had to do.

In the barn, the sporting gentlemen set their trap. Their main purpose was to ambush Tom and Hackett. Any gold would be a bonus. The ladies would be a gift to the dropouts from the camp. The main thing was that the ladies in the barn should be unharmed and on display if Tom and Hackett arrived. The dropouts must stay hidden.

The tall, lean, dark figure of the duel master was in charge. He was Gordon Hill. He was the enforcer and rarely visited the Harbour rooms because Madam Helena thought his presence too menacing and out of keeping with the elegance of the rooms. He played his cards with the fur hunters and made money. He had made the plan and he would see it through. He sat on top of a broken wagon and watched like a hawk. If he could kill the Englishmen, throw the women to the dropouts and blame them, he could solve the immediate problem and move back to their life in St Louis. The duel had been a vain mistake but perhaps he could pull it all together.

Denis Roach was small, thin and shifty. He was rat-faced and without any redeeming features, except that he was mathematically brilliant. He had a three-dimensional understanding of the cards and the odds that they implied. At the rooms, he was a secret weapon, controlled by Gordon Hill. He lived off scraps of cash and women thrown to him by Gordon Hill. He had an evil interest in women, unmatched by any capacity to engage for more than a few cruel minutes of failure and shame. But he remained obsessed.

Guy Davenport was medium sized, dark, plump, witty and charming. He was a cool poker player and he was wary of Gordon Hill. He was happy to stay outside the barn with the dropouts to organise the ambush.

The ladies were tied on a ledge at the back of the gig. Denis Roach could not resist feeling in their bodices and up their skirts. He would not be able to satisfy himself until the Englishmen had been killed. Gordon Hill had warned him, and he must do as he was told. But in the meantime, he groped and exposed himself.

"It's just like a penis, only smaller," said Elizabeth, haughtily.

"If he let go, he would lose it," laughed Nell. They were appalled by his attentions but had guessed that they were safe until Tom and Hackett were killed. This infuriated Denis Roach, and his lust and rage built up.

Guy Davenport organised the dropouts. There were seven of them, led by a burly old boatman who punished any disagreement. He had earned their respect. Guy Davenport worked with him to set lookouts and maintain order. They were working for a little gold, all the weapons and the women.

Tom and Hackett arrived before dawn. They tied the horses far away from the barn. The dawn chorus tuned up and hid the sound of their arrival.

Hackett carried his rifle. Tom carried the tin trunk. The barn was set among trees and they were able to approach quite close. From one hundred yards, back in the trees, they could see into the barn. Mainly there was gloom, but through the part-open doors, Hackett could make out the ladies on the back of the gig. Outside, they could see Guy Davenport flitting around the barn organising the dropouts.

So, the sporting gentlemen were intending to lure Tom and Hackett into the barn and to ambush them with the dropouts when they were trapped inside. The bait would be the ladies. Gordon Hill regarded the activities of Denis Roach with contempt. But that could be the catalyst that triggered the attack by the Englishmen.

Tom and Hackett agreed to scout the sides and back of the barn. Hackett took the left and TK, on a war footing, took the right. They had worked together many times before.

The sun was beginning to glint through the new leaves, creating light and shade. Hackett took great care. He skirted wide around the barn and approached from the rear, intending, then, to get a view of the left side. The shaft of the stave hit him across the head and shoulders and then the butt hit him in the kidneys and shocked him into immobility.

As with many around St Louis, Bill Johnson had been a river man and may go back to it again. At present, he was resting at the camp on the river. He was square. Not particularly tall but almost as wide, with a deep chest and broad shoulders. He had a flat head and was bald. So, he wore a round hat and they called him "Mr Johnson".

He could use guns, axes and knives but for today's adventure he had chosen a hickory stave, and that is what he had used to fell Hackett when he crept up behind. He strung Hackett up before re-joining the rest of the group and reporting to Guy Davenport. As instructed, he had not killed Hackett. That would be left to the ambush.

As his head cleared and his breath returned in little gasps, it took Hackett some time to realise that he was upside down with his long dark hair hanging over his eyes. He was suspended from the bough of a tree. His hands had been tied with the end of a rope, then his feet were tied with a double clove hitch. His weight was taken on the knots at his ankles. His wrists were tied but not supporting any weight. The rope had been strung over the bough and tied off to the trunk. His attackers had left him in order to join in the hunt for TK, then he would be led into the ambush.

TK had always imagined that Hackett was made of whipcord and wire. He was not tall, and he was not heavy. But he had incredible strength in his hands and limbs. The bang across his back was nothing compared to what he had suffered in the past when the legend grew that he never took a step back. He had eyes like a hawk, a nose like a beak and hands like talons. His head started to clear, and his breathing became regular. He was aware of a blackbird flitting in the tree, trying to distract attention from its nest.

When his hands had been tied, he had instinctively tensed his wrists. Now, he relaxed his hands and wrists, taking his full weight on the rope at his ankles. He pointed his fingers together and pressed his wrists together. Slowly, he worked his top hand out of the bind. It stuck. He repointed his fingers and wriggled his top hand. It was still stuck. Ah, he strained to bring his elbows together and wriggled again. The hand started to come free and then he easily pulled it clear. He used his free hand to release the ties from the other hand and the rope fell away.

So, Hackett was still upside down tied by his feet. However, his hands were free and he was able to rub his wrists to restore the circulation. And then he sat up. The rope that extended from the bough to his feet now became a facility. He jack-knifed at the waist and took hold of the rope below his feet. Then he pulled himself up to grasp the tight rope above his feet from which he was suspended. For anyone else, this could be a problem. For Hackett, with his gripping hands, it was less difficult. Even so, he had to work hard, a few inches at a time, to reach the bough. At last, he hung over the bough at his waist and leaned down to release the hitch on his ankles. Without tension, it released easily with his strong fingers. He kept hold of the rope and slid down to the ground. Then he crawled on hands and knees into the undergrowth. He was vulnerable. If the ambushers returned, he was unarmed and very stiff.

He took his time, waiting quietly for the circulation in his ankles to return. At last, he got some feeling in his feet and began to wiggle them. He did not hurry. He would be of no use without his legs. He knew that most of the strength in a fight came from his legs. He had lost his rifle, ammunition and knife. But Hackett always regarded weapons as a distraction. He could kill with his hands.

He sat quietly as his strength returned. He heard,

above him, the pigeons, always early starters, billing and cooing and fluttering. They were not being disturbed by any approach.

TK had found the main team guarded by a lookout on the right side of the barn. Here was a chance to use the bow to reduce the numbers. There was a slight disruption when Guy Davenport and his companion arrived to give the warning. But they stayed together, relying on numbers. They posted lookouts to warn of any attack.

The rifle would be too slow and too conspicuous. TK strung the bow and fitted heads to ten arrows. Then two more. With Guy Davenport there were eight targets. The lookout was the obvious first shot. If he hit him well, there may be no noise. After that, he would take his shots and take his chance. His gamble was that the sporting gentlemen would not move until he was dead or captured. He feared for Hackett, but had to fear for the worst but hope for the best. He would never give up on Hackett but he could not wait.

With so many shots, he would need the glove to take the pain out of the bowstring. If his judgement was correct, and they were waiting in ambush until he attacked the barn, he could stand here in the shadows and take his time before his targets started to move. He was shooting across a sunlit glade at clear targets. They could not attack in the open across the glade and they could not see their attacker.

He hit the lookout and fitted the second arrow before the target fell. He wanted the sporting gentleman but had to take an easier target. The gang were alerted, and TK managed one more hit as they took cover. Then, as they looked out, he aimed two feet below the eyes. If the eyes did not reappear, he counted a hit and looked for the next. He took a snap shot at Guy Davenport as he drifted away, and missed.

He aimed two feet below the back of the head of a dropout who had looked up to see Guy Davenport drifting away. The dropout died in anger.

After Davenport had left, the last two or three dropouts, including Mr Johnson, drifted off. The tables had been turned without warning. They had been brought to make an ambush but instead, they had been ambushed.

Tom waited. At last, he sensed a presence and reached for his knife. Hackett put his hand on his shoulder. Now the tables would indeed be turned. The last two sporting gentlemen were trapped in the barn with their hostages. They did not know that they had been deserted.

Tom and Hackett considered their strengths. Their location gave a good view of the barn and the groves around it. One rifle could command the area

Two gentlemen were trapped inside. Hackett took TK's rifle and TK crept forward with the bow. At the doorway, TK notched an arrow and looked through a gap. Clearly Gordon Hill was in charge, but the little rodent guarding the ladies could not be relied on not to do something stupid. TK nodded to Hackett to open the door by one foot. The rat came into view and, as he turned, the arrow hit him in the centre of the chest. He fell back transfixed, unable to move.

Gordon Hill realised that the tables were turned but he

was still in a commanding position. He had a rifle and two pistols. But he was exposed. He sat on a broken wagon thirty feet from the ladies. As Tom prepared to shoot him, he pushed one pistol into his belt, seized the other and ran to the gig.

Now he stood behind the ladies with two pistols, ready to kill if he was challenged. It was a stand-off. If Tom shot him, he could shoot a lady. He had not seen Hackett.

He called out, "Out there, I can shoot a lady if you shoot at me, or even if you hit me. I want you to rig up the gig and the ladies will drive us out. If you try to kill me, I will kill a lady. Come into the barn and rig the gig. I will drop the ladies off in the road."

For Tom, this was a new experience. He had had situations of life and death with his men in battle. He could weigh the options. He could balance the lives of his men against the possibility of victory. This was different. He had everything to lose. One bad choice and Nell or Elizabeth would be killed. He had to let Gordon Hill believe that he could succeed.

"Very well. You have not killed anyone yet, but not for want of trying."

Tom asked Hackett whether he had a clear shot. He nodded. Hill stood high on the gig with two duelling pistols. One had killed Otto and the other had killed Richard Price. They looked small in his big, raw hands. With his wide shoulders and bushy black hair, he was a commanding figure.

Tom asked Hackett to wait until Hill swung the pistol towards him and then aim for the head. He stepped into the barn and then started to step away from the gig.

Whether through instinct or intent, Hill swung the duelling pistol towards Tom. Hackett fired and Hill instantly lost a tonsil and a rather troublesome wisdom tooth. Tom dived towards the gig and Hill's shot went through the space that he had just vacated.

Hill remained tall and commanding, apparently unconcerned by his wounds. He spat blood and bone and turned to where Tom had dived. Hackett's second shot performed the lobotomy. And yet, Hill still stood in domination with his second pistol cocked. Tom could not reach him. He could draw his pistol but if he managed to shoot Hill, the momentum could drive Hill towards the ladies and a shot from the pistol could go anywhere.

It was a bizarre stand off. So long as Hill had what was left of his mind on shooting Tom the ladies were safe. If Tom peeped out and fired his pistol the ladies would be endangered from Hill's fall. If Tom showed himself Hill would fire but Tom could be hit. The last option was beginning to seem the best. If he rolled fast, Hill might shoot and might miss. That seemed to be their best chance.

In the meantime, Hackett realized that Hill was fixated with Tom. He bent low and ran up to the gig, jumped between the ladies and reached for the arm holding Hill's pistol. He knocked it up and it exploded bringing down dust, dirt and debris from the old roof. Aptly, he hit Hill in the big, prominent, Adam's apple with terrible force. Hill fell down choking as Tom emerged from under the gig. Hill may be dying, but he was not dead. To be certain, Tom drew the broad dark knife and stabbed Hill through the heart. Even then, Hill remained standing. But, at last he sank to his knees and finally fell in the dust of the barn floor. There he lay, with his wild black hair plastered with blood and brains, all coated with debris from the roof.

Dennis Roach was not dead. He had an arrow in the middle of his chest. TK later thought that it was his best shot, ever. Roach could not move but he could see and hear. And he was terrified. He made a mewing sound. The ladies went to him. They saw the pistol lying on the step of the gig within reach but beyond his capability.

Nell said, "Perhaps we should shoot him in what passes for his manhood."

Liz laughed, "It would be a difficult shot dear, it's so small."

Hackett spoke from behind them, "*Infra dignitas*, ladies. It is below your station."

And he picked up Roach's pistol and shot him between his beady little eyes.

"*Semper in rectam*, as always you are right, Hackett my dear. We would have been diminished," said Elizabeth. And Hackett groaned. One day she might leave him with the last word.

"And where's the fun in that?" said Nell.

They dragged the bodies to a dilapidated shed. Four dropouts and two gentlemen. They went through their pockets to retrieve some of Otto's losses but the gentlemen seemed to have been saving for the next hand of the game. They hitched up the gig and led out the three horses of the gentlemen. Then they set fire to the shed.

As the fire glowed behind them Elizabeth said "I think Hill had half a mind to kill us."

Nell said "No his mind was on other things."

Hackett said "He was just mindless."

Nell said "Tom…."

Elizabeth said "Come on Tom."

Tom understood that, for the ladies, this joking was a sign of the relief after their trauma. However, it was not his way to joke after battle. Banter and battle were two separate things. But he relented and said "I'm not sure about his mind, but I know that in the end, he did not have the heart for it."

And the fire glowed behind them as they headed home.

Ambush

Guy Davenport had drifted away. Mr Johnson and the surviving dropouts had waited for a call from the barn. But when none came, they assumed the worst and crept away. It was a long walk back to town. They hid in a copse until dark. They saw the glow of the fire from the barn. Then they went down to the quay. Mr Johnson took a boat. The oars had been taken away to prevent theft. This was no problem for Mr Johnson. He found a long pole, launched the boat and drifted on the current, using the pole to steer from the stern.

Guy Davenport went back to the house that he had shared with the other gentlemen. He went to his room and lit a lamp. He packed his trunk. Not much to show for his time in St Louis. He added the rifle and ammunition taken from Hackett's pockets. Finally, he lifted a floorboard and put a purse with his money in the chest.

He went to Gordon Hill's room and tried the floorboards. No movement. He moved the furniture. Still nothing. He tried the bed. Nothing. Finally, he pulled out the drawers of the cabinet and found the wallet at the back.

Next, he went to the room of Richard Price. He found the hiding place, but it was empty.

Finally, he went to Roach's room. There was nothing under the boards or in the bed or behind the drawers. In desperation he looked under the commode and there it was. Typical. And it contained twice as much as his own and Gordon Hill's wallets. Roach had been a thief among thieves.

So, the chest was finally showing a bit more for his time in St Louis and he locked it and went down to the quay.

He went to a steamer that was undergoing repairs. This was not unusual. It would take three or four days for spare parts to come upriver on the next steamer, to complete the fitting and take on a cargo. He had time to arrange his affairs before leaving for New Orleans. He would deal with the Englishman and move on. He went on board and noticed the familiar smells of polished wood and burned coal. He paid in advance for a cabin and he paid a little extra for his presence to be kept secret.

He went to the lads who ran the handcarts for the steamer passengers, led them to his room and led them down to his cabin. He used a carrot and a stick. He paid a little extra for secrecy. And he added the threat of whipping if his place on the steamer was revealed.

He sent a lad to Madame Helena with a request for him to visit at night. The message came back to "Come tonight. Come to the garden door."

That night he rented a horse and went up. He went through the garden to the door. In the dark, he could not see the flowers, but the scent was beautiful. He crept in.

Madame Helena had heard about the duel and had heard about the ambush at the barn. She believed that she could choose whom to support between the

Englishman and the gambler. She was confident of her position.

Guy Davenport was scared. He feared for his life. And he had only one card. He played it. He was hiding in a steamer. If the Englishman could be killed, he would stay in St Louis and restore order at the Rooms. If not, he must run downriver back to New Orleans. So, if Madame Helena would set a trap, he would spring it and the problem would be resolved.

Madame Helena quickly decided to keep her options open. Guy Davenport was clearly in trouble. Her first choice would be to bring the Englishman in to restore the dignity of the Rooms. And Guy Davenport could make his own arrangements to escape.

However, if she could not reach agreement with the Englishman, then Guy Davenport could take his chance with the ambush and she would him bring him back to the Rooms.

So, Madame Helena agreed that she would invite Tom Kynaston to the house for a chat. She would send him away and Guy Davenport could spring his ambush on the road down to the town. Madame Helena would pay the river people for the ambush.

Guy Davenport went to Mr Johnson. It took all of his charm and a lot of money to arrange the ambush. The dropouts would be paid well and could keep whatever they could find. For each it appeared to be a good deal. But Mr Johnson did not intend to let Guy Davenport live. He and Madam Helena were going to die and, as the sailors would say, there would be no loose ends.

There was no sign of Guy Davenport in the town. So,

eventually, the ladies emerged to resume their daily ride in the gig.

Hackett talked with the fur hunters. Frankly, he was not impressed with their manners and values. But he learned that they were all backwoodsmen from the east. They were rough, tough, mountain men. St Louis was the frontier. The last base before adventuring up the Missouri to the Rockies. So they had stories to tell and he was pleased to listen. He and Tony Parsons were forming a quiet understanding based on untaught experience and skills from two different continents. On top of this, Hackett had found some booksellers who were feeding his interest.

Tom received a summons, thinly disguised as an invitation, from the Governor's office.

He was greeted by a deputy. The Governor was away on governor's business.

"Thank you for coming, Kynaston."

"Colonel."

"I beg your pardon. From where do you claim that rank?"

"His Majesty's British Army."

"Well, the British Army has withdrawn from the Louisiana territories."

"Then I, also, will withdraw. Good day."

"I apologise. I over-stepped my position. I am the Deputy Governor, and on behalf of the Governor, we would appreciate your advice."

"Very well. It is polite to allow some minutes. Use them wisely."

"Did you reach the Pacific Ocean and the British base?"

"Yes."

"Is the base well established, well-ordered, and at peace with the natives?"

"Yes."

"How has this been achieved?"

"The British are traders. Fort Vancouver is held by the Hudson's Bay Company. They are traders. They trade with the natives for furs, weapons, tools and trinkets. They trade with the hunters for supplies and money."

"Did you see the territories east of the Continental Divide?"

"Yes."

"Were you attacked?"

"Not in the Rocky Mountains. We were not stealing furs. But anyone who steals furs will be attacked."

"Did you have friendly relations with the natives?"

"Yes. We were able to establish friendly relations with the nation south of the Yellowstone River. We helped each other. Two of their warriors led us to Fort Vancouver. They have good trading relations with a community of Dutch farmers. It's all based on trade."

"Apart from the furs, we may need to move them from a part of their lands."

"Then you must expect to fight."

"Where would you stand in the event of a fight?"

"With my native friends. They would not need much help from me. They have great manpower and they are very wealthy. However, if they needed help, then I would give it."

"You would fight against the U.S. Army?"

"Yes. If the U.S. Army attacked my friends, I would

help them. I would lend them my skills learned fighting with the British Army. However, they may not need my help. They are strong, resourceful and wealthy. The American government has no fight with those people. I would advise you to leave them in peace. In particular, stay away from the land to the south and west of the Yellowstone River. Thank you for the coffee. Good day."

On his way back to the inn, he was interrupted on his way along the boardwalk by frontiersmen ridiculing the well-dressed slave of Madame Helena. The slave was standing tall and dignified in the face of insults from the frontiersmen. They ridiculed him as a slave dressed up as a gentleman. Worse, he was a slave employed by a woman and dressed up by a woman. He was called Walter and he was standing defenseless in the face of this ridicule. It was not hostile, but it was demeaning. Clearly, Walter was taking it as part of his position and was weathering the storm. He had no defense, except his dignity.

Tom stopped. And waited. And watched. And waited. At last, the ridicule stopped, and the frontiersmen grew quiet. Then, one of the fur hunters from their voyage along the River Platte asked why he had stopped. Tom looked at him and did not say a word. He looked at the group and tilted his head and raised his eyebrows.

At last he said, "This gentleman is a slave. He is dressed by his owner and he does the work of his owner. He has no choice."

One of the frontiersmen said, "Look, maybe we were going too far."

Tom waited.

"Perhaps we should apologise."

Tom waited.

"Very well, we're sorry."

Tom nodded. Everyone stepped back. Walter walked on and Tom walked away.

Life settled down. The ladies trotted out, and Tom and Hackett wandered around the frontier town. The whole economy appeared to be based on the fur trade, the hunters, the factories, the traders and the investors. There was a constant undercurrent of trade. Furs came in from the west and went out on the convoys going east, and on the steamboats going south. Issues flared up and died down. The dispute with the sporting gentlemen and the ambush at the barn seeped out, circulated and died down. Tom and Hackett seemed to have gained a new respect, but no questions were being asked.

There was no sign of Guy Davenport. Tom was concerned to know that he was possibly out there, carrying a St James rifle. He mentioned this to Tony Parsons. Tony made some enquiries and heard that nobody had seen Guy Davenport since the day of the ambush at the barn. He could by lying low in the town. There was no indication that he had gone to the river camp. Tony Parsons asked his contacts to look out for him.

Tom received a note from Madame Helena inviting him for coffee. Reluctantly, he accepted and rode up to Madame Helena's fine house outside the town.

Madame Helena had arrived by steamboat, without trace. She assumed the status of a lady and nobody dared challenge her. She had bought the Harbour Reception Rooms and established a respectable venue for tea, coffee and polite card games at the tables. She was not accepted into polite society but there was so little polite society in the town that her wealth provided all the introduction that she needed. She bought a fine house on low hills outside the town and managed very well.

A group of sporting gentlemen arrived by steamboat from New Orleans and started to frequent her rooms. They provided some professionalism to the games but also a sharpness that was out of place among the elegance that she was trying to present.

Each of the sporting gentlemen had tried to endear himself to her but she wished to maintain her independence. She had allowed the challenger to escort her occasionally but, generally, kept her distance. Then Otto had arrived.

Tom handed over his horse to Walter and a pretty maid led him into an elegant reception room. He stood up when Madame Helena swept in wearing a deep red dress. Her dark hair was finely curled, and the dress was cut a fraction low, but her jewellery was discreet. She graciously invited him to sit at a coffee table with armchairs.

The pretty maid served coffee in porcelain cups from a silver pot. Tom slowly saw that the performance was intended to intimidate him and to establish her superiority. As if he had not seen such a fine reception before. And he smiled.

The performance continued. Madame Helena graciously offered sugar from a silver bowl. Tom sat back and drank coffee black, without sugar.

Madame Helena said, "I am so sorry that circumstances have prevented me from inviting you earlier. I was very fond of your friend, Otto. Then he got involved in that dreadful duel. I really believed that if Otto had made a proposal I may have been tempted. Seriously tempted. Those sporting gentlemen from New Orleans were becoming beyond my control. Of course, they resented Otto. It was very unpleasant. And then five kings, on one of my tables. It was a scandal. Dear Otto tried to restore some order but it was not to be. I regret the confrontation and I regret the outcome. I had thought that Otto might stand beside me in so many ways. But it was not to be. However, in a strange way, some good may come of it. Perhaps we can start again."

She leaned forward slightly, showing a little extra frontage, and placed her arm close to Tom's hand.

"I wonder whether I may count on you for support at this difficult time." And her brown eyes looked down with tears forming. Tom patted her hand and she leaned forward further to put her other hand on his.

Tom was a fighting man. Ladies' sentiment and tears were weapons against which he had no defence. He started to feel a strange protective emotion tinged with sexual awareness. Then he thought of Nell with her crazy laugh. This performance was not part of his world. Then he thought of the cards, the sporting gentlemen, the duel and the loss of dear Otto. He realised that he was being seduced by these tearful eyes. He withdrew his hand and sat back.

"Madame Helena, I am on my way to New York. I do not think that I will be able to help you."

The effect was dramatic. Madame Helena sat back. Her eyes, so recently filled with tears, now blazed and she rang a small silver bell.

"Mr Kynaston is leaving."

Walter met him with his horse. "Don't ride down the town road, Mr Tom. There is river trash from the camp hiding up in wait. Ride out through the fields."

Tom said, "Thank you, Walter, I know the men from the river camp. I thought I had seen the last of them. I will take the field paths."

So, Tom went through the fields and descended down the farm lanes into the town.

For Madam Helena, this was not in the plan. Either she expected Tom Kynaston to join her venture or she had expected him to ride into the trap. She was scared. She took her valise and rode down to negotiate with the dropouts. Guy Davenport had drifted away.

Tom, Hackett and the ladies dined well and there were no signs of trouble. The camp dwellers had received the visit of Madam Helena and Guy Davenport had drifted away.

Next morning, the ladies rode out in the gig. Hackett walked around the town looking for books. And Tom went to the county office to ask about the freeing of slaves.

St Louis had not abolished slavery, but ownership of slaves was not so onerously enforced as in the South. Slaves were working up on the steamboats to earn their freedom and then staying in the town to work as free men. Being black did not mean being a slave.

Tom had started to ride up to a grove above the

harbour to watch the sun set. He was fascinated to see the steamboats manoeuvring in slow motion for position on the jetty and lighters barging for business on the river and carters jamming up for trade on the quay. And all the time the muddy brown river flowed south, connecting growing towns on its journey to the sea, a thousand miles away.

That evening, the group ate supper together. Tony Parsons joined them. They were relieved that they had survived the vengeance of the sporting gentlemen and the dropouts from the river camp. Madame Helena may have set a trap with the dropouts, but Walter had foiled that. They discussed how soon they could leave for New York and agreed that it could be a mere matter of days. Elizabeth smiled.

The next morning, after breakfast, Tom found a visitor waiting for him. Walter had been waiting patiently.

"Mr Tom, Madame Helena has disappeared. She was not home last night after you left. She has been meeting trash from the river camp. I think they were making an ambush yesterday. After you left, she went to meet them and has not come back."

"How can I help?" asked Tom.

"Well, Mr Tom, if she has come to harm with the river trash, I need to have my papers. Also, Mr Tom, I need to register that my owner has disappeared. Mr Tom, will you come with me to the county office?"

This man had probably saved Tom's life and now he feared for his own life.

"Of course, I will come with you, Walter. We will borrow the lady's gig. Please wait two minutes and we will be on our way."

Tom returned with Hackett. They went to the livery yard and collected the gig. Tom had ridden H2 out whenever he could. She needed the open plains and had been neglected. The ride to New York would suit her. Hackett was amused that he would be holding the horse for a slave. He enjoyed the irony.

As they drove to the county office, Tom explained the order of business and asked Hackett to contribute. First, they must record that Walter had no part in the disappearance of Madame Helena. She had left the house soon after Tom. Also, the maid could confirm that Walter had remained in the house. Next, the county office must confirm the papers that had been recorded with them when Walter arrived with Madame Helena. Finally, in accordance with the papers, it may be possible to take the steps necessary to obtain Walter's freedom.

Hackett rehearsed Walter's movements after Tom had left the house and offered to go up to collect the maid, Martha, to add her testimony.

Walter said, "Thank you, Mr Hackett, she is too worried to come with me and too worried to stay."

At the courthouse they agreed that Hackett would return to the hotel in the gig to pick up Nell and/or Elizabeth to go up to the mansion to pick up Martha and bring her to the courthouse.

In the meantime, Tom and Walter went in and declared their business. There was some delay, and as Tom and Walter sat together Walter told his story.

As Tom understood it, of course, Walter had been born

a slave. His father had been owned by a merchant in New Orleans. He had served diligently and had been well treated and promoted to foreman. In the next generation, the merchant's son took over the business and offered to take on Walter. So, at the age of ten, Walter had been indentured for twenty-eight years. His notional pay would be set off against his manumission and he would be free at the age of thirty-eight. That was the way in New Orleans at that time and, for Walter, it could have been a lot worse in the plantations.

His new master had prospered and built the trading business into one of the most prosperous in New Orleans. Walter had inherited his father's acumen and in due course he was promoted to bookkeeper, secretary, office manager and finally, general manager.

Walter's master, Edward Sumption, had married a lady from France. She had arrived in New Orleans with no bona fides, only her claim to be of the French nobility, her beauty and her self-assurance. She styled herself Madame Helena Biencours.

Soon, Madame Helena had established a brilliant circle in New Orleans. Their receptions were the pinnacle of social life in New Orleans. And Walter was the manager.

Then, when it appeared that their position was established, a scandal erupted. Her husband, Edward Sumption, was in dispute with another merchant, Nicholas Pontiers, regarding a delivery of logs down the river. At one of their receptions, Nicholas Pontiers was caught by Edward Sumption with Madame Helena. Sumption hit Pontiers on the nose.

Rumours were rife. They had become lovers. Madame Helena was seducing Pontiers. Pontiers was humiliating Sumption. Pontiers did the only honourable thing. He paid a team of stevedores to rough up Sumption. It was not too bad, but as they kicked him into the harbour, his head hit a mooring post. He gasped for breath, choked and drowned. There were hangings. Pontiers paid a fine. Mrs Pontiers denounced Madame Helena. Factions formed and the social status of Madame Helena was destroyed.

Nicholas Pontiers refused to pay the disputed debt because of the fine. Madame Helena closed the business, sold their mansion and took passage on one of the new steamboats to St Louis. She asked Walter to go with her. He agreed, provided that she would register his papers in St Louis. She agreed.

Madame Helena had bought the Harbour Rooms and fitted them out in the best style of New Orleans. Walter managed the rooms. He was black but he was tall and handsome, finely dressed and he carried himself with great dignity. Also, he knew his business. It was all very polite. Ladies and gentlemen would meet for tea and coffee in the rooms and the gentlemen played cards with great style. Madame Helena bought a fine house above the town. It appeared that she had reinvented and re-established herself as Madame Helena Biencours to perfection. Then the sporting gentlemen stepped off the steamer and her world changed. The handsome Richard Price tried to steal her heart. Gordon Hill took over the games. Guy Davenport played with charm and made it fun. Denis Roach set up a blackjack game and quietly took his percentage.

Otto had changed all that. His tall, handsome, lazy, self-assurance had been irresistible. Here was what Madame Helena needed to establish her position. Otto did not stand a chance. He thought that he was winning with Madame Helena. She thought that she was managing him beautifully. Then there was the duel. Madame Helena had not been the same since.

"So, Mr Tom Madam Helena had been meeting Guy Davenport secretly after the ambush at the barn and he brought up the river camp trash. After you left the house Madam Helena rode down alone to meet the river camp trash on the road. I never saw her again."

Hackett arrived with Martha. She was very pretty and, at Elizabeth's suggestion, had tidied herself up and put on her best dress.

The clerk was shocked to receive so many visitors, but they offered to limit the numbers to two at a time. They started with Tom and Hackett going through the procedures that must be followed. Tom always outranked Hackett. However, he had run away from school. Hackett had received a good education before his father's business led him astray. Tom had always turned to Hackett for help with the administration. Tom had the big picture, but he relied on Hackett to fill in the details. So, they asked the clerk to tell them the procedure. Tom helped him to set out the stages that must be followed and at each stage.

Hackett was available to help with the detail. Step by laborious step, they went through the detailed procedure. When the clerk hesitated, Hackett gently helped him.

When they needed detail, they called in Walter or Martha to help. At last it was done. The amount for Walter's freedom was settled. It was not impossible. He had almost served his twenty-eight years. Tom paid, and the papers were issued. Hackett had provided many of the words and he felt some pride of authorship. Finally, Walter was free.

Martha was different. She had more years to serve and was still a valuable asset if Lady Helena wanted to sell. In the absence of Lady Helena and any papers, Martha was just an unclaimed asset. They delivered Walter and Martha to friends in the town.

Now, they were finally closing their business in St Louis. Tom went with Tony Parsons to the wagon yard and sold the trailer. At the livery yard they checked the horses and mules. They sold a couple of horses that had struggled on their journey to St Louis and bought replacements. They double checked the saddles and bridles and ordered replacements.

In the evening, Tom went up to the copse on the hill above the harbour. He sat under his favourite tree. He watched a paddle steamer manoeuvring in the channel heading downriver for New Orleans. What was the cargo? Who were the passengers? What were their hopes and fears?

He was content. But as Captain John Phipps would say, there was one loose end. Guy Davenport was still at large with a St James rifle.

Guy Davenport

Tom, Hackett, Tony and the ladies met over dinner. They were ready to go. But, Tom could not leave the loose end.

Nell and Elizabeth pleaded with them not to take any risks. They had come so far, and they were nearly back to civilization.

Tom said, "There is one loose end and we have to do what has to be done. It is our code."

The next day, Tom and Hackett went to the house where the gentlemen had lived. They saw the signs that the hiding places had been looted. The owner came from next door to complain that the rent was overdue, and she had seen the lads from the quay taking a trunk away in a handcart. She feared that her tenants had flitted. They went to the quay and Hackett saw the youth who had tried to steal the valise of Madame Helena all those days ago. He placed his hands on the young man and whispered in his ear. Then he leaned to hear the whisper of the reply.

The quay had been built up to prevent flooding of the town and served well for mooring the steamers. Now it was busy with loading and unloading, embarking and disembarking. The steamer that the boy had pointed to was undergoing repairs to its engine. Heavy parts were being swung in and out. Workmen lifted and lowered, pushed and pulled all around the gang plank leading into the steamer. Tom and Hackett decided to come back later. They would wait for evening.

Mr Johnson was a river man. Just like seamen, he did not like loose ends. Now he had two loose ends. Guy Davenport had drifted away from two ambushes that he had asked Mr Johnson to set up and left Mr Johnson to fend for himself. Mr Johnson had decided that the death penalty would be appropriate. Tom Kynaston had escaped from both the ambushes which hurt Mr Johnson's professional pride. Unfinished business.

Many of the boys from the river camp worked the quay. They cheerfully broke their deal with Guy Davenport and told Mr Johnson where he was staying on the steamboat that was being repaired. He decided that Guy Davenport would be the priority. there was no time like the present. He would go to the steamer tonight. He would take his butcher's knife. There was a full bright moon casting deep shadows.

Guy Davenport was terrified. He knew that Mr Johnson could not forgive his desertion. Also, the Englishmen were relentless. He had been using the boys from the quay to bring him food and news. So, he knew that both Mr Johnson and the Englishmen were looking for him. And had grievances. He was counting the hours until the steamer would leave. In the meantime, he locked himself in his cabin and sat with the rifle and his pistol loaded.

Mr Johnson arrived first. He stayed in the shadows until he saw the steamer captain stroll down the gang plank and head for the tavern where the river captains met. A new steamer had arrived and the captain was keen to hear the news. Mr Johnson stayed in the shadows until he reached the gang plank and then heaved himself into the boat.

Tom and Hackett arrived in time to see Mr Johnson go aboard. Was Guy Davenport employing Mr Johnson for another ambush or had Mr Johnson lost patience? They waited for him to pass through the boat and then followed silently.

The cabins were on the top deck at the bow of the boat. They were in two rows either side of a central passageway and had an external deck-way with doors to the passageway and the deck-way. They heard voices from the foremost cabin on the river side. Mr Johnson had gone down the passageway and kicked in the door. It was hanging open. Tom took the passageway and Hackett took the deck-way.

Mr Johnson had stood in the doorway and seen twin barrels pointing at his chest. But Guy Davenport did not fire. He wanted to use his best weapon and charm his way out of the situation, as usual. Unfortunately, he was not looking the part. He was unclean and unshaven, his shirt was dirty and his coat was crumpled. On balance, Mr Johnson was looking more presentable and became more confident.

Guy Davenport started to explain that he had left the ambush at the house because he did not want Madam Helena to recognise him in case he could step in to mediate at some point. Mr Johnson said "Cut out yer big words and lower yer gun." Guy Davenport pointed the rifle between Mr Johnson's feet and asked what had become of Madam Helena.

"Ah, I left 'er with the boys and went 'ome to Mrs Johnson"

And he gave a yellow, broken grin at the mention of his domestic arrangements. In fact "'ome" was a canvas and wood construction that had started as a tent and been reinforced and repaired with planks and posts and spars to take on a shape of its own. "Mrs Johnson" was the latest in a succession of camp girls who served his needs.

Tom could see through the gap between the inner edge of the door and the frame. He saw Mr Johnson reach inside his jacket for the butcher's knife. Mr Johnson intended to step forward inside the arc of the rifle barrels and then use the big knife. Guy Davenport was a card player and a gambler. He recognised the movements of hands and eyes. He saw Mr Johnson glance at the rifle and saw his hand slip under his coat. He jumped back as Mr Johnson drew the knife. He raised the rifle and pulled the trigger. The effect was spectacular. He had cocked both hammers, so both barrels fired. Mr Johnson sat back against the side of the cabin with the knife in his hand and Mrs Johnson became a widow. Guy Davenport fell back the other way and sat against the chest. Still a bachelor with the rest of his life ahead of him.

Tom drew the pistol and stepped across the cabin to open the deck-way door. It opened outwards. Hackett stepped in and moved Guy Davenport's pistol on the desk away from his outstretched hand.

Tom was wondering how they should deal with Guy Davenport when he bolted. He dived past Hackett on all fours, out of the door to the deck, through the rail and into the river. Hackett had seen the situation, but

Davenport's dive took him by surprise. They heard the splash as Davenport hit the muddy, cold waters of the Mississippi river. Then came the gasp as he took in air and a little water. Davenport set off fast away from the steamer.

Tom and Hackett went to the point where Guy Davenport had left. Was it a dive or was it a jump? He came up, gasped and splashed towards the quay. Then he went down and did not reappear.

The heavy pistol came through the passage doorway first. Tom dived and slammed the cabin door onto the wrist. Hackett stepped aside and twisted the pistol away through the thumb. It did not go off. He threw it into a corner and it did go off. A chair at the desk sagged on three legs. Hackett pulled the empty hand into the cabin. It was the captain.

Tom pushed the captain back into the cabin and ordered him to send a few spectators from the door.

He said, "That man had tried to kill us twice. We would have killed him, if necessary, because he would have tried again."

Hackett picked up the rifle, went to the trunk and pulled out the ammunition and the wallets. He poured the money onto the table. Among the large pile of cash there were four gold coins. Otto's coins.

Tom said, "The rifle is ours. These four gold coins were stolen from our friend. You can have the rest, if that accords with your view of the rules of the river. Are you satisfied?"

The captain held his wrist and agreed. He did not want any further delay. He wanted to leave early next day.

Together they dropped Mr Johnson over the side.

It was a trick that Guy Davenport had learned as a boy in the warm waters far down river without clothes and without boots. He managed to keep down and swim back to the bow of the boat. Coming up would be harder, and he could not breathe out. He kicked frantically and, at last, came up under the bow. He breathed out and rolled on his back to breathe in, desperately. He listened for sounds above. He heard voices and the splash of Mr Johnson's disposal. Then only the lapping of the current.

He stayed close to the hull of the boat and worked his way to the stern. Then, another underwater dive to reach the next boat along the quay. Then he worked his way along to a slipway and crawled out very slowly to rest among the canoes and rowboats. He wrung out his coat and shirt and decided that they were better on than off. He knew that in the cool evening breeze he would need to act quickly. But he knew what he had to do.

He scrabbled, looking for a piece of heavy wood like a broken paddle. He was in luck again. He found a short iron bar tied through a ring to secure a boat.

He knew a tavern with stables, outbuildings and, importantly, a privy twenty yards from the back door. He squelched through the shadows and waited near the privy. He was tempted to test the warming quality of a couple of horses in the stable as he started to shiver, but he hung on. Clients strode, waddled and staggered to the privy. But he was waiting for a man of his size, walking alone. He was shivering badly when a heavy old man set off alone. When he reached the privy door, Guy Davenport raised the bar and hit him with all the strength that he could muster. He fell immobile.

Perhaps dead. Guy Davenport did not really care. He quickly pulled his victim into an empty stable and waited for the secondary residents to scrabble and flutter away. And then he stripped his victim. The clothes were old and worn and fitted loosely. The boots would not fit but the socks could replace his wet ones. His borrowed clothes smelled of tobacco. He bundled up his sodden clothes, threw a horse blanket over his victim, and crept back into the shadows.

It was a long walk up to the house of Madame Helena. He dumped the sodden bundle in a ditch under a bridge. Then he walked on in the shadows. He did not meet anyone.

He had warmed up by the time he reached the house. It had been shuttered up, but a side door had a weak bolt and he got in.

He found some hard cheese and water in the kitchen. Then he went straight up to Madame Helena's study. There was space behind a drawer in the bureau but it was empty.

The study led into the bedroom. A massive wardrobe almost covered one wall. There were hat boxes on the shelf above the dresses and there were shoes underneath. But below them there was a row of drawers. He pulled them out and saw that one was shorter than the others. He cleared the space above it and used Madame Helena's silver letter opener to lift the lid of a compartment. He smiled.

This had been only her reserve fund and she had taken a lot of money down to the river people to buy off the ambush – with fatal consequences. However, there were four small bags of gold coins and that would be enough.

He took a quilt from Madame Helena's bed and set off into the moonlight. He would go through the fields and find a place to sleep in the shadows.

He woke at dawn and was the first customer for a bath and a shave. He was early into the store to buy new clothes. The storekeeper raised an eyebrow when he was presented with a gold coin.

"Hard work paying off at last," said Guy Davenport. He wore the new clothes out of the store, carrying the stolen clothes in a bag.

At last, he could present himself for breakfast at an inn on the quay. They directed him to the next boat to leave. The boys saw him board the boat but could only wait for enquiries and possible tips. But none came.

He slept through the bustle of the loading of the cargo and woke on the river at last heading south. They passed the camp on the river and he saw urchins playing on the shore.

Two miles downstream they passed a bend where the current slowed and dropped flotsam on a dirty beach. Lying in the shallow water, nudged by the weak current, was a woman in a dark red dress. Her skirt was lifted, and her bare legs floated pale in the dirty water. A little further along, under the branches of a dead tree, Mr Johnson floated on his back, bloated from the wind in his large stomach. His hat had travelled further but now sat among the rubbish. The captain thought that there may be a story there. But not for him. He increased speed and the wash of the paddles pushed the bodies further up the dirty beach.

Guy Davenport looked back and smiled. It had all turned out nicely after all.

Leaving St Louis

Walter paddled hard against the current. The long canoe was making progress. He wore dungarees, slave clothes, but around his neck he wore a small, corked flagon with his papers and a few coins. He was a free man heading north, for Canada. At the back of the canoe, behind the other paddlers, sat Martha, a slave, on the perilous underground route north. Both were heading for Canada and hoping for a new, free, life.

At Fort Vancouver, John Potts left the Partner's dining room and went down to his new boat and his assistant.

At the Settlement, the first mules were born and the Dutch families wondered about the fate of the English people who had left this long eared legacy. And so much more.

Harry thought that it was time for him to make one of his regular visits to the Settlement. In particular, it was time for another reading and writing lesson. Jack and Jill and their cat and dog were changing his world. And his teacher was turning it up-side down.

The team put on their buckskins. They would be riding the last part of their journey on horseback. They loaded the spare horses and the mules with their back packs. The mules did not know that they were carrying hat boxes. Elizabeth hoped that Ben Horseman would not have forgotten their understanding. Nell was looking forward to taking New York by storm, but she was feeling a little off colour this morning. Tom, Hackett and Tony looked forward to exploring the potential of the railways, the investment opportunities and the chance for adventure. These were their thoughts. With just one thousand miles of open prairie to travel, what could go wrong…………..

…………….Well, quite a lot, actually.

****

They camped in the open on the plain on the first night. They had completed sixty miles. Nell and Elizabeth were sure that they could maintain this pace.

The next morning, Nell was too ill to move, never mind ride. She and Elizabeth read the signs and declared that she was with child and the sickness would continue. She could not go on.

They agreed that TP would ride back to St Louis to collect a trailer. The others would follow the trail back if Nell could manage it. They expected to meet on the trail and to transfer Nell to the trailer for the return to St Louis.

TP cantered away and the others waited for Nell to recover a little. Eventually, Tom and Hackett decided to repeat the procedure that the Smiths had used to save Hackett all those years before. They made a cushion on the front of Tom's saddle and wrapped Nell in a blanket and rested her in Tom's arms. Then they began to walk back.

Hackett changed places with Tom after a few hours and they kept going until evening. They camped in the open air on the open plain. In the morning they would wait for Nell to recover enough to set off again.

They Met TP in the late morning. They transferred Nell to the trailer and rested her on buffalo robes among the hat boxes.

They reached St Louis in early evening. It was a beautiful time and people were walking out and meeting in the lanes and squares in the French tradition. TP had reserved rooms at their hotel and Nell immediately took to her bed apologizing to everyone all the way.

Downstairs they held an emergency meeting. The lovely lady who owned the hotel came in to tell them that the Governor had returned and the Deputy Governor had called with soldiers. She had told them that her guests had left for New York. There was no reason to provide an update. TP arrived with more news. The Deputy Governor had made his report, including his hostile interview with Tom, stories of the feud with the sporting gentlemen and the disappearance of Madam Helena. He had been ordered to bring Tom in for interview. It would not take long for news of their return to reach the Deputy Governor. Reluctantly, they concluded that they would have to leave. The only way for Nell to travel would be by steamboat. But could they afford it?

They put their money on the table. It had a fine embroidered cloth. The coins looked few and poor when Tom and Elizabeth had contributed. Hackett's contribution improved the picture because he had not been buying hats. Finally, TP added a bag of coins that was all that he had to show for risking his life on the prairie and in the mountains. Tom and Hackett said that they would repay him double. Elizabeth straightened her shoulders, "treble."

Now they had a chance. But could they find a boat before the Deputy Governor found them? And even if they found a boat, they would have little left when they arrived in New Orleans, to pay for passage to New York.

Elizabeth pointed out that if one or two of them could ride to New York they could deliver letters to the bank and perhaps, with a slight blush, to Ben Horseman and

Adam Hillstrider, to help the bank with the transfer to a bank in New Orleans.

Brilliant. They looked at the options. If TP could ride H2 to New York with the best spare horses, to New York, he could carry the letters, and the others could take a steamboat to New Orleans. They agreed that TP could ride alone. Hackett's urban skills may be needed in New Orleans.

TP went to his contacts. He kept H2 and the two best horses. He sold the other horses and the mules. Even tough old TP had become fond of those mules. He got a promise that they would be well treated and he would need to borrow them one last time. He would be back and would not want to be disappointed.

Tom and Hackett went down to the harbour and found the inn where the steamboat captains met. They remembered the night when they had watched Guy Davenport's fate unfold. It had started with his visit to the inn.

Tom remembered the inn where the captains met in Liverpool. The same fog of pipe smoke. The same quiet talk of experienced men talking among equals. And the smell of rum punch.

He went to the innkeeper and asked whether any of the captains had a boat leaving for New Orleans in the next few days. The innkeeper pointed the stem of his blackened pipe at a small, grey-bearded man in a captain's coat on this warm evening. "E'll be next out". Tom and Hackett went over to him and introduced themselves. "Ham Coyne" growled the reply in a strong Glaswegian voice. "Me boat's the River Belle." Tom asked whether he could take four passengers and when he would be leaving. "Aye I've got space. I leave at dawn, day after termorrer".

Before Tom could speak, Hackett took over. It was not a negotiation. It was a gentle growling contest. The result was that they had two standard cabins at the standard price and Hackett told Tom to pay.

Tom asked how long they would take to reach New Orleans. "Bout three weeks. I last by saving me boilers. Also, need to make a couple a stops." Tom suppressed, a smile. On full board, while he waited for his money, Ham Coyne could take as long as he liked. So long as he left at dawn on the day after tomorrow.

Back at the hotel, they added TP's money from the livery. There was not much left. Ben and Adam would look after TP in New York. But they would not last long in New Orleans. "If they have pawn brokers, we may survive" said Tom, "How much are the hats worth?"

So they wrote the letters late into the night. Elizabeth had the best handwriting and the best spelling, but they used a lot of paper. The first letter was to Tom's bank asking them to send the full balance of his account to the bank's chosen bank in New Orleans. The next was to Ben Horseman asking him to follow up the instructions to the bank. Elizabeth added a PS. The last was to Adam Hillstrider, asking him to liaise with Ben to raise the money and pay TP as much as he needed. They were rich, with large credits with HBC and they needed to get home.

TP picked them up at dawn with the trailer and mules, now on loan. TP's contacts had reported that the Deputy

Governor had heard of their return and was planning a visit.

They checked out of the hotel and spent the day and night in a copse, dreading the sound of military horses. But none came. The Deputy Governor was directing operations from his desk. He had learned that they had left again for New York with a trailer, so he could pick them up on the plain. No hurry.

TP would bring the trailer and mules, to pick them up before dawn. If all went well, at dawn Tom, Hackett, Nell and Elizabeth would be on the boat and TP would be on the ferry. It might be a close-run thing. Would the boat leave on time? Was the Deputy Governor an early riser?

Nobody slept that night. Before dawn TP arrived with the trailer and the mules. Tom carried Nell. TP and Hackett loaded the saddle bags and rolls. Elizabeth added the hat boxes with a lovely smile. And they went to catch a boat.

On the quay, the sun was touching the tops of the boats and slanting into the spaces between them. At the River Belle, they moved quickly. Tom picked up Nell and ran up the gang plank. A fierce lady barred the way. "What's the illness?" Elizabet dropped the hat boxes. "Morning sickness. She is with child." The stern lady smiled and led the way to the cabin. She and Elizabeth made Nell comfortable. "Don't ye fret yersel, we'll make her fine. Breakfast in the saloon in an hour. Two fine guests and two others yet to come if they get outer bed". Tom was ignored. TP and Hackett brought up the saddle bags, rolls and, with big smiles, the hat boxes. Tom handed the letters to TP. TP nodded and left. Tom heard the creak of the trailer and the jingling tapping of trotting mules as they left, the sun was bringing dawn along the quay. A clock chimed the half hour. Tom asked Ham Coyne when they would leave. "Afore six." Came the reply but nothing happened. Tom walked along the quay watching for the fine guests and the Deputy Governor and his escort. But nothing happened. The Quay was calm and the sun crept forward.

At last, he heard the rattle of iron on stone and dreaded the arrival of the Deputy Governor, but the fine guests had arrived and were led to the master cabin. Tom's heart sank when he saw the luggage piled on the coach. The two coachmen carried the cases up one at a time. Tom fought off the temptation to offer to help. He just had to stand and watch, case by case always listening again for the rattle of iron hooves on the cobbles signaling the arrival of the Deputy Governor and his escort. But it did not come. At last, the final couple of bales were lowered into the hold. Would Ham Coyne now wait for the last two passengers?

At the hotel, the soldiers learned that the guests had left for New York. At the Deputy Governor's residence they waited for him to finish breakfast and mount up. At the ferry, they saw the pale blonde hair of TP, touched by the early sun, on the other side of the river, with three horses, loping east. They clattered to the harbour. The clock struck six. At the harbour, they saw the River Belle complete her turn and start to drift south, her paddles turning slowly. And two passengers arrived late. Time, tide and Ham Coyne wait for no man.

The boys on the quay confirmed that the English had left. The Deputy Governor was not sorry to see them go. It saved him a lot of trouble in a lot of ways. His timing had been perfect.

On the boat, Tom and Hackett saw the Deputy Governor arrive, followed by the late passengers. They could not relax. Ham Coyne might turn back or the Deputy Governor may choose to follow them along the river and call on Captain Ham Coyne to pull in. Then what would he do? Tom found himself edging towards the wheelhouse. But Ham Coyne did not turn back and the Deputy Governor did not follow.

The River

Tom and Hackett were not sorry to see St Louis grow smaller in the early morning sun. They saw the camp in the wood by the river and watched the first activities of the day with fires starting and children being set to work. Further down river, they passed the beach where all the debris from the river washed up. As they drew level a crowd of vultures and crows took to the air screeching and cawing. They left a mess of carrion with bits of black and red cloth and the white glint of bone in the water. Hackett raised an eye brow and Tom shook his head. The boat paddled on. At last they had left St Louis behind them.

In the saloon: "Mr Kynaston, I hope". They were sitting at the table with the other passengers.

"You have the better of me, Sir".

"I am George Maine. This is my wife, Frances. We have been living in St Louis for a few months and have heard a lot about you. I have been hoping to meet you but the Governor "borrowed" me to choose a location for a new fort on the river. By the time that I returned, I heard that you had left. Then, I heard that you were back, but leaving again soon to avoid the Governor. I gambled that you would leave by river and advanced my departure."

"Well, my wife is with child and ill in the morning. We hope to sail gently to New Orleans to embark for New

York. That said, we will be pleased to exchange a few pleasantries along the way." Tom introduced Hackett and Elizabeth who explained that Nel was lying down and may emerge to demand larks tongues or whatever else was her fancy for the day. Frances Maine smiled and gently started to join the ladies group.

In the meantime, Mrs Coyne produced a good breakfast. Ham Coyne came in to complete the introductions. His son, Robbie, was the Assistant Captain, Assistant Engineer and Stoker. There were a couple of deck hands – and don't get in their way. He explained that they would be travelling slowly on the current and saving the boilers. They would stop for a couple of days in Memphis. Otherwise, they should spend their time in the cabins, on the foredeck and in the saloon. It would become very hot and he would arrange sun shades on the foredeck.

Mrs Coyne and Frances Maine set out the areas where the ladies would arrange themselves. The gentlemen were left to make do with the rest.

George Maine really wanted to talk to Tom. But gradually, he started to see that Hackett had been by Tom's side throughout, was well read and had studied the terrain on their journey. He provided a different perspective. Frances Maine recognized that Elizabeth had been well schooled and had a sharp intellect. When Nell started to add her own outrageous alternative perspectives, Frances was enthralled.

George Maine was short and round with wavy dark hair carefully brushed against his head. He wore a cotton jacket with a cotton shirt and a stock tied in a bow. A straw hat completed the picture. He brimmed with self-confidence. He led the conversation by explaining that he originally came from Boston. He was a designer of major works that created economic opportunities. He had been in St Louis to look for opportunities. Clearly, the levee and harbour could be expanded without limitation. The steam-boats carried away furs downstream. But where were the opportunities upstream? Who would buy boatloads of cargo from New Orleans? That is why he wanted to know the situation in the west. Could St Louis grow crops? Was there a railway opportunity? Always, what were the opportunities, what were the limitations?

Tom explained that the HBC had fought for, and won, a monopoly of the fur trade on the west of the Rocky Mountains, the Columbia river and the sea routes. From St Louis it was two thousand miles of open country to Fort Vancouver. From there it was thousands of miles by sea to China to the west or round Cape Horn to New York and Europe to the east.

Tom asked whether it was worth investing in railways to cross the continent.

"The time and cost would be a big risk. The limitation, now, would be whether the furs would last and whether the fashions would last. Thirty years ago people were wearing felt hats with feathers and buckles." George looked closely at Tom. "Gold might do it".

"Right now, the potential for railways is to build on known markets, to link with steamboat routes and to connect cities that are already trading. The limitations are iron, coal, water and, surprisingly, wood. The trains can carry everything that they need except, perhaps, sufficient water. I am going to take a very close look at railways next."

Hackett said, "Add rivers, mountains, swamps and natives to your list of limitations."

George said, "That is why I wanted to meet you."

So, George returned to his questions about the prairie between New York and the Missouri. The answers to his questions about the land to the west of the Missouri seemed to have convinced him that there were no opportunities in that direction. Too many limitations perhaps.

Hackett had been taking a close interest. Later he asked Tom whether George could be trusted. He must know about the gold. "Let's wait and see."

Nothing can be decided until we reach New York. And our team will be waiting. In the meantime, if he asks us to invest in something that is too good to miss, the river will be waiting. But I think he is a genuine enthusiast and good company."

While George questioned Hackett, Tom took the opportunity to chat to Ham Coyne at the wheel of the boat. Ham had a strong Glasgow accent, which Tom liked. He had started as an apprentice in the Glasgow ship yards and had seen the start of the steam age. His career had coincided with the development of the technology. He became an expert in the building of steam engines. He had been asked to bring an engine to New Orleans and to supervise the fitting to a paddle boat. It had gone well and he and Mrs. Coyne had fallen in love with the river life. He had been given a share of the boat. The next step may be to move to St Louis and start a repair business. The climate would be better and he could buy a nice house, but all the broken down boats would naturally float on the current to New Orleans, so he would be working against the natural order. Tom asked whether Ham could build steam engines in America. "Yes," said Ham, and continued in his broad brogue "if there was a forge with iron and coal. Also, you would need lathes, drills and other machines. The British have been reluctant to allow them to be exported. But now it seems easier and they are being made in New England. I could build the engines but you may have trouble transporting them. They are big and heavy. It would all depend on the location." Tom asked whether Ham could build small steam engines. "Yes", said Ham and he took out his pipe and smiled. The smile was the same colour as the pipe. Perhaps, at one time, they had both been white. "Even the small ones are heavy."

Ham pointed out the hazards of the river. There were islands and shoals. Even on these upper stretches broken logs were a major danger. As they progressed south, more and more cut logs would be encountered. Boys with canoes strung three or four together in small rafts and navigated them on the current, dancing on the trunks and steering with a long pole. Lower down, the rafts got bigger, with shelters built on. These were hard to manoeuvre and a real hazard. Also, lower down, the tributaries had log jams formed by trees washed into the river in storms that got wedged and caused a backup that could be almost a hundred miles long. Now and then a block rotted free and washed into the main river. They could sink you.

The summer days on the deck in the ladies' section were a joy. Frances Maine brought new experiences from new locations and really wanted to know about London and English country life. In turn she told about the eastern cities and, of course, New Orleans. Nell and Elizabeth added a flavour of life at the settlement. The mule breeding brought out Frances's fan in a flutter.

Each day Nell recovered a little earlier and the smile widened a little and the laugh grew louder. But now the mosquitos were beginning to bite in the evening. Mrs Coyne and Frances Maine did their best but the result was that the laugh now emerged from a bundle of cotton. Even so, Nell was laughing again.

They arrived at Memphis. George had helped to choose the location for the town. He explained that, after taking account of the limitations, it was the best place to build a harbour connecting the Ohio River with the Mississippi. Tobacco, cotton, coal, timber and sugar flowed down the Ohio for transport to New Orleans and beyond. He had helped to design the town. He was very proud of this and his investors were very pleased. George showed them round and explained the reasons for various features. He showed them the saw pits where logs floated down river were cut into planks. One man stood above the log with the top of the saw. He was the "top dog". Another man stood below at the bottom of the saw, covered in saw dust. He was the "under dog".

For the English team, it was a shock to see how much of the work was being carried out by slave labour. How much of the cargo was being loaded by slave labour. The working of the town depended on slave labour. Surely slave trading was illegal and the British were enforcing an embargo. George explained that the whole economy was founded on slave labour. Some slave traders beat the embargo. But, mainly, the existing slaves were extremely valuable. They were part of the economy. Emancipation provided a little respectability. But new generations born into slavery would continue to power the plantations and provide more and more of the workforce. Even after they were emancipated, they had no real alternatives and their labour was cheap. Tom did not ask about the limitations. He would not invest in the businesses of the Mississippi.

One evening Ham Coyne announced that they were "in for a blow". They would anchor for the night close to the shelter of an island. They would also run a mooring rope to one of the pines on the island. Otherwise, supper passed as usual with the exchange of information from Europe to New York to New Orleans and Fort Vancouver. As they retired it started to rain. In the night they were woken by shouting from the river and shouting from the boat. Tom and Hackett went on deck to investigate. They had to go down to the lower deck to see the frantic activity. Robbie was supervising the hands to be ready with quant poles. A raft was coming. Tom and Hackett picked up poles and peered out into the rainy night. At last, they saw it. Four logs, each five feet wide and fifty feet long had been secured together and were being pushed towards the boat on the current swirling round the island. They had to push it away. They worked frantically with the crew and it seemed that they would succeed. But the back of the raft swung in at the last moment and hit the boat in the worst possible place – the paddle wheel. From the boat, someone called "Why didn't you drop anchor?" and through the dark and rain they caught the reply, "We aint got no anchor".

At breakfast George observed that Ham must have been pleased to push the raft off. "We din't push the raft off, we pushed the boat off, and it's damaged".

Luckily, the damage was mainly to the woodwork, the ironwork was bent but not broken. Ham supervised the repairs with loving care. He got the boat ready to leave the next morning. Just another day on the river.

As they edged closer to New Orleans, George asked what they were going to do next. Tom said that he had thought that they might look at contributing their experience to building railways to the west. However, it looked as though there would be too many limitations. They did not know if there would be any other opportunities for their experience. "So you expect to go to work?" said George. Tom smiled and Hackett said "We would not invest in anything that we did not control. That is our way." George laughed, "Well, perhaps you may be able to start a little closer to home. Closer to New York there may be the opportunities for building railways without the limitations of going west. I will be coming to New York. Perhaps we can meet." So, no tempting offers at this stage. They would have been disappointed. Hackett, in particular, was warming to George.

Between Tom and Hackett, there was beginning to be a change. Into battle there was no question who would lead. Into business, there was more discussion.

George asked them where they would be staying in New Orleans and for how long. Tom hesitated, shrugged and then explained that it was all a question of time, money and paper. They would need to live modestly on their money and the money that they could raise by pledging some valuable items, until paper arrived from New York. They must play safe. "Nonsense," said George, I will pledge credit at my bank." Tom shook his head. "I have travelled twice across this continent without borrowing a cent. I am not going to start now. It is a matter of pride. We have lived hard and we can endure a little more hard living to get home. However, if you can introduce a modest hotel, an honest broker and a sound shipping agent, we would be grateful. Then we will know how well we may live." George had learned enough about this independent spirit not to argue. "Very well, please don't kill anyone before you talk to me."

New Orleans was a shock. Half the population was black and half the population spoke French. The heat was intolerable, the humidity was exhausting and the smell was appalling. The ladies stayed on the boat while arrangements were made.

George knew what to do. Money first. Tom wrapped up the rifles and they visited George's broker. The broker called in the gunsmith. The gunsmith admired and gave a value. George suggested a second opinion. The gunsmith improved his valuation. The broker offered a rate which would last for a period before the loan would expire and the guns would be sold. George negotiated a longer period.

The advance could keep them in style for a few

months. But if the papers did not arrive from New York, they would need to curtail their visit in order to buy passage to New York. And they would lose the guns. George recommended the hotel and they booked in. The shipping agent gave them the price for a passage to New York. After setting aside the cost of the passage they would need to leave in three months. That night Elizabeth wrote again to New York. In theory they had plenty of time for letters to New York and credits to New Orleans, and what could go wrong….Well, for a start, the British were not popular in New Orleans. George promised to keep them out of trouble.

Tom went down to the quay to thank Ham. He got the address of Ham's agent in New Orleans. Nothing was promised, but they hoped to meet again.

*****

King George was one of the senior residents of New Orleans. He was twenty five years old, almost fifteen feet long and weighed about one thousand pounds. He had a nest deep in the roots of the swamp. He spent most of his time there with the rotting remains of his threats. Today, he was down to the last few scraps of a large dog and a boy was almost ripe. It was time for him to add a new meat into the sequence. His territory included the bayou swamp between New Orleans and the lake.

New Orleans was being built on islands of higher land, stretching from the centre. King George patrolled the areas where the islands met the water. The town was bringing food to him. He usually took domestic animals but he was getting a taste for the residents.

Each day they visited the banks to ask whether their papers had arrived and each day they were disappointed. The bank staff were becoming disrespectful towards these desperate Englishmen. One morning, after they had visited the banks and, as usual, found no credits, George suggested a walk into the old town, in particular the French Quarter. He had not been involved in the original construction or subsequent improvements. The French Quarter was a testament to the building of the town by the French, ownership by the Spanish, return to the French, and now the Americans. Much of its original character had survived. The colours and the smells were distinctive. The architecture was unique, particularly on the upper floors with verandas and walkways decorated with flower pots.

They looked into shops selling French and Spanish delicacies and bottles. They sniffed into restaurants with distinctive local menus. Cajun spices predominated. George said that the flavours were extreme and he had been protecting them against them at the hotel. As you went west along the coast into Texas and Mexico, the food became hotter and hotter. It became so fierce that a new arrival might need to exist on bread and water. Even then, the bread might be spiced and the water might be bad.

Girls of all shades and shapes and sizes displayed themselves at upper windows.

On the stalls they saw exotic animals and reptiles. There seemed to be a lot of snake. On the fish stalls they saw the huge ugly catfish and other strange specimens from the swamps.

They looked into a gambling hall and came face to face with Guy Davenport. And Guy Davenport bolted.

Tom said urgently that they must follow him. They had to know where he lived, or at least felt safe. He told George that Guy Davenport would find a way to kill them if he could. He would explain later.

They hurried through the streets, keeping Guy Davenport in sight, but he was getting further away. George panted that they should not worry. Guy Davenport's alternative destinations were narrowing. As the town had grown outwards onto the islands of higher ground, causeways and bridges had been constructed. Guy Davenport was heading out that way and would have to use one of these links. There was no hurry.

At last, they came to a causeway with bridges leading to a group of wooden houses at the edge of the bayou, surrounded by swamp. They could see Guy Davenport almost at the end of the causeway. Tom said that they must stop. If Guy Davenport had a gun in one of the houses, they would be an easy target on the causeway.

But Guy Davenport did not go into a house. He headed off along a path at the edge of the bayou, leading to a small beach with a canoe pulled up above the water. He had reached the beach and was launching the canoe when he met King George.

It was all to do with the tail. That was where King George got his speed and strength. One huge thrust of the tail lifted King George up towards Guy Davenport. King George snapped his mighty jaws on Guy Davenport's right leg. Then a reverse thrust of the tail dragged Guy Davenport down into the bayou. It was the death roll that Guy Davenport could not avoid. This time there would be no drifting or bolting. He was bashed down onto the bed of the bayou. He breathed out air and breathed in swamp water. Another roll and another bash, and he lost the last of his air, took in more swamp water and lost consciousness. When Guy Davenport stopped struggling, King George swung the tail and set off back to his nest. Guy Davenport would join the food rotation in the larder. He would follow the boy. Guy Davenport had drifted away for the last time.

"That would be King George," said George Maine. "This area is in his territory and it was risky to splash out to the beach."

"So Guy Davenport finally ran out of luck," said Tom.

"And his charm seems to have failed him," said Hackett.

In the meantime, Tom was finding it difficult to keep up appearances. He was becoming desperate. He had enough money to pay for the hotel for a few more weeks. But the date for redemption of his beautiful rifles was becoming uncomfortably close. Months had turned to weeks and now he was counting the days. Unless the credits arrived from New York the guns would be lost. The financial loss would be painful but the emotional loss of those lifesaving weapons would be unbearable. He would have to swallow his pride and ask George Maine for help.

One morning, about a week later, the group were sitting in a large airy reception room at the hotel under fans worked by slaves. Nell had made her morning entrance and, from under her cotton defences, was beginning to set the reckless tone among the ladies. Frances and George were now regular visitors. Today, Hackett was asking about steam engines and George was asking about ferries. Tom had made up his mind to raise the subject of the rifles when an opportunity arose. The happy chatter continued, but Tom did not join in.

Then the chatter subsided as a tall, dark figure stood in the doorway. Elizabeth hesitated until she saw the smile that was just for her. Then she ran. It was not mule breeding, but it was close. As she came up for air, Elizabeth said "Don't you bother with them. Just you come along with me." And she led him away.

"I think our money has arrived," said Tom. "Then we must find you a ship said George. New Orleans in summer is no place for visitors." Nell said "Take me away from these mosquitos before I turn into a strawberry." Tom said "What about the sea sickness?"

Nell said "Anything, as long as it doesn't itch."

The next morning, when Elizabet and Ben had composed themselves, the group met again and introductions were made. George was thrilled to meet a well-respected New York lawyer with business connections. He led them to the bank where Ben presented the bank papers and collected the money. It was more than Tom had expected. Ben explained that, on their return to Baltimore, Mr and Mrs Paul Delamaine had been ambushed, robbed and ransomed. As instructed, he had offered the emerald ring at the reserve price and Paul Delamaine had gladly paid the price. Unfortunately, he heard later that Mrs Delamaine had had a fatal riding accident. Mr. Delamaine had hanged a couple of slaves. So, had ended the story of the emerald ring.

Next, to the shipping office to find a big ship bound for New York. It was not difficult. They seemed to be sailing every day. They chose one of the biggest that could ride steadily on the currents and the winds. It would leave in two days' time.

Then to the broker to redeem the rifles. There would be some delay. The rifles were in safe custody and there would be procedures for their release. Tom started to speak quietly and clearly. Hackett stood beside him. But George Maine stepped forward and took the broker aside. He returned to say that the broker would have the guns available for redemption the next morning, without fail. And the rates would be calculated to today's date.

The following evening, their last before departure, they held a dinner at the hotel. When they had booked in, George had given instructions about the menus. No local foods could be served. No local shellfish or prawns.

Deep sea fish and imported beef would be best. They had survived.

Today, George had sent to the markets for the best fillet of beef and the best lobsters. They would be grilled. The French had left some vineyards up river so some expensive wine was served. It was a great party. Nell's performance from under the swathes of cotton and stuff was the highlight.

At the end George added a sombre note. He had heard that news of a rumour that there was a great British swordsman in the city and the young gentlemen had been choosing their champion. Normally, New Orleans was cosmopolitan and forgiving but the last invasion by the British had left a bad taste and the people of New Orleans were ready to remind the British that they had been beaten here once, and would be again. Civic pride was aroused and to be chosen as champion was a matter of great prestige and carried the expectation that the British would be defeated. Tom said, "Normally, I would shoot him from fifty yards, but I don't want to delay our departure. We may need to be slightly ungallant."

The next morning they paid the hotel bill. The redemption of the rifles had been completed. The money from New York had arrived in time. At last they were going "home" and they were in good spirits. They hired hand carts and set off for the ship.

The Challenger stood in front of the gangway with his hand resting on a long sword. He was very tall and had a fine moustache and beard. He cut a handsome figure, standing proud. He was barring their way. His supporters stood on the quay, well dressed for the entertainment.

There were even a few ladies in hats with parasols adding to the scene.

Hackett opened the tin box and threw the sword in its scabbard towards Tom. It fell short and skidded on the stones towards Tom's feet. The Challenger sneered as he watched it slide to a halt. As he was watching the sword, Hackett stepped forward and took his right hand, which was holding the top of the sword, and twisted. The sword fell onto the quay and Hackett steered the challenger towards his group of supporters. Then he jerked and the wrist popped. There would be no sword fight today.

But the supporters started to converge on the lone figure. Hackett broke a couple of outstretched fingers and delivered a couple of gentle throat chops, but they continued to press forward. He could not afford close combat with so many without starting to kill.

Then he heard the familiar sing as Tom drew the dark sword. Tom used the back edge to crack at outstretched hands. "No blood, no deaths" called Tom. Hackett picked up the Challengers sword and started to use the back edge. Knives, pistols and sword sticks appeared, and wrists were broken.

So, there was the sight of Tom with deep red gold hair in the morning sun, broad shouldered, deep chested and light on his feet, cracking with the back edge of his dark sword and Hackett, straight as a ramrod, his long black hair thrown back, his fierce nose and chin thrust forward, never taking a step back and thrashing down with the back edge of the Challengers sword. Then Hackett fell, knocked over by two falling supporters. The others moved forward. Tom saw his dear comrade go down.

"No, no, no" he screamed and attacked with a violent fury, crashing relentlessly with the back of the dark sword against shoulders, arms, wrists and knees. Hackett managed to throw off the fallen supporters, got up and resumed his thrashing. In the face of the renewed assault, the supporters turned. Now the uninjured were helping the injured to withdraw. They were a sorry sight. But one heavy old man with bushy whiskers and a tall hat continued to roar his defiance. Tom used the sharp edge of the sword to slice the top off the hat, and remove one half of a pair of pork chop whiskers. A boot in the backside sent him on his way, half hatted and half whiskered.

Later, the companions drank rum and said that it would have been different if they had known what to expect. Only the Challenger was silent. He felt lucky.

So, after a brief burst of sheer violence it was all over. The challenger's sword lay on the cobbles with an assortment of discarded weapons and the dark sword was back in the tin box.

Ben helped the ladies up the gangway. The boys pushed the hand cart with the cases – and the hat boxes. Tom and Hackett guarded the rear. They held the rifles but no weapons were raised from the supporters. They had come for a party. But it had turned into a rout. There were broken bones, but nobody had been killed. No honour had been satisfied.

So, the team they were on their way. George waved from below, raised his straw hat, said that it had been a privilege, and he hoped he would see them in New York.

The voyage went well. Light winds and low seas helped Nell to recover.

The team took the opportunity to discuss the future, without pressure. They showed Ben the HBC papers. He was amazed. He confirmed that he could arrange for them to be fully honoured in New York. They could live elegantly and make large investments if they chose.

In the context of investments, they discussed George Maine and his intention to promote investment in the railways. Ben explained that George would have to produce a prospectus. He and Alan Alexander would examine it in fine detail with the new breed of bankers, who raised funds for wars and major projects.

Tom mentioned, quite shyly, that he would like to start a business building small, fixed steam engines to pull ferries across rivers, pull wagons up hills, power saw mills and hundreds of other small scale operations. He had no idea how to start. Ben said that it would be another exciting opportunity and, with the right team, the potential could be developed or disproved. Tom would not be alone.

New York

The team that that disembarked in New York was very different from the team that had embarked in New Orleans.

Nell was radiant with clear skin and her reckless smile. She was now Mrs Tom Kynaston. Elizabeth and Ben were engaged to be married, soon. Hackett stepped off the gangway as Mr. Mark Hackett, business partner.

Elizabeth had transformed Hackett on the voyage. Her new status as a fiancée had given her new confidence to show her affection for Hackett without fear of misunderstanding. She made him cut about ten years off his hair and told him that he was good looking and wealthy. He should step confidently into the new life. As always, Hackett did as Elizabeth told him.

So, they arrived in New York in good spirits and full of confidence for the future. Nell and Elizabeth demanded the best hotel and ordered a gig. They chose a red one with a tall high stepping black horse. They wore riding outfits with hats and drove fast. Their assault on New York had begun.

Ben presented the HBC papers at several banks (spreading the risk) and ensured that they were honoured. Tom and Mark had to swear oaths about the death of Otto to complete the credit to Elizabeth. The banks were delighted to receive the business.

The big reunion was held at the Plymouth Inn. The old

team were so pleased to be reunited, and in such happy circumstances. Elizabeth was dazzling in a bright red dress.TP was the guest of honour. They told him that his ride would go down in history with Dick Turpin and Paul Revere. He shook his tanned blonde head sadly and told them that he had had to leave H2 lame on the plain.

They drank a toast to H2 and wished her luck. And the party went on. A couple of new ladies were quietly introduced, not knowing what to expect, but were made welcome and soon entered into the spirit. Miss Hawkeye was shyly introduced by Adam Hillstrider. His advances were now being well received. Miss Hawkeye mentioned that life at the top of the hill was becoming difficult for her father. Tom was greeted with silence when he said "Mules"..................

Elizabeth cornered Mark Hackett. "Mark my dear, I will need to choose a couple of bridesmaids and I want you to help." Then Nell cornered him. "Mark, my dear, I would like you to be godfather to my child. To continue to look after us." He was being bound into a family that he had never known. And he smiled. There was a buzz of hope and excitement in the air.

A couple of days later Tom and Mark sat drinking coffee in the Plymouth Inn, which was now their headquarters, wondering how to involve TP in their business proposals without offending his proud spirit. Some sort of partnership looked best. Then, the man himself came in and announced that H2 had trotted home, sound.

THE END

Please do not lend this book to anyone.

Printed in Great Britain
by Amazon